No Strings Attached

a novel by

Nancey Flowers

In the Beginning

I didn't start out being the other woman. I started out as the girl friend. Then I matriculated to the status of fiancée and eventually graduated to wife. Now I proudly present myself as the other woman and firmly believe in a lifestyle of no strings attached.

Every woman I know hates the other woman. You know the one that your man gets his freak on with regularly. She's also the person that your husband is really thinking about during sex while pretending to be satisfied with you. On some occasions the wife may even want to trade places with that other woman, but she can't. The wives and so-called girlfriends in these monogamous relationships are curious to learn what it is that their man sees in that other woman. That woman is me, and I'm here to tell you it's good to be me. That's right; I said it! It's damn good to be the other woman. You can handle your business without worrying about getting hurt, because everyone knows the deal upfront, and there are no feelings involved.

Let me tell you something: the same way a man desires variety is exactly what we women want—a little spice in our lives! Think about it for a second…why not have three, four, or even five different men? You can have one for every need. Some men don't like to engage in cunnilingus, but a man like that would be a waste of time anyway. Another may not know how to lap the breast properly, and who has time to teach? Then there is always that toe sucker; and if you haven't had your toes sucked, then you don't know what you're missing. Shit, I'm no stickler for a commitment. As far as I'm concerned, I'm glad that the flava of the moment has a place to go home to. Go back to your wifey. I don't need that responsibility anymore. I'm not washing your dirty-ass clothes; ironing and starching them after they've been washed, cooking and slaving over some hot-ass stove; cleaning the house that we both live in; or having babies. Imagine that, nine months of walking around fat as a damn house and *you,* the wife, will still be underappreciated. Yet you are carrying the baby that both of you lay down to make. Imagine that! Instead of your man worshipping the ground you walk on, he's laid up over my house, sweet-talking me. In between rounds he complains and confides, "I don't find her attractive anymore." Hell no!

I am fierce. I will screw your man without a second thought and trust me, after the first time he will get hooked. I can celebrate a different man every day of the week if I choose. Make that one for every month, and I have responsible sex. Felice Monét Jackson has little time for foolishness, and most men talk nothing but foolishness. Take it from me; I've got a Ph.D. in menology. Men will do and say anything to get into your thong and it's pathetic that women fall for it time and time again. Now, if I decide to be with a man, it's not because of his weak-ass game. No. It's because I made a conscious decision to lay with him, and there are no strings attached. I've been burned once—no make that twice—and they both hurt more than hot oil in a frying pan.

I was married for several years to my business partner, Bedford Jackson, whom I call B.J. B.J. and I dated for two years while we were in college. We were the perfect couple; you know the type. We were both drop-dead gorgeous and yes, we fought over the mirror when we were together. B.J. and I were both business management majors with minors in finance. As a couple we were a powerhouse. Unstoppable! Then everything came to a crashing halt the day I came home to find him in bed with another woman.

I remember that afternoon as if it were yesterday. The reason I keep it logged in my memory is just as a reality check. No sense in getting my hopes up and falling for one of these knucklehead men again. As soon as that picture appears, I remember that all men are liars. All men are cheats. All men are dogs. The constant reminder of B.J. in bed with another woman keeps me sane and levelheaded. Sick, but true. Everyone deals with pain differently, and this is my way of handling it.

Jackson and Jackson Financial Consultants, Inc., was established in 1995. B.J. and I had always dreamed of opening our own firm. When that day came I felt that nothing could stop us. Nothing could separate us. Nothing could stand in our way. There was no obstacle that we couldn't overcome together. The love between us was stronger than any current from the Red Sea. We were closer than gum stuck to a shoe, so where did the love go?

Now, I'm single, sexy and very satisfied. Like I said, I was married to B.J. for several years. I was very much in love. During the last year of our marriage if you had so much as told me that he was out there having an affair, I would have kicked your ass. I would have whipped you good for lying. I would have come two seconds short of putting you underground. Let's just say that I would have done a lot. I worshipped the ground that man walked on, and I believed he did the same for me. After all, this is the man with whom I believed God had ordained me to be with. Was I ever wrong! I honestly don't know how B.J. found the time to be with anyone else. However, he apparently did. It's time for a little replay. Please accept this invitation to:

Event: Termination of marriage
Reason: Misplaced dick in another woman
Time: 3:40 P.M.
Day: Wednesday
Date: May 20, 1999

The morning sun was brilliant. B.J. and I were going into our sixth year of being in business and it was a little slow, but we expected it to pick up soon. What with all of the technology companies that were springing up, we were bound to get more business. We weren't bad off, but it was still a struggle. Right before B.J. decided to take that leap of faith and I was laid off, we purchased a beautiful brownstone in the Stuyvesant Heights section of Brooklyn. It was on a gorgeous tree-lined block. There were a few houses that were abandoned, but I'm an optimist. I figured in five to ten years, Stuyvesant Heights would be a well-sought-after area. Our community would be the place to be.

From the moment we walked into that house I knew that we had to have it. B.J. felt the same way. It was supposed to be a three family, but we didn't want anyone living with us. At the time, B.J. and I both made good money at the companies that we worked for, so we decided immediately that tenants were out of the question. There were so many horror stories about tenants not paying their rent on time and sometimes not at all. Or at the signing of the lease you believe that it is a family of three. However, as soon as they moved in, the family size swelled from three to six. Then there was the noise factor. We would have to tolerate footsteps above us because the floors were wood and would often settle or creak even with the least amount of pressure.

We took the entire mortgage on ourselves, and it was fine. B.J. and I never believed in biting off more than we could chew and could more than afford the payments. But I digress…back to sordid details of B.J. and the other woman.

I've always been an early riser. Sometimes I feel like I was born with my very own internal alarm clock. No matter how late I fall asleep, I still manage to get up between 5:30 and 6:00 A.M. B.J. was still snoring when my body buzzer sounded, and he didn't like to be bothered until after I had gotten out of the shower and had freshened up. He wanted to get in as much sleep as possible. When I finally completed my morning routine of yoga, shower, body pampering and hair-styling, I nudged him softly. B.J. scrunched up his face, began coughing loudly and turned his back to me. This was his morning ritual, with the exception of that awful cough, so I shook him harder the second time. B.J. pulled his body even farther away from me. He coughed longer and louder, and his body heaved like he was in pain. At this point I became concerned. B.J. rarely got sick. He had the best immune system known to man, so this coughing fit wrestled my attention. I was in the process of hauling my foot into my pantyhose and was startled by his bronchial spasms. I immediately returned my attention to him.

"B.J., honey, are you okay?"

B.J. didn't answer right away. He hocked up some phlegm and reached over to my side of the bed for some Kleenex. He looked at me with water-filled eyes, caused by his bout of coughing.

"I'm feeling sick, baby. I don't think that I'll be able to go in today," B.J. answered, sounding extremely nasal.

"Oh, you poor baby. Would you like Mama to make you some tea?"

"Mmh-hmm," he answered, bobbing his head like a five-year-old.

I didn't even bother to finish putting on my stockings. Instead I removed my foot from the nylon toehold, kissed him on the forehead and headed down to the kitchen. While down there, I contemplated if I should remain home with B.J. or go in to the office. Neither of us had taken a day of sick leave since we started Jackson and Jackson, so I didn't see how one day would hurt. The sing-song of the kettle startled me out of my thoughts. Hastily I turned the gas burner off and began looking for B.J.'s favorite Sylvester the cat mug. After searching high and low, I finally realized that it had to be in the dishwasher. I walked over and opened the door and there Sylvester was, looking at, me spitting "Suffering succotash, you found me!"

I returned to the bedroom and found a pile of crumpled pale blue Egyptian cotton sheets and an empty bed. Then, from the adjoining room, I heard the toilet flush. I placed the blend of mint and Tension Tamer teas on his nightstand. The bathroom door opened and a pitiful-looking B.J. walked out. Tissue was stuffed into his nostrils and he was breathing from his mouth.

"B.J., baby, I made your favorite tea." I extended my arms to embrace him. "My baby looks so sickly. You know what? I should stay home with you today. You need Mama to give you a little tender loving care. I'm going to leave a message with both Davonna and Shirley; the office will be fine without us today. That's probably why you are so sick in the first place. It's plain exhaustion. You've been running yourself ragged. What else could it possibly be? It's been in the high seventies, low eighties for the past couple of weeks, yet you have signs of the flu? That's strange."

"Felice, baby," B.J. said in between breathing. "I need you to go in today."

"B.J., baby, the office will be fine without us. One day won't hurt."

"It's not that. I have a meeting this afternoon with Mr. Rich Dennis from Nubian Heritage. I can't cancel on him because he's coming from out of town. However, you can see him in my place. . .please."

B.J. was at my, mercy and he was batting those long, luxurious eyelashes that framed dark, brooding but sexy eyes.

"Is that today?" I asked.

"Yes, it is," B.J. said, caressing my hand to seal the deal. When he felt that I had given in, he let go and crawled back into bed like an infant. Instead of drinking the tea he removed the tissue from his nostrils and attempted to sniff it. He dipped his index finger into the liquid to determine the temperature.

"Don't you think I know you by now? Why do you always do that? Do you really think that I would serve you scalding-hot tea?"

"I don't know. I remember that time when you made that fried chicken and fed it to me right out of the frying pan and—"

"Damn, B.J., will you ever let me live that down? We were in college and I was just excited to be cooking for my man."

"Yeah, well, my tongue was scorched for several days."

"Have I done anything like that since?"

"No, but you can never be too careful," B.J. replied and then sipped the tea. Apparently I passed the temperature test.

"Whatever," I said and softly punched his shoulder.

♀♂

10:30 A.M.

"Good morning, Shirley. You look stunning today. I've never seen that outfit before. Going on a hot date?" I asked.

Shirley was always well dressed. Her attire was classic and always enhanced her look. Today she donned a salmon-colored two-piece skirt suit. The color was brighter than her normal choice of clothing and the shirt beneath her blazer had a neckline that was a little more revealing than her usual taste. It also looked like her shoulder-length hair had been recently cut and freshly relaxed. For a woman in her late fifties, Shirley didn't look a day over forty and could put the women that claimed to be forty or even in their late thirties to shame.

"Child, please! You know when you run out of your good clothes because you're too darn lazy to take your everyday favorites to the cleaners and you have to wear what is left? Well, this is what was left. I'm glad that you like it though. I may have to pull this one out more often," Shirley said chuckling.

"I know exactly what you mean. Anyway, how are you today?"

"I'm doing just great. I already miss the mouth on that husband of yours. It's just been so quiet. I can't believe he's sick. Can you believe that all the time that I worked with him at Becker and Coles, not once, and I mean not one time, did that man call in sick. I've worked with him for nearly ten years now."

"I know. I said the same exact thing to myself this morning. If I weren't there to witness his being sick I wouldn't have believed it, either."

Shirley bobbed her head in agreement.

"I need your help with something. Bedford has a meeting this afternoon with Mr. Richlieu Dennis of Nubian Heritage and I have to sit in his place today. I need their file to review the portfolio and the location that they're scheduled to meet at."

"Oh, I have all of that information right within reach," Shirley said, turning to her in box for a file labeled NUBIAN HERITAGE in bold italics. "The meeting is for 12:30 P.M. at Caribbean Spice on Forty-fourth Street and Ninth Avenue. The reservation is under Bedford's name." Shirley placed the file in my hand and just when she was about to ask me a question the phone began to ring.

"Shirley, I think that this should be fine. If I need anything else, I'll be sure to buzz you."

Shirley waved okay and returned to her call.

I headed back to my office and the first thing that I did was call home to check on B.J.'s prognosis and update him regarding my findings on the Nubian Heritage account.

"Hello," B.J. answered. His condition sounded like it was worsening.

"Sweetie, you sound awful. You should probably call Dr. Barnes's office to find out if he's available today. You may have the flu, or strep throat, and might need antibiotics. The last thing we need or want is for your condition to worsen."

"I'll be fine. All I need is a good day's rest. I'm going to take a nap, so if I don't answer the phone, don't get alarmed." Bedford paused to clear the phlegm in his throat.

"Okay, you get your rest. I'm going to finish preparing for the meeting this afternoon. I've already started to review the file, and I even have a few suggestions that I believe Mr. Dennis will like."

"That's great. Well, tell me all the details of your meeting when you get home later. Good luck!"

"Thanks. Feel better. I love you," I said, blowing kisses into the phone.

"I love you too."

The day continued, and the meeting with Nubian Heritage was flawless. We went over their financials and what Jackson and Jackson could do for their organization as well as a financial forecast. Mr. Dennis was pleased with the presentation and the suggestions regarding the strategic growth of his business. After the two-hour briefing and discussion, there was no doubt in his mind that he wanted to hire our firm.

I was so excited that I didn't even bother to return to the office. I stopped at the pharmacy to get B.J. some cough medicine and ibuprofen and picked up some homemade soup from a little restaurant in the Park Slope section of Brooklyn.

The cab pulled up in front of our brownstone at approximately 3:30 P.M. I was surging with excitement. I couldn't wait to tell B.J. of our latest accomplishment.

I entered through the ground level of our three-family brownstone. I decided to warm the soup up since it had gotten cold during my travel home and give B.J. a nice tall glass of orange juice to accompany the medicine that I bought, since he was so adamant about not going to see a physician.

I silently crept up the stairs to the third level where we had our bedroom to surprise B.J. The tray was balanced in my hands as I tip-toed to my destination. I remember having a hard time turning the knob of the bedroom door due to the weight of the tray in my left hand. After jiggling the handle a few seconds more the moisture from my hand caused the door to fling open. The door made a harsh sound as it slammed against the back wall. Apparently B.J. had been sound asleep and the noise startled him. He jerked up in the bed and less than a millisecond later, so did his bedmate. Her name was Davonna, and she was my secretary. Davonna had also called in sick that day. Evidently she came down with the same illness as B.J.—fuckingitis. The tray that I managed to balance like a model with a book on her head went crashing to the floor. Can you believe they had the audacity to be lying up in our marital bed? Apparently they had already had sex and had the nerve to cuddle and take a nap together.

Well, needless to say, I was shocked. I didn't know what to think or feel, but in that instant I knew that someone was going to feel my wrath. I leaped onto the bed and proceeded to choke B.J. He managed to grab my hands from around his neck, so I clawed his face with my nails and he reflexively flung me to the floor. Davonna hurriedly put on her undergarments. How very stupid of the woman to allow me time to come after her. I quickly pounced on her like a lioness attacking its prey. She wailed a thunderous noise. Davonna had the most fearful look in her eyes. I couldn't tell if she was afraid of the fact that she knew she was going to be on the unemployment line the following morning or if she was scared of the ass beating I was about to give her. Either way, I wasn't about to pity her. I may not have been able to beat B.J.'s ass right then, but someone was going to get knocked the fuck out, and that person was Davonna.

Davonna stood still, as if she was dumbstruck, for a good moment. By the time she decided to run, I had her cornered. I wasted no time pummeling her face and banging her head against the wall. She didn't resist or try to fight back, which took the joy out of whooping her ass, but that didn't stop me. B.J. finally managed to drag me off her because I was exhausted, crying and hurt. I can only remember feeling that way one other time in my life and that was something that I managed to suppress for years.

My head pounded loudly and my heart throbbed with anguish. I heard a loud banging and thought that it was either my head or my imagination. However, our nosy neighbors must have called the police, because they were knocking on the door.

This is my story. The beginning of why I decided to pledge my allegiance to a life of no strings attached.

Secrets

The walls were canvassed in a soft mauve pastel and the spread of paintings by Keina Davis and Bernard Stanley Hoyes blended evenly with the lavender hues. The CD player hummed the smooth sounds of Julie Dexter's *Dexterity* album, played repeatedly on track four, "Faith." It was the only thing that helped put Felice to sleep lately. Her return to New York brought back the nightmares that she had left behind two years earlier. Only now they were worse and more bizarre.

The dream started out pretty simple, but vivid. The afternoon rays dazzled against the soft blue skies. The sun kissed Felice on her ten-year-old cheeks as she sat on the porch with her great-aunt Leslie. Aunt Leslie always wore the same colorful house dress that resembled a smock with white snap buttons, with her knee-high stockings rolled down to her ankles, and pink house shoes. She steadily tapped her foot to a beat that only she could hear. Occasionally she would hum to that same beat. Felice could smell the pungent odor of her aunt. It was a mixture of fried chicken and cigarettes. Aunt Leslie eyed Felice carefully before digging into her bosom for her change purse. She peeled off four single dollar bills, handed Felice the money and nodded her head. Felice knew exactly what her aunt wanted: one pack of Pall Mall Reds, a 7-Up, a bag of pork rinds, and a pickle. She always left Felice with just enough money to buy a twenty-five-cent bag of Bon Ton potato chips and a quarter water.

Felice took the same route to the bodega every day. When she arrived at the store the owner automatically put the pack of cigarettes on
the counter and waited for her to return with the rest. He smiled at
Felice as he bagged the items and gave her a complimentary pepper-
mint ball candy. Felice took the bag and returned the smile. On her way
back home the route somehow changed and outside was pitch black.
Felice ran. Without warning the street turned into an alleyway. She
refused to turn around for fear of what she might see, but she could
hear the footsteps chasing her. Felice ran her little heart out, but the
footsteps were gaining on her. She wanted to drop the bag with the
items, but Aunt Leslie would be upset if she came back without her
cigarettes and pork rinds.

The brick walls had Felice trapped and she heard the sounds of a
baby wailing. She was tired and couldn't run anymore. She decided to
hide beside a Dumpster. The cries of the baby increased as she kneeled
next to the large garbage bin. The Dumpster reeked and Felice held her
breath. The baby was now laughing as if someone was tickling it. Felice
wanted to laugh, too, but she knew she couldn't. The foul smell coming
from the trash seemed to be getting stronger and Felice felt herself
beginning to suffocate. She closed her eyes, exhaled and then quickly
inhaled to hold her breath again. In that instant he appeared. He was a
nameless face that lived in her neighborhood. The boy was about fourteen or fifteen years old. Felice always saw him hanging around the
corner of her block and others, and he was usually up to no good. He
was much bigger than Felice. He reached for her small, sweaty hands,
but she screamed and the laughing baby began wailing again. She didn't
take his hand. Instead she wrapped her hands tightly around her small
frame. The boy grew frustrated and ordered Felice to remove her
clothes. He threatened to tell Felice's Aunt Leslie that he saw her smoking on the porch when she wasn't around, if she refused. Felice knew
how disappointed her aunt would be so she did as she was told. Slowly
she got up. She removed her tank top and the tears spilled from her
water-filled eyes. The boy moistened his index finger as if he were
preparing to turn the page of a book, then he planted the finger on her

underdeveloped nickel-sized nipple and fondled it. Fear and disgust filled her. Felice was very afraid because she was instructed never to take her pants off for any boys or men. The boy threw her down on the concrete, and he and Felice struggled as he pulled her pants off. He quickly maneuvered his zipper and pulled out his penis. Felice gave up the fight, but her sobs grew louder with each thrust. The tears started to crust in the corners of her eyes.

Suddenly the boy was gone and Felice was huddled in the corner next to the Dumpster again. Her clothes were on, but the crotch of her pants was stained with blood and urine. A woman in a white lab coat appeared and opened up the lid to the Dumpster. She took the baby into her arms, smiled and cradled it. Felice couldn't determine the sex of the baby. She didn't even want to see the baby. Felice just wanted to go home and eat her potato chips, drink her quarter water and watch Aunt Leslie chain smoke and smack on her pork rinds. The woman extended the baby to Felice, but Felice shrank back further into the crawl space. The smile vanished from the strange woman's face and she spoke loudly, "Take your shit, bitch."

This night was different and void of all dreams. Felice took a hot bath before turning in and drank a nice cup of honey vanilla chamomile tea. She even had a copy of Michael Presley's new book *Tears on a Sunday Afternoon* to read until she fell asleep, but she never even got to flip a page. The chime of the phone caused her to stir from a decent night's rest and eventually turn over. It was the last sound that Felice wanted to hear. Without even turning to look at the fluorescent dial on the clock she knew that it was too early. Hell, anytime at this point in her life was too early for callers. Her bad dreams were causing her to have one too many sleepless nights, and insomnia had claimed her normal sleep pattern.

"Who is it? What do you want and it better be good?" Felice answered. After four rings she was almost fully conscious and the sharp lash of her tongue could surely be felt by the caller on the other end.

There was silence on the other line.

Felice held the phone a few inches from her face and stared blankly at it. For a moment she thought it might be her lover Jermaine Gray's wife, Marissa. Over the last few weeks he had been spending far too much time with Felice and she was forced to kick him out before dusk.

"It's too early in the morning for this crap," Felice said. She placed the receiver back to her ear.

"Hello?" she said again.

There was still no response.

"You know what? I don't have time for games. Whoever this is, lose my number."

Just as she was about to place the phone into the cradle she heard a voice.

"Felice, please don't hang up."

She immediately placed the phone back to her ear. The voice was one that she had avoided for two years. How could it be? Where did he get her number? It wasn't listed and she went through great lengths to make sure that not just anybody had her home phone number.

Felice's brain was on pause. The only thing she could think of doing was hanging up. She was not ready to confront the ghosts of her past. She had given up so much and it had been painful, but she had promised herself that she wouldn't look back. Looking back was never a good thing. Her therapist even said that she needed to let the past remain there. Although she hadn't been exactly honest with her therapist. Well, it wasn't that she wasn't honest; it was more like she had omitted what one might consider pertinent information. It wasn't like she killed someone, but she had come close.

Felice was numb. She could hear him breathing on the other end of the phone.

"Hello, Felice."

"You must have the wrong number. Sorry," Felice replied and hung up.

Felice pulled her legs from beneath the comforter and hugged them to her body. She rocked back and forth. She knew that he was going to call again. Felice knew that he had recognized her voice, but was simply giving her time to recuperate.

How did he get her new unlisted home phone number? Who gave it to him? Had he hired a private detective to track her down? Why was he reaching out to her after all this time? What did he want from her? She had severed all ties with him and had made it clear that she didn't want any further communication once she left. That was almost two years ago.

Felice immediately turned her answering machine on. She never bothered to personalize her message, which played in her favor that morning. No sooner did she hit the button than the phone rang again. The machine picked up after the third ring and the automated recording played.

"Felice, don't play games with me. I know this is your number. It's been long enough. Don't you think we need to talk? You can't avoid us forever. My numbers haven't changed, so call me or I'll continue to call you."

"Is that a threat, muthafucka?" Felice yelled. She knew that he couldn't hear her, but she wished he could.

Felice stopped rocking and extended her legs above the comforter. Although it was winter and she was anemic, she was boiling hot. She was determined to go back to sleep. All she asked for was one peaceful night of slumber. One night of no interruptions.

Felice didn't even enjoy being with her lovers anymore. It wasn't that they didn't satisfy her sexually—that was never the case. She just felt like they were all demanding too much of her time. They all wanted more than she was willing to give, especially Jermaine, and she wasn't willing to give much anymore. Not after all of the failed relationships she had been through. She had tried the marriage thing, and that was a complete bust. Then she had attempted to try again and got kicked in the teeth. Felice was no glutton for punishment, so she decided to quit while she was ahead. Now her motto was simple: the other woman was the true champion, because she lived a life of no strings attached. Everybody knew the deal upfront.

After all of the bullshit to which she allowed herself to fall prey, Felice sat herself down and wrote in her journal. She hadn't written in it for more than a year, but from time to time when she felt that she was getting too deep she would read the first page of her journal: *Every woman I know hates the other woman.* The last line ended with *I pledge my allegiance to a life of no strings attached.*

Felice looked at the flashing light on her answering machine that indicated a new message. She quickly hit the "erase" button and almost immediately some of the tension eased from her body.

She was curious to know how he found her. Why couldn't he leave her alone? Felice finally looked at the time. She had to know who the snitch was. The first person she dialed was her best friend, Sylvah Lawrence.

Sylvah picked up the phone on the second ring.

"Good morning," Sylvah mumbled, the sleep walking through her lips.

"Hey, girl! How are you doing?" Felice asked.

"Girl, do you know what time it is?"

"Oh, I'm sorry. Did I catch you at a bad time?"

"Not really, but it sure is early as hell. I feel like I just went to sleep. I was up packing the remainder of those boxes. Speaking of which, I know you're coming over to help me out, right?"

"You know that I got you, girl."

"Okay, what's bothering you? This is not a social call. This is one of those something-is-bothering-me, I'm-tired-of-men-bullshit, I'm-having-bad-dreams or I'm-depressed calls."

"Sylvah, you need to stop, because you are not funny. I told you that I've been having a hard time sleeping lately. I just wanted to talk. Damn, a sister has been MIA for more than a year and you would think that you missed me."

"MIA, my ass. I visited you in Cuba twice and stayed for a week the first time and a month the second, so don't give me that crap. Maybe you're having a hard time adjusting to this harsh weather again, or maybe you miss the Cuban *papis.*"

"Girl, please, there are plenty of *papis* right here in America, but I must admit the *mujeros* in Cuba were much more attentive."

"Speaking of Cuba, how is your father? Have you spoken or written to him lately?"

"Mr. Hernandez is doing just fine. I don't call him anymore because

I swear the government is tapping my phone. Every time I call I hear this clicking sound on the line, and I only hear it when I speak to him."

"Seriously? Well, maybe it's not what you think. It is overseas and sometimes the wires get crossed and what not."

"No, it's what I think it is. The damn government taps any and everybody's phone when you call a communist country. They say that we live in a democracy, but that's a bunch of bullshit. I saw freer people in Cuba. No hunger, no poverty that exemplifies our lifestyle here in America, and there was plenty of harmony. This nation could take a lesson from Cuba."

"For real! Anyway I better get back to sleep. It's now five-thirty and I expect the movers to be here between ten and eleven."

"Okay. Well, have you spoken to or seen Bläise lately?"

There was a long moment of silence and then a deep sigh.

"No. Why, have you?" Sylvah asked.

"Oh no. It's not what you think. I was just curious, you know. I mean well, he may have called you. You know how fickle these men are. One minute they don't want to be bothered by you and the next they come crawling back."

"Well, he hasn't called me and I haven't called him. I don't see him or his friends anymore or much of anyone from our past. That part of my life is cut off. He contacts the kids directly. I have one last piece of business to finalize and then it will be all over. Felice, I really have to get to bed. Call me when you get up in the morning. Try and get some sleep, okay?"

"Yeah. By the way, Sylvah... "

"Yes?"

"I'm sorry if I opened up old wounds. I didn't mean to."

"I know. Good morning."

"Good morning."

Felice sat and stared at the clock. She counted the seconds for each minute that passed. She did this and allowed her mind to wander for exactly eleven minutes. Eleven minutes of trying to decide if she should make that next call. Eleven minutes of her stomach doing flip-flops. Eleven minutes of wondering if she really wanted to know, or if it even mattered at this point. Did it really make a difference who gave him her number? The fact remained that he now had it. The growing concern was what else did he have on her? She should have stayed her behind with her father in Cuba. She had had no concerns and no real worries. Her biggest worry had been what her diet would be for that particular day or how hot the temperature was going to be, because if she curled her hair the humidity might make it limp.

Felice got up from the comforts of bed to retrieve her Palm Pilot from her handbag. She found it and mosied back to the warmth of her comforter. She dialed the number and waited for the phone to ring. She was about to lose her nerve and hang up, but someone picked up on the third ring. It was too late anyway; her number was sure to appear on the Caller I.D. display since the recipient didn't accept calls from private numbers.

"Good morning, Pryce residence," a groggy voice answered.

"Good morning. Is Samantha available?" Felice asked.

"Who's calling?"

"Felice."

"Hold on a moment. Sam, Sam," the voice called out.

Felice was disgusted.

"Sam. Sam, get up. It's Felice."

"Wha…what? Tell whoever it is that I'm sleep."

"Sam, I said its Felice."

Felice heard the phone exchange hands.

"Felice? Is everything all right? Are you okay?"

"Yes, I'm fine," Felice answered solemnly.

"Then what's wrong. I know you don't miss your dear old mother."

"Listen, Samantha, or Sam, or whatever it is that you want to be called."

"No, you listen! I'm still your mother. You called me at a quarter to six in the morning, so you can spare me the damn attitude. Now, I'm glad that you went to Cuba and created a bond with your father, but you will not come back here and disrespect me."

"I'm sorry. I'm just a little rattled. All I want to know is if you gave anybody my new phone number?"

When her mother couldn't offer her an immediate response Felice already had her answer.

"Mother, why? Why did you give him my number? I specifically asked you not to give it to anyone. I'm not ready to deal with everybody yet. These things take time."

Felice heard her mother breathing heavily and the person who answered the phone was questioning if everything was okay. She knew her mother must have been on the brink of tears.

Both Felice and Samantha were sobbing.

"Felice, it wasn't easy. He came to me pleading to speak to you. I told him that I didn't know where you were. For months I told him that you were away. And when you were gone it was easy, because I wasn't lying. But he was unrelenting in his pursuit."

"You know that he's a sweet talker. That's what he does best."

"Felice, it wasn't the sweet talking that got to me. I could care less about that or him." There was a long pause. "Felice, why didn't you tell me? Why did I have to hear it from him?"

Felice's chest heaved heavily. The sobs racked her body, causing temporary paralysis. Her body was numb and she felt a prickling sensation in the sole of her feet. She imagined her mother going through the same pain. Felice knew that she would one day have to face the ghosts of her past, but she didn't want to run into them.

"Mother, please don't. Please don't. I can't right now. I have to go," Felice said and hung up the phone, but not before she heard her mother say, "You can't run forever."

2

Moving Day

A thin slice of light peeled through the windowpane. The glare woke Sylvah long before the alarm, which was set to blast at a quarter to eight. Too lazy to disarm it, she allowed the non-syllabic sounds to spill into the air. Wearily she reached over to cease the clock and in another swift motion she flicked on the reading lamp. It was almost one year to the date that she and her husband, Bläise, parted ways. The yellow manila envelope containing the divorce papers sat on the bedside table. It had been there for more than two weeks, still awaiting her signature. She left it on the nightstand to serve as a blatant reminder that her marriage was really over. "I'll sign and mail you some-time this morning before the movers arrive," she voiced to herself.

Sylvah sat upright and propped her body on the cushioned head-board. She wasn't quite ready to leave the comfort of her California king–sized bed or her beautiful four-bedroom home. This was the same bed that tore her marriage apart. It was the place that she grew to love and despise almost simultaneously. It seemed almost impossible to hate a piece of furniture. After all, what could it do to you other than provide you with a fitful sleep or a little bit of discomfort? But this was Sylvah, and she was anal in that manner. She wanted badly to blame something other than herself for the disposal of her marriage, so she used the bed as a scapegoat. Sylvah felt that its purchase was the beginning of the end of her twenty-year marriage. Prior to its acquisition, the troubles between her and Bläise had been practically non-existent. That was a little less than five years ago. They were better off cramped up on top of each other in their queen-sized bed. At least then they still made physical contact with each other. Once they got the California-king, they stayed on their respective sides of the mattress—Sylvah on the left and Bläise on the right.

Truthfully Sylvah knew the bed wasn't the reason her marriage dissolved. Their problems began well over ten years ago. It probably started when her sex drive disappeared. It vanished the day she looked in the mirror and actually noticed her excess weight. She had managed to gain twenty-five pounds in a matter of two years. That was the beginning of the end of a wild and adventurous sex life. Her desire fizzled. It felt as if the pounds had crept up on her. There was no warning. She couldn't run for shelter. No one else in the family had a weight problem, so why was this happening to her?

Prior to the weight gain, she and Bläise had fucked like rabbits. There wasn't a time or place that was inconvenient for them. They enjoyed indulging in impulsive sex. They had done it in several places, including a bathroom stall, the subway, the roof, a public library, the stairwell in college, a swimming pool, and she had even given him head in an elevator. The most memorable experience was when they had made love in the sauna during the Black Ski Summit. Another couple walked in, but exited once they saw what was going on. The act of getting caught actually heightened the experience, causing spontaneous combustion and eruption from both. Sylvah always wore clothes with easy access, because with Bläise she just never knew. Bläise always told her that he loved that little spark in her. On the exterior Sylvah appeared to be reserved, but that was all a façade. Sylvah definitely had some freak in her, and Bläise knew how to whet her appetite. When he felt like being adventurous he would arch his eyebrows and pucker his lips in that sexy way that Sylvah adored and without a word he'd be driving her like a nail into a wall. The kids didn't even slow them down. Sex between Sylvah and Bläise was one of their favorite pastimes, however, all of that abruptly came to an end.

Her first two years of law school were the hardest and once she managed to get through them she didn't do anything to lose the weight. Bläise still complimented her and even voiced his satisfaction by saying, "Baby, it's just more cushion for the pushing. You know I like it from the back, and you could never have too much ass for me."

She would laugh at his coy remarks and knew that he meant well, but still she wasn't content with her appearance. Her body went through some kind of metamorphosis and she didn't come out looking like a beautifully painted butterfly. She went from a size six to a size fourteen. The change actually required a brand-new wardrobe. Her bra size even increased. Sylvah who barely had a mouthful before the weight gain went from a 34B to a 36C. Her back got broader and her breasts grew fuller. That was the only thing that she didn't mind.

Their children even commented on her heaviness. Kenya and Zaire, who were pre-teens at the time said, "Mommy, you're fat." The weight gain and the words that poured from her children's mouths were a huge blow and Sylvah was too entrenched in her studies to recover physically. Whenever they went out to dinner as a family, Kenya and Zaire would caution their mother against after-dinner sweets. It was all out of love, but children merely spoke the truth, no matter how heartbreaking it was. When she finally started to accept her shapeliness, it was simply too late. Bläise began finding other pastimes, and they didn't include her. He'd go bowling with his coworkers and even began watching football games at bars. Bläise hated bars and complained about the smoke. He wasn't much of a social drinker either, but anything was better than being around a sulky Sylvah, and with time he adjusted. Adding insult to injury, they owned a sixty-inch television with Surround Sound. Nevertheless, he got tired of her constant complaints about school, her job, money, the kids, and the weight gain. He told her that her mouth was like a fish swimming upstream—it never got tired.

Those were things that she needed to put in a chest and place in the attic of her mind. The fact that she and Bläise managed to share twenty good years was a blessing, however, she did have the good sense to finally walk away. It wasn't healthy to stay in a failing relationship. She witnessed the volatile situation that her grandparents had, and it was horrible. It was painful and awful to be involved with someone whom you no longer loved. The kids were both in college and were old enough to understand, so it was time to move on with her life. A friend recommended that they seek counseling, but Bläise being headstrong and heart wrong refused. Deep down she was afraid of letting go. Afraid of starting over. Afraid that there wasn't anyone out there suitable or as compatible with what she and Bläise shared before things went awry. Afraid of another heartbreak. Afraid that no one would find her attractive, but that was the least of her worries.

The day before as she strutted down the street talking on her cell phone to her hairdresser, Kennedy Hudnell, she caused a car accident. A three-car accident at that! It wasn't every day that a thirty-nine-year-old woman caused cars to come to a crashing halt.

"Woman, are you causing accidents again?" Kennedy asked, chuckling on the other end.

Sylvah merely laughed it off and kept her pace; however, the man in the third car jumped out and stated, "You know that you caused this accident, right?" He was looking directly at Sylvah. She blushed, smiled, and kept walking. Kennedy was still on the line, eavesdropping.

"See, I told you," he replied.

To make matters worse, the same man who accused her of causing the accident began calling for her attention again.

Oh great, Sylvah thought and said aloud, "I hope they don't need me to become a witness. I didn't see what happened anyway, and I'm not lying for these people."

"I hear you," Kennedy replied. "Tell them those exact words and keep rolling."

"Kennedy, I may have to call the police or find one out here real quick. This man is following me," Sylvah said as she spun her head around to find the man a step away from clipping her heels.

"Pardon me, miss. I'm sorry for bothering you. I just wanted to ask if you'd be interested in dinner and the theater."

Sylvah's bottom jaw hung open and her upper lip rolled, exposing the gap in the top row of her teeth. This was far from what she thought he had in mind. How could this be happening to her? Why was this man tripping? The fact that someone struck his car seemed to be the least of his worries, and from the look of it, that little ding was going to cost someone a pretty penny. He appeared to be more interested in getting his mack on.

"Excuse me," Sylvah replied still in awe at the scene that was taking place before her.

Kennedy remained on the other end of the phone saying, "*Mmph, mmph, mmph.* Handle your business, Ms. Sex Goddess. What do you have on today, anyway?"

"Kennedy, shut up," Sylvah said, laughing.

The man began to back away and a genuine look of embarrassment covered his face. The only words he heard come out of Sylvah's mouth were *shut up*. He was oblivious to her phone conversation. Unaware and unable to see the headpiece neatly camouflaged by her long hair, he hung his head in shame for taking up her time. Realizing that he thought she was talking to him, Sylvah pointed to the cord of the phone and he bared his teeth in a slight smile.

"Well, would you consider going out with me for a lovely evening of dinner and possibly a play?" he asked again. He bounced back like a rubber band and seemed to really be on a mission.

Sylvah looked over at the other two drivers who were exchanging information. One of the men beckoned the man who stood in front of Sylvah. "We need you over here," the man chided in an unpleasant tone.

"Give me a minute, will ya!" Sylvah's new friend replied.

This man was dead serious. Sylvah was in a good mood and Kennedy was urging her to give the man a response. A positive one. Sylvah didn't know what to do. He was a good-looking man, but she was still married—scratch that, soon to be divorced. What was a woman to do? Sylvah had never dated a white man before. For that matter, Sylvah had never really dated. She had been with Bläise for more than half of her life. She had two lovers before Bläise and those encounters took place during her teenage years. She couldn't even remember the touch, feel, smell, or taste of another man. Yet, here this man was expecting to taste some of her deep, dark chocolate. It appeared that he liked his women strong and black.

A white man! He wasn't your typical white man either. He was nicely dressed in an expensive navy blue pinstriped, double-breasted Italian suit. Probably Armani. A tie that resembled something that she could have easily picked for Bläise in a heartbeat. He was driving a Lexus. It wasn't the current year, but it was definitely top of the line. There was no sign of a wedding band—not even the shadow of a ring. His shoes were either new or recently polished and his hands were beautifully manicured. Sylvah allowed the thought to run through her mind once more before answering: a white man. He had a Brad Pitt/ Pierce Brosnan/Johnny Depp appeal. Damn what was the world coming to? It wasn't like he was asking her to marry him. He was polite and merely offered to take her out to dinner and the theater. She couldn't even remember the last time she visited the theater. Oh yeah, *The Lion King* in 2000.

Sylvah reflected that too much thought could damage the mind. She had a way of overanalyzing situations, but that was part of her being. That's what lawyers did. Sylvah dipped her hand into her handbag and retrieved a business card. Even before the Tango-colored nails with the acrylic tips could reappear, he handed her his information. She quickly glanced at his business card and read his name aloud.

"Hunter Bolton. That's different," she said in a singsong voice.

"My parents are eccentrics. They loved the sixties. My middle name is Grey," Hunter replied, smiling like he had just scored a goal.

"Really. Well here's my number." Sylvah placed the card into Hunter's open palm.

"Sylvah Lawrence, attorney at law. I may need to retain your services right now. Are you any good?"

"Well, Mr. Bolton, wouldn't you like to find out?" Sylvah said teasingly, knowing that Kennedy was taking all of this in.

"If you give me the time, I have every intention of finding out," Hunter said as he backed away and headed toward the site of the accident. "I have every intention of finding out," he said once more with a grin that gave Sylvah goose bumps.

"Woo!" Sylvah gasped. It was the only word that escaped her lips as she proceeded down the path and picked up where she left off with Kennedy.

Sylvah walked away from that accident with a confidence she hadn't felt in years. She was a conservative dresser. Her attire was simple but elegant—black pants that were fitted but not tight, a soft brown knit turtleneck, three-quarter-length camel-colored suede jacket, matching handbag, and brown python boots with pointed toes and sizeable heels. Though she wasn't a prude, Sylvah strongly disliked it when women chose to bare all of their goods, leaving nothing for the imagination.

When Sylvah entered the hair salon forty-five minutes later her arrival provoked standing ovations. After all, it wasn't every day that a beautiful lady like herself was able to cause a multiple-car accident.

The events of the day before caused a smile to dawn on Sylvah's face. She was so ready to move on with her life. A year of sulking was definitely enough. Her friends complained because she was always in a funky mood. It was almost as if she had PMS (personal man shit) for an entire year, but she suddenly felt renewed. Refreshed. Rejuvenated. And in less than two weeks she would celebrate her fortieth birthday. Her best friend, Felice, was treating her to a five-day, four-night vacation in Jamaica. Their reservations were at the Hedonism II hotel located in Negril. It was a much-needed respite from her life of drudgery. Hopefully, she'd be able to do away with her friend Barry McKnight for the week. He had been her lover for the past year. When they made love he swooned like Barry White and he strongly resembled Brian McKnight—at least he did in her dreams, but she wanted and needed the physical, the real deal, and she was ripe and ready for some actual fun and loving.

"Lord, let me sign these papers," Sylvah spoke into the air, allowing the words to ricochet off the walls and back into her ears. Rolling over to the untouched side of the bed, she located a pen in the drawer of the hand-crafted beechwood nightstand. The document was long, but she knew exactly where to sign. She had her lawyer look it over with a fine-tooth comb. Obtaining a lawyer made practical sense. Doctors have doctors, so why shouldn't she have a lawyer? She had reviewed the papers but didn't want to risk missing pertinent information. She knew the law, but a corporate edict was different from divorce law, and Sylvah wasn't about to handle her own case. There was a slight possibility that she might overlook something.

♀♂

Sylvah entered her marbled bathroom dressed in a gentle green terry-cloth robe monogrammed with her initials. Standing directly in front of the large sixty-by-seventy-two-inch silver-framed mirror she undressed and admired her new body, which was now a firm size eight.

The steam from the shower made the mirror hazy, fogging up Sylvah's view. She extended her hand under the water to test its temperature before stepping in. Once inside, the water pelted her like a dose of heavy rain in a tumultuous storm. The high output shower massager was set on level three, the most therapeutic of the six settings. The fact that the massager was also handheld made it an invaluable asset to Sylvah. She was in need of an invigorating shower session. There were knots in her back that needed kneading and a twinge between her legs that demanded the pulsating water's attention.

Sylvah had recently purchased another showerhead just like hers for Felice. All of her friends thought her to be crazy when she told them the pleasure that she received from the massager, and, just like the skeptics they were, they laughed. But one weekend Felice came for a visit. Her curiosity was piqued after hearing Sylvah's incessant chatter about her shower massager, so she decided to give it a whirl. Sylvah was in the laundry room located next to the bathroom washing clothes when she heard a squeal. Tempted to yell and check if everything was all right, she decided against doing so. She figured that Felice must have forgotten to adjust the water temperature before stepping into the shower. Sylvah put another load of clothes into the washer and was adding fabric sheets into the dryer when she heard Felice cry out, "Oh, my fucking goodness! Oh, shit. . .help me!" Sylvah slammed the dryer door shut and ran three paces to the bathroom door. She turned the knob and the warmth of the steam grazed her face, and the fog hazed her vision.

"Sylvah, is that you?" Felice asked in short, steady breaths.

"Yeah. Is everything all right?" Sylvah asked, concerned although she remained standing in the doorway.

"Yes, I'm fine. I'm fine." Felice was still experiencing the after-shocks that accompanied her orgasm.

"Are you sure? Because I thought I heard you screaming for help."

Sylvah laughed to herself as she reflected on that day.

As she exited the shower she heard her phone ring. She quickly glanced at the small clock above the commode and saw that it was only eight. Who could be calling her this early in the morning and why? If it was Felice again, she was going to kick her ass when she arrived. It was bad enough that she had already called her earlier that morning. Sylvah grabbed her robe and sprinted into her bedroom. She had to get to the phone before the fourth ring, otherwise the machine would come on. A lot of people had a tendency to hang up on answering machines.

"Hello," Sylvah said, kneeling forward and leaning on the bed to catch her breath.

"Is Mrs. Lawrence available?" the voice on the other end asked. It was way too early in the morning for telemarketers, Sylvah thought and was tempted to make her reply in the negative. But she decided not to be hasty.

"This is she. How may I help you?"

"This is Jason from Keep It Moving and Storage. I'm calling to confirm that our movers will be there at eleven this morning. Do you have any special needs that I should let my drivers know about?"

That was the wrong question to ask Sylvah after she just got out of that steamy and body-relaxing shower. She had lots of special needs, but was sure that that wasn't what the caller had in mind. Besides she didn't know if any of the men coming this morning would be able to help her out anyway.

"Jason, is it?" she asked, not really waiting for a response. "Everything is packed and ready to go. I have a few small items that I need to put away, but those things will be done by the time your men get here."

"Okay, but just as a precaution we'll bring extra boxes. You just never know. You know?" Jason said and laughed.

"Yeah, whatever," Sylvah said, getting antsy. She was ready to cut him off.

"Okay. Well, your final bill will be… *blah, blah, blah.* If you should need any additional services, it will cost you extra. *Blah, blah, blah.* So, we'll see you then. Thank you for using Keep It Moving and Storage."

Why in the hell did he feel the need to call her so early in the damn morning? The movers weren't due to come for another couple of hours. Damn, she definitely could have missed that call. Less than a minute later the phone rang again. This time she let it ring until the machine came on. If it were important, whoever it was would leave a message. The extended greeting played while she applied the mango-scented lotion to her legs. She made a mental note to take Bläise off the recording when she moved into her new condominium. Now that she was going to be single she didn't want men thinking that she was still attached. Although that had its appeal, that wasn't the type of man that she was looking for.

"Pick up the damn phone!" It was Felice. "You know that your ass is home, so stop screening the calls."

Sylvah grabbed the receiver before Felice could mouth off any more crap, because she could and would take up the entire ten minutes of recording time if she wanted to.

"Woman, you really have issues! First you call me at five in the damn morning disturbing my peaceful sleep. Now, suppose I had a man laying here with me?"

"Hello, may I please speak to Sylvah?"

"Anyway. I don't know why you're trying to play me. I could have a man in here if I wanted to."

"Sweetheart, no one said you couldn't, but I know you and it's been how long since you and that man parted ways? And when was the last time you got your groove on? Barry McKnight don't count."

"You better stay tuned and don't touch that dial, because sister is hot. As a matter of fact, I'm hot to death! Sister is causing car accidents and turning heads of white men these days. Girl, you betta recognize."

"What! You can give me the details when I get there. I'm on my cell and on the way now. Do you want anything from Junior's? I'm about to stop in for coffee and some breakfast to go."

"As a matter of fact, yeah. I don't have any food left. I cleaned the refrigerator two days ago and gave away all of the food, and all of the canned and boxed goods are packed away. Get me coffee and a bagel with lox."

"Girl, this is Junior's, not Lawrence's Delicatessen. I'll get you something good. See you in about thirty minutes. Call waiting, gotta go."

"Who is it?" Sylvah asked.

"It's Jermaine, girl. Who else?"

"You got that man whipped. If he put as much effort in his marriage as he did to you, maybe things would work out. Anyway, hurry."

Felice arrived in record time. They were able to eat their scrambled eggs, toast and corned beef hash before the movers arrived. Sylvah was sipping on the last of her fresh-squeezed orange juice when the doorbell rang. Felice popped up like a jack in the box upon hearing the chimes.

"Girl, you act like you expecting company," Sylvah teased.

"Let's see. . .you hired a moving company that is black owned, so you know these brothers are bound to be beautiful and buff. They lift heavy things, so they've got to be in shape. So to answer your question, yes, I'm expecting some company."

"I should have known that was why you volunteered to come over here and help. You always have some kind of ulterior motive."

"Don't act surprised," Felice said as she hightailed it to the foyer to answer the door.

Sylvah picked up the bags and the remains of their breakfast to place the items into the garbage. She could hear Felice flirting with the movers as she took the bag out of the trash bin and tied the drawstring handles into a knot. Felice led three bronze-colored men to the kitchen. On sight none of them really appealed to Sylvah. The first brother was well built, but couldn't have been more than an inch or two taller than she was, and Sylvah never liked dating men close to her height. The second brother had it going on and he was the perfect height for Sylvah, but he could use a serious tan. He seemed to be lacking in the melanin department, and Sylvah liked her men to be at least golden-brown. The third brother had the height, the complexion, and the body, but the gaps between his teeth were so wide you could use his mouth as a dish drain to rest plates. To make matters worse his head was disproportioned. It simply appeared too small for his body.

Sylvah watched as Felice fawned over all three of the men and she knew that if her friend could have her way she'd be doing all three of them right there on her kitchen floor. Hell, and from the way the men were responding, Felice would get no rejections. All three of them were salivating.

Felice was a freak. There was no hiding it, and for years Sylvah had lived vicariously through Felice to learn new tricks of the trade. Felice was a tall beauty with skin the color of raw sugar and a naturally curly hairdo. Her figure required a sign that read "sharp curves ahead." Sylvah hadn't really noticed it before, but she realized that Felice's attire was a little on the skimpy side. Her friend was wearing a sky-blue baby tee that more than accentuated her ripe breasts and revealed her navel ring. Felice wore a 34D bra and for whatever reasons her nipples were never at ease. They stood at attention 24/7 and since her breasts stood firm and upright she rarely wore a bra—and today was no exception. She had on tight black low-rider stretch pants and because her pants were low, Sylvah could see the powder-blue lace of her thong panties. If Felice were to make an attempt to bend over the movers would get a clear view of the crack of her ass.

Sylvah politely greeted the men, told them that they could get started in the kitchen, and walked past them to take the garbage outside. She trusted that her girl would be able to entertain them in her brief absence.

She took the large aluminum trashcans that displayed her house number on the side to the curb, then she walked back into her concrete yard and closed the gate behind her. Just as she was about to reenter her house she heard the gate creak and slam again. Sylvah quickly turned around to see her intruder.

"Hi. Are you Mrs. Lawrence?" the stranger asked.

This brother looked good, and there were no complaints this time around. Sylvah was mad at herself for not looking her best. She had a scarf on her head; a sweatshirt from her almamater, Morgan State University; and tight, torn jeans. Sylvah wasn't going for the sexy look, because she wasn't planning on meeting Mr. Umm Damn today. Mr. Umm Damn was about six feet one. His complexion was like a pancake when cooked properly and his body was banging. Mr. Umm Damn's hair was cut very low; he had beautiful teeth, which were showcased by an alluring smile; long eyelashes; and thick silky eyebrows. Where did men like this come from? Sylvah wondered, trying not to froth at the mouth at this beautiful creature. Sylvah would've slammed herself into a wall if she were still walking.

"Miss, are you Mrs. Lawrence?" he asked once again.

"Are you talking to me?" Sylvah asked, realizing shortly after that her question was extremely silly. After all, he was standing in her front yard and she was the only person besides him in it. Never in life did she think that anyone could look better than her now-estranged husband, Bläise.

"Yes, I am," he said, giving her an odd look.

"My mind is elsewhere today, so please pardon me. Yes, I am Mrs. Lawrence. Actually it's Ms. Lawrence. As of today I'm no longer married, and since I don't believe that I'm old enough to be your mother, please call me Sylvah."

"Oh, I'm sorry. I wasn't trying to insult you or insinuate that you were old, because you don't look a day over twenty-five."

Sylvah knew that this bronze Adonis was bullshitting her and what he really meant to say was that he wasn't a day over twenty-five, which was fine by her. The late, great singing sensation Aaliyah sang it best: age ain't nothin' but a number. She was flattered and didn't bother to suppress the burgeoning smile that tugged at her lips due to his very forward compliment.

"If I had my paint, paintbrush, and canvas, I would capture that celestial smile that you just laid on me. Your smile is past beautiful, it's divine."

Okay, Mr. Umm Damn was definitely interested in sampling the goods that stood before him, because he was stroking the oil on her canvas pretty thick. Sylvah became curious and wondered if he stroked up and down, round and round, slow and steady, or fast and hard. Inquiring minds wanted to know.

The usually reserved Sylvah decided to step out of character and play along with her new friend. "Is my smile all that you like?" Sylvah inquired with a sly grin. "What's your name?" Sylvah could tell that she put her new young friend on the spot by the way his cheeks turned blush red.

"My name is Jason. I spoke to you on the phone earlier."

"Oh, so that was you. Well, please come on in," Sylvah said, leading him into the house. "So how long have you worked for Keep It Moving and Storage?" Sylvah asked, trying to get an idea of how old Jason was without coming out and asking the question directly.

"I've been working with this company since it was established five years ago."

"Really? So how does it feel to work for a black-owned organization? Is it all that it's cracked up to be?"

"Yeah. It's that and then some, especially since it's my company," Jason responded.

Sylvah stopped dead in her tracks, put her hands on her hips, and swung her head around one hundred and eighty degrees after his last comment. Now she was confused. Jason had to be in his early to mid-twenties and here he was professing to own one of the most successful African-American–owned moving and storage companies in the five boroughs of New York.

"Come again?" Sylvah said.

"Keep It Moving and Storage is my company. I opened it up when I was twenty-two, which was shortly after I graduated from college."

"Really? I'm impressed. Who helps you run it? Your parents?"

"I keep it running," Jason answered smugly and rightfully so. Sylvah's line of questioning was unwarranted. "I'm an artist by trade, but I realized early on while in college that my art wouldn't support me until I made a name for myself so I was a double major. I studied business management and art history."

Sylvah made an attempt to retract her query. "I didn't mean to make it sound as if you couldn't run this company alone. It's just that you appear to be so young, and I just assumed… well we all know what assuming leads to. Please accept my apology."

"Apology accepted," Jason said, extending his arm so that Sylvah could once again lead the way.

When they entered the kitchen Jason immediately surveyed the amount of work that needed to be done. He walked over to his employees and gave them directions on which rooms to begin clearing first. Within seconds the men divided into two teams and began doing their work.

Felice walked over to Sylvah with a huge smile on her face. Sylvah smirked back at Felice, because she knew that her girl had something up her sleeve, and whatever it was she wanted no parts of it.

"I'm going to start organizing the boxes that are upstairs," Sylvah announced. "I still didn't put all of my clothes in the garment box yet."

"Well, wait for me. I'll come help you. After all, that is what I'm here for," Felice said.

"Oh, really? I thought you were just here as a showpiece today. Besides, I thought that you'd want to stay down here and keep these men satisfied—I mean occupied. What is wrong with me? I guess it's just a little slip of the tongue."

"Sylvah, you are not funny. Anyway, I still want to know what's going on with you and these white men. You still didn't tell me what happened."

"Oh, yeah. Well, bring your butt on upstairs and I'll tell you," Sylvah said. She walked over to Jason.

"Jason," Sylvah said coyly. "We're going upstairs to finish packing the remaining items. If you need anything, please feel free to come upstairs." *Another uncharacteristic move, what is getting into me?* Sylvah thought.

Jason stood and smiled giving Sylvah his undivided attention. "Definitely. I'm sure I'll need your assistance shortly."

Sylvah could feel the red filling her cheeks. Why was she blushing? Damn! She turned quickly so Jason wouldn't see her face. She sashayed, softly swinging her hips and without glancing back, she knew he was looking.

Sylvah and Felice entered the master bedroom. They both went into the walk-in closet and began transferring clothes from the wardrobe into garment boxes. Within twenty minutes they were finished and the only thing left to be done was to move the items into the truck. While they waited for the men to complete their work downstairs, Sylvah told Felice all about her episode from the day before. Felice suggested that Sylvah pursue a relationship with Hunter, at the very least a little rendezvous, at which Sylvah scoffed. Hunter was far from golden-brown. Although her curiosity piqued about the prospect of being with a white man, the thought of being with a sexy, strong, ambitious younger black man was even more appealing. Sylvah was lost in her thoughts when Jason appeared. Felice had to tell her to snap out of it and brought her attention to the sexy visitor who stood patiently in the doorway.

"Ms. Lawrence. . .I mean Sylvah, I wanted to take a look up here if you don't mind, so we could begin taking these items out to the truck."

Sylvah cleared her throat and pulled herself together. She didn't realize how much she desired this luscious young man. When she stood she could feel the moisture that had begun to form between her thighs. Now that he was standing only a few feet away, her clitoris was experiencing a slight titillation of excitement. She was feeling a bit embarrassed, but she quickly realized that no one else would know that her panties were wet or that her pussy was throbbing. Sylvah felt like a bitch in heat, and she knew that Jason could be the dog that she needed him to be.

"By all means. Please take your time and look around. I tried to organize things to make it easier for you guys. I put the larger boxes to the front and the smaller ones are back there." Sylvah pointed and Jason shifted in the direction of her finger. He moved closer to Sylvah, and she could feel the warmth of his body. Unconsciously, Sylvah began fanning herself, and Felice choked up a laugh.

"Girl, I'm going downstairs to let them know that they can begin clearing some of the upstairs rooms and to see if *I* can be of any assistance. It appears that there are too many black folks in this space and you know how we can draw heat."

Before Sylvah could object, Felice was gone.

"Umm, are your guys almost done downstairs?" Sylvah asked as Jason circled the room.

"Yeah, just about. I have another worker who just showed up, so we have more than enough hands now."

"That's good. You'll be able to do your job a lot quicker and then you all can go home early."

"That's true, but I'm in no real rush."

"Oh, you don't have another job after this?"

"I have a job that I want to complete right here, right now," Jason said as he walked up behind Sylvah and put his hands on her waist. "Sylvah, if you don't mind me saying so, you are beautiful. I haven't been able to take my eyes off you from the moment I arrived."

Sylvah was startled and quickly pulled away. She wanted him, but she had never been involved in a one-night or even a one-afternoon stand before. This was all happening too fast. She had to regain control of the situation.

"Jason, I don't know if I gave you the wrong impression, but I'm still a married woman."

"I thought you said earlier that you weren't married. It doesn't matter, and I apologize if I've overstepped my boundaries. I don't usually behave this way. I was just so attracted to you," Jason said as he walked off sheepishly.

"Jason, wait," Sylvah called.

Jason stopped in the doorway and turned around to face Sylvah, who walked over and took him by the hand, closing the door behind them.

Sylvah craned her neck to invite Jason's mouth to meet hers. Jason's tongue moved with such precision that it felt like he was making love to Sylvah's mouth. His thick lips were pressed softly against Sylvah's and his mouth was warm and sweet. Jason looped his tongue around hers and did something that Sylvah had never experienced before. Then he kept her tongue in his mouth and slowly sucked on it the way Bläise used to suck on her clitoris. Sylvah could feel herself melting in Jason's massive arms. The kiss was intense, and Sylvah felt another jolt of excitement in her vagina. When he was through, Jason pulled back and gazed into her chestnut eyes, causing Sylvah to swoon. She didn't know how and when things got so hot and heavy, but they had and she wanted more.

Kissing was usually considered personal, private, and very passionate. Sylvah couldn't remember the last time she shared a kiss like that with anyone—not even with Bläise. Yet here she was kissing Jason, this young brute of a man. She still couldn't get over his age. It really shouldn't have been an issue. Sylvah felt she deserved this young treat. Plenty of men dated younger women. As a matter of fact many men only dated younger women. What difference did it make if she decided to date a younger man? The important thing was that he treated her right. Hell, why was she getting so carried away? It was only a fuck!

Between breaths and on the way to the bed, Sylvah spoke, "Jason, I'm almost old enough to be your mother." After further calculation she realized that she would have been a very, very young mother.

"Then teach me, Mommy. Teach me, because I'm willing to learn," Jason said as he bent to his knees and began unbuttoning Sylvah's jeans. Slowly he slid them off her full hips and sumptuous ass. His hands moved freely about her body, and Sylvah laid back to enjoy the company and pleasure of Jason's hands, which seemed to be extraordinarily soft for someone who moved furniture for a living.

Sylvah's body yearned for the touch of a man, and she wanted this man inside of her. It had been almost two years since her body was caressed. Jason's fingertips grazed the damp crotch of Sylvah's panties, which he removed with his teeth. Sylvah wriggled as Jason darted his tongue in and around her vagina, using it as a probe. Sylvah wondered how someone so young could be so good. Bläise didn't even please her like this. Jason moved his hands against her smooth, bare legs, and Sylvah's chest heaved from elation. She chewed on her lower lip to keep from moaning aloud. After all, Felice or one of Jason's employees could come knocking on the door at any second. Sylvah's breathing intensified when Jason's tongue hit her spot. She wanted to stop him, but it felt too good. Bläise was a good lover, but he never hit the spot that quickly. A moaning sound passed through her lips. Sylvah bucked her head forward. Jason used that as an indication and slowed his tongue down a few notches.

"Not yet," he said as he held up his head. "I want to taste some more of this sweet nectar."

He kissed her vulva and licked on her clit some more. From time to time he would stick his tongue in and out of her vagina to stop Sylvah from climaxing. When Sylvah could stand it no more, she held his head on her spot, forcing him to bring her to orgasm. Sylvah's body flinched and her legs locked around Jason's head. As Sylvah continued to cum Jason stroked his tongue in strong, circular motions, and she imagined that he handled his paintbrush in the same manner.

A rush of cum gushed out of her vagina as her body continued to jolt. When her legs relaxed and her body became tranquil Jason moved up onto the bed to join Sylvah, but she wasn't quite ready for him to enter her. Sylvah wanted to taste Jason as well. Their lips touched briefly before her descent. She positioned her body upright and headed straight down south. She quickly unfastened his belt and pants, and before long his large and very attractive penis filled her mouth. She utilized the strength in her jaws to suck his shaft and used her hand to jerk what couldn't fit into her mouth. She marveled over his beautiful piece of equipment, which was indeed a masterpiece. Sylvah could tell from Jason's expression that he was thoroughly enjoying her warm, soft lips and mouth wrapped around his penis. On occasion he would look at her and moan his pleasure, and she kept her eyes on him the entire time. She placed her free hand on his balls and fondled them for further stimulation. This action seemed to turn him on even more, because he began pumping into her mouth faster and harder. The head of his penis was now touching the back of her throat. Sylvah could feel the life throbbing and the veins pulsating in her mouth. His penis became thicker, so she slowly removed her lips in preparation for her ride on the downtown express. The next stop was Sylvah Street.

Jason reached for Sylvah's hand and pulled her to lay beside him. Gently he pried her legs apart and bent down to get one last taste. He rubbed his fingers over her clit before sucking them. With tender thrusts he made his way past the gated region. Sylvah moaned and Jason covered her mouth with his lips. This kiss was even more passionate than their earlier one. Sylvah held on to Jason's neck and wrapped her legs inside of his to intensify the penetration. She found his rhythm and they waltzed to the same beat. Jason gazed into Sylvah's eyes as he put picked her up by the ass. Within seconds he was standing and lifting her up and down, plastering her slickness onto his condom covered dick. Sylvah's ass was damp, and he could feel her moisture trickling down his thigh, which heightened his arousal. Jason's breathing came faster as he inserted Sylvah's large, ripe nipple into his mouth. He suckled her breast like a nursing infant, fast and feverishly.

Sylvah could feel another orgasm beginning to surface, and she made no effort to hold it back. She pulled her body closer to his and clawed her fingers into his flesh. She bawled for the Creator as her body gave way to the bottled-up pleasure. Sylvah's seeping river caused Jason to lose total control. His body convulsed as he filled her with his hot liquid. His movements became languid. Sylvah closed her eyes, lay her head on his shoulder, and collapsed into his cozy embrace. Jason kept Sylvah in his arms as he walked them both back to the bed. He lay her down and faced her, planting soft kisses on her forehead, cheeks, chin, and lips.

A few moments lapsed before either one of them made a move and time seemed to stand still. Neither of them wanted to disembark their passionate excursion. Sylvah felt refreshed and didn't know if anything would ever become of her and Jason. But one thing she knew for sure was that her next stop was to Jamaica, West Indies—Hedonism II.

3

A Few Things About Men

Felice was exhausted. She had a long day watching all of those good-looking men move boxes up and down, in and out of the house. And thanks to her early-morning caller her one night of peaceful sleep had been interrupted prematurely.

Slipping out of her fitted jeans, she threw them in the hamper in the bathroom. She drew herself a nice bath and turned the jets on in the whirlpool tub. A modest amount of Mango Cocoa Shea Body Wash from Nubian Heritage was poured into the circle of water. Felice was in dire need of an invigorating bath because she still had a lot of things clouding her mind that she needed to clear.

Upon returning home to New York, Felice realized she couldn't run from her past, but she needed to handle things in her time. It had only been three and a half months since she returned. In that short time she had to handle multiple problems. When she left New York she had decided to sublet her condominium. It was against her better judgment, but her mortgage had to be paid and she hadn't seen the sense of depleting her funds; especially since she had plans to stay indefinitely. Apparently, in her absence the individual to whom she leased the apartment received a nine-month assignment in Switzerland. Without notifying Sylvah, who Felice left in charge in case of emergency, he decided to rent it out on his own. He sublet it to a couple with children so when Felice came back, her place looked like a tornado had claimed it. The walls displayed all sixty-four colors compliments of Crayola. Her appliances, which were new when she left, now looked like they had been repossessed from a junkyard and her furniture was beyond repair. It was a good thing that she put her antiques and good stuff in storage.

The family who resided in her apartment had changed both the locks on the door as well as the phone number, so Felice had to camp out in front of her condominium to give them notice to vacate the premises in one month. During that month, Felice stayed at Sylvah's town house. It was fun, but she longed to be back in her own domain. She wasn't really comfortable bringing her male companions to Sylvah's home. Although Sylvah never passed any comments about Felice's houseguests, it showed in her mannerisms and behavior. Felice knew that Sylvah was probably saying, "Damn, how many men do you have?" Felice was a grown-ass woman and didn't need to seek anyone's approval or endure another's judgment. She also didn't need anyone to be knee-deep in her business, because it was just that, her business.

Felice dipped her toes in the steaming tub and the water was just right. She allowed the rest of her body to follow and sunk beneath the bubbles, leaving only her head above water. Leaning back, she let her mind wander on the day's events—to be more specific, the movers, Shechem, Lavan and Brick. She laughed when Brick told her his name and knew that he had to be kidding. But she learned that his other occupation was boxing and Brick was the name that he went by. It was also his last name. Felice had to decide which one of them she would pursue to rendezvous with. All three of them looked good to Felice, but Sylvah snagged the best-looking one, Jason. He was all of twenty-seven years old. Felice could have taught him a thing or two, but instead she had three men to choose from to teach. Not a bad situation.

In two days she would be in Jamaica celebrating Sylvah's fortieth birthday. But Sylvah had done a little early celebrating of her own. Felice couldn't believe her conservative friend and her little tryst that afternoon. If Felice weren't there to hear it with her own ears, she wouldn't have believed Sylvah. This was not the Sylvah she had left behind two years ago.

That previous time was a lot different for both she and Sylvah. Felice had no idea that Sylvah's marriage was in trouble. She was aware that Bläise and Sylvah had disagreements, but that was common in all relationships. Felice couldn't understand why they allowed their friendship to disintegrate the way they had. Bläise and Sylvah had stopped communicating. They stopped listening and they stopped loving. All of those things could have been repaired. It wasn't as if Sylvah caught or ever heard of Bläise cheating, and he wasn't disrespecting her. Their biggest problem was neglect, and both of them were at fault with that. It was almost as if they were waiting for the kids to turn eighteen so they could split up. As soon as Kenya and Zaire went away to college, Bläise and Sylvah separated. Felice felt like she was losing a part of herself as well. She always looked at Sylvah and Bläise as the perfect couple. Now Sylvah was selling her house, the only place in which Felice always felt comfortable.

In Felice's own little way she was envious of Sylvah and Bläise's relationship. It appeared to be perfect, but that was the problem: the operative word being *appeared*. However, there were certain things that, as a married woman, Sylvah never bothered to share with Felice, and Felice respected that. After all, she was once married herself and understood the necessity of keeping some things private. However, when Felice's commode began to overflow, she needed someone to help her clean her ass. Felice decided to shed her pride and share her agony with her best friends, Sylvah and Candace Farewell. Felice needed their support, and it wasn't something that she felt comfortable telling her mother, Samantha.

The relationship between Felice and her mother was strained for more reasons than one. Felice felt her share of betrayals and the more she was forced to endure, the less mercilful she became. The first bout of betrayal came when she was just a child, and Felice shuddered when the vision forced its way into her psyche. The second came from her mother during Felice's first year of college. Although she resolved herself to the fate that her mother chose, she never felt that she could truly forgive Samantha. The biggest hurt came from her ex-husband, Bedford. In Bedford she felt she could put all of her past pains to rest. Felice trusted him in a way that she never thought she could ever depend on another human. Felice was always one to safeguard her feelings. However, when she met Bedford, she opened up her shutters and let the daylight consume her gloomy past. Bedford and Felice were a match made in heaven—or so she thought.

Then she did the hardest thing a woman could ever do. She left him. Felice picked herself up, pulled the pieces together and didn't look back as far their marriage was concerned. Nevertheless, she was smart enough to remain amicable so that their business relationship could continue to flourish. Felice wasn't about to let her bank accounts suffer because of this mishap. There was no reason to punish herself. She came to the conclusion that her life would always be filled with tempests. At first it was hard to pretend with Bedford. After all, he hurt her. Immediately after the divorce she took a month's leave of absence. Felice moved out of their brownstone and didn't argue with Bedford about selling it for profit or ownership. Her first step to recovery was to leave the place that caused her pain. During that month she stayed with Sylvah, Bläise, and their children. In less than a week she found a new residence. It was a beautiful three-bedroom located on Eastern Parkway and Underhill Avenue. It was a prewar building with huge apartments. Management was renovating the residences into condominiums or allowing buyers to purchase the apartments as is. Felice liked the sound of as-is. This gave her the opportunity to design and create her own space. Felice had a vision about her new living arrangements and allowed this to occupy her thoughts. The mortgage and closing took less than two weeks, and one week later she was moving in.

The first week back at work had been the most difficult for Felice. She tried her best to avoid Bedford. It was hard because their office space at the time was small. They only had six other people who worked with them—Shirley, her former secretary Davonna, three account executives and an assistant. Felice resorted to residing in her office, bringing her lunch to work and keeping her door shut. Everyone in the office felt the tension. It was impossible not to, considering that they were all once such a close crop. They would go to lunch together or order in, sit in one another's space and shoot the breeze, laughter filling the air, and the staff meetings were filled with humor. The tone changed to serious and the members of Jackson and Jackson had resorted to just being cordial toward one another. Everyone respected Bedford and Felice too much to take sides, and no one really knew why the fairytale suddenly ended with the exception of Shirley, who always knew things. No one had to tell her and when Davonna didn't return to work, her theory was confirmed. That didn't dissuade Shirley from being loyal to Bedford, and though she had her opinions about the situation she didn't feel the need to share them with anyone, not even Bedford.

The second week was just as agonizing, but Felice made an effort to be more sociable with the staff. She didn't want the work environment to be stiff and uncomfortable, and she knew that hostility decreased productivity. Her only problem was interacting with Bedford in a civil manner. It was hard for her to speak to him in closed quarters without making a snide remark. Felice had a mouth that could shoot off rounds quicker than a machine gun, and it didn't come with a safety.

Her third week back was less painful. Over the weekend she had gone with Sylvah for a full-body massage and makeover. Felice left the spa feeling refreshed and rejuvenated, and her mind was clear. Later that evening her girls took her out to a private celebrity-laden soiree, and she received so much attention that she almost forgot that her soon-to-be ex-husband was a mongrel. By Monday morning she was still grazing on the remnants of her weekend.

Bedford didn't make it any easier for Felice. He was unrelenting in his pursuit of trying to get Felice back. He fawned over her every chance he got. Bedford showed up at all of her favorite spots, bought her gifts, and wooed her to death. This behavior lasted for more than three months and almost broke Felice because regardless of his infidelity and betrayal she still loved Bedford. He was also still her business partner.

Jackson and Jackson kept Felice busy. At least she allowed the job to occupy her every waking moment. The thought of being alone was frightening, though Felice wasn't alone for long. Felice attended an after-work mixer with her girls Sylvah, Alana Wright and Candace Farewell. The scene was nice and the clientele professional. Alana was getting her flirt on while Sylvah and Candace danced to the latest songs and Felice was at the bar getting another drink. She was about to walk away when she felt someone pull her arm. Quickly she turned around to face whoever had the nerve to grab her.

"Felice Pryce?" the man asked.

"Yes," Felice said trying to place the face. He looked familiar, but she didn't remember his name right away. He must've attended high school or college with Felice, especially since no one called her by her maiden name anymore.

"Jermaine. Remember me? We dated senior year in high school."

"Oh, Jermaine Gray. You look so different with your goatee, and you filled out some." At six-feet-two, Jermaine could have been a model. He was tall and lean with a slight muscular build, bald head, gorgeous teeth and butterscotch skin tone.

"I hope that's a good thing."

"Yes, it is. You were a string bean in high school. You were cute, but you were so thin. Now you're looking really good," Felice said as she viewed the entire package.

"You're looking pretty nice too. I see so many of our old classmates and they have either gained weight, look older than they are or look like they're leading a really rough life."

Felice nodded her head and laughed, because not too long ago she, too, saw an old schoolmate who looked haggard.

"So what are you doing these days?" Jermaine asked.

"I have my own business, Jackson and Jackson. Well, I have a partner. He's about to be my ex-husband."

"I'm sorry to hear about the ex-husband thing. How long were you married?"

"Too long. Anyway what about you?" Felice asked, nursing her drink and admiring Jermaine's half-moon dimples.

Jermaine rattled off bullet points of his life as if he were being interviewed. "I'm an accountant for Bad Boy Entertainment and I've been there for six years. I'm married with two kids, but things are kinda shaky between my wife and me, and I don't know how much longer it will be before one of us just walks away." They shared a moment of awkward silence. "Are you here alone?"

"Well, I hope things work out for you, especially since children are involved. Oh, I'm here with three of my girls." Felice pointed to Sylvah and Candace in the center of the dance floor. She couldn't spot Alana. "Come on. Let's join your friends." Jermaine took Felice by the hand and guided her to the dance floor. They dirty danced for nearly two hours straight and were glued together even when the deejay played hip-hop. Neither wanted the night to end. They parted ways, but not before exchanging information. Shortly thereafter Felice and Jermaine began seeing each other, even though Felice knew it was wrong. It was a distraction from what she was going through with Bedford. Jermaine's easygoing personality and attentiveness were soothing to Felice. The adulterous affair persisted much longer than it should have and Felice felt herself falling for Jermaine. He was just as sweet as he was in high school, but he was a married man and she was in the process of a divorce. In spite of everything, Jermaine kept telling Felice he would leave his wife if she just said the word. None of it was right, but when they were together it felt lovely. Felice came to the understanding that Jermaine was only an intermission and nothing serious could ever ensue between them.

One year later she met Aaron Cane. Aaron was a beautiful man who happened to be a professional basketball player. He played basketball overseas in Europe. Aaron was six feet, five inches, two-hundred and twenty-five pounds, twenty-nine years old, with a salary of $750,000 a year, not including his endorsements. He was black and Spanish, smart, charming, and sexy. Aaron appeared to be all of that and then some. He didn't seem to be lacking in any area, especially in the bedroom. Felice quickly learned that there was a world outside of Bedford. This man allowed her to discover herself in more ways than one. He taught her to be uninhibited and in return she became willing to please and in the process found the male G-spot. Sex couldn't get any better than what Felice was experiencing. The only flaw in their relationship was that Aaron was overseas, but he wanted to devote himself to Felice. He flew her in to see him regularly, and she soon became a member of the Mile-High Club. One and a half years later he professed his everlasting love to Felice and proposed to her with a four-carat ring.

Felice was floored and felt she had no choice but to respond in the positive. Although Felice wasn't single very long she believed that Aaron was actually saving her from a life of unnecessary bull and the dating— scratch that, mating—ritual.

Aaron and Felice met through a mutual acquaintance. Felice was having lunch with a colleague who happened to be an attorney. The client invited Aaron along to discuss business as well as to introduce him to Felice so that she could give him some sound financial advice. Felice and her associate arrived before Aaron, and when Aaron entered the restaurant, Felice almost forgot her name. She was stupefied and her eyes followed him until he arrived at the table. Felice had no idea that this was the man to whom her comrade had planned to introduce her. She was almost tongue-tied during the introductions, and Aaron laughed and made light of the awkwardness that encased them. Aaron was only scheduled to be in New York for three days, but after hanging out with Felice he extended his stay for a week and she showed him the time of his life while he paid for it all. He lavished her with gifts and attention and said all the right things. He was a sweet man from a small remote town in Florida. Aaron put her mind at ease. When he finally had to return to Europe, Felice thought that would be the end of their free-fall weekend. Then Aaron proved her wrong by sending her a plane ticket to visit him the following month. Felice accepted, and it was on that trip that she knew that she loved him. Felice allowed herself to open up and feel again. Her heart was almost fully recovered and was about three quarters to complete restoration.

There was a slight problem, however. Felice had begun having an affair with her ex-husband again and occasionally Jermaine came by. The relationship with Aaron was good, but it was very fickle. Although he sent for her, it was only once a month and sometimes bimonthly. Besides that, she wasn't going to invest herself a hundred percent until they were living in the same country and married. She loved Aaron, but the fact still remained that he lived thousands of miles away and trust had to be earned. Yes, she trusted him, since she had no reason not to, but he was still a man. Bedford taught her a few things about men, trust, and relationships.

First, just because you lived with a person didn't mean you always shared the same opinions or views.

Second, you could know a person for many, many years and still not really know them.

Third, if you can't account for a person's whereabouts then their alibi could be false.

Fourth, man is only human and should never be held on a pedestal or idolized.

Fifth, if given too much leeway your pet/man might stray.

Sixth, what you liked about the person in the beginning could very well turn your stomach later as the relationship begins to dull.

Seventh, you cannot change a man. You have to love him for the person that he is.

Eighth, true relationships are built on friendship not sex.

Ninth, every man lies.

Tenth, niggas ain't shit!

These were harsh lessons, but words to live and stand by. Felice thought that her relationship with Bedford was flawless. Apparently it was all her imagination. At first, Felice tried to find out where she went wrong. Then she later realized that no matter what, it was really Bedford who went wrong and the blame ended there.

Knowing these things saved Felice when her relationship with Aaron began to be tested. Felice knew that she shouldn't have resumed a relationship with Bedford, sexually or otherwise. But Felice enjoyed sex, and Bedford was good while Jermaine was passionate. Aside from that it felt good to have Bedford chasing her. He knew that Felice was the best thing to ever happen to him, but he still chose to risk it all. By the time Felice hooked up with Aaron, Bedford was already involved with a sweet southern belle named Sandy Beulah-Mae Dixon, whom he married a year later. He claimed to have loved Sandy, but never issued Felice her walking papers. By then Felice was in way too deep to even care. She never questioned him about why he continued their affair, and what did it really matter? They were simply having fun. It was a cool arrangement. They were great in business together and excellent in bed together. It was a match made in heaven with no strings attached. Each party knew the risks involved. They had been through enough together to weigh the consequences of their furtive actions. Felice met Sandy on numerous occasions and thought that she was nice. Extremely nice, but naïve as all hell!

Sandy and Felice had the pleasure of meeting at one of their client's celebrations. Sandy was about the same height and complexion as Felice. She had a neat figure and an accent that sounded like she should have been on that old television program *Designing Women*. Felice laughed at the resemblance between her and Sandy. She even mentioned it to Bedford jokingly the following day. It was then that Felice realized her true power over Bedford and knew that she could never be replaced. The relationship persisted for the greater part of Bedford and Sandy's marriage. However, it was off and on, and once Aaron became a fixture in her life, it was more off than on.

Aaron made Felice happy and Felice made Aaron happy. Their relationship was fun. They never really had time for arguments because early on in the relationship they agreed to keep the outside world where it belonged, outside. The time they spent together was marvelous. They did plenty of sightseeing, dining out, dancing, partying, and lovemaking. That was generally all a three- or four-day trip allowed. The trips were short, but both agreed that they were well worth the long hours on the plane. The arrangement suited Felice just fine. She was so caught up in her work that a demanding relationship with a different suitor would have been impossible. Jackson and Jackson was demanding her time. If she and Bedford were to continue to flourish and attain goals they set for themselves then she couldn't afford much more than she was giving to Aaron, and he understood that. The same went for Felice with Aaron's career. He could be traded at any time.

Aaron continued to send Felice tickets to visit him, and on one occasion she even surprised him by attending a game at the Olympics in Barcelona. When she showed up, the look of astonishment on Aaron's face was incredulous. His shock was understandable, because who would have thought that Felice would go out of her way to come so far just to see him play? She had never done anything like that before. Felice had a full-scale plan ahead for them. She booked the honeymoon

suite at a five-star hotel and ordered oysters, chocolate-dipped straw-
berries, a can of whipped cream, blueberries and two bottles of chilled
champagne. Felice planned to do everything that would please Aaron
and then some. Aaron was extra relieved that she had her own room in
a different hotel across town. He said that he wanted them to have
their privacy, but needed to get back to his hotel by 6:00 A.M. He couldn't
afford to miss practice and roll call. It was bad enough that he was
missing curfew. Felice was understanding and wasn't interested in
jeopardizing his job. She was simply interested in getting her Aaron fix.
Aaron's team had won the game, so he told Felice that he would meet
her in an hour or two at her hotel. Felice knew Aaron felt bad abandoning the team and not celebrating their victory. He was quickly becoming
a habit, and she enjoyed the way he smoked her ass like a cigarette.
The good thing was that no one would get lung cancer from this particular habit.

As promised, Aaron arrived exactly two hours later at Felice's room.
He was a man of his word, and she didn't doubt that he would be late.
She was laid out on the bed in her new Claire Pettibone lace lingerie.
Aaron was always very appreciative of the effort and time that Felice
took in making herself smell and look nice for him. Felice knew that it
wouldn't be long before her Claire Pettibone was removed and dis-
carded on the floor, later to be found beneath the bed or in a corner
somewhere. Nevertheless, the look of approval and satisfaction on his
face was more than worth it.

Aaron allowed the rhythm of the music to guide him into the bedroom the way a cobra followed the mesmerizing tune of a flute player.
His eyes bulged as he entered the room. Felice was spread-eagled
across the bed, shaved and dressed and ready to be eaten. His penis
shot up like a speeding bullet and within seconds he was buried in Felice's
sweetness. Felice was drenched from head to toe from Aaron's tongue
work. He was masterful as he gave her multiple orgasms. She was so
overwhelmed with pleasure that she experienced a minor headache. It
wasn't a migraine. It was more from having one orgasm too many—
back to back. Aaron was ferocious as he made love to Felice over and
over.

Felice was not about to be outdone and reciprocated as good as she received on the bed, on the floor, in the shower, on the sink basin, on the balcony, and on the food service cart. Four hours and five condoms later both Felice and Aaron were sapped. They both slept as sound as bears during hibernation. Felice was smart enough to order a 5:00 A.M. wake-up call for Aaron. Felice remained for the weekend, but Aaron was occupied with photo ops, press conferences, and parties. Felice was disappointed that she didn't get to spend as much time with him as she had hoped, but understood, especially after Aaron was voted Most Valuable Player. This was great for him because he was still in his prime, and there was a good chance that he could be recruited back to the States or even Canada. He even had a meeting with Isaiah Thomas, who at the time was coaching the Indiana Pacers.

After Aaron proposed to Felice, the one thing that stayed on her mind was where they were going to live. She didn't want to move to Europe. Felice could almost deal with Canada, but Europe would take major adjusting. Her roots were planted deep in American soil. She proudly claimed her African heritage, but Felice knew that she'd be lost anyplace other than America. She wasn't against trying something new, but it would get tired after days of no communication with family and her real friends. How many black people really lived in Spain? There were people of African descent there but they didn't share the same culture or ideals. It just wouldn't be the same.

When Felice returned home she was feeling good, like she wanted to conquer the world. Aaron sent her twelve dozen white and red roses. He thanked her for coming out to surprise, support, and sex him. He emphasized the word *sex* and said that she was welcome to do that more often. Her office looked like a small florist shop. Felice was so ecstatic that she walked around the office smiling all day. She ended up giving ten dozen of the roses to office personnel. There was no way that she was going to be able care for all of the flowers. Felice loved and appreciated the roses, but Aaron went overboard. She took one vase home and left one in her office. The rest of her week went pretty much the same. She continued to receive wonderful gifts from Aaron, gained new business for Jackson and Jackson, attended girls night out with her closest friends, and Bedford was even on her good side.

Two weeks later she was introduced to misery. It started with a phone call she received from her mother. Felice and her mother weren't the best of friends. They actually weren't friends at all. They simply had an understanding to stay out of each other's path. Felice had never forgiven her mother for keeping secrets from her, and at age thirty-five she was to learn that when it came to her mother, such a thing never ceased. The first secret she discovered on her own and never quite pardoned her mother, but Felice didn't live her mother's life. Therefore, Samantha could do as she pleased.

Samantha had called Felice with disturbing news. She had a mammogram and lumps were found, and it couldn't be determined if they were malignant or benign. The shield that Felice often wore around her mother was disarmed. This was the first time that she really ever needed to be concerned about her mother. As much as Felice hated to admit it, her mother was the iceberg in her ocean. Samantha was big, steady, solid, strong, tenacious, and anchored. These were all qualities that she admired in her mother when Felice was a child and even as an adult. Therefore, Felice was worried. It never dawned on her before that she could lose her mother. Finding masses in her mother's breast at her age wasn't a good thing. Cancer was linked to their family. Felice's grandmother died from uterine cancer, two of her uncles died from leukemia, and her mother was to be diagnosed with God knows what.

The following week Samantha was scheduled to go through a series of examinations where she would be poked and prodded. The week after that she was to undergo a lumpectomy. Felice tried to attend every appointment with her mother, and if she were unable to go, she visited Samantha in the evenings after work. It was a stressful time for everyone, their family especially.

It turned out that the lumps were benign. Felice was relieved. As much as she hated her mother, she loved her equally as much, if not more. There relationship was sweet and very, very sour. Shortly thereafter their relationship returned to the way it was prior to her mother finding out that she had cystic breasts.

Soon Felice knew that something was wrong with her. She was

feeling lethargic. Her breasts were painful and she was retaining water. In a matter of one month she had gained five pounds. Felice was a regular at the gym and the entire staff at Bally's knew her by name, so why was she steadily gaining instead of losing? Felice had an idea, but was praying that wasn't the case. Felice paid her doctor a visit, and to her disappointment she found out that she was pregnant. She was saddened because she knew that it wasn't Aaron's. According to the doctor, Felice was two months pregnant. Either way, it didn't matter since she and Aaron used condoms religiously. On the other hand, she and Bedford rarely used condoms. Also to her recollection, the condoms never broke when she and Aaron had sex. They never slipped off and as far as she knew, they were never punctured. She doubted that Aaron would purposely try to get her pregnant. He never mentioned anything about wanting kids or starting a family. They were both comfortable with the way things were.

Felice didn't know what she was going to do. She kept the pregnancy to herself for one month trying to figure out a way to tell Bedford. Felice didn't know how Bedford would react, but she figured he wouldn't be happy. After all, he was still married to Sandy. Most importantly, how was she going to explain this to her fiancé? She could lie to Aaron and say it was his, but that would be extremely deceptive. The foundation of the relationship would become weak, which would cause the structure to crumble, ending a wonderful thing. How could she possibly get around this? She could have an abortion, but at thirty-five she risked the chance of becoming infertile. Felice had never been pregnant her entire life and always thought she was either lucky or barren. Now that she knew she wasn't infertile, what was she going to do? Besides that, she was now three months pregnant since she wasted so much time trying to find a way to tell Bedford.

The memories flooded back to Felice as if it were yesterday. It was a Monday morning when Felice had to practically corner Bedford in his office. He reacted the way that she hoped he wouldn't, but what else could she expect? It wasn't like she had just told him that he had won a million bucks. She was telling him that he was the father of her unborn child. The conversation went semi-smooth. Bedford didn't say or do anything irrational, immediately. She sat him down and broke the news to him as best as she knew how.

"Do you want the good news or the bad news first?" Felice asked.

"I'll let you decide which one you want to give me first."

"Okay, fine. Be that way. Here goes…" Felice said, pausing for an extended amount of time as Bedford looked on. "I'm pregnant."

"That's great! Your boy Aaron must be happy. So what's the bad news?"

"You're the father."

Bedford appeared constipated. He looked almost hysterical, but there was nothing funny. He kept mumbling something under his breath, and Felice wasn't quite sure what he was saying. However, it sounded like "fucking nightmare."

After the bewildered look disappeared from his eyes they resumed the conversation. Bedford started out denying that it was his child and treating her coldly. He even stooped so low as to say that it was one of her many partners. The only other partner she had besides Aaron was Bedford. Jermaine hadn't been in the picture in months. Then he told her how much he wanted to start a family with Sandy. Felice didn't want to cry, but the tears that fell from her eyes decided they didn't need her consent. Hearing Bedford talk about beginning a family broke her heart for several reasons. The first was, it should have been her five years earlier, before things between her and Bedford went crazy and before the demise of their relationship. Felice and Bedford were so career- driven that they never discussed starting a family. Two, the pregnancy wasn't with the man that she was about to be married to and finally, there was a strong possibility that Aaron would break up with her. Bedford made it clear that there was no way Aaron would accept knowing that she was pregnant and it wasn't his. Bedford broke the code of honor between men and shed light on her situation.

"Let me be blunt with you. Aaron may know that you are over here getting your groove on, but there has never been any proof to substantiate that. Aside from that, no man wants to know that someone else is tapping his piece of ass. We may know the truth deep down, but once it comes to light, we no longer want the soiled goods. We toss them to the side and move on to the next. That is a man by nature. We can do it, but our women cannot."

It was a harsh delivery, but Felice knew all of this prior to Bedford's discourse. She just needed to hear it aloud.

One week later she received an express parcel marked URGENT, but it wasn't from any of her clients so she wasn't in any rush to open it. Felice allowed the package to sit for a few days. Finally on Wednesday after her desk was clear and she was close to resolving her earlier situation with Bedford she decided to see what was so urgent. The yellow envelope inside of the express package read in large capital letters, "DO NOT BEND." Now Felice's interest was piqued. She removed the letter and the contents fell out onto her desk. There were three sets of pictures. The top one was of a cute little boy. Felice didn't recognize him, so she picked up the note that accompanied the pictures.

Dear Felice,

There are a few things that I thought you should know. Since my husband failed to tell you that he was married, he left me the honor. Aaron Cane is my lawful husband. He has been and will continue to be until I say otherwise. We have been married for seven years and have two children and another on the way.

Aaron and I are high school sweethearts from Lincoln, Nebraska. I recently learned about you when you paid him a visit in Barcelona. I heard from one of the other wives that you two were an item. I knew from day one that Aaron wasn't faithful, but the fling between you all has gone on far too long.

Stay away from my husband. I'm not leaving him and contrary to what he may tell you, he's not leaving me. We love each other and have another baby on the way to prove it.

My advice to you is walk away now before you get your feelings hurt. Stay away from my family. You are an unwanted element. You are a home wrecker!

Sincerely,

MRS. CANE

P.S. Even if Aaron tried to leave me, his money would be tied up in child support for eighteen more years and let's not forget about all that alimony I'd get!

Lincoln, Nebraska? Black people lived in Nebraska? Felice was shocked. She thought Aaron was from Pensacola, Florida. That muthafucka was another lying bastard. He was just like every other man. Aaron Cane was no better than the rest of them.

Felice had enough going on in her world and could have done without this little revelation. How could Aaron do this to her? He was supposed to be her knight in shining armor. He was supposed to rescue her from insanity. Instead he was pushing her through the revolving door of Bellevue. When was he going to tell her that he was married? What was he waiting for? Perhaps, after the invitations for their wedding went out or maybe during the nuptials.

Felice thought she and Aaron had something special. He said he loved her. He didn't have any pictures of his family in his home. Felice separated the pictures and lined them across her desk. One of them displayed a young Aaron and his wife on their wedding day. The other was a smiling Aaron with his wife and what must have been their first baby. Then there was the first picture that she held before she knew who the little boy was. That must have been their second child. The little boy looked to be about three years old.

The last thing that Felice wanted to do was break up a happy family. She knew that if she called Aaron he would have some lame excuse. Felice didn't want to hear it, so she decided not to speak to him right away. If she had the wrong thing would have flown out of her mouth.

Felice sat at her desk contemplating her next move. She was stunned and her body was numb. She began to tremble, and she was just about to cry when she heard a commotion. Felice tried to snap out of her trancelike state to see what was going on in the office.

Feet scuffled toward the other end of the hall. Felice pried herself away from the desk. Her pant leg got hitched on a big splinter that was hanging from the side of her desk, causing a snag in her linen slacks. She found the scissors and cut the hanging thread and ran to see what the fuss was about.

Sandy, Bedford's wife, was beating the mess out of the woman Felice had walked to the elevator with before she and Bedford went to lunch. This scenario was all too familiar to Felice. *Damn, Bedford! How could you be so foolish twice?* Felice asked herself. She felt bad for Bedford and even worse when Sandy threw one of his precious and very large Ming vases at him. Bedford didn't expect or see it coming. The vase cuffed him right on the side of his head. Bedford wobbled before dropping to the floor with the help of Sandy charging at him like a bull to a matador.

Felice instructed everyone to return to their office. The employees were very hesitant, but no one wanted to openly disobey the boss so they did as they were told. Another woman was there and Felice didn't recognize her, but she must have been Sandy's friend. She tried to pry Sandy away from Bedford but wasn't very successful. Less than two minutes later security entered and hauled a hysterical and rebellious Sandy along with her friend, out of Bedford's office and out of the building.

After everything had cooled down, Felice went into Bedford's office to console him. That was the second time she had seen Bedford brought to tears. The first time was after his nephew, Shiloh, was killed. Felice was hurting, but for all of the wrong reasons. She wondered if Bedford had cried after she left him. Did he really love Sandy that much? If so, then why didn't he ever love her like that? Well, it didn't really matter now, because he fucked both of them over. He was just a sucker for pussy—new pussy, old pussy, it really didn't matter, just as long as it was pussy.

Bedford was too smart a man to keep getting caught in the same stupid situations. He was the poster boy for stupidity. Smart in business, dumb in love. Felice held the father of her unborn child and spoke soothing words to him. There was no reason to throw acid at him when he was already in hell. He was sure to burn anyway. While she rocked Bedford in her arms, she felt a true connection. Felice realized that deep down, she never really stopped loving him. In the process, he rubbed her belly and for the first time throughout this fiasco she felt life. There was life in her belly. It was a life that both she and Bedford created together.

They talked and neither Bedford nor Felice left the office until very late that evening. Felice was well aware of the fact that she could never return to the life that she and Bedford once had, but it was nice to feel wanted.

Eventually, Felice contacted Aaron. She didn't let on about the package, however, she could tell that he sensed something was different between them. Aaron kept inquiring whether everything was okay. He told her at least twenty times how much he loved her, which was nineteen times more than usual. Aaron was privy to something, but Felice wasn't going to confess what she knew right away.

"Aaron, I was thinking about us having a summer wedding. Wouldn't that be nice?"

"Yeah, it would be. That would give us a full year to prepare."

"A year. . .no silly. I meant this summer. Two or three months from now, like July or August."

"No, baby!" Aaron said, alarm threading through his voice.

"Why not? I don't want to wait a whole year to get married to the man that I love."

"Felice, you know that I have training all summer with the Raptors. I can't just go off and get married."

"Aaron, all we need is a weekend. We can hold off on the honeymoon because once we're married, every night will be our honeymoon."

"Damn, if a man could travel via phone, I'd be there sopping that sweet ass of yours up right now with my biscuit."

"I know you would," Felice said giggling.

"What are you wearing, beautiful?" Aaron asked, trying to seduce her over the phone.

"Aaron, don't try to change the subject. I didn't call you for phone sex. I want to set the date for our wedding now. We can get married before you go to training camp. We should do it the weekend of the Fourth of July."

"Nah, that won't work. I got stuff to do."

"Stuff like what, baby?" Felice inquired. She laughed quietly as Aaron continued to back himself into a wall.

"Just a little business. Nothing for you to worry about."

"I hope it's nothing serious."

"Everything is good. I just have some loose ends that I have to tie up."

"With your wife and kids?"

"Wha-what did you say?"

"I said, your wife and kids."

"Wife and kids?"

"Yes, baby. You know, the wife who has been your sweetheart since high school? The one who has two of your children and another on the way."

"Who told you that?"

Felice couldn't believe Aaron. Who told you that? Was this the best he could come up with?

"Does it really matter? When in the world were you going to tell me you were married with children? I mean damn, Aaron, you asked me to marry you. Were you planning on becoming a polygamist?"

"Did whoever you spoke to tell you I filed for a divorce earlier this year?"

"Was this before or after you got your wife pregnant again?"

"Felice, listen. My wife came here to discuss the divorce and the terms. She told me she was going to contest it because she didn't like the deal my lawyer was cutting her. I begged her not to because I haven't been in love with her for years now. Aside from that, the settlement was more than fair. She threatened to take me for everything I have. I didn't want a messy divorce. She asked me to sleep with her one last time. I agreed, but I didn't know she was ovulating and had all of this planned."

Felice listened to the story. It sounded plausible, especially after the letter she received from Mrs. Cane. She ended the letter with *P.S. Even if Aaron tried to leave me his money would be tied up in child support for eighteen more years and let's not forget about all the alimony I'd get!*

Those were the words from a very desperate woman. Nevertheless, Aaron's wife was trouble. She would always be trouble, and Aaron would never be rid of her. Felice had to think of whether she wanted or was ready to be involved with a man who had overweight luggage. Generally, one had to pay a hefty penalty for excess baggage.

"Aaron, let's just say I do believe you. The fact still remains that you have a wife you never, ever told me about. We've been a couple for more than two years. Not only do you have a wife, you have a family." Felice was fuming.

"I would have told you about my kids. I love my children."

"You don't even have pictures of them in your home. What kind of love is that?"

"Felice, don't be so quick to judge me. I have my reasons for not telling you right away, and I'm sure there are things you haven't told me as well."

"I don't have secrets with such enormity." Felice said, lying.

"Felice, I didn't tell you because my wife is vicious, and I wanted to resolve this as soon as possible without her getting to you."

"Aaron, thanks for being so considerate and trying to protect my feelings, but let me tell you something. We couldn't possibly enter a marriage under these pretenses. This wasn't just some little lie. You painted a brilliant picture for me when really it should have had dark clouds surrounding it and lightning bolts darting from each one."

"I'm sorry that you feel that way," Aaron said, sounding remorseful.

"Not sorry enough, Aaron. I thought you were better than this, but you're no better than the average dog. No, you're a mutt, Aaron. Have a nice life," Felice said as she hung up the phone.

Yo Ma, It's Your Birthday

Sylvah was relieved that she had packed for Jamaica before moving. Her new apartment, which was only a medicine ball's throw away from Felice's, was fabulous. The movers were kind enough to remove the larger items out of the boxes, leaving her less work to do upon her return. She was psyched about her trip and intended to have lots of fun. Most of her chores were complete, so she didn't have to worry about things unraveling during her travels.

The expanse of the apartment suited Sylvah well. True, she had to give up a few things, but none of the items really mattered anymore and didn't have much impact on her here and now. She still had enough room for her children to come home during their school breaks. Kenya went to Spelman College in Atlanta, Georgia and Zaire attended Tuskegee Institute in Alabama. Kenya and Zaire had the option to stay with her or their father. Both parents had opened their homes to them.

Bläise had called Sylvah earlier on her cell phone, but she was preoccupied with Jason, so she made the conversation brief. He was calling under the pretense of the divorce, wanting to know if she had signed the papers yet. Sylvah told him that she had, earlier that day, and had even returned them via certified mail. Bläise went on and on about making sure that they took care of the situation right away, but all he was really doing was keeping Sylvah on the phone. At the end of their conversation he had the nerve to wish her a happy birthday.

It was rumored that Bläise was living with another woman who was his junior. Sylvah didn't know how true this was, but never bothered to investigate or ask him if the rumor was true. Besides, what he did with his life was his business. Jason was younger than her and he managed to teach her a thing or two earlier, so she hoped Bläise was just as lucky. Speaking of Jason, Sylvah couldn't get him off her mind. She hoped she wasn't falling for him. Sylvah knew sex could only complicate matters.

Sylvah heard her cell phone ringing, but didn't know where it was located. By the time she found it, the ringing discontinued. However, she read the display and it was her son, Zaire. Sylvah hit the resend button and automatically dialed him back.

"Hello, Zaire."

"Hey, Ma. Did your move go okay?"

"Why yes, it did. Thanks for asking. I'm sorry I missed your call earlier. I couldn't find the phone. So what's up? You miss me?" Sylvah asked, smiling. She loved her children. They made her proud. Zaire was in his third year of college at Tuskegee, where he was studying to become an engineer. Ever since Sylvah could remember, Zaire wanted to get into aeronautics and build space shuttles. He was smart enough to get into a program that would give him this opportunity, and over the past two summers had interned at NASA in Florida.

"Nah, not really," Zaire responded.

"Ouch, that hurt," Sylvah said, trying to sound upset. She knew how unattached her son could be. He was even moodier now that she and Bläise were getting divorced. Zaire was taking it much harder than Kenya, at least on the outside. Kenya seemed to be absorbed in her own world. She was in her first year at Spelman College and didn't have much time for anyone except Kenya.

"You know what I mean. Anyway, I know you're going away with your friends tomorrow and I just wanted to wish you a happy birthday before you leave."

Sylvah was almost moved to tears. She was so emotional lately and didn't know what it was all about. It must have been an age thing. Next she'd be having hot flashes, and that really was only a few miles down yonder.

"That is so sweet of you! Thank you for remembering."

"Mom, stop overreacting. You know that I wouldn't forget. By the way, did Kenya call you yet?"

"No, why? Did you speak to her? Is everything all right?" Sylvah asked, sounding panicked.

Kenya and Zaire had their differences, but secretly they adored each other, and Sylvah and Bläise were privy to this. They played the sibling rivalry thing for years, but once they found things in common, like Kenya wanting to date Zaire's friends and vice versa, they began getting along fantastically. Zaire played the role of big brother and wouldn't allow Kenya to date anyone whom he considered a knucklehead. In the beginning Kenya detested her brother for getting into her personal business, but in the end loved him for protecting her. Zaire helped her prepare for her SATs and apply to colleges, enabling her to get into her top three choices. Kenya wanted to be close to Zaire, but far enough so that she could live her own life. They were just a few hours away from each other by bus or car.

"Ma, I'm sure she's fine. I just wanted to know if she beat me and called you first."

"Well, you beat her and it's still pretty early. I'm sure that she'll get around to hollering at her mother."

"Ma, please stop trying to sound young and cool. You're like going on fifty," Zaire said, laughing.

"Well, if I'm going on fifty then you must be going on thirty. My, how time flies! That means that you've graduated from college, had time to get your master's, and can now support yourself because you have a great job. Do you have a wife and kid on the way yet? I need grandchildren now."

"You got me."

"I do, huh? Next time you decide to say something smart you better think twice. I may be getting older, but my brain is just as sharp."

"Whatever."

"Speaking of school, how is everything? How is your girlfriend, Fuschia?"

"Ma, her name is Lavender and well, we decided to put the brakes on things for a while."

Sylvah knew that her name was a color of some sort, but Zaire changed girlfriends quicker than an Indy 500 racecar driver switched lanes. Sylvah didn't have the time or the memory span to keep up with him and his wild ways, of which she highly disapproved.

"Another one bites the dust, huh?" Sylvah said, sucking her teeth. "Maybe you should put more emphasis on your studies and stop getting involved in these relationships. You have plenty of time for that." Sylvah began unpacking boxes of perishables in the kitchen. She opened all of the pantry doors and began placing the canned and bottled foods in the cupboards. Two days prior to moving, she had hired a service to come in and clean the place thoroughly, so she didn't have to worry about the place being sanitized.

"This time it was her idea that we take a break. Lavender is a premed student and said that she couldn't afford to be distracted."

"Smart girl," Sylvah said as she dipped a spoon into some peanut butter. "Well for what it's worth, I love you, and you can distract me anytime you want."

"I have something that I want to tell you, but I don't want you to get mad," Zaire said.

Uh oh! Sylvah thought, the spoon was sticking to the roof of her mouth. This was beginning to sound serious. The last time Zaire told her that during his freshman year of college, she found out that he had been arrested for being in the wrong place at the wrong time. Apparently he went joyriding with a few friends, but Zaire didn't know that the car was stolen. Sylvah had called a couple of her attorney friends and they were able to absolve Zaire of any wrongdoing.

"Should I be concerned?" Sylvah asked, trying her best to remain calm.

"Nah. It's nothing for you to really become concerned about."

"Okay, so shoot," Sylvah took a deep breath and held her hand to her chest for relief. In the brief moment that it took Zaire to continue she said a silent prayer for her family and herself.

"Well, I've been thinking lately, and I'm not all that sure engineering is what I'm really cracked up to do. I mean, sometimes I feel overwhelmed."

"Zaire, listen to me, we all experience anxiety. It's okay." Sylvah wanted to reassure her son. She knew that the divorce was affecting him, but she never realized that it was this extreme.

"Ma, my grades are really slipping. I'm not really interested in the stuff that's going on around me right now, and I'm tired."

Sylvah wanted to be there for her son. She needed to be there for him. If she could blink, twitch her nose, snap her fingers, or wiggle her behind and be in the presence of Zaire, she would.

"Zaire, the semester will be over in a few weeks. Try your best to keep it together. Baby, I don't want you to jeopardize your scholarship. You've been doing so well and you're so close to finishing. You only have two more years. There's very little that you can't accomplish in this day and age. The world is a jungle right now. Everyone's a little confused about something—terrorism, war, unemployment, the stock market falling, drugs, and poverty—but, Zaire, you have so much going for you right now. The world is at your feet. Take advantage of it all."

Zaire was still on the other line. Sylvah could hear him breathing, but he wasn't responding and that was fine with her. She wanted him to let everything she was saying sink in.

Sylvah wondered if Zaire had spoken to Bläise about this yet. Bläise would be highly upset if he knew that Zaire was thinking about dropping out. Well, he didn't exactly say that he wanted to drop out. Maybe he just wanted to change majors, but he was only two years from getting his degree. If he played his cards right he would also be hired by NASA. They had already shown an interest in having him join their ranks after he graduated.

"Did you speak to your father yet?"

"Kinda. I told him, but he didn't hear a word that I said. All he kept saying was, 'We'll discuss this when you get home during your break.' And you're not really listening to me either. I don't know why you two even broke up. Neither one of you listens." Zaire sounded frustrated.

Finally Sylvah was getting somewhere. She would have to speak to Bläise after all. They had a common problem that needed to be solved.

"Zaire, your father and I listen. We just have the same concern and that's you. We want to make sure that you're getting the education that you deserve."

"I gotta go," Zaire said abruptly.

"Sweetheart, please take everything that both your father and I have said into consideration. Don't make any hasty decisions or do anything that you'll regret later. You know that I love you, and if you need me to visit when I get back, I will."

"You don't need to visit me. I'll be all right."

"Are you sure?"

"I'm sure."

"Do you need money?"

"Nah."

"Now I know you're not all right. Z, I love you!"

"I love you too. Have fun on your trip, and don't be like Terry McMillan and try to get your groove back."

"You're funny."

♀♂

Sylvah was worried. Why didn't Bläise tell her their son was in trouble when she spoke to him earlier? They spoke for what felt like forever, and he babbled about nothing in particular or of importance. This was important. Sylvah hopped on the counter in her kitchen and dipped the spoon in the peanut butter again.

Now she had the urge to speak to Bläise. Of course she could confide in Felice or Candace, but they weren't Zaire's parents. Sylvah felt responsible for the anguish through which her son was going. She wished she knew what to do in order to reverse this spell that was taking over Zaire's mind, body, and emotions. She knew what would ease his pain. Still, reuniting with Bläise was not really an option anymore. The only thing that seemed important to him nowadays was the status of the divorce. Hell, she wanted the divorce just as much as him, but she wasn't in a haste or anything. Her freedom meant just as much to her, but Bläise acted as if he was suffering a slow death—if this divorce didn't get finalized soon.

Sylvah changed her mind regarding calling Bläise. Their earlier conversation began to upset her, and she didn't need to get on the phone sounding distressed. Instead, she walked out of her spacious kitchen and went into her half bathroom. She needed to wash her face and rid herself of the residue that tears were leaving beneath her eyes.

"Pull yourself together," Sylvah said aloud. She began thinking of strategies of intervention for Zaire. Maybe if she could get her parents, Bläise's parents, Bläise and Kenya together and discuss everything openly in a group setting, things would work out. This way everybody could say whatever was on their mind. The family should have had this forum before they decided to separate. This could have resolved any bad feelings and heartache right from the very start. Now Sylvah was on to something. As soon as she returned from her trip she would call Bläise and setup everything. He wouldn't be opposed. It wasn't as if they had walked away from each other as enemies. They simply grew tired and out of love with each other. Sylvah would never deny that she cared for Bläise. He would always be her first, but neither was in love with each other anymore and that made all the difference in the world.

Her cell phone was ringing again and this time Sylvah saw it, but on her way over to the counter she tripped on a plastic shopping bag that was in her path and busted her ass. *Damn,* Sylvah thought, lying on the ground unwounded, but both her back and behind were aching from the fall. All she could do was laugh out loud.

"What a damn tragedy!" Sylvah remarked to no one in particular as she continued to laugh and rub her rear end. She would definitely need that full-body massage from Dexter St. Slong, that Felice kept bragging about when she arrived in Jamaica.

The phone began ringing again and this time Sylvah walked over to get it.

"Hello?"

"Happy early birthday, Ma," Kenya sang into the phone.

"Thank you, sweetie."

"Go Ma, it's your birthday. You better party like it's your birthday. Get your groove on, 'cause it's your birthday," she sang.

"What in the world has come over you?" Sylvah asked, laughing and trying to rub away the pain in her lower back. At the same time she was doing a little move that Kenya had taught her the last time she was home on holiday. If Kenya could see her, she would crack up.

Eventually they would both end up rolling on the couch holding their stomachs from so much laughter.

"Nothing, I just figured that since I'm not there to celebrate with you that I would bless you with my beautiful voice over the phone."

"Did someone down there lie to you and tell you that you can sing?"

"Ma, you know I can throw down. I could be the next Mary J., Faith, India Arie, or Alicia Keys."

"Or how about the next Kenya C., short for Kenya can't sing."

"We'll see about that, o ye of little faith. So, are you excited about your trip? Did you get the gift that Zaire and I sent you? We need you to take plenty of pictures while you're in Jamaica."

"I'm very, very excited about my trip. I haven't been on a vacation with my girls in years. Oh, and yes I did get the digital camera. Thank you. I forgot to tell your brother thank you earlier when I spoke to him."

"That punk called you already?" Kenya asked.

"Yes, and stop calling your brother a punk. By the way, when was the last time you spoke to Zaire?" Sylvah asked.

"I think it was like earlier today." Kenya paused for a brief moment. "Yeah, it was today. You know that we speak all the time, so I get confused."

"Did he mention anything to you? Did he sound upset or anything?"

"Nothing more than usual. He was a little upset about him and Lavender breaking up, which was strange. I think the only reason he's tripping is because she called it off first. Zaire is used to being the one handing the walking papers, and this time the tables were turned on him."

"I bet that you're right. Otherwise, he was fine? And please be honest with me."

"Ma, I'm always honest with you."

"Really, did you lose your virginity yet?"

"Let's stick with the subject at hand here, shall we?"

Sylvah laughed because Kenya never answered that question for her. As close as they were, when it came to sex Kenya balled up like a snail in its shell. On the other hand Zaire, who she really didn't want to hear it from, told her more than she ever cared to know. There was a point that he would even come to her and show her any abrasion or strange mark on his body, including his penis. Thank goodness those days were past.

"I'll let that slide this time, but you'll stop avoiding my question at some point and will even come to your ma for advice."

"Ugh, I don't think so. Anyway, what you really want to know is what's bothering Z? Truthfully, I don't know. He's talking strange about not wanting to continue with school and how he's tired of this professor and being at Tuskegee, but I think those things are all excuses. For what, I'm not sure."

"Do you think it's the divorce?" Sylvah asked, getting concerned again. She felt a weird bubbling in her stomach, which indicated gas. "Damn, where are the teabags when you need them?

"Ma, are you okay?"

"I'm good. I'm just trying to locate the teabags."

"Okay. Well, I don't know. I mean, I'm okay about the divorce. I spoke to Daddy today and everything is cool."

"Are you sure?" Sylvah asked, dipping her hand into the box marked COUNTER AND PANTRY ITEMS. She knew that the tins that held the assortment of teas were at the bottom of the box. By the time she reached them she had to wipe her brow from the thin line of sweat that had begun to form. Sylvah really needed to get back in shape, especially if dancing for one minute and reaching into a box caused her to sweat.

"Ma, I told you that I don't need to lie to you. I'm fine. If you want to hear me say something different then I will. I really hate that you and Dad decided to give up on each other. You are a good woman and he is a good man. You two were a team and yes, I'm disappointed, but if this will make you both happier then so be it. Eventually you will both come to your senses and realize that the world is full of lunatics and that you two locos belong together. There, I've said my peace," Kenya said and awaited a response from her mother.

Sylvah mentally recited the speech her daughter had just given her and she was flustered. She and Bläise were responsible for raising this feisty, smart, beautiful, and courageous young lady. They were equally accountable for raising their handsome, smart, and bullheaded son. Up until this point in his life they never experienced any major problems with Zaire. He was always respectful to his lady friends, kept decent friends, worked, maintained good grades, and excelled at whatever he put his mind to. He got into a few fights at school, but that was to be expected. His first major scuff was the incident in college with the stolen car. As far as Sylvah and Bläise knew, he didn't do drugs, so what more could a parent ask for?

Maybe Sylvah was putting up false alarms and taking her conversation with Zaire overboard. Perhaps he just needed to vent, and this was his way of crying for attention.

"Thank you for being so sweet and honest as usual. I just want to make sure that both you and your brother are fine."

"We're both fine. Zaire is just a little depressed, and I think the Lavender thing is a great deal of it."

"So you would tell me if you knew otherwise, right?"

Kenya sighed on the other end. Sylvah knew that she was getting tired of the interrogation.

"Don't get huffy with me. I'm just trying to make sure, Kenya. I don't know what I'd do without you two. You are all that I have, and I love you both to death."

"We know that, and we love you too. And we are not all that you have. Dad is still there for you too."

"You're not going to let this one go, are you?"

"Nope, not until you two are either committed to each other again or in Bellevue together."

"I think that it might be the latter."

"Oops, call waiting. Ma, I gotta go," Kenya said, sounding excited and eager to go.

"Hot date?" Sylvah asked.

"Wouldn't you like to know?"

"Make sure that you make him use protection."

"Ma, I love you, but I gotta go!" Kenya responded and clicked over quickly.

Damn, Sylvah thought. She had two grown children and she was about to turn forty. She didn't quite know where the magic carpet was flying her off to, but she was able, ready, and willing to see and taste what the other half of the world had to offer.

5

Felice the Brick Slayer

Felice was tempted to call one of her girls. She was so excited to be going on vacation with the three of them. It had been a long time since they all hung out together, but she'd see them in airport the following morning.

Candace now had a house in the 'burbs and a luxury car. It was Felice who now teased Candace about living the American dream. She had a fine setup with a great husband and 2.5 kids. Felice always asked, who in the hell came up with 2.5? Was that the retarded kid? The child who made up the .5 and wasn't quite whole? Did he ride the short yellow school bus? Felice knew exactly what 2.5 stood for, but realistically no one had 2.5 kids.

Felice had a sensation that required a lot of gyration. Who would be the lucky subject? Jermaine quickly came to mind and departed just as swiftly. It was definitely time to call it quits between them. He was seriously considering leaving his wife with the intent of having Felice full time. Felice wasn't ready to be anybody's fulltime, much less have a married man leave his family on her behalf. She flipped through her trusty little red book to select the winner. The book consisted of men Felice had met at different functions revolving around work, social gatherings, clubs, networking events, and such. The entrants were potential suitors if Felice were ever interested or just a good lay though she had only slept with a handful—she was promiscuous, not a slut.

Felice decided to begin with the letter A. She had them alphabetized by first name. Aaron's name and number were still the first one listed. She located her black pen and drew a line through his name.

"Good riddance," Felice said aloud to herself. She continued to go down the list: Abe, Aiken, Alan, Andre, Andrew, Anthony, Antonio. The A list was short, so she moved on to the B's. Barry, Ben, Blake, Brandon, Bryce and her latest addition, Brick, the moving man she met at Sylvah's. She wondered how stacked Brick really was. Was it a long brick? Short? Wide? Narrow? Would it stack up to meet her needs? Felice decided she would soon find out as she picked up the cordless receiver to dial his number.

"Hello?" Felice said it more like a question, because she didn't even hear the phone ring. "May I please speak to Brick?"

"This is Brick, but why are you asking for me when I just called you?" Brick asked.

"I just dialed you."

"No," Brick responded. "I heard you pressing numbers and then you came on the line.

"Oh, what a coincidence. Like minds," Felice said as she laughed.

"That we were thinking about each other at the same time?"

"Exactly."

"Well, what exactly were you thinking about?" Brick asked.

This was interesting. Brick wanted to play question and answer. Felice wanted to play jockey and horse.

"You," Felice answered. She knew quick one-word answers would get him over there quicker or vice versa.

"What about me?" Brick asked. Felice could sense the smile burgeoning across his face while he tried to play coy and sexy.

The flipping gaps between your teeth, Felice thought. *Now get the hint and bring your butt over here!*

"You coming to my place and paying me a visit." Felice figured cutting to the chase was the quickest route. No map necessary, at least she hoped.

"And where do you live?" Brick answered, suddenly sounding out of breath.

"Are you okay?" Felice asked, concerned. She hoped he wasn't asthmatic. The last thing she needed was for him to have an attack from over-exhaustion or from too much excitement, which she was known to cause on several occasions. She also didn't need anything interfering with her trip to Jamaica.

"I'm cool," Brick reassured her. "I was just doing my last set of pushups while I talked to you."

"You have me on speaker?" Felice inquired.

"Yeah, no disrespect to you or anything."

"No problem. It's just that you sound so clear. Anyway, I live on Eastern Parkway and Underhill Avenue."

"I think I know where that is. The West Indian parade passes by there on Labor Day, right?"

"Uh, yes. It's directly across the street from the large Brooklyn Public Library and the Botanical Gardens. Near Grand Army Plaza."

"Yeah, I know where. That's a real nice area," Brick exclaimed.

"Right," Felice answered, getting impatient with the conversation. "Enough with the small talk, so what time should I expect you over?"

"I just got in from work about twenty minutes ago. I have to shower, get dressed, call my daughter, and drop a gift off to my mom. Her birthday is today and you know how you women can get, especially if we show up late with the gift."

Felice made a note in the empty space that was provided next to Brick's name in her red book: *talkative and chauvinistic*. Felice didn't plan on calling him too often, not unless he did something absolutely phenomenal in bed. She knew one thing for sure: Brick had a baby momma, which definitely meant off limits. Baby mommas were sometimes worse than wives.

Brick never did answer her question about coming over. It sounded like he had a lot of running around to do. Perhaps stopping by her place would be an inconvenience. His mother probably lived in Queens, the Bronx, or Long Island, all of which were a trek from her apartment in Brooklyn.

"It sounds like you have a lot of things going on," Felice said.

"Nah, my moms lives in Bed-Stuy and I live in Bushwick. I'll speak to my daughter on my drive over to my mom's. It's eight o'clock now. I can be there by 9:30. Is that a'ight with you?"

"That's fine. I'll see you at 9:30. Oh, and I live in Apartment 10A. I'll tell the doorman that I'm expecting you."

"Cool. I'll call you when I'm near."

♀♂

Felice was curled up on the couch munching on green grapes when her intercom buzzed. She picked up the receiver.

"Yes?"

"Ms. Jackson, there's a Mr. Brick here to see you," the doorman announced.

"Send him up."

Brick was five minutes early. At least he knew how to be prompt. Felice made a mental note to add *prompt* next to his name. Felice was in the middle of watching one of her favorite movies, *The Usual Suspects.* She walked to the door backwards, not wanting to remove her eyes from her fifty-inch flat screen television. She knew this movie like the beauty marks that were mapped across her body, but she loved the scene where Kevin Spacey left the police precinct appearing to be crippled, and then in an instant he was walking regular among the other pedestrians. "Who is Kaiser Sose?" she said, laughing to herself.

The bell sounded again.

"Damn, you got up here quick," Felice said, simultaneously unlocking the door and turning the television off with the remote.

"Hello," Felice said, looking Brick over thoroughly. "You clean up nice."

"Well, thank you." Brick kissed Felice on the cheek. "You're not too bad yourself."

Wrong response, Felice thought.

"Just kidding." Brick smiled offering Felice a bouquet of lilies.

"How thoughtful of you," Felice said, bringing her nose toward the flowers.

"You are very welcome. I couldn't forget my lady."

"Your lady?" Felice asked, curiosity peppered her voice. *Did something occur between us during my absence?* Felice looked around the room to make sure that he was indeed speaking to her. "You are such a kidder!" Felice replied, a fake smile plastering her face. "Come on in."

Brick stepped in and removed his jacket.

"Let me get that." Felice extended her arm to take the jacket from Brick. "This is a nice jacket. Oh, and I see you got it from Moshood on Fulton Street. He does nice work."

"Yeah. I dig his work. I get a lot of clothes from him. He even custom makes outfits if you ask him."

"That's real nice."

"So, what were you doing before I arrived?"

"Watching a movie," Felice said as she sauntered over to the coat closet.

"Which one?" Brick walked over to the couch and got comfortable.

"The Usual Suspects."

"Word! With Kevin Spacey?"

"Is there another one?" Felice answered, becoming annoyed. If it weren't for the pulsing between her legs she would have just said to hell with Brick. However, he was there and he was stacked, looking good and smelling nice.

"Do you have something to drink?"

"What would you like?" Felice asked, changing directions and heading to the kitchen instead of back to the living room.

"Do you have beer?"

"I have Guinness Stout, Smirnoff Ice, cranberry juice, water, orange and apple juice."

"I'll take a Coke."

"That's not an option."

Felice felt like she was dating that model Torrence. Now that was a nightmare. Torrence was as handsome as Boris from *Soul Food,* a great shopping buddy, knew how to invest his earnings, but not much more going on upstairs or in the bedroom area either. Torrence had a big dick, but little action. His forte was eating her, which was cool but a good meal came with steak and potatoes and, if you were lucky, grilled vegetables. Torrence only offered hors d'oeuvres, and dessert was definitely out of the question.

"My bad. I'll take a Smirnoff."

Felice grabbed two Smirnoffs and went to join Brick. She handed him the drink and sat beside him.

"You smell nice. What's that you have on?" Brick asked.

"I'm wearing Olive Butter lotion from Nubian Heritage."

"Word. I get my shea products from them. Their stuff is off the chain," Brick quipped.

"Yes, its very good stuff." Felice twisted the cap off the bottle and took a sip before placing it on a coaster on her Italian glass center table.

Brick drank the entire bottle and followed suit by placing his empty bottle on a coaster. He reached for the universal remote and turned both the television and the DVD player back on.

"This apartment is huge and real nice," Brick said, taking a glimpse at the place. "How long you been living here?"

"A few years."

"It must cost a grip to live here?"

"You could say so. Brick, what are you here for?" Felice asked curiously.

"To hang out with you, of course."

Felice got up from her plush sofa and untied the belt around the waist of her robe, allowing it to fall open.

"You came to do what?" Felice asked seductively, her 34Ds ready, aimed, and prepared to fire.

"Damn," Brick replied, astonished at the glorious sight before him. His eyes bulged slightly.

"You like?" Felice asked, taking a seat atop Brick's lap facing him.

"I love," Brick said, licking his sumptuous lips.

"I can tell," Felice said as she felt an immediate rise in Brick. It felt like he was hiding a small third world country in his pants. This wasn't such a waste after all.

"It's all for you," Brick said, palming Felice's ass. He stood with Felice still wrapped around his waist and carried her over to the bar. He placed her on the counter and sat in one of the chairs. He hungrily pulled her thighs apart. It was a good thing Felice was limber.

Brick's three-inch tongue was doing somersaults around the perimeter of Felice's pussy. *Elation* was too small a word for the feeling that washed over Felice.

Felice's toes began to curl and Brick was only three minutes into the meal. She didn't want to interrupt the appetizer, but she didn't see much of a choice.

"What the fuck are you doing, Brick?" Felice screamed out in ecstasy. She took quick breaths like a pregnant woman about to give birth.

"You like that shit, huh?"

Felice didn't answer. Instead she hopped off the bar and walked back into the living room, wagging her index finger for Brick to follow, which he did.

Brick kicked off his boots, removed his pants, and practically ran over to Felice.

Felice lay across her off-white mohair carpet. Brick took off his boxers and what was before Felice only made her more anxious. Jackpot! Brick was at the free-throw line and he couldn't possibly miss this shot.

Brick removed a condom from a gold wrapper and securely placed it on his other person.

♀♂

Felice learned a new term—*wax on, wax off*—because Brick surely waxed her ass and good. She was having a sound sleep and must have been on dream number three. The first two were *Felice the Brick Slayer I and II*. This dream was different, and it made her body feel strange, like she was being licked by a puppy. It was cute at first, but the puppy settled for licking the crack of her ass. The dream was becoming annoying, forcing Felice to wake from a fitful slumber.

Felice turned over from her stomach and saw it was no dream at all. Brick was licking between her butt. Felice gathered her senses and wiped her eyes to make sure she was seeing correctly. Brick wiped his mouth and was about to kiss Felice on the lips.

"OH HELL NO!" Felice screamed. "Look where your mouth just came from! Why were you licking my ass? You don't even know me like that."

"I-I thought you'd like it," Brick stammered defensively.

"You know what I'd like, Brick?"

"What?" he asked.

Felice turned on her side and looked Brick square in the eyes. Brick looked so pitiful, but she wasn't in the business of keeping strays.

"I would like for you to get your clothes, put them on, and get the hell out of my apartment."

Brick and his six-plus, toffee-brown frame and gorgeous body moved from away from Felice and off the bed. She watched him as he walked out into the living room. She pulled her robe from the side of the bed and followed him. Felice entered the living room and watched as Brick put on his pants, undershirt and finally, his pullover sweater.

Felice retrieved his jacket from the coat closet and handed it to him.

"Felice, I didn't mean to offend you," Brick said.

"You should have thought about that before placing your tongue in the crevice of my ass. Think before you lick next time. You can't just go around licking just anyone's ass."

"I hope we can still be cool." Brick extended his hand to Felice.

"Yeah, sure," Felice said, accepting his handshake. She didn't see any reason to remain hostile. After all, he was leaving without much discussion.

Felice opened the door for Brick.

"Take it easy," Brick said, walking backwards as he took a final glance at Felice.

"You too," Felice replied, closing the door. She headed straight to the nightstand in her bedroom and took out her red book. She located Brick's name and wrote a new entry in the tiny space: *ASS LICKER*.

6

Membership Has it's Privileges

As usual Felice waited until the last minute to look at her plane tickets to check which airport she would be leaving from and the exact time. The driver was already downstairs waiting for her, and the doorman had the nerve to buzz her twice in the last ten minutes. He acted as if he were the one about to miss his flight.

"All right, already! I'm on my way down," Felice yelled into the intercom. She didn't bother to wait for Jeeves's reply, but instead slammed the receiver back into its cradle, grabbed her bags and keys and headed out of the door, plane tickets in hand.

On Felice's way down in the elevator she glanced at her tickets. She saw just what she was hoping not to see. The paper ticket read LGA. Felice hated LaGuardia Airport. It was farther to get to and always jam-packed. The flight wasn't due to depart until 9:15, but that two-hour-prior-check-in crap for international flights would surely make her late.

The doorman ran to the elevator to help her with her bags and when they got outside, the driver took over. She gave Jeeves a small tip and hopped into the car.

Felice took out her compact and began to apply her lip liner, lip gloss, and a little bit of eye shadow, which she didn't have time to do that morning. After Brick left she had a horrible sleep. She couldn't clear her mind of him and his nasty tongue. Perhaps not nasty, but he didn't know her well enough to be engaging in the stuff that he was doing. That was a major turn-off. Felice was all for receiving and not having to give, but that was more than she was willing to deal with.

When Felice lifted up her head she noticed that the driver was headed toward Bedford Avenue and Fulton Street. Where in the world was this man taking her?

"Driver," Felice said, but he had his Pakistani music near full blast. She resorted to tapping him on his shoulder. The man turned the music down a few notches and proceeded to face Felice.

"Yes, ma'am," he answered with a smile.

"Where exactly are you taking me?" Felice huffed.

"I be tekkin' you to de airport, ma'am."

"Which one?" Felice asked curiously.

"LGA. . .La Guardia of course. This is nottin de airport you wish to go?"

"Yes, it is, but why are you taking me this way? We should have gone straight down Eastern Parkway to the Jackie Robinson Parkway. The expressway would've gotten us there quicker."

"No, no. I be drivin' dis way and it is much, much quick. Of this I can assure you."

"Listen, I don't have time for you to be rerouting me. It's already a quarter after seven. I should already be there, so please don't make me lose anymore valuable time."

"You will not be of disappointment, ma'am."

"I swear you better not make me late," Felice said under her breath, leaning back into the comfort of the Lincoln Town Car.

When Mr. Habib or whatever his name was saw Felice sink into her own resolve, he turned his radio back to full blast.

Felice began feeling chills. She was only wearing a halter-top, which belonged to her bathing suit and the bikini was beneath her jeans and a matching jean jacket. It was early in the morning and the temperature was only in the low fifties. It was October and the temperature wasn't going to increase much more than it was now. New York's Indian summer was just about over. They were now tossed into the arms of fall. Now was a great time to be going away since the climate was beginning to change. Felice had gotten so used to the year round warm temperature of Cuba, she had almost forgotten how cold it could actually get in New York. Felice only wished she could stay in Jamaica through the winter, but upon her return she had major business to take care of, things she knew could no longer be avoided, and her first action was Jackson and Jackson.

"Driver, sir." Mr. Habib couldn't hear Felice, so once again she tapped him on his shoulder. He repeated the same ritual and turned down the music and then faced her.

"Yes, ma'am. What is it now dat I can be helping you wid?" His heavy accent smothering Felice.

"Can you turn the air off? It's pretty cold outside already without the help of the air conditioner. Would this be all right with you?" Felice asked, trying to remain polite.

"That will not be problem. I turn off for you." He tapped the button that read "A/C" and again turned the music up.

"Thank you," Felice said, relieved, not really caring if he heard her over the music. She immediately began feeling her body temperature increase. What was wrong with men? They didn't like heat. In the dead of winter they would turn the ceiling fan or the air conditioner on. *If your ass is so hot, go the heck outside and play in the cold, but please don't freeze me out. Was that too much to ask for?* Felice fumed to herself.

Felice looked at her watch and it was 7:40, and they were stuck somewhere on the Brooklyn Queens Expressway in the middle of traffic. Why in the world didn't she just tell Mr. Habib to turn the vehicle around and go back toward the Jackie Robinson? How much longer before she arrived? She couldn't blame this totally on Mr. Habib, but she was going to do her damn best and try. Twenty-five minutes and no airport signs yet. Now she was fuming. Yelling at Mr. Habib wasn't going to make the car move any quicker. He wasn't driving Herbie the Love Bug and this vehicle couldn't fly. Instead of tapping him on his shoulder for a third time and getting absolutely nowhere, she dipped into her travel bag and took out the book that she had been trying to read for the past few nights, *Tears On a Sunday Afternoon* by Michael Presley.

Felice hoped she could concentrate enough to read despite the loud opera banshee singing mixed with tambourines and reggae beats that Mr. Habib insisted on.

Fifteen minutes and two completed chapters later, they arrived at LaGuardia Airport in front of the Air Jamaica terminal. Felice looked at her watch and was relieved. She was late, but at least the flight hadn't taken off yet.

Mr. Habib popped the trunk, jumped out of the car and walked swiftly to open up Felice's door. He then went to retrieve her luggage out of the car. While he did that, Felice removed her jean jacket and tied it around her waist. She was late, but knew exactly how to garner some attention. Felice peered down at her watch and began to count backwards from ten. She didn't even get to seven before one of the baggage-check men ran to her aid. It was just as she figured. Large perky breasts exposed for all to see, membership had its privileges.

"Will you be needin' anyting else, ma'am?" Mr. Habib asked.

"No, I'm good. Thanks." Felice went into her handbag to fetch a few dollar bills. She handed them to Mr. Habib, who tipped his head politely, closed his trunk and returned to his car.

The baggage-claim man immediately took over where Mr. Habib left off.

"Do you have your ticket, ma'am?" the older gentleman, who must have been at least sixty, asked Felice. He was drooling worse than a baby as he stared at Felice's very ripe breasts and hard nipples.

"Why, yes I do," Felice said, leaning over the counter to hand him the tickets, showing him enough cleavage to give him a hard-on.

"Thank you," he said, clearing his throat and coughing.

"You're welcome."

"Okay. You're on Air Jamaica Flight 360, which is scheduled to depart at 9:15 A.M." The man whose name badge read Mr. Brown looked at his watch. "Ms. Jackson, you don't have a lot of time, but don't worry, I'll get you fixed up."

"I appreciate it." Felice flashed him her million-dollar smile, which was well received. "Aren't you forgetting something?" Felice asked as she handed him her passport.

"Oh, yes. Thanks," Mr. Brown said and looked at Felice and then her passport. He then went down the assigned line of questions with Felice.

"Did you pack these bags yourself?"

"Yes, yes, and yes to all of the questions that you are about to ask me."

"Ms. Jackson, I know that you probably get tired of these questions, but I still have to ask." He went on and asked her the other questions and then returned his attention to the computer.

Mr. Brown obviously hadn't taken typing classes, or maybe they weren't offered when he went to school. Either way, Felice watched painfully as he typed at a turtle's pace.

"I'm almost done," Mr. Brown said, holding his head up to reassure her. "Shit! Hey Henry! Get over here, man! I can never seem to get this right. Excuse my language, Ms. Jackson."

"That's okay," Felice said, wishing he would speed things up.

"What's up, man?" A younger man who must have been Henry answered, but he was busy assisting another passenger.

This is great, Felice thought, *just what I need. Mr. Ben-Gay messing up my itinerary.* She could probably go behind the podium and fix whatever it was he kept screwing up on the computer. She took enough flights, and saw enough airline personnel punch in the codes and everything else, to instruct a class.

Henry joined them.

"Hey, what's up, man?" Henry asked. He gave Mr. Brown a pound and then stood beside him. His frame towered over Mr. Brown's.

"You see this right here?" Mr. Brown asked and pointed to the screen. "That's not supposed to happen, right?"

"Nah, it's not, but it looks like the flight is overbooked," Henry said, looking over at Felice for the first time. His eyes said "damn," but his tongue remained in his mouth.

"What exactly does that have to do with me?" Felice asked, getting impatient.

"It's nothing for you to worry over, sweetness," Henry replied. He stared Felice over from head to foot. "We need to get you out of this cold," he said focusing on Felice's breasts. "It's a might bit chilly out here, don't you think, Mr. Brown?" Henry said and chuckled. Mr. Brown just nodded.

Felice didn't respond, but instead chose to listen to Henry for her next step. At that moment she loathed him, but he was going to be her ticket to getting onto this flight and to her gate on time. She definitely brought it on herself, flaunting her wares like she was, but it was going to pay off.

She began rubbing her arms briskly as the goose bumps began spreading across her upper body.

"Let me get this, Mr. Brown." The older man stepped aside and allowed Henry to work on Felice's flight information. A few minutes later he said, "Okay, boom. I got it. Now it looks like your flight will begin boarding in about twenty minutes, so let's get rolling."

"Great," Felice said, relieved.

Henry tagged Felice's luggage and put it on the conveyer belt. Felice gave Mr. Brown two dollars for trying to help her out earlier. She had about five more singles left, which she would give to Henry once he delivered her safely to the gate. She snatched a quick look at her watch and shook her head. It was already late. Henry saw the worry on her face.

"I told you, don't worry. I got this." Henry stepped into one of the airport shuttle carts and signaled Felice to get in. They drove past a slew of people until they got to the security gate and the metal detectors.

"Give me your ticket and passport," Henry ordered and Felice obliged. Henry pulled one of the guys to the side and they started talking about something, but the next thing Felice knew she was next in line to be searched. She made certain to remove all keys and change from her person before going through. Felice didn't want to waste time having them do any unnecessary searches on her. A woman who was about to step through the gate before Felice was told to wait and allow Felice passage first. The lady, who appeared to be sophisticated at first sight, became irate and started cursing and making a fuss over the fact that someone skipped her. Felice went through, cut her eyes at the woman, and didn't bother to look back.

Henry was waiting on the other side of the metal detectors. He laughed as he saw and heard the ruckus.

"All that commotion and for what?" Felice asked Henry as they continued to walk.

"Stupid bitch!" Felice heard the woman scream as she continued to walk. Felice still didn't turn around, but held her middle finger up behind her back.

"Let me make this quick stop over here," Henry said, walking a few steps ahead of Felice. She had to make sure that she took her ticket and passport back from him before he left her. Felice looked at her watch and this time she began to panic. Her flight was supposed to leave out of Gate 42 and they were somewhere between 20 and 24. Why was Henry chilling on her time?

Felice started to walk over to him. He was taking something from one of the ticket agents behind the desk when she arrived.

"Is everything all right?" Felice asked.

"I told you from the beginning, I got this. Stop worrying, ma. I do this every day."

"Okay," Felice said as she took the ticket and her passport back from Henry. "I really appreciate you walking me down here and helping me get through the security gate so quickly. If you weren't here, I'd more than likely still be waiting on that long line and end up missing my flight."

"Probably, and probably not. See, what you have to do when you are in a situation like that is alert them that your flight is departing. Someone will try to usher you to the front and from the security gate you are pretty much on your own, but never wait on those long lines, especially if your flight is nonrefundable."

"Okay," Felice said, suddenly feeling in awe of Henry.

Henry reached over and took the travel bag that must have weighed at least thirty-five pounds off Felice's shoulder.

"Let's hustle," Henry said and began to jog down the walkway. Both he and Felice dipped and dodged through a gang of people. They were only steps away from the gate now. Felice could see the number 42 getting closer.

"We will now begin boarding Flight 360 to Montego Bay, Jamaica," Felice heard over the loud speaker.

"Thank God!" Felice said out of breath. Nonetheless, she was smiling when they arrived at the gate. She was flustered. They ran from Gate 30 to 42, which was a little bit of a distance considering how far apart the gates were.

"Who got this?" Henry said as they stopped to catch their breath.

"You got this," Felice answered and laughed. She went into her purse to pull out the money to tip Henry. "No, Ma. I don't want your money," Henry said, waving away the ten-dollar bill Felice was handing him. She had decided he deserved more than five.

"Are you sure?" Felice asked.

"He's sure," Sylvah said, coming up behind her and hitting Felice in the back with her carry-on bag.

"We thought that you would never make it," Alana commented.

"You know Felice, always late," Sylvah replied. "What in heaven's name are you wearing, girl?"

Candace merely waved from her seat.

"Girl, you've got to come prepared. I plan to soak up the sun as soon as I get off the plane," Felice retorted.

"That's not all you gonna soak up," Sylvah said mischievously.

"Ms. Lawrence, please don't let me pull your card right here, because you know that I will." Felice threatened. "Happy birthday, girl!" Felice finally got her bearings and reached to embrace her best friend. Sylvah obliged her.

"Thanks for the trip," Sylvah whispered in her ear.

"You're welcome."

"We are now boarding all first-class seats," the agent announced over the speaker.

"Let's get out of these people's way," Alana and Sylvah said in unison.

"Felice, that's you," Henry said still standing by.

"Huh? I didn't purchase first-class seats," Felice questioned.

"I know, but I had your tickets changed to assure that you didn't get bumped off the flight. Remember when I stopped back there at the desk? That was to change your seating arrangement."

"Oh my goodness," Felice said, beaming. "Thank you, thank you! You didn't have to do that for me."

"A lady like you deserves to fly first class only."

"Oh, what a bunch of shit, I think I'm about to gag," Alana said.

Felice looked over at Alana. "While you're busy hating on me, sistah, I'll be sipping on mimosas in first class. Ba-bye!" Felice tilted her head obnoxiously while waving and headed toward check-in and Henry continued to walk by her side.

"Listen, ma…I wanted to know if I could have your number," Henry said. For the first time Felice looked at Henry as a man instead of just some worker at the airport.

"Turn around for me," Felice said. "Slowly."

Henry looked at Felice strangely, but did as he was told. There were still four people ahead of Felice. She looked him over thoroughly.

"Mmh, tall, ruggedly handsome, nice smile, nice cinnamon complexion, employed, speaks English, your lips don't look like you smoke. Are you married, in a committed relationship or single?"

"I'm currently separated."

"How long?"

"For a minute."

"That's not really an answer, but I'll let it slide for now. Any kids?" Felice continued to question.

"Yes, I have a son."

"Who has custody?"

"We share the responsibility."

"Do you and your baby momma have an amicable relationship? Because I don't want any baby momma drama."

"We're cool. You don't have to worry about no drama or nuthin'."

"Okay, I'll give you my number," Felice quipped.

"Damn, ma, you kind of rough. I like that in a woman." Henry laughed as he took the business card from Felice.

Felice was next up at the podium. Henry slipped her his business card as well. She smiled as he walked away backward, trying to get a final glimpse of her before she disappeared on to the plane.

"When you getting back?" Henry asked, his voice rising slightly so Felice could hear him.

"In five days," Felice replied, walking onto the plane. She looked back and waved at her girls and Henry.

♀♂

Felice was already on her second mimosa as her friends began to board the plane. First Sylvah, then Alana and Candace followed. They all stopped when they got to her row.

"Well, welcome ladies," Felice said as she stretched into the empty seat beside her.

"Flat leaver. It's okay though, because when we arrive you'll be right back with the rest of us second-class citizens," Sylvah said and hit Felice with the pillow that was in the seat beside her.

"Showoff," Alana pouted.

"Felice, does this mean I get the row to myself?" Candace asked.

"I guess so," Felice responded. She laughed so hard it hurt as her friends walked by.

"Forget you," Sylvah said as she walked through the curtain that separated first class from coach.

"I love you too," Felice replied.

♀♂

Asphyxiating was the only way to describe the weather clenching Felice as she disembarked the aircraft. Now she was feeling over-dressed and couldn't wait to remove her bikini top. Hedonism II was just the place to do that. Felice couldn't wait. She went inside the muggy but air-conditioned terminal and listened to the group of singers belt out Jamaica's welcome song as she waited patiently for her friends.

Five minutes later a groggy-looking Sylvah, a disgruntled Alana, and a rested Candace entered the terminal.

"Damn, it's hot out there," Sylvah commented. She removed her shades and placed them atop her head and began fanning herself with a magazine.

"It's that damn menopause," Felice joked.

"Girlfriend, homeboy who escorted you through the airport will be buying Depends for you sooner than you know it, so you better warn him," Sylvah whipped back.

"Temperamental? That's another sign," Felice said.

"Ladies, let's be civil," Candace said and went over to Felice for an embrace.

"Candace, watch out for cooties, girl," Sylvah said, laughing.

"If I have cooties, I got them from you," Felice replied.

All of the ladies headed to baggage claim to get their bags and begin their five-day voyage.

7

Whatever Happens in Jamaica...

Day 1

Candace, Felice, Sylvah and Alana were all occupied with Bahama Mamas, daquiris, and rum and Cokes while soaking up the sun for delicious-looking tans. Both Alana and Felice opted to remove their tops on the nude beach. Square Sylvah and Conservative Candace opted to remain fully clothed.

The sun pierced the summer-blue sky while the clouds sketched an indiscernible pattern throughout. The scent of fresh saltwater filled the air. Passersbys walked in droves, kicking sand in their wake, occasionally glancing at the four women.

The beach was packed with nude sunbathers, the majority of them Europeans. Old and young Caucasian men alike walked by, their flaccid turtle penises barely covering sagging balls. European women with large, medium, small, real, and fake breasts strolled by seeking attention with bodies that were dusted with freckles and sunburn.

Sylvah read a book, choosing to ignore the scene; Candace was turned on her side listening to her CD player, while Felice and Alana lay on their stomachs.

Felice turned onto her back exposing her breasts for the world to see. She was sitting between Alana and Sylvah while Candace sat on the opposite side of Sylvah.

"You and your damn titties. Why do you feel the need to show them to the world?" Sylvah asked, refusing to look away from her book.

Candace turned around to join them.

"If I weren't so modest, I'd do it too," Candace said.

"No one knows you here, Candace, and I won't tell anybody. You know the old saying, 'whatever happens in Jamaica stays in Jamaica'" Felice said.

"Leave me and Candace alone, crazy lady," Sylvah said.

"No one said anything about you and your saggy bags. I was talking to those of us with perky breasts."

"You know what? Jason didn't complain two days ago," Sylvah scoffed.

"Who the hell is Jason?" Alana asked, turning to join the rest of the crew.

"Yeah, who is Jason?" Felice mocked.

Felice knew how private Sylvah was about her sex life, so to hear her mention Jason aloud in mixed company shocked her.

"Jason is someone that I conjured up. He's a fantasy of mine," Sylvah countered.

"Oh, that's what I thought," Alana said. "I can't imagine you with anyone outside of Bläise."

"It is possible for me to be with another man," Sylvah said.

Candace, being the savior she was wanted the vacation with her friends to be commotion free, so she decided rescue Sylvah. Besides, she knew Sylvah didn't light her pipe just to blow smoke, and that Jason must have been someone with whom she was recently involved. However, she probably didn't feel comfortable sharing the details with them at this time.

"Felice, tell us about your little sabbatical in Cuba," Candace beckoned.

Felice wanted to make sure that she had everyone's full attention. She wasn't in the business of repeating herself unnecessarily. She gazed at her friends and saw that all eyes were now on her.

"Cuba is *muy simpatico!*" Felice said, kissing her fingers to her lips.

"Did you go to Cuba or France?" Sylvah asked.

The ladies all laughed at Felice's poor Spanish accent.

"Whatever. Now do you want to hear my tales or not?"

"Go on, but please spare us the Spanish. I know *muy simpatico*," Sylvah said mocking Felice's hand movement and the kiss, "means very nice, but the accent is killing us."

"Fine, be that way," Felice said, trying to garner sympathy. "Well throw out any preconceptions that you have of what a communist society is or should be. The country is truly beautiful. The people are nice, and it's one of the best Caribbean islands that I've ever been to. Yes, they have poverty in Cuba, but I didn't see homeless people on the streets the way we do in America or even here in Jamaica. Even the poorest of people have shelter, and they most definitely have a class system of the have and the have nots."

"Really?" Candace asked savoring everything Felice said.

"I thought Castro had everybody wearing khaki or dingy colors of gray and working in factories," Alana said.

"That's exactly why I said remove anything you may have heard. It wasn't like that when I visited China and it's surely not like that in Cuba. These are the misconceptions America would like for you to believe."

"You visited China after the Communist reign," Alana said.

"Yeah, I know, but the society that I saw didn't just spring up overnight. Russia, on the other hand, is a completely different story. Even the Cubans don't care for Russian communism. Now, where was I? Oh yeah, they wear every God-given color in the rainbow. Apparently no one told them cigarettes could cause lung cancer, because smoking is second nature to them. They don't need to ever take their vehicles in for emissions tests. They don't find them practical or necessary. You can die from walking in between two cars, the exhaust is so thick. They love old American cars like Chevys and Fords, the fifties models. They have the most beautiful Catholic churches you have ever seen, but get this: the majority of the population doesn't believe in God."

"Now that's a real sin," Candace said, shaking her head.

"All of this sounds great, but you haven't told us what we've all been waiting to hear," Alana said, looking weary.

"I see some of us are a little impatient. Well, they love everything sweet. Oh, for your information, Alana, that includes their women. You wouldn't do well there with your funky attitude," Felice toyed.

"Ha, ha…very funny," Alana responded and turned up her nose at Felice.

"I had this fabulous fling with a soccer player. His name was Guillermo. He wasn't as tall as I usually like my men, but he was cute nonetheless. We had a hell of a time trying to understand each other in the beginning, but the important thing was we both understood the language of love."

"Oh, give me a break!" Sylvah said. "However, I must admit, Guillermo is definitely a cutie. I wonder what he's doing now?" Sylvah asked as she repositioned herself on a beach chair and placed the novel across her lap.

"Please, I'm sure he isn't having a hard time finding a replacement," Felice said, a hint of laughter traipsing her words. "When I first arrived in Cuba looking for my father I stayed in Havana at a hotel. My first week there was a struggle. I barely knew how to say, *No hablo espãnol* and *me llamo es Felice*. I was walking down this road called Five Mile when a tour bus with passengers pulled up beside me. This dark-chocolate brother opens the door and begins speaking Spanish faster than a speeding bullet. I tried to explain to him that I didn't speak the language, but he kept talking. Finally I told him as best as I could, English only. You should have seen the dejected look on his face. Well, he kept driving the bus beside me as I continued to walk and when I got in front of my hotel he closed the door. He held up his hands in the universal 'I'm sorry' mode, and I simply blew him a kiss. After that shit, I was determined to learn more than two sentences."

"Shit, I don't blame you," Alana countered.

"So, how was it meeting up with your father?" Candace inquired.

"It was cool. It took a while before I was able to track him down. Communication was a major problem. People do speak English there, but very little. I learned that I'm definitely a cross between both parents as far as looks. I believe myself to be smart like my father and witty like my mother. Every place I went they called me mulatto. Now here in the States we don't want to be labeled such, but in Cuba it simply means I'm not light and I'm not dark."

"You compare yourself to your mother now?" Sylvah asked.

"She's still witty," Felice answered.

"What does your father do?" Candace asked, sipping the last of her drink.

"He's a biochemist and works for this Cuban pharmaceutical company. They get a lot of people who come from overseas for medical attention in Cuba."

"Damn, and I read somewhere that there medical is free," Alana stated as she rubbed more suntan lotion on her already burnished skin. Her light cocoa complexion was now a toasty brown.

"Yeah, but not for Americans," Felice added. "Considering the United States doesn't have a treaty with Cuba.

"Felice, did you attain what you were after in Cuba?" Candace asked, her voice filled with sincerity.

"I never really thought about it, but to answer your question, yes. I wanted to build a relationship with my father, and I did. I got to live with him for a while and know him. For so long he was just a figment of my imagination. So many unanswered questions and closed doors that I never had the keys to gain access to, you know? But for the most part I managed to put closure on a lot of things relating to my parents."

"Then it sounds like your mission was accomplished," Alana said, nodding and listening intently.

"I guess it was," Felice answered, shaking her head with satisfaction.

"Ladies, I'm starting to bake," Sylvah said. "Let's go inside to the bar."

All of the ladies got up and followed. As they walked to the bar they spotted someone who looked remotely familiar.

"Oh my goodness, is that who I think that is over there?" Alana asked excitedly.

"It all depends on who you think it is," Sylvah said clueless as to who the young man was, although she did find him dangerously attractive.

"You know, umm…that model guy. The one who's in all of the commercials and magazines." Alana was snapping her fingers and racking her brain trying to recall his name.

"Clayton Breeze," Candace answered.

"That's right. That's him, and he's coming our way. Oh my goodness, I'm not wearing a top!" Alana said as Clayton headed over to the bar where they were sat.

"And you're just now realizing this?" Sylvah smirked, placing her book on the bar.

"Girl, hold your head up proud and aim those 34A daggers at him," Felice said, poking fun at Alana's petite, erect breasts. "He can blow his breeze in my direction any day. Mmm, the things I could do with him," Felice pondered aloud.

"We can imagine," Candace said, choking on her drink. Surprised stares were aimed in Candace's direction. "I'm not the prude you all think I am," Candace said. "I do have a husband and kids to prove I know how to keep my man happy."

"Well, excuse us!" Alana said.

Clayton arrived and took the vacant seat beside Candace. She swiveled the chair to face her friends, turning her back to Clayton.

"Oh my goodness," Candace whispered. "He's even better looking up close."

"Is that possible?" Alana asked, trying to lean over to get a better look.

"Hey, back those things up off me," Sylvah said, pushing Alana and her breasts off her shoulder.

"Sorry," Alana said apologetically.

Sylvah shuddered.

"They're only titties," Alana said defensively as she watched Sylvah overreact.

"And as you can see I have two of my own. I don't need yours rubbing against me."

"Good afternoon, ladies," Clayton said, looking at all of them, but focusing attention on Candace.

Clayton Breeze was very easy on the eyes. He wasn't as tall in person as he looked in his commercials, billboards, or photos, but he was easily six feet tall, maybe six-one. He had a nice bronzed complexion with red undertones, compliments of the sun and a face that looked like the god of beauty himself chiseled it for the entire world to marvel. He wasn't a pretty boy, but he was remarkably handsome with a clean-shaven head and the shadow of a beard cloaking his face. His eyebrows were rich with sheen and texture and were perfectly arched. His rose lips were full and enticing and although his cheeks didn't possess dimples, his chin offered a small cleft.

"Hello," they all replied in unison.

"Beautiful island, isn't it?" Clayton asked.

"Yes, it is," Candace answered before everyone else.

"So what brings four beautiful women like you down to the tropical island of Jamaica?" Clayton looked at each woman, giving each one the same amount of enthusiasm with his gaze. He didn't look at Alana or Felice's breasts any longer than necessary.

"We're celebrating our friend's birthday," Felice answered

"Really? Which one of you?" Clayton looked them over as if the word *birthday* was going to magically appear across one of their foreheads.

"Me," Sylvah said, blushing and raising her hand like a pupil in school.

"Really? Let me get you a drink. What are you having?" he asked, waving the bartender over.

"Well, I don't know. What would you suggest?" Sylvah asked, a smile creeping across her face.

"They have this drink called Lady Marmalade. It has a touch of honey, Grand Marnier, Sweet and Sour Mix, and Jamaican rum. One of my coworkers couldn't get enough of it while she was here."

"Ooh, Lady Marmalade sounds good. I'll try it," Sylvah replied.

"And you ladies?" Clayton asked.

"I'm game," Felice said.

"Me too," Alana added.

"I'll have a virgin daiquiri. That drink sounds a little too heavy for me," Candace said.

Clayton gave the drink order to the bartender along with an order for steamed shrimp and lobster tails.

"Oh yeah, the non-drinker. How could I forget?" Alana commented.

"That's cool," Clayton said. "I don't drink either. As a matter of fact, being in the business that I'm in and not partaking of the alcohol scene definitely makes me the oddball of the group."

"Well, it seems you two have something in common," Alana said, trying to suppress her resentment.

"It seems that we do," Clayton said, not being the least bit bashful about his interest in Candace.

"Excuse me, people, I have to go to the rest room," Candace said stepping off the barstool. "I'll be back."

Felice could tell Candace was a bit uncomfortable with the attention that Clayton was giving her.

"You know what, I'll come with you," Felice offered.

The two ladies went in the direction of the restroom. Once inside Candace headed straight to a stall and locked the door.

"Candace, I think Clayton likes you," Felice teased.

"I know, but I'm married. It's not like I can like him back."

"Listen, girl, we're on vacation. Have a little fun. It's okay to flirt, just don't get carried away. Besides, I'm sure Clayton won't bite—or maybe he will."

"Felice, get your mind out of the gutter," Candace said, flushing the commode and opening the stall door.

"Seriously, we're all here to have some fun. Let him buy you a few drinks and just talk. Just don't do what I would do in your situation." Felice patted Candace on the back. "No harm, no foul."

"I guess so," Candace said, washing her hands.

"Come on, let's go."

When they returned to their seats the drinks had already arrived. The group was in lively chatter and everyone was laughing at a joke. Candace returned to her seat beside Clayton and Sylvah and tried her best to avert her attention to the drink.

"I don't bite," Clayton whispered into Candace's ear.

"I never said you did," Candace replied.

"Mmh, this is good," Sylvah said taking a sip of her drink. "What did you say this was called again?"

"Lady Marmalade," Clayton responded.

"So you never did tell us what brought you down here, mon," Felice said, throwing in a little Jamaican-flavored accent.

"I was here for a photo shoot, but it ended yesterday. I don't have anything else scheduled until the end of next week, so I decided to extend my vacation until Monday."

"We leave on Monday too," Felice said.

"We were never formally introduced," Sylvah said. "I'm Sylvah. This is Candace." Sylvah turned to her other side. "This is Alana, and this is Felice. I also want to thank you for recommending the drink and for getting us appetizers before I get ripped and forget my manners."

"No problem, and I'm Clayton Breeze, but my friends call me Clay." Clayton stood and proffered his hand to each of the ladies.

"You must be like putty in a girl's hand," Alana said, sounding like a schoolgirl with a crush.

"Some might say that," Clayton said, returning to his seat.

"Vain too," Felice added.

"Others might say that too." They all laughed.

"Clayton is a colonial name, right?"

"Yes. My parents are actually from Jamaica," Clayton said.

"Oh, great. So are Candace's parents," Alana said, envy coating her words.

"Really, Candace? It seems that we do have a lot more in common than I thought."

Clayton continued his conversation with Candace for more than an hour. It was as if Felice, Sylvah, and Alana weren't even present. Alana was scorched as Clayton and Candace soaked each other up in discussion.

Candace and Clayton found out they had more in common than even she thought. Both of them had to spend their summers in Jamaica as children. They majored in advertising while attending college and were both excellent swimmers. By mid-afternoon they were both riding jet skis, enjoying the waves and each other's company.

♀♂

Day 2

"She's married," Alana scoffed, drink in hand as she stared at Candace and Clayton on the dance floor. When Candace and Clayton first started dancing they were a safe distance apart, but at some point, Clayton's body blanketed Candace's like a sheet on a mattress.

"It's not like she's fucking him," Felice defended.

"Married people shouldn't dance with other people like that," Alana remarked with disgust.

"Married people shouldn't do a lot of things, but they do!" Sylvah said.

They definitely do, Felice thought, reflecting on her relationship with Jermaine.

Felice, Sylvah and Alana stood like wallflowers at the Hedonism Pajama Wet N' Wild party. The music was jumping and so were the people on the dance floor. Bodies were intertwined and contorted in positions that Felice often tried behind closed doors, but never on a dance floor. All of the ladies received invitations to dance, but none of the men were up to the women's standards.

Sean Paul's latest hit penetrated the dance hall. Bodies crammed every available corner of the room. The space was air conditioned, but people were perspiring from the heat being generated.

On one side of the club, scantily dressed women danced atop the bar and the men sat below, getting free feels. There was a pudding licking contest taking place at the far end of the bar. Naked men and women raced to lick pudding off each other while onlookers rooted them on and snapped pictures. No one gave this scene a second thought, because this was what Hedonism was known for.

Felice, Sylvah, and Alana stood and observed the scantily clad partygoers. Most of the men wore swim trunks or briefs; the really risqué wore what appeared to be G strings with faces of animals like pigs, giraffes and elephants and the snouts and trunks housed their penis. The women were garbed in one- and two-piece bathing suits; sheer gowns revealing mounds of flesh; netted material; and other very creative ensembles.

Sylvah wore a very sexy black lingerie top and fitted white Capri pants with strappy sling-back sandals. Alana sported a two-piece pink teddy that left very little to the imagination, and Felice donned a glittery red halter-top and batty rider jean shorts. All of them were pleasing to the eye and received a great deal of attention, but the only man worthwhile was Clay, who was occupied with Candace.

"He's probably gay, anyway. He didn't even stare at our breasts yesterday. Hmm," Alana said, changing her pose against the wall.

"Alana, stop freaking hating! The man probably sees breasts all the damn time. After all, he is a model. Now Candace is out there having fun, and I damn sure don't need to continue being a pillar to this wall any longer than necessary. I'm going to dance," Felice said and headed to the floor.

"We're gonna slow it down a little bit," the deejay announced as he changed the tempo of the music. A few more people entered the party and all eyes were fixed for good-looking men.

"Can the music get any slower?" Alana asked, getting upset and scanning the room for likely prospects.

"I'm going to join Felice on the dance floor," Sylvah said, growing tired of Alana's complaining.

♀♂

Day 3

"Goodmawningladies," the waitress sang. "What can I do you for today?"

"I'll have a cup of Blue Mountain coffee with cream and sugar. Thanks." Candace handed the waitress her menu. "I'm going to get me some salt fish with ackee and dumplings from the buffet."

"A glass of grapefruit juice, please," Sylvah said. "Do you know if they have French toast and hash browns today?"

"I believe we do," the waitress said, turning her attention to Felice.

"I'll take a tall glass of fresh squeezed orange juice. I feel like having a fruit salad with lots of mango and kiwi today," Felice said.

"Will dat be h'all?" The waitress asked as she completed writing the drink orders.

"Yes, that will be it." Sylvah confirmed.

"Okay," the waitress said and sauntered away.

The ladies got up and walked to the buffet table for their food selection.

"So where is Alana?" Candace asked.

"She got wasted last night. A couple of guys kept getting her drinks, and Felice and I warned Alana to stop drinking, but she kept repeating 'I'm a big girl.' That big girl must have thrown up at least three times last night, and guess what?" Sylvah asked, not waiting for a response. "I stood by and watched her."

"Big girl," Candace said, laughing.

"Speaking of missing, what happened to you last night? One minute you were on the dance floor and the next you were gone." Sylvah commented.

"Me, missing? No, you tw-two just did-didn't look hard enough," Candace stammered.

"Oh my goodness, you fucked Clayton!" Felice screamed.

"Oh shit, no you didn't!" Sylvah said surprised. "You stuttering skank." Sylvah laughed.

Candace's face was flushed from embarrassment. She was hoping they wouldn't ask about her whereabouts. She didn't mean for it to happen. She was attracted to Clayton, but she didn't mean to sleep with him. Candace had never had a one-night stand before much less cheated on her husband of ten years.

"Is he packing?" Felice asked.

"Was he any good?" Sylvah asked eagerly.

"Was who packing and was who any good?" Alana asked, walking up behind them at the table. She looked at everyone's face and then at Candace and instinctively knew what they were talking about.

"Candace, you fucked Clayton? You cheated on your husband?" Alana asked disdainfully. "I always knew you weren't shit. You have a good husband and children at home. I can't believe you."

"Shut the fuck up!" Felice said.

Candace left the table and walked swiftly toward her room. Tears began to stream down her face. She didn't mean for it to happen and she didn't intend on anyone finding out. Now, Alana of all people was privy to this information. What else could go wrong in her life? All she wanted to do was visit the island, see the sites, take a few pictures, capture some sun, enjoy lively conversation with her friends, purchase a couple of souvenirs for her family, and relax. Fucking Clayton Breeze wasn't on the list, but somehow it got penciled in.

"Candace, hold up," Felice yelled, trying to catch her.

Candace didn't want to hear what anyone had to say. Not even her dear friend Felice. What she did was wrong, and she was going to have to live with it. The heading *adulterer* would replace her former title of wife. The scariest part was she enjoyed her experience with Clayton the first, second and third time.

Candace knew things were going too far when she felt the room begin to spin and their dancing remained slow, regardless of the selection played.

"I think they gave me regular daiquiris instead of the virgin ones," Candace commented to Clay, grinding her behind deeper into Clay's groin.

"Are you going to be okay?" Clay asked, his hands circling Candace's waist.

"I think I need to lie down. I have a slight headache."

"I'll walk you to your room," Clay offered.

Clay and Candace headed toward her room, but she threw up before they could arrive.

"How far is your room?" Clay asked, holding her thick, long hair away from her face.

"On the other side." Candace pointed to the suites in the opposite direction.

"My room is in the building over there. You can rest there if you want. I have a couch and you can have my bed," Clay offered.

Candace wasn't really comfortable with Clay's offer, but she didn't want to inconvenience him by asking that he accompany her to the room, so she agreed.

Clay's suite was even nicer than the one Candace and Sylvah shared. When they entered the room, Candace bolted to the bathroom and closed the door behind her. When she came out Clay was sitting on the couch.

"You all right?" Clay inquired.

"I messed up my shirt, and I think I got vomit in my hair," Candace said, embarrassed. "I need to take a shower and wash my hair. Do you mind?"

"No, not at all," Clay said, coming to her aid. He went into his bedroom and returned with a clean T-shirt and boxers for her to change into.

"Here you go," Clay said, handing Candace the clothes through the cracked door.

"I've never done this before, Clay. You've got to believe me. I'm so embarrassed."

"I believe you, and you have no reason to be embarrassed," Clay said, reassuring her.

Candace showered, washed her hair, and tried to rinse out her soiled top. When she came out of the bathroom Clay had coffee prepared for both of them. Candace took a seat beside Clay on the couch and helped herself to the steaming cup of Blue Mountain.

"Everything Irie, mon?" Clay joked.

"Uh, I'm feeling a little better. My head was pounding and I should have known that something wasn't right. Instead I went and asked for another drink. That Jamaican rum is no joke."

"It's pretty serious. When you ordered your drink, you did specify virgin, right?"

"I'm quite sure that I did, but they never really pay attention anyway. I'm feeling pretty tired." Candace yawned and snuggled into the crevice of Clay's very open and extended arm. Candace wasn't really paying attention to the fact that she was with Clay and not with her husband, Shane.

Clay gave Candace an innocent peck on the forehead. Candace gazed at Clay and her lips were directly beneath his. He dipped his head to align their lips, and they shared the most intense and gentle kiss either one of them had ever experienced. When the kiss ended, their lips lingered and continued to brush across each other's. Their breathing became labored as Clay pulled Candace closer into his embrace and that marked the time when things started to spiral out of control.

Three condoms, four "oh fuck me's," and the best oral sex Candace ever experienced later, Candace had broken one of God's holiest of ordinances.

♀♂

Day 4

"She won't come out of her room," Sylvah announced.

"She hauled ass so fast yesterday I couldn't catch up with her," Felice said.

"She fucked up, that's why she's locked up in that room. Guilt was stamped all across her face before she jetted out of the restaurant yesterday. I may have been hungover, but I knew what was up. Candace has everything—a fine-ass husband, kids, a cushy job—and she jeopardizes everything to screw the first good-looking man she spots on the island."

"You talk too much," Sylvah stated and cut her eyes at Alana.

"I'm only speaking the truth."

"Tell me again why we even speak to you?" Felice asked Alana. "You are so judgmental and jealous, it's disgusting, and guess what? If given the chance you would've fucked Clayton, too, but you couldn't, so you have to dig into Candace. Get a damn man and a life."

Sylvah, Felice and Alana shared looks. Felice and Sylvah shook their heads in disgust at Alana. Both women grew frustrated at Alana and her attitude toward Candace. They thought that over the years Alana would eventually grow up and stop behaving so iniquitous toward Candace. High school was well over twenty years behind them and still Alana chose to act like she was sixteen. She was forever playing the role of a bully when it came to Candace. It had always been like that. Sylvah and Felice figured that Alana was insecure because in actuality, Candace was considerably more attractive than Alana. However, Candace was demure and never flaunted her beauty. Without ever trying, Candace always received more attention than Alana even with her glasses and natural braided hair.

Felice had numerous boyfriends in high school. She was pretty, popular and smart. People clamored to be in her company because of those qualities. But mostly they loved her aura. Felice let off good vibes and always had a kind word for everyone who managed to waltz in her presence.

Although she was an only child, Felice was never alone. She had more friends than a deck of cards, but she was no fool. Out of the school of fish that swam through her pond every day she knew if anything ever went down, her real girls were the ones who would be at her aid. Her true friends were Sylvah, Candace Farewell and Alana Wright. Alana was a little questionable at times, but for the most part Felice believed that she would be there. All of the other people were faking the funk. They hung around because A, they wanted to be seen with the in-group; B, they wanted to use Felice for one reason or another; or C, they simply wanted to be up in her business. People were funny that way, wanting to find dirt on you to bring you down to their acid hell. Back then there was no dirt to be found on Felice. She hung out with her friends, worked at a department store part-time during the week and had a boyfriend, Kadar Landry who adored her to death. He was tall, dark, and too manly for his sixteen years. Kadar was a roughneck, but had his wits about him. Felice reciprocated Kadar's adoration and everyone envied their relationship. They dated for a little over a year, and during that time they never consummated the relationship. This was a little strange for someone of Kadar's stature, but was the case. Felice allowed him to do many things, but intercourse wasn't one of them, and surprisingly as hard as Kadar was around his boys and at school, he never pressured her. Samantha, Felice's mother, raised Felice to have a free mind and spirit, but strongly impressed that once a man made his deposit and withdrawal, the account would remain open and the dividends would dwindle, decreasing the value. Felice wasn't about to be labeled "easy" or "slut" like so many of the other girls she knew. Felice listened to her mother's words, which at the time made a great deal of sense.

Felice knew how to learn from example. She observed her peers. She wasn't going to fall in love and give her goodies away. She had heard the stories about how girls gave up their virginity and then one month later the guy moved on to the next chick doing the same 'ol shit, leaving them crying and wondering why he left.

Kadar might not have been content waiting with the possibility of never getting to home base. Nonetheless, he respected and loved himself some Felice, and most importantly, didn't want to run the risk of letting her go and her having a change of heart and giving it up to the next brother waiting behind door number one. And there were plenty of contestants waiting to take his place. These young men made their interests known to Felice on many occasions when Kadar wasn't present. Felice was always cordial to them while turning down their propositions, and she always made Kadar aware of the people who approached her. Their relationship was cool like that. Neither of them was on a jealous jaunt and appreciated each other for that quality. Kadar also told Felice when girls flirted with him, even when it was her girl, Alana, which Alana denied. Felice was no idiot and let it slide, but the level of trust for Alana went from one hundred percent to fifty. Felice confided the hurt to her mother, and Samantha advised, "Never trust your man around your female friends. Otherwise, if you blink twice they would've handled their business and then pretended as if nothing ever happened."

Moving forward, Felice was leery of everyone with the exception of Sylvah. She and Sylvah met under circumstances that would forever allow Felice to trust Sylvah with her life. Alana, she learned, was distrustful and Candace was quiet, almost a recluse. Candace's quietness and demure demeanor got under Alana's skin and made her suspect of Candace's behavior. Alana thought it was impossible to live without drama and that Candace had to be hiding something. The other funny thing about their friendship was that the only reason they were friends was because of Felice. She was the zipper which kept them fastened.

Sylvah was two years their senior, just as popular and pretty as Felice, loud but had an I.Q. that made the clouds appear low. She got along with everyone. Alana was a straight-up hater, but was always well dressed, smart, and after hanging around so much, just became a fixture. Alana enjoyed drama, and if she could be the center of said drama, all the better. Candace was one of the first people Felice met upon entering high school. They shared so many classes together it was inevitable they would become friends. Candace was cute, but didn't know her own potential. She wore glasses and her mother refused to perm her thick, long hair. She wore cornrows before they became stylish. Alana loved to pick on Candace's hairstyles and glasses. Yet Alana's hair was so short that if your breath was hot enough you could dry it with a mere cough. These belittling occurrences didn't take place when Felice was around. She always heard about them secondhand from Sylvah who usually came to Candace's rescue. Felice may have been nice back then, but she rarely minced words and would have told Alana about herself in a heartbeat.

Kadar and Felice broke up when Kadar went away to college before Felice's senior year of high school. Felice was heartbroken. Kadar would always be her first love. He attended Georgia Tech and was there on an engineering scholarship and got a spot on the basketball team. Kadar was a very good center and eventually even made it to the pros. In his senior year he was drafted to play with the Atlanta Hawks, but his career was short lived because of a motorcycle injury. Apparently he still had that roughneck streak in him. To this day, Felice always felt that Kadar was the one who got away. Perhaps if they had stayed together, she would still be a good girl, a one-man kind of woman. Ha! Who was she trying to fool? The one-man shit got tired real quick! Those days were long gone. They evaporated with Bedford, who did end up being her first, her last, her nothing. He helped Felice morph into the beast she had become. He created the disorder that permeated in her world and was intent on continuing. Felice learned a hard lesson, and she'd never mix business with pleasure again. It took her nearly fifteen years to learn, but better today than tomorrow.

♀♂

The women picked haphazardly at their food. Each woman was in her own world and could care less about the beautiful weather outside or that they only had one more day on the island when Clay pulled up a chair to join them.

"Good morning, ladies," Clayton said.

"Good morning," Sylvah and Felice answered. Alana mumbled something inaudible under her breath.

"I didn't see you all yesterday. What did you guys do?" Clayton asked, unaware he was an uninvited guest.

"We went to Dunn's River Falls, toured Rose Hall Mansion, and went shopping in town," Felice replied.

"Sounds like fun. Did you get a lot of pictures and souvenirs?"

"A few," Sylvah answered nonchalantly.

Clayton placed the menu down and scanned the room not really interested in continuing the small talk. When he couldn't find what he was looking for he returned his attention back to them.

"Where's Candace?" he asked.

"You should know, you fucked her," Alana responded.

"Excuse me," Clayton said, stunned.

"Never mind her," Sylvah said. "She's in her room."

"Oh, she must be wiped out from yesterday, huh?"

"Try the other night," Alana said.

"Did I do something to you, Alana?" Clayton asked, looking at Sylvah and Felice, confused.

"Yeah, you didn't fuck her," Felice said as she pointed at Alana. "so she's upset."

"Okay, this conversation is getting a little too weird and much too personal for me," Clayton said scooting his chair back and rising from the table. "I'm sorry if I disturbed you all and your morning," Clayton removed the napkin from his lap and placed it on the table and left.

After Clayton left Sylvah also rose from the table.

"You know what, I agree with Clayton. The conversation did get strange and much too personal. We are supposed to be friends. This was supposed to be my birthday weekend celebration. Instead I've been surrounded by negative energy ever since we arrived, and it's generated from one source." Sylvah scowled, directing her poisonous glare at Alana. "I'm going to my room to talk to my friend and try and convince her to join me for a swim on our last full day in Jamaica."

"I'll come with you," Felice said.

They walked out, leaving Alana sitting at the table alone.

♀♂

Day 5

"No first class this go-round?" Sylvah teased, turning around to face Felice in the seat behind her on the plane.

"Go back to your book," Felice laughed as she reclined her chair all the way back. She had a restless night filled with more bad dreams.

Felice and Sylvah were the only ones in talkative moods. Candace still hadn't said more than two words to anyone and no one cared whether Alana spoke.

The day before, when Sylvah and Felice returned to the room for Candace, she had already left. She wrote a brief note for Sylvah stating that she needed to clear her head and was going out.

Candace took a cab to visit her aunt in the parish of St. James, Montego Bay. She loved her friends, but didn't want to indulge any of them right then. She didn't need their words of consolation, the pity stares or anything else. Candace just wanted to be. Besides, she knew her mother must've already informed her aunt Sugar that she was in town, in which case she would be awaiting Candace's arrival.

Candace made sure to dress real simple and didn't bother with any jewelry. She loved her Jamaican people, but they were also known to be thieves, especially if they smelled the scent of foreigner on you.

Candace had the cab drop her off at Barnett Street. She overpaid the driver in American dollars and he couldn't stop thanking her. Candace closed the door and waved good-bye. She stopped in a small bakery near her aunt's house and purchased a beef patty with coco bread and a Ting soda. She passed the colorful shanty businesses and the people selling fruits and vegetables in the marketplace. Candace turned to see if her small purse, which was clipped to a knapsack, was securely fastened, and it was. Before turning the corner to her aunt's she reached into her pocket to retrieve a few dollars and purchased a piece of sugarcane and a bag of tamarind candy. Once she got to her aunt's she knew her uncle would peel the skin off the sugarcane for her.

Aunt Sugar was sitting on the porch, almost as if she knew to expect Candace. When she spotted her she yelled to her husband that Candace had arrived, raced down the steps, and crossed the road to greet her. They embraced for what felt like an eternity, and it made Candace feel good. It took her back to the summers of her childhood.

"I almost tink dat I wusn't goin to see yu!" Aunt Sugar exclaimed, pulling back and taking a good look at her grown niece.

"No, mon. I couldn't du dat, auntie," Candace said with her synthetic Jamaican accent.

"Lawd, hab mercy. . .look pon de chile," Aunt Sugar said as they entered the house. Her uncle gave her a bear hug, causing Candace to drop her items.

Candace spent the rest of the afternoon relaxing while her aunt and uncle fussed over her. Her aunt made her a complete meal of Escovitch fish, rice and peas, steamed cabbage, and plantains. After the meal, Candace had no choice but to take a nap in the spare room. She was too full to wheel herself out to catch a cab. When she awoke her aunt was back out on the porch reading the *Gleaner.*

"You're up," her aunt said, acknowledging Candace.

"Yes, I really needed to rest."

"Candace, I know we haven seen each otha in a long time, but I sense sumpting is wrong."

Aunt Sugar was one of Candace's favorite aunts, and they shared a very special bond. The distance never ripped that apart. When Candace got married to Shane, her aunt flew to the States to help out with the wedding and even baked the cake.

"You're right," Candace said, giving in instantly.

"Talk," Aunt Sugar said, biting into a piece of cane.

"I did something really bad and can't forgive myself, and I don't think God will either." Candace paused waiting for her aunt to comment, but she didn't. "The other night I slept with another man."

"Goodness. Yu haven marriage problems?"

"No, and even if we were, what happened still wouldn't make it right."

"True." Aunt Sugar held Candace's hands in hers. "But let mi tell yu a story," Aunt Sugar said. They sat over a glass of carrot juice and Aunt Sugar told Candace of a time between her grandparents. She learned that her father and aunt were, of course brother and sister, but didn't share the same mother. However, when her grandfather brought Candace's father home his wife, Candace's grandmother accepted him, forgiving her husband of his infidelities. Candace's grandmother raised her stepson as if he were her very own until the day she died.

"The Bible tells us to ask the Lord to 'forgive us our debts, as we forgive our debtors," Aunt Sugar said, closing out her story.

When Candace left her aunt she felt ten times stronger than when she first arrived. At the hotel, she started to the bar to get a soda, but saw Clay and decided to detour to her room instead. The suite was dark and Sylvah's room door was closed, so she went into her bedroom. She took a nice long shower, packed her clothes in preparation of the following day, and went to bed. But before her head hit the pillow she bent down on her knees and prayed for forgiveness. Candace lay comfortably in her bed and upon closing her eyes knew the next day would be her resurrection and whatever happened in Jamaica stayed in Jamaica.

8

Suppose Your Wife Goes Into Labor?

The return flight was tiring and turbulent for several reasons. Nothing felt the same between the foursome. Prior to leaving for Jamaica, they were all anxious to go, but by the fourth day, they were all anxious to leave. On the plane, Sylvah read a book, Alana listened to a CD player, Felice watched the featured movie, and Candace feigned sleep. There was no laughter or idle banter. Only silence.

The trip from the gate to the other end of the terminal felt eternal. The four women stood around the luggage carousel waiting impatiently for their bags. Felice and Sylvah were the only two briefly exchanging conversation. Alana allowed a few strangers to stand between them, and Candace stood aloofly to the side. Heat, tension, and suffocation filled the air as they avoided contact. Felice and Sylvah decided to give Candace her space and they purposely shunned Alana, as to avoid an unnecessary debate at the airport, which would cause Candace additional stress. They knew Candace found the occurrence in Jamaica to be sinful and embarrassing and that it would take her a while to get over it. When Candace shut down the way she had it was best to leave her alone. Twenty years of friendship made them privy of one another's flaws and taught them how to deal with such situations. Generally, for Candace, it was space and time.

Candace's husband and children arrived at the airport to take her home. Tension misted the air as she departed and words were left unsaid. Alana caught a cab and Sylvah and Felice were about to do the same when Jermaine pulled up. Felice didn't recall giving him her flight information. Nevertheless, he was outside waiting and looking really good. Blue jeans never looked better, and his baldhead glowed against the moonlight. Five days of celibacy had been enough. Just when Felice thought she was going home alone, Jermaine decided to surprise her. Deep down Felice couldn't help but love him. Nevertheless, she had a rulebook and planned to stick by it. Their current situation suited her just fine.

"Good evening, ladies. Would you care for a lift?" Jermaine asked.

"We sure would," Felice answered, giving him her carry-on bag.

"How are you doing tonight?" Sylvah asked.

"Great, now that my sweetheart is back," Jermaine said, kissing Felice's full lips. Jermaine opened the car door for both ladies, relieved them of their luggage, and put everything in the trunk.

Jermaine entered the car, got comfortable, and started the ignition. "Put That Woman First" by Jaheim played. The message rang clear. Jermaine was no longer subtle with his quest to have Felice in his life on a permanent basis anymore. Upon her return from Cuba, he had purchased her a very nice and expensive ring. Felice couldn't help but gasp as the eloquent four-carat solitaire diamond ring surrounded by baguettes beamed at her. The radiant diamonds glistened against the light as he placed the ring on her finger. Felice wondered if Jermaine had taken a picture and her handprint to the designer, the ring fit so well. The comfort level of accepting such a gift had its penalties. Felice was reluctant, because she didn't need Jermaine thinking their fling amounted to more, but it was tempting. After much debate, force, and insistence for Felice to take the ring as a gift with no expectations, she had to accept. For someone with no expectations, Jermaine sure had a way of constantly appearing unexpectedly, blowing up her cell, and keeping tabs on her whereabouts. Felice loved him, but ignored him whenever he behaved this way.

"Did you ladies pack for five days or five weeks?" Jermaine joked.

"Those bags are Sylvah's," Felice said, laughing.

"Oh, whatever," Sylvah said, rolling her eyes.

"So how was your trip?" Jermaine asked to no one in particular.

"Eventful," Felice answered.

"How so?" Jermaine asked curiously.

"You really don't want to know," Felice replied and Sylvah giggled.

"Did you get yourself into something you had no business doing?" Jermaine asked, sounding a bit jealous and curious at the same time.

"Sweetheart," Felice said, caressing Jermaine's inner thigh, "you need not worry. This trip, I was a good girl."

"Well that's good to know. So is someone going to tell me what was so eventful?"

"It's really not important, but I'm really glad to see you tonight. I wasn't expecting you."

Jermaine appeared to be blushing. "You knew I'd be here to pick you up. I don't want you catching cabs if you don't have to."

"I still appreciate it."

"Thanks from the backseat, too. You saved me from having to dish out money for a taxi, and I was already running low."

"Oh, you can chip in for the gas," Jermaine said, laughing.

"Forget you," Sylvah replied.

♀♂

Jermaine dropped Sylvah off and carried the bags to her apartment. Five minutes later he was searching Felice's end of the block for parking. Eastern Parkway was not conducive to drivers. It really didn't matter what time of day it was, when a spot became available you almost preferred not to move the car again. However, Jermaine lucked up and located a spot less than a block away from Felice's building.

Upon entering the apartment, Felice began unpacking all of her luggage. Souvenirs were labeled and put away until they arrived at their destinations. Felice liked to get everything out of the way immediately so that she could work on other projects. While she unpacked, Jermaine kicked back on the sofa with a drink and a movie. Felice never worried about entertaining Jermaine since he always made himself comfortable.

"Jermaine, what have you been up to lately?" Felice asked, her voice rising slightly as she finished up in her room.

"Missing you," Jermaine replied.

"Isn't that sweet. How's your mom?"

"She's doing okay. Last week was the second anniversary of my father's passing and she always gets into a slump. It's real hard for her, especially since they were married for so long."

"I'm sorry to hear. How long were your parents married?" Felice asked.

"Forty-two years. They got married right out of high school."

"Damn, forty-two years is a long time. Marriages barely last ten years nowadays. Anyway, how's work?"

"Busy. I have another business trip to make in a few weeks. P. Diddy is starting another business venture. I have to go over the finances, etc. Otherwise, same old stuff. I have Alicia Keys concert tickets for next week Tuesday. Do you wanna go?"

"No, I can't. I already have plans. Why don't you take your wife?"

"She's due pretty soon, and the last thing we need is for her water to break while we're at the concert."

Felice fluffed the pillows on the bed and completed her tasks in the room. She walked through the corridor and entered the living room to join Jermaine. There were things bothering her. If Jermaine knew his wife was due, why was he there with her? Secondly, if his wife was pregnant, their unhappy home couldn't be too unhappy. They were still having sex. Jermaine claimed it was a moment of weakness, and according to his wife, she was on the pill. Either way she became pregnant and would have the baby at any given moment.

"Jermaine, suppose she goes into labor tonight?" Felice asked as she stood directly in front of him, arms folded across her chest.

"Everything is copasetic. Anyway, she's really not due for another month, but she always delivers early. Marissa or her mother will call me on my cell and I'll meet them at the hospital," Jermaine said nonchalantly.

"So where do they think you are now? It's a quarter to eleven."

"Out, and I don't owe them any explanations. I still provide for my family. I'm there when it counts."

"It counts right now, Jermaine. Your wife is about to have *your* baby, and you are here with me. Now don't get me wrong, I enjoy your company, but right is right."

"If it weren't for this whole baby thing, I would have been long gone and Marissa knows this. What we have is not a relationship. We simply exist in each other's space. Now, what you and I have is real."

"Jermaine, what you and I have is the beginning stage of a relationship, and it's called infatuation. It makes us feel euphoric. The whole wanting to be around each other all the time, long telephone conversations, gift giving, sex, and romance is where we are. You and Marissa experienced the same thing when you first began dating. You both failed to continue working on the relationship and allowed it to falter. Who is to say the same wouldn't occur with us at some point?"

"You're different. Remember, Marissa stepped out on me first and with a co-worker at our job. The brother came to me and said he didn't even know Marissa was married and let me listen to a message she left for him. Then she lied even though I had proof. Felice, I loved my wife and tried to be the bigger person because of the children."

"So now you want to hurt her by being with me, because she did it to you? I understand you're hurt. I've been there, but you need to get to the core of why she felt the need to go outside of your marriage. Something went awry with your relationship. Seek therapy. Do something, because no matter what it is I feel for you, I'm never going to be your wife. I'm telling you this up front." Felice had to be blunt. Things were becoming too serious between them. At least it felt that way.

Jermaine sat quietly as if to fully digest Felice's words. It struck him like a steel bat hitting an eighty mile-per-hour baseball and he was flying fast toward left field. Felice had always been direct with him and their situation. Felice and Jermaine were in a standstill relationship. Nothing further would ensue.

Felice took a seat beside Jermaine. He sat with his body hunched over and his elbows resting on his knees while his clasped hands supported his chin. The torture creasing his face tore at Felice's heart. However, her words needed to be said.

"Jermaine, the last thing I want to do is hurt you. We have history together, and perhaps, under different circumstances, things, would've been different. But they're not. You have to stop putting me on a pedestal because I'm not the person you believe me to be. There are things you don't know about my present life."

"Those things are not important. What I do know about you, I love."

"I'm not going to dispute whether you love me or not. Your love for me is not the issue. All I'm saying is don't worship me, because I'm no saint. Do you understand?" Jermaine pulled back to look at Felice. Her expression revealed more than the words exiting her mouth.

"You make it sound so serious, and nothing can be all that bad. I've known you since high school and unless you've killed someone or committed some heinous crime, I think you're fine."

Felice offered a nervous chuckle. "You have to stop holding on to the past. Back then, I was seventeen-year-old Felice Monét Pryce. Today, I am Ms. Felice Jackson. In high school I was a girl child. In college I became a young lady and graduated to the woman standing before you today. A lot has happened in between."

"A lot like what?" Jermaine asked, looking Felice in the eyes.

"You know what? Let's change the subject. You came to pick me up from the airport to relax and for a little loving, am I right?" Felice said as she moved onto the couch and kneeled beside Jermaine to give him a shoulder massage. Jermaine repositioned himself to accommodate Felice, making her job a little easier.

"You'll get no argument from me. I'll take all the loving from you I can get. Changing the subject, okay, let me ask you. Why did we ever break up?"

Felice briefly stopped her massage, waiting for Jermaine to face her. The look on her face was incredulous.

"Are you serious?" Felice asked, resuming the massage.

"Yeah, why wouldn't I be? We get along fine, and I can't recall us behaving much differently in school."

"Jermaine, I can name three reasons. We were in high school. Aside from that, we ended up attending different colleges and when we were a couple you badgered me to death for sex. If it weren't for me trying to get over Kadar, we wouldn't have lasted nearly as long as we did. You ran every game in the book trying to get me to sleep with you. It was pathetic."

"Damn, Felice, that was cold. And I don't remember begging you for sex."

"You may not remember, but you did."

"Well, I don't have to beg anymore," Jermaine said, grabbing Felice's hands from behind his neck and pulling her into his lap.

"This much is true."

Felice and Jermaine's lips locked while their tongues sensuously tangoed. The room temperature began to swelter, and Felice began feeling sticky. Pushing off Jermaine she brought the kiss to an end with another soft peck.

"It's beginning to feel a little warm," Felice said while she swiftly tugged at her shirt, using it as a fan. "I'm going to go draw a bath for myself because the plane ride has me feeling a little less than clean right now."

"Sounds good. Can I join you?"

"I expect you to, or you can watch me," Felice said naughtily.

"Tempting, but as much as I enjoy watching you, participating is always more fun. Everything with you is always fun, Felice. You're such a free spirit."

Felice rose and held Jermaine by the hands. "Come on—let's go find some creative ways to get clean."

"I have some ideas," Jermaine said.

"I'm sure you do, Mr. McNasty."

"And you'd have it no other way," Jermaine said as he patted Felice's butt.

9

In Black and White

Sylvah was beat. There wasn't a box left to empty, with the exception of the ones that she never unpacked at the old house. She would have to look through those to see if the items were even worth keeping. The fact that she didn't even remember what was in them was clue enough she probably needed to throw them out.

It was only one day since her return from Jamaica and instead of feeling relaxed, she was stressed. Both Sylvah and Felice tried reaching out to Candace with no success. Candace wasn't accepting calls at home or at work. Her secretary said she had been in meetings all day. Both Sylvah and Felice knew that was a crop of lies. No matter how busy Candace had been in the past she always took their calls. Sylvah just wanted to make sure that her friend was okay, but she would simply have to wait until Candace came around on her own.

The thing that bothered Sylvah most about the situation was that Shane hadn't wanted Candace to go in the first place, but Sylvah and Felice made such a big fuss he just stopped fighting. It wasn't as if he could have stopped Candace from going, but she wanted to receive his blessing before she left. Candace was very superstitious about things like that. She once told Sylvah that she and Shane never went to bed upset, they never left their house with bad feelings, and they made sure to say they loved each other at least twice a day. To Sylvah, that was a real marriage, and she could respect that. Now Sylvah was feeling like shit for asking Candace along. Sylvah just thought the trip wouldn't have been the same without her, and sadly, she was right. Sylvah felt that she was partly to blame. She didn't encourage Candace to sleep with Clay, but if only she had left well enough alone. If Candace had never gone, none of this would have ever happened. Of all the people to get their groove back, she hadn't expected it to be Candace.

Sylvah had been working on a case that was due in court the next day. She decided to occupy her time reviewing her briefs. The case was actually hilarious to Sylvah. A woman was suing her husband, and she was the one who was caught in an adulterous relationship. Sylvah found the situation to be a comical oxymoron; the scandalous cheating wife sues the faithful husband. The soon-to-be-ex-wife wanted $3.5 million in damages, alimony, and the house.

Felice who was once Dr. Scott's financial planner and who had made him a ton of money, which his grimy wife was trying to get her hands on, referred him to Sylvah. Dr. Scott came to Sylvah in tears and told her the sordid details about his wife cheating on him.

Being a doctor was a very demanding job. Dr. Scott worked twelve- and sixteen-hour shifts as a surgeon at NYU Medical Center. He had been married to his wife for seven years. They had met at an upscale restaurant where she worked as a hostess. Dr. Scott rarely got out but his sister and brother-in-law were celebrating their wedding anniversary, and since Dr. Scott was early, instead of being seated, he chose to kill the time talking to Glenda, who caught his eye when he entered the restaurant. He described Glenda as dazzling and the most beautiful woman he had ever set eyes on. Sylvah saw Dr. Scott as an average-looking man who didn't make you say *wow* on sight. *Not like the guy from her accident, Hunter Bolton,* Sylvah thought, a smile tugging her lips. Nonetheless, Dr. Scott was still a good catch. Glenda told Dr. Scott she had dreams of becoming a Broadway actress and he believed her. They began dating, fell in love, and within months were married.

It had been a slow evening at the hospital. No medical emergencies in the city of New York, which was a rarity. It was still reasonably early so instead of going to his usual coffee spot with peers Dr. Scott stopped at the florist shop, purchased a dozen red roses and hopped on the Long Island Rail Road home.

This was the first time he made it home on a weekday before night-fall in months. He saw a car parked in his driveway, but didn't think twice about it before entering his home. He opened the door and said, "Surprise, honey, I'm home early!" Only he was the one who was surprised. His wife was being mounted by Mandingo. Dr. Scott said he stood there for a good minute before walking back out the same door he came in. Glenda was having sex with a black man. He sobbed like a baby in Sylvah's office and she tried her best to console him without laughing. Sylvah didn't know if he was crying because she cheated or because it was with a black man.

Glenda's claim was that had Dr. Scott spent more time with her, she wouldn't have had to cheat on him. She was suing him on grounds of negligence and failing to perform husbandly duties.

The day she became Mrs. Scott was the day she quit her job. She never had to cook, clean, sew or stitch anything for Dr. Scott. She took acting class after acting class and never completed any before the term ended. All classes were paid for, compliments of Dr. Scott. She took endless trips with friends and family, compliments of Dr. Scott. She received an allowance of five thousand dollars a month, compliments of Dr. Scott. Glenda had plastic surgery on her nose, lips, and breasts, again compliments of Dr. Scott. She had drawn his blood when he found her cheating; now she was trying to put him on life support and eventually pull the plug. It was Sylvah's job to make sure none of this happened. If it weren't for Felice, Sylvah would have turned down this case. She hadn't worked on a divorce settlement in years, but this was an interesting case and there was money to be made.

♀♂

Sylvah didn't know when she fell asleep or what time it was, but the phone alarmed her. She was too disoriented to determine whether it was her cell phone or her land line, which was installed earlier that afternoon. The phone was already on its third ring, so she took a chance on the home phone since it was closest.

"Hello," Sylvah said.

"Hey, Sylvah, are you still mad at me?" the voice asked.

Sylvah wished she had selected the cell phone instead. That way she could have avoided her caller.

"Hey, Alana," Sylvah replied despondently.

"I sense that you are still a little upset," Alana said, sounding tense.

Sylvah was too tired to remain upset with Alana. She was ready to let bygones be just that. She should have been use to Alana's behavior. This wasn't the first nor would it be the last time she would turn a parade into a funeral procession. Twenty years later and they were still tuning into the same station. This was actually mild in comparison to some of the other things that she pulled in the past.

The first despicable thing Alana had done was hit on Kadar, Felice's boyfriend in high school. Felice was offended to say the least, but still allowed Alana to remain in her circle.

The second was a minor offense. Nonetheless, in high school Felice's age was a secret. No one wanted to be younger than their classmates. Sylvah and Kadar were privy to the fact that Felice was skipped a grade in elementary school. This was unbeknownst to anyone else, until Alana found out and told the entire school. Then there was the time Alana didn't want Sylvah dating her older brother, so she did everything in her power to break them up. Or the two times she left Candace stranded. The first time was right after the prom. Alana and Candace's dates had split the cost of the limo, but Alana wanted to leave early and go to a hotel with her date. She took the limo and left Candace and her date in the middle of Long Island at 2:00 A.M. Candace had to call her parents to come pick them up, and the following day Alana acted as if nothing ever happened.

The other incident occurred when Alana became pregnant by a young man who denied responsibility. Alana didn't want to tell her parents and needed someone to accompany her to the abortion clinic. Sylvah was already away at college, and Alana was too afraid to tell Felice. That left Candace, who accompanied her to a clinic in New Jersey. Candace stayed the entire time and when the procedure was over, the guy who had impregnated Alana unexpectedly came to pick her in a two-seater car. Alana was so excited to see him that she hopped in the car, never asking Candace how she intended to get home. The only thing Candace knew was that she was somewhere in South Jersey and nowhere near Amtrak or the PATH trains. She had to use her last thirty dollars to catch a cab to the train station and from there had to beg her way onboard the train.

There were many other episodes, but those were the few that stuck out. None of them were immune to Alana's malevolent ways. Felice had made a good point while they were in Jamaica when she asked, "Why do we even speak to you?" This sounded strange coming from Felice's mouth, because she was always the forgiving one of the group, but Sylvah guessed she was just fed up. Felice also said aloud the question that crossed all of their minds at least one time or another.

"Do I have a reason to be upset with you?" Sylvah asked as she busied herself with the papers from the case.

"Well, I realize I said some mean things, and I wanted you to know that I'm sorry," Alana said, sounding almost pitiful.

It finally appeared that Alana was coming around, Sylvah thought. "Yes, you did say some rather harsh things."

"I know. Will you accept my sincerest apology?"

"Actually, I'm not the one that you should be apologizing to, because…"

"I already planned on calling Felice too," Alana said, cutting Sylvah off in mid-sentence.

"I didn't mean Felice. I meant that you should be apologizing to Candace. You were wrong for saying the things you said to her and the comments that you made afterward to us regarding her situation."

"Candace?" Alana said in mock surprise. "You want me to apologize to Candace? For what? She's the one who cheated on her husband. She should be begging Shane for forgiveness. You know how many women would die for a good man like him? Oh, there is no way in hell…"

Sylvah heard her cell phone ringing and tuned Alana out as she went to find it. When she located it beneath a pile of clothes on her bed she didn't even bother to check the Caller I.D. Instead she pressed the call button to answer delighted for the distraction. She was growing tired of

Alana and their conversation, which was headed toward a cul de sac of nothingness.

Sylvah pulled the home phone receiver away from her head as Alana continued her banter and replaced it with the cell phone.

"Hello, just one moment. I'll be right with you." Sylvah didn't wait for the caller's response, but returned her attention to the home phone.

"Alana, I have another call. I have to go. Goodbye" Sylvah didn't await Alana's response either and cancelled the call.

"Hi, I'm sorry," Sylvah said into her cellular phone. "I was on another call." She still didn't know who the party was on the other end.

"I hope I didn't catch you at a bad time," the caller said.

Sylvah tried to find a comfortable position on the bed while tring to recognize the voice, but remained clueless.

"Ugh, no I wasn't busy. By the way, who is this?"

"It's Hunter," he said as if they were old friends.

Sylvah still waited for further explanation.

"Hunter Bolton. . .the guy from the car accident the other day."

"Oh, Hunter, how are you?" Sylvah smiled as she remembered the circumstances that brought them together that day.

"I'm doing well. I called your office a few days ago and was told that you were on vacation. Then I called your cell and left a message, but I didn't hear back from you."

"Oh, I went away with my girlfriends for my birthday."

"That was nice. Where did you all go?"

"We went to Jamaica."

"That sounds like fun. I've never been, but maybe one day in the near future…" Hunter said.

Sylvah finally settled for a cozy spot in the center of her bed and she nuzzled the phone to her ear. She didn't actually think that Hunter was going to call her.

"The island is beautiful," Sylvah commented. "So to what do I owe the pleasure of this call?"

Hunter hesitated as if he had to give serious thought to his answer. "I was wondering if you gave my invitation for dinner and the theater any further thought."

"Really! Why would you want to go out with me? I mean what do we have in common?" Sylvah asked, interested in hearing his explanation.

"Well, let's see...you're a woman and I'm a man. What more do we need to have in common?" Hunter retorted.

"You're forgetting one thing."

"What's that?"

"I'm black and you're white," Sylvah said as if this was a new discovery.

"Okay. At present it's dark, by morning it will be light. You're beautiful and I'm handsome. You're an attorney and I'm a businessman. My point is, what relevance does any of this have if we like each other or enjoy each other's company? Sylvah, it's just a date. If it doesn't work out, no hard feelings. Is that all right?"

Sylvah listened intently as Hunter babbled. He did have one good point. It was just a date. How harmful could it be?

10

Hunting For the Devil

Upon Felice's return from Jamaica the dreams once again commenced. She'd wake up in an agitated state and when she finally managed to return to sleep, the dream would simply pick up where she had left off. Felice knew that if she visited her therapist she would only tell her that Felice needed to face her past. Felice was well aware of this and didn't see the sense in spending two hundred dollars an hour for someone who probably had more issues than she did.

New segments had been added to her dream. After Felice refused to take the baby from the woman in the white lab coat, Felice moved from beside the Dumpster and began to flee. She ran faster than that little show-off boy in her sixth-grade class, Derrick Row. However, she was still in an alleyway. Far away a hint of light glowed, but in the distance there was a figure, which appeared to be a man. He beckoned her to continue in his direction.

Felice was trapped and didn't know if she should continue down the same path or run into one of the side doors of the abandoned buildings. She was afraid of the man ahead and didn't want to meet another dead end. She was anxious to get home to her grand-aunt Leslie. Felice couldn't seem to find a safe haven. Suddenly, among the dark bricks, an opening presented itself. It looked like a hideaway and Felice heard voices that sounded familiar, so she entered. Felice held tightly to her packages as she tiptoed toward the voices. Each passageway felt like a maze as Felice continued to amble closer to the voices. She was growing weary trying to locate what she now identified as her grand-aunt and one other person. Felice wanted to call out her grand-aunt's name, but didn't want to gain any unnecessary attention. She knew her aunt Leslie would be upset enough when she saw her soiled clothing. How could she possibly explain that without getting into trouble?

The wooden floorboards creaked as Felice came to a set of stairs. The voices had to be upstairs because she had checked almost every room on the lower level. She looked around the perimeter of the room before climbing the stairs. The place looked oddly familiar, but was lackluster. The walls were empty, the paint was peeling, the fixtures were rusted, water stains covered the ceiling, and the house was barren. Still, Felice knew this place. The banister was the only thing polished and was shinier than a brand new show room model car. Felice ascended the stairs and firmly held the railing as the steps grew narrow and steep. Upon her arrival at the top, she glanced down at the floor under her. It was then that she realized that the quarters below were Aunt Leslie's house minus the furnishings, warmth, and spray of scents that defined their home.

Felice's feet were glued to the outside of Aunt Leslie's room. The voices rose as she pressed her ear against the door to eavesdrop. The discussion on the other side was intense and the door eased open from Felice's weight. Their backs were turned to the door as Felice stepped into the room, which was filled with all the memorabilia and furnishings that were absent from the rest of the house.

"When you gon' tell your chile the truth?" Aunt Leslie grunted, swaying in her rocking chair.

"She's still a child, Auntie. Besides, what I do don't concern her none."

"Samantha, when will you learn that light sheds in every dark corner?"

"Auntie, you tend to over exaggerate."

"You'll live to regret it if she finds out on her own. Don't say I told you so."

The crackle of the fireplace startled Felice and caused her to gasp.

Both her aunt and mother twisted in her direction. Neither adult spoke immediately. No one commented on the state of Felice's clothes or the fact that she had been gone for quite sometime. Caterpillar minutes crawled before Aunt Leslie eyed Felice in the same manner she had earlier before Felice took off to the store and said in a faint, weak voice, "I have to go. I'm tired and I can't hold on no more."

The emotions that coursed through Felice's body made her limp. Her small frame began to heave as tears rushed, dampening her cheeks. Something deep inside told her that she would never see her aunt again. "Don't go," Felice whispered. She attempted to reach for Aunt Leslie, but the woman drifted farther away beyond her grasp. Felice's taupe complexion darkened from fatigue and lament. When Aunt Leslie pulled back and turned to walk in the opposite direction she knew she'd never see her again. The lone tear that channeled down her mother's face confirmed that notion.

When Felice awoke she knew exactly what she had to do to rid her of these horrid trances. Her first chore would be to hunt for the devil.

Not Your Average White Man

Sylvah didn't know why she was so nervous. It was just a date. Hunter didn't ask for her hand in marriage. He didn't have two heads, a tail, hooves, floppy ears, or anything out of the ordinary, and he didn't appear to be psychotic or neurotic.

A full week had passed and Sylvah busied herself with her work. She was dealing with Dr. Scott, who offered Glenda one million dollars and half of her monthly allowance in alimony. He wasn't willing to give up his home because it was to be passed down from generation to generation not to be lost in some trivial divorce settlement. Dr. Scott was adamant about his family's property. If anything was to be lost it couldn't be the Scott house. Sylvah agreed and was just as determined as she put through due diligence to ensure that Glenda only received the alimony.

Sylvah didn't agree with Dr. Scott's generosity of one million dollars. In the state of New York, Glenda was not entitled to half of anything. They weren't married for a full ten years and she hadn't borne him any children during their shaky seven. From everything Sylvah gathered, the marriage was a travesty to begin with. Glenda never really loved him or intended to keep house with Dr. Scott any longer than necessary. She was merely using him. Throughout the entire marriage she used one form of contraception or another and called her husband impotent, which he later discovered was not true. Dr. Scott's mother had a strong distaste for Glenda before they were married and once the nuptials were sealed, Glenda made him choose between the two. Dr. Scott hadn't spoken to his mother in more than three years and his work made it easier for him to disconnect from the rest of the family. Glenda allowed countless members of her family to reside with them months at a time. The last straw was when she insisted that Dr. Scott convert from Catholicism to The Church of Scientology, where they believe that God exists, but do not have a specific belief about the nature of deity and reject the concept of eternal life in hell and heaven. This made him lean closer to Glenda, because his family thought they were crazy for converting to Scientology and she was the only thing he had left in the world besides his career.

Listening to Dr. Scott made Sylvah recall her marriage to Bläise. None of the things Dr. Scott had endured even crept into their matrimony. So where did they go wrong? They had two beautiful children, prosperous careers, a home, and love. Sylvah never stopped loving Bläise, but she was no longer in love with him. She still liked him as a person. Didn't that count for something? Sylvah was more than sure that Bläise shared similar feelings. Still the question lingered.

♀♂

Sylvah came home after a long afternoon at work. Hunter was due to pick her up at seven-thirty. There were less than forty-five minutes to prepare. The train ride home was event filled and exhausting as usual. She rushed to her closet to select something elegant and simple for their date. They had spoken on the phone every day. Hunter even called to check the type of diet to which Sylvah adhered. She couldn't help but laugh into the phone. Sylvah was thrilled at the lengths he was taking to make their date perfect. Yet she hoped that he wasn't a perfectionist.

The closet was filled with outfits that still donned tags. Sylvah was in the habit of acquiring items with hopes that she would have somewhere special to wear them, but she rarely went out. Sylvah was truly a homebody. The only clothes receiving any action in her closet were her two-piece suits and dresses, which she occasionally wore to church. She sifted through several garments she didn't even remember purchasing. Her hand grazed something which felt like satin. Sylvah pulled it out and she was faced with a beautiful blood-red, knee-length, sleeveless dress that had sequins on the bodice and a modest oval that would reveal her back. She held it up for inspection and checked the size to make sure it would still fit. The dress met her approval and Alana had purchased a shawl for her birthday that would compliment the dress perfectly. It was a nice evening and she didn't want to wear a jacket over the dress.

This date would be a reprieve to her afternoon, where she had to play therapist to Dr. Scott, Felice, and half of the office staff. Glenda's attorney rejected the offer that Sylvah had presented on behalf of Dr. Scott, which meant that the case would drag out unnecessarily.

Felice was having strange dreams that had her talking in riddles and tongues. The only thing that Sylvah could decipher was that Felice had to stop running from her past and deal with her demons. Sylvah didn't feel comfortable telling her friend what to do, especially under the circumstances. Felice's past was more than sketchy and when she ran off to Cuba, she left a lot of loose ends dangling and returned with others tied.

The intercom buzzed and the doorman informed Sylvah she had a guest. Hunter had arrived on time and Sylvah had to apply her makeup during the ride down on the elevator, and she only lived on the sixth floor. Nonetheless, by the time she stepped into the lobby Sylvah was picture perfect. Hunter practically drooled as he held the door open for Sylvah to enter the car. Hunter was even better looking than she remembered. His dark hair had been freshly cut, his hazel-green eyes matched his cardigan sweater and black pants hung on his six-foot frame just right.

Sylvah was greeted with the soulful sounds of R. Kelly. That was different. It was R. Kelly's second album, but with all of the negative news surrounding the artist Sylvah was surprised. It was probably the only black artist Hunter owned, and he was simply using it to impress Sylvah. She was tempted to press another selection to see what other CDs he had in his changer.

Before driving off, Hunter gave her a peck on the cheek and presented Sylvah with a sizable box of Godiva chocolates, her favorite.

"Sylvah, you look absolutely gorgeous this evening and that scent you're wearing is delicious," Hunter said, briefly sniffing the air as they sat at a red light.

Flattered, Sylvah smiled and blushed under his gaze.

"You're even more beautiful when you smile," he added.

"Thank you," Sylvah said. "Do you mind if I change this CD?"

"Of course not. You don't like R. Kelly?"

"He's good. I'm just not in an R. Kelly mood right now. What else do you have in your CD changer?" Sylvah asked curiously.

"I have Maxwell, Joe, Tracy Chapman, Celine Dion, and Eric Benét.

"That's a nice selection. I wouldn't mind listening to Maxwell. How long have you been a fan?"

"I've been listening to him for a few years now. A friend of mine is in the music industry. She's worked at Sony, Arista, Atlantic, and Island records in the urban markets division, so she gives me a lot of complimentary CDs."

"So did you always like rhythm and blues or did you grow an affinity for it?" Sylvah asked.

"A little bit of both. I was familiar with all of the older players like Aretha, Natalie, Diana, and the late great Barry White, and I used to love Rick James when I was in junior high, but then she turned me on to the younger generation and now I can't get enough of the stuff."

"Very interesting," Sylvah said as they crossed the Brooklyn Bridge. "You say younger generation as if you're old."

"I'm not that old, but I'm sure that I don't exactly fit the demographics that the record executives count as part of their listening audience. They usually target the black market, sixteen to twenty-four years old, salaries between twenty and thirty-five thousand dollars, etc. etc.

None of that criteria fits me."

"Interesting way of looking at it," Sylvah said thoughtfully. "I guess the only thing that matches my description is the black part." They both laughed and continued their banter for the remainder of the ride to the restaurant. Before long Hunter was pulling the car into a parking lot.

♀♂

They entered Zanzibar's, located in the heart of the city. It was a few blocks north of the acclaimed Forty-second Street and a few blocks south of Fifty-ninth Street, Columbus Circle. There was a short line of people waiting to get inside, but Hunter took Sylvah by the hand and guided them to the front. A fairly large man met them at the door. Hunter gave his name, and he ushered them inside, leaving them with the hostess. Sylvah was impressed. The hostess saw Hunter and gave a broad smile. They made small talk at which time he introduced Sylvah to the hostess, Marilyn. She was polite, but it was obvious that she didn't approve of Hunter's choice for the evening.

The front of the restaurant offered a long bar where people talked, laughed heartily after a hard day of work, drank, and smoked. Conversations burst forth in every direction. An eclectic mix of chairs and oddly shaped tables filled the opposite side of the domain. Expressive and vibrant sounds charged the expansive and colorful room. A long, red carpet along with a plush deep-red velvet curtain separated the lounge from the dining area. Hunter and Sylvah were lead to the section for dining.

Once seated a waiter appeared, handed them menus and took their drink orders. Sylvah inhaled the rich ambiance of the restaurant. Scents mingled beneath her nose, reminding her that she hadn't eaten in seven hours. Her dress matched the décor to a tee as she briefly swept her hand across the red velvet chair. The triangular silver table separating Sylvah and Hunter was uniquely polished in some areas and dull in others. Large silver frames with abstract art clutched every wall. After much appraisal Sylvah finally turned her attention to the menu.

"Have you decided what you'd like?" Hunter asked.

Sylvah was trying to narrow her choice down to braised lamb with curry and ginger or the Mahi Mahi in mango sauce.

"What are you having?" she asked, her eyes still pasted to the menu.

"The stuffed lobster is one of my favorites."

"Sounds good," Sylvah said, making up her mind. "I think I'll have the Mahi Mahi. It sounds pretty tasty." Sylvah put the menu down and placed her attention on Hunter, who was gazing at her in a childlike manner.

"Is there something on my face?" Sylvah asked, feeling a little shy under his gaze.

"No. I just can't get over how beautiful you are," Hunter said.

"Thank you. I appreciate the compliment, but you can stop staring at me like that. It's a little jarring."

"I don't mean to offend you," he said, reaching across the table to take her hand. Sylvah noticed the smoothness of his palms, and it felt like Hunter had never done a day of hard labor in his life. She allowed him to caress and stroke her hand as he continued to speak. "I know that this sounds like something from a textbook, but from the first moment I saw you I was taken. I was at that stoplight staring at you, and I guess those other guys weren't paying much attention to the road either, because they rear-ended me."

"Then I'm truly flattered," Sylvah said, offering her close-up smile.

"No, I should be flattered. You're the one who agreed to accompany me on a date. So since I have you captive, tell me a little about yourself."

Sylvah didn't see much to tell. The one thing that she learned from Felice was that you didn't fill the evening with your history or your problems, especially not on a first date. She didn't have much of a life except that which she had built with Bläise and her children. Life after marriage didn't really offer too much other than work. Sylvah didn't have Kenya and Zaire to look after anymore as they were both away at college.

"I work at a law firm, handling anything from real estate to divorce.

I have two children, and I'm presently going through a divorce."

Hunter continued to massage Sylvah's hand as she spoke. The waiter arrived with their drinks, breaking up their union. He took their appetizer and dinner orders and was off again.

"Is that the world of Sylvah Lawrence? Tell me more about your children," Hunter urged.

"My son, Zaire, is twenty going on midlife crisis and my daughter, Kenya, is eighteen going on becoming my mother." Gentle laughter was shared between the two. "Zaire is having a hard time coping with the divorce. He's more than a few hundred miles away in college, and it's hard for me to see him react this way. My daughter, on the other hand, is a trooper. She's expressed her displeasure regarding the breakup, but is a lot more understanding."

"I see," Hunter said thoughtfully, but he seemed bored.

Sylvah looked into Hunter's eyes and again he was looking at her with the same gaze from earlier. She couldn't tell if it was lust, admiration, or longing. She moved her eyes from him to the small oil lamp that burned on the table.

"I'm doing it again, aren't I?" Hunter asked. "It's not intentional."

"So tell me a little bit about yourself," Sylvah said, steering the conversation into his driveway.

"I'm a businessman, single, no children, and once upon a time I was engaged. Unfortunately, the young lady broke my heart and left me for another. Both of my parents are still alive, well, and together out of comfort and not love," Hunter stated matter of factly.

"Okay, tell me the type of business you're in. Is it legal?"

Hunter chuckled at Sylvah's cheeky inquiry.

Sylvah felt a splash of embarrassment tinge her face as she interrogated Hunter. She noticed that he constantly defined himself as a businessman, but never stated or described his work. As an attorney, Sylvah hadn't gotten this far in her career from being sloppy and didn't plan on adding any blemishes to her résumé. She was trained to pay attention to detail and that one iota of missing information didn't depart her mind for a moment.

"I can see you are a woman who speaks her mind." Hunter paused and cleared his throat. "I use to be in the construction business."

"Are you Italian?"

"No. My last name is Bolton, not Bolio, Barone or Bonaducci. I'm white Anglo-Saxon. You don't need to worry, I'm not tied to the Mafia or anything, though if I were Italian I'd probably get a better tan." Hunter examined his pale hands. "I sold that business and bought a chain of auto mechanic shops, got bored with that and now I develop computer programs for large businesses. I'm sort of a jack of all trades. I get bored with one thing and move on to the next."

"Is that what you do with your women as well?" The expression on Hunter's face told her that he felt like a blind man walking with shades on at night. He didn't see that coming.

"No. I only do that with my business. I do believe in long-term relationships. Remember I told you that I was engaged and she left me. Not the other way around."

"True. I'll ease up on you a bit," Sylvah said. "What happened to you and your betrothed?"

"Long story, but I'll make it quick. I was thirty-one and ready to sow my oats, and she was twenty-three and not quite ready to be plowed. Now let me ask you a question. Why would anyone want to divorce someone as beautiful and strong as you?"

"We married young and twenty years later realized we fell out of love," Sylvah answered, thinking back to her earlier thoughts of her and Bläise.

"I don't understand how people let that happen. I mean I saw it happen with my parents, but I don't understand why."

The food arrived before Sylvah could respond. She had her own set of theories. The waiter set the plates before them and without asking he also brought refills on their drinks. Sylvah and Hunter almost completed their meals without uttering a word. The meal was scrumptious as they shared their cuisine with each other. The evening went on with much lighter conversation, and Sylvah found Hunter to be quite comical. The waiter had long cleared their table and refilled their drinks twice. They stayed at the restaurant well over two hours and neither wanted the evening to end. When the music switched from alternative to salsa, Hunter stood and pulled Sylvah to the small area to dance with him. Their bodies collided as they tangled and intertwined their movements to suit the rhythm that hissed from the speakers. Hunter twirled and dipped Sylvah so many times she felt like a tortilla chip. His swift and choreographed dance style fascinated her and for a moment, she felt like she wouldn't be able to keep up with him. By the time they left from the dance floor, Sylvah's dress clung to her like a wet bathing suit and Hunter's face was moist.

"Where did you learn to dance?" Sylvah asked curiously as they took their seats.

"Everywhere and nowhere, really. I never took any instructional dance classes if that's what you mean. I learned from going to clubs when I was younger and then I did a small stint in Puerto Rico. I went out dancing almost every night and learned to master it."

"You can really move."

"Surprised that a white man can dance?"

"No, just surprised that a white man has rhythm. There is a difference. You can show someone dance steps and they can get it, but if they lack rhythm then it looks pretty painful."

"I never thought about that, but I guess it's true," Hunter said, nodding. "So what do you want to do next?"

Sylvah looked at her watch and saw that it was a few minutes to eleven. The next day was Saturday and she didn't have to be at work, but she did have several errands to run. Nevertheless, she was having a good time and enjoying Hunter's company more than she ever imagined.

"I think it's time for me to go home and get some sleep," Sylvah announced.

Hunter looked disappointed. "I thought we were hitting it off?"

"Trust me, I am having a great time, but I have things to do in the morning, and I'm sure you do too."

"Okay," Hunter said, not wanting to challenge Sylvah or push her away. "But, you have to promise me that we can do this again some-time."

"Definitely," Sylvah replied with a smile. "I'm wiped out." She swiped her brow for emphasis.

"Don't tell me you can't hang," Hunter said. Sylvah gave him a stare that asked, "where did you learn that from?" and laughed.

The ride home felt too quick. Hunter parked the car outside of her building and they chatted for another thirty minutes. Sylvah learned Hunter was thirty-six and born and raised in various sections of Brooklyn, which explained his cultural awareness. He loved fishing, basketball, tennis, took care of his parents who had retired to Miami, Florida, and took one month off a year to vacation. Sylvah didn't have much to share with him, but promised she'd find something interesting to tell him on their next date.

When Sylvah was about to open the door to leave the car, Hunter bolted out to open it for her.

"I hope that you continue to spoil me like this, because I can get used to it," Sylvah joked.

"You'll never have to worry as long as you're with me. I will continue to open doors for you."

"Thank you," Sylvah said, accepting his extended hand as he assisted her out of the car.

"Let me walk you to your door."

"That's not necessary," Sylvah stated.

"Yes it is," Hunter said, arming the alarm on his car.

"Okay, but only to the elevator," Sylvah conceded.

Hunter agreed and continued to hold her hand as they entered her building. They passed the doorman, who greeted both Sylvah and Hunter as they sauntered by. Hunter pressed the elevator button for Sylvah and they waited silently for its arrival.

When one of the three elevators finally arrived, and before Sylvah could enter, Hunter turned her for an embrace and without warning his lips grazed hers. The warmth of his lips gently pried Sylvah's mouth open, and Hunter's tongue smoothly traveled the interior of her mouth while her tongue followed. The earth remained silent as Sylvah felt her body stir against his. His arms were swathed around her waist and pulled her close for an intimate embrace. Sylvah could feel his body hardening as she wrapped her arms around his neck. Their breathing was choked. When the kiss ended they both had to steady themselves to remain balanced.

Sylvah was glad she had told Hunter to walk her to the elevator only. She wasn't quite ready for what he was offering.

"I'll call you," Hunter said before the elevators doors closed.

"I'll be waiting," Sylvah whispered behind closed doors, still tipsy from the kiss. She knew one thing for sure: Hunter Grey Bolton was definitely not your average white man.

12

Saturday Night

Giddy would have been an understatement for they way Hunter was making Sylvah feel. It was only ten o'clock Saturday morning and Hunter had already called her. He claimed he couldn't wait to hear the sound of her voice again and invited Sylvah out for a breakfast morning rendezvous, which she declined. As enticing as it sounded, Sylvah didn't want to become attached too early in the relationship. For years Sylvah had watched Felice and the one thing she learned was that it was okay to play hard to get. The less available a woman made herself, the more the man seemed to desire her company. Sylvah was up for that.

"So are we on for next week?" Hunter asked.

"Yes, Hunter. I wouldn't flake on you unless it was something beyond my control. It's not my style to set plans for an engagement and then cancel. I don't believe in being inconsiderate." Sylvah replied.

"Well, you don't seem like the inconsiderate type, so I won't press the issue. So tell me what night works for you?"

"I'm free on Friday night. We can hang out a little longer this time."

"My goodness woman, are you trying to kill me?"

"What do you mean? We don't have to go dancing again. If it's too strenuous for you, we can take it easy."

"No, no. Dancing isn't the problem. My issue is, having to wait an entire week to see you again."

The expression of concern that was on Sylvah's face was immediately replaced with a wide grin and bouts of laughter, which Hunter joined in on. It relieved Sylvah to know it was nothing serious, but most importantly he also had a good sense of humor.

"You are something else." Sylvah said toying with the telephone cord. She was still hanging out in the bed even though there were tons of chores and errands to complete.

"Seriously, I don't want to wait an entire week to see your beautiful face again, or to taste those lips either."

"Mmh, sounds tempting, but you are going to have to wait. And I'm standing my ground on this one."

"Are you absolutely, positively sure we can't go out later on this evening?"

"Hunter, stop making this so hard for me. I have tons of things to do today and I haven't started anything on my list yet. Instead of visiting the gym this morning, I'm still laying in bed talking to you, so already I'm behind. I have to pick up clothes from the dry cleaners. Finish reviewing the research my paralegal gave me for pending cases, and I still need to go food shopping. I have a long day ahead of me and fun isn't in the game plan."

"Well, I'm willing to change that if you'd let me. All work and no play can make Sylvah a pretty dull gal."

Wow, Sylvah thought. She had been wondering when the white in Hunter would come out, and his last statement showed it.

"Hunter, I'm far from dull, so I don't think you need to worry about that. If I were, you wouldn't want to see this sister again, right?"

"Good point. Okay, I won't push my luck, because…"

Beep.

"Hunter, hold on a moment. My other line is ringing," Sylvah interjected. "Hello," Sylvah answered.

"Good morning, scrumptious," Jason replied.

Sylvah's heart raced. She hadn't heard from Jason in a few days. They had spoken earlier in the week, but he had business to take care of out of town and she had been busy with closings most of the week. Therefore, they had been playing a wicked game of phone tag.

"Well, hello stranger," Sylvah giggled.

"How are you doing on this beautiful Saturday morning?"

"Better, now because you called."

"Is that right? Jason asked rhetorically. "Well you just got a rise out of me, and it's not just because I just woke up either."

"You are so nasty."

"Only with you," Jason teased.

"I wish, but with your sexy butt, I doubt it."

"Trust me, I have no reason to lie to you."

"If you say so! Oh my goodness, I have another call on hold. Do you want to wait or should I call you back?"

"I'll wait all day for you," Jason replied.

Sylvah clicked over. She felt horrible for making Hunter wait while she chatted freely with Jason. It was plain rude, but it wasn't intentional.

"Hunter, I'm so sorry. I didn't mean to place you on hold so long."

"You're forgiven, but you owe me."

"What do I owe you?"

"Drinks after work on Tuesday?"

"Hunter, it's very tempting, but I don't hang out during the week unless it's work-related. I really need my rest. My hours at the office are exhausting and the only thing I want by days end is to be home, but we'll talk."

"No problem. I enjoy our little a tête-à-tête."

"Nice. Well bye," Sylvah said not waiting for a final response from Hunter. She quickly clicked over to return to Jason.

"Jay, are you there?"

"I told you I wasn't going anywhere. You don't believe me when I tell you things do you? Tell me what a brother has to do to gain your trust?"

"Earn it. We'll see what develops over time."

"Sylvah, I have time. But you should know I want to be with you. I like being with you."

"Jason, we've only been together twice and the first time was purely sexual."

"You know what?"

"What?" Sylvah asked curiously.

"I think you're still hung up on our first time together. I know it was a bit unusual for you to take such a step with someone you didn't even know, but I'm still here. I'm not going anywhere unless you instruct me otherwise."

"Jason, you're right. It's just that even though I enjoyed our little tryst, it made me feel a little whorish."

"Question, and don't take offense."

"Okay, I won't."

"Do I treat you like a ho?"

Jason's last question threw Sylvah for a loop, but it gave her something to think about. They had been on one date since their little frolic and there was no sex involved. As soon as she returned from Jamaica, Jason found his way to Sylvah's office. He presented her with a lovely bouquet of flowers and six crystal wine flutes as a house-warming gift. Sylvah was flabbergasted, because she didn't expect him or the gifts. They had a nice cozy dinner at an Indian restaurant in the East Village and then caught a foreign flick. When they arrived at Sylvah's apartment building he didn't ask to come up, which Sylvah half expected and secretly wanted. Instead, Jason kissed Sylvah slowly, parting her lips and gently easing his tongue inside her mouth. He intertwined and occasionally sucked the tip of her tongue until she became lightheaded. Then he left. When Sylvah returned to her apartment she jumped into the shower and allowed the massager to bring her to ecstasy. Jason's behavior was extremely respectful.

"No, you haven't treated me with anything except respect. You've been quite the gentleman."

"You say it like you expected differently. Is it because of my age?"

Sylvah didn't respond. Didn't want to reply, because she knew the answer was yes.

"Sylvah, I'm going to say this once. I'm a man who has accomplished a lot in his twenty-seven years. I own my business, home and I still follow my dreams of becoming an acclaimed artist. I make time to do the things I deem important. I know what I want in life, because I'm a man on a mission."

"Really," Sylvah replied.

"Really, and part of that mission is having you in my life. I like you. I want the opportunity to know you better on every level. I already know you are a great lover."

Sylvah blushed. She was happy Jason wasn't there to witness the change of color on her face. That was a compliment she hadn't heard in years. Considering lovemaking with Bläise became so tedious and stiff. It was amazing either one of them could spare a grunt or a moan during their last years together.

"I guess the question is—do you feel the same way and would you like the opportunity to know me better?"

Jason was definitely young. Not many men were willing to wear their heart on their sleeve. They were having an open and honest exchange, which was rather refreshing. It wasn't as if she and Hunter didn't have open dialogue, but this was different. Or somehow Sylvah wanted it to be different. She was trying to be candid and unbiased with each man, giving them both a fair chance. She was fond of Hunter and Jason, but the fact that she and Jason were intimate made her favor him more, so the judge wasn't quite as impartial.

Sylvah liked Jason. Liked him so much it confused her. He made Sylvah feel like she was twenty-five all over again and this felt frightening, because she was the mother of an eighteen year old daughter and a twenty year-old son. When Jason touched Sylvah, goose bumps covered her flesh. When they kissed she became dizzy, he made the crotch of her panties sopping wet and his voice made her heart skip a beat.

"Yes, I'd like to learn more about you. Spend time with you."

"That's what a brother wanted to hear. You just made my day. Listen I gotta' run, but I want to take you out tonight, say, around seven o'clock for dinner?"

Sylvah was in a Jason trance. He could have said, *I want to come over there and fuck you right now,* and Sylvah would have girlishly replied, *okay.*

"Seven is fine," Sylvah said, neglecting her chores.

"Dinner, and I have an invitation to an art gallery opening in SoHo."

"Should I wear something nice?"

"Is it possible for you to wear something and look anything but nice?" Jason complimented and chuckled. "I'm wearing slacks and hard-bottomed shoes if that gives you any ideas."

"It's helpful," Sylvah answered.

"Good. I can't wait."

"Neither can I," Sylvah teased.

"I can always change my plans and come over now."

The mere thought of Jason coming over and making her cum made Sylvah's secret spot salivate.

"Sounds good, but go handle your business, Mr. Green. Let's not change our plans."

"I'll make it worth your while," Jason said adding bass to his already deep, but velvety smooth voice.

"And later, I'll definitely make it worth yours," Sylvah replied.

13

Freak

The restaurant hummed with churchgoers, Saturday night party hoppers, late risers, and those too lazy to cook on Sunday morning. This was the crowd that filled the space of Akwaaba Café.

Felice, Sylvah, and Candace shared a table for four over steaming plates of macaroni and cheese, baked apples, collard greens, turkey bacon, fried chicken, muffins, scrambled eggs, a mixed leaf salad, and fried fish. In the background a live band played old familiar tunes.

The four women normally convened monthly for Sunday brunch, though this was the first time they'd gotten together since their return from Jamaica, which was more than a month before. Everyone's calendar suddenly became too filled to attend their regularly scheduled outing. Sylvah had been occupied with settling into her new apartment; work; Zaire; Jason; and Hunter. Candace figured if she continued avoiding her friends, she could stamp out the Jamaica incident. Felice was busy fighting her own personal demons. Alana was being the spoiled brat she was.

Felice stuffed a forkful of macaroni and cheese in her mouth. "What happened to Alana?" she asked her mouth full.

"I don't know," Sylvah answered. She stared blankly out of the picture window while she poked at her food.

"Didn't anyone call to remind her?" Felice looked at both Candace and Sylvah.

"You know that I'm not going to call her," Candace replied.

"I left her a message. Besides, since when did we need an invitation to come here? We do this every month rain or shine. Well, except last month that is," Sylvah said.

"She called me a few times after we got back, but I wasn't in the mood. You know how Alana can get when she's on a tangent."

Sylvah thought back to the first conversation she had with Alana after their trip. As far as Alana was concerned she could do no wrong. Sylvah spoke to her a few times after avoiding long conversations. Alana was dangerous and unstable. Sylvah had never realized how jealous Alana was before this incident. She was truly upset that Clay slept with Candace and not her. Alana suddenly developed a sense of right and wrong and refused to be around Candace. Sylvah was sure that Candace could care less whether Alana chose to be in her company. More than likely Candace was fed up with Alana anyway.

"So anything new going on, ladies?" Felice asked.

"I went out on a date," Sylvah announced, twirling a piece of bacon.

"Really? Good for you, Sylvah." Candace sat up enthusiastically.

"With who?" Felice asked.

"Hunter Bolton." Sylvah smiled bashfully.

"Who?" Felice asked.

"You know, the man I told you about from the car accident."

"You mean the white guy?" Felice asked. She paused and focused on Sylvah.

"That's the one."

"Sylvah, I'm glad to hear that you're dating. So, tell us about Mr. Hunter Bolton. He sounds interesting," Candace said.

"He owns his own computer company, developing software for businesses. He enjoys dancing, which he does well, and he's eligible."

"Single, owns his own business, hmm. Does he have any children? Any excess baggage?" Felice asked.

"No children and no excess baggage to speak of, so far. He was once engaged and claims his fiancée broke it off."

"Why would she do that?" Candace asked.

"I don't know for sure. He says she found another and dumped him."

"He probably has some kind of nasty habit or he took too long to walk down the aisle. You know, he did the honorable thing by proposing and giving her the ring. Then three years pass, and still no date is set for the wedding. Then there's always the NP syndrome and he cheated on her."

"I'm afraid to ask, but what is NP?" Candace asked.

"New pussy," Felice said, laughing.

"That would be your explanation, wouldn't it?" Sylvah replied. "Not every man cheats. I don't, for one minute, believe that Bläise ever cheated on me."

Candace remained silent.

"That may be true. Bläise is truly one of a kind. I still don't understand why y'all broke up. All I have to say is, if you two can't make it, then there's no hope for anybody else," Felice said.

"Please, you can't base the world on our marriage. We were far from picture perfect and of all people you should know, Felice. Are you kidding me? We were like Frick and Frack. Bläise and I argued every other second. He was like a dictator." Sylvah retorted.

"You knew that when you guys first got together," Felice said.

"Then I grew tired of it. What we liked about each other in the beginning suddenly became our Achilles' heel."

"Well, this happens. It's just that you two seemed so right for each other, like a perfect fit."

"I know, but nothing lasts forever. The most important thing is that we made the best of the years we had, and the result is two beautiful children, who we wouldn't trade for the world. Zaire is now a man with a good head on his shoulders, and Kenya has blossomed into a beautiful young woman. They're both healthy and smart. Neither of them has made us grandparents yet. What more could we ask for?"

"Very true, Sylvah" Candace said thoughtfully. "By the way, how are they doing?"

"Good. Zaire is rebelling against the divorce and Kenya seems to be handling things all right. Otherwise, by any parent's standards they are doing quite fine."

"So do you intend to continue seeing your new white knight?" Felice inquired.

Sylvah thought about her entanglement with Jason. She wasn't sure how to juggle two men. She and Jason had gone out again last night to City Island and had a great time over dinner. Afterwards they went to S.O.B's in lower Manhattan to see a wonderful new R&B artist, Jully Black. They had decided to forego sex because they wanted to get to know each other. However, Sylvah didn't know how long she would be able hold out; they were starting to see each other regularly. This was all so very new to her. Even so, it was exciting. Her divorce wasn't even final yet and she had two men to pick from. There were women who never had the opportunity to marry, much less have two men at their beck and call. All the same, it was too soon to say where either of these relationships was headed. The choices were somewhat difficult, although Sylvah had no intention of forfeiting the race. As far as she was concerned, may the best man win!

"Hunter did ask me out again. We've been having such a good time. Prior to Hunter, the last time I went on a date, I was eighteen years old. The next thing I knew, I was pregnant, dropping out of college and getting married. Everything happened so quickly with Bläise and me."

"That's true. The one thing I can suggest is that you have fun with it. Let the man wine and dine you and enjoy yourself in the process," Felice said.

"I agree," Candace offered.

"I definitely plan to."

"So did you do it?" Felice asked.

Candace looked at both Felice and Sylvah. The question didn't startle her. She just wanted to see Sylvah's reaction.

"Only you would ask me about sex on a first date." Sylvah glared and Felice returned an even sterner gaze. A look that read "you can't fool" me. It appeared as if Candace had picked up on the glances, but Sylvah was almost certain she was clueless.

"My goodness, Felice! You're speaking about a one-time occurrence. You will never let me live that down, will you? Neither my first, nor is my middle name, Felice."

"People who live in glass houses shouldn't throw stones," Felice quipped.

Candace looked baffled and curious at the same time. Sylvah wanted to clue Candace in, but wasn't use to sharing such intimate details regarding her sex life.

"No, I did not sleep with Hunter," Sylvah finally responded. "But we did share a really nice kiss. I didn't even know what hit me. When I got to my apartment I rushed to my medicine cabinet for my spare oxygen mask," Sylvah joked.

"It was that good, huh?" Felice asked with a toothy grin.

"Yeah, but I have to watch myself. I don't want things to move too quickly between us. I want to savor this."

"I don't blame you," Candace interjected.

"Savor my butt. You better check out the produce now to see if you're wasting your time. Nobody wants to purchase a small cucumber or tiny plums."

"Is dick all you think about?"

"Is there anything else in this world worth giving thought to?" Felice asked, laughing.

"Freak!" Sylvah lashed out.

"And you say that like it's a bad thing."

Candace laughed at both of them. "Y'all are hilarious."

Felice's cell phone rang. Reaching in her purse she retrieved it and looked at the LCD display. The phone continued to ring after she identified the number and placed it back in her bag. Jermaine was trying to keep tabs on Felice, calling two, sometimes three times a day. He began questioning Felice's whereabouts, leaving long, obtrusive, messages, and was starting to show up at her home unannounced. Fortunately, the doorman never let anyone up to her condominium without her consent. Their fling would soon come to an end. This possessive trait Jermaine had begun exhibiting didn't sit well with Felice. Quickly she returned to the conversation.

"I guess you didn't want to speak to whoever that was," Candace said.

"Not really, it was Jermaine," Felice answered.

"Mmm," Sylvah grunted.

"Jermaine who?" Candace asked.

"Jermaine Gray, the guy I dated senior year in high school."

"The one we saw at the mixer? Y'all still kicking it?"

"Something like that, but he's starting to become too attached."

"Girl, Jermaine is handsome and a good catch. What's wrong with him being a little attached?"

"He's married," Felice said, exasperated.

"Oh," Candace replied, a bit surprised. Sylvah laughed at the exchange.

"Besides, I'm not interested in becoming involved in a serious relationship. Anyway, moving right along, we are certainly glad you've decided to rejoin us in the land of the living. You were starting to worry us," Felice said.

"No need to be concerned. I'm simply staying focused on my husband, kids and career. I know you both believe I've been avoiding you lately, but I'm not. Shane and I have spent a lot of time reconnecting. The kids are becoming a handful, and I recently got a promotion at the job, so I've really been busy."

"Congratulations," Felice said, reaching to hug Candace.

"Congratulations, girl!" Sylvah squealed. A few heads in the restaurant turned in their direction. She, too, embraced Candace. "I can't believe you're just now telling us this. When did it happen?" Sylvah asked.

"Three weeks ago. They were talking about promoting someone prior to our trip. I didn't think I was even a candidate. Then, when I got back, the seniors had a luncheon and announced that I was the account director for new accounts."

"Really? Spike Lee actually releases the reign and gives promotions over there at DDB Needham?" Felice asked. "You know how he likes to write, act, direct and produce all at the same time. "That's where P. Diddy gets it from."

Candace laughed. "Yes, he does. He treats his account teams and staff very well. We're really growing pretty nicely. Now I have a team of people who report to me. At first it felt funny, but it feels right, like I was born to lead."

"You probably had leadership abilities in you forever. They were just sitting dormant," Felice said, winking. "All of my friends are take-charge kind of women. Why do you think you were my friend all these years?"

"Because every assembly needs a conservative," Candace laughed.

"Then what would you consider me?" Felice asked.

"You're the Liberal. Sylvah is the Democrat and Alana is an independent party."

"I like your analogy," Sylvah commented. They all laughed heartily.

Felice, Candace, and Sylvah continued to enjoy each other's company. Each one of them got up to refill their plates and ordered drinks to celebrate Candace's new promotion. Felice shared her Brick experience with them, after which they had a good laugh.

"I'd like to honor the spirit of true friendship!" Sylvah held her glass in the air. "Twenty-some odd years of happiness together, boyfriends, shopping, celebrations, marriages, careers, children, sickness, health, tears, and plenty of other adventures and more to come." They clinked glasses. They didn't seem to care that Alana was missing such an auspicious occasion and no one poured a glass to say, "This is for my homey who couldn't be here today," either.

Mr. Fix It

Felice was still bursting with energy after leaving Akwaaba's. Everyone had left in good spirits since Alana wasn't present to bring down the momentum. Felice found Alana to be very disappointing lately. No matter how much Sylvah or Felice tried to enlighten Alana, it never seemed to make an impact. It was actually tiring. Shortly after their trip, Alana tried to convince Felice how wrong Sylvah was for attacking her over the phone. Felice listened to the entire story, and in the end agreed with Sylvah. It was common sense. Alana had no right to judge anyone, especially not Candace. Unfortunately, the only person who had to deal with what transpired during their vacation was Candace. Besides, Felice knew for a fact that Alana slept with a few married men in the past. Therefore, how in the world could she criticize someone? Felice didn't understand why it even bothered Alana so. Why would she be so jealous when they were all supposed to be friends? Maybe it was simply time to move on and keep Alana at a distance. Unfortunately, some people would never change, and it appeared Alana was one of those people.

Instead of immediately returning home, Felice decided to leisurely walk through the area. It wasn't long ago when she lived nearby. When she was married to Bedford, they had purchased a home on Decatur Street, between Stuyvesant and Lewis. At the time there were a few abandoned houses on the block, but now there were none. Bedford lost the house to Sandy in their divorce settlement and she sold it for triple the amount in a matter of months. People were buying real estate like it was free government cheese being handed out and the prices had sky-rocketed from $200,000 to $600,000 and, in some cases, even $800,000-$1,000,000. The area had charm and concealed beauty and was being recognized by many, though the price increase was still unbelievable.

There was a good friend, Calvin Hamilton, who lived a few blocks away from where Felice stood. It was early afternoon and he was probably still at home. Calvin was a certified Mr. Fix-It. Anything Felice needed repaired, Calvin was her man. When Felice had originally purchased the condominium it needed loads of renovations, since she bought it as-is. Although the building handled certain maintenance issues, plumbing and installing new fixtures were not their responsibility. Calvin came highly recommended to Felice by her dentist. She preferred getting referrals than using strangers who would possibly overcharge and still not do a competent job.

Felice's apartment had still been a bit of a wreck as the interior designers were still in the middle of painting. The kitchen cabinets were being installed and the bathroom remained unsightly. Felice had wanted a complete overhaul of her bathroom. When she mentioned to her dentist she needed emergency work done, he quickly provided her with Calvin's information. It was unimaginable to know that the family before her actually lived in such conditions. The state of the apartment was one step up from the projects. Prior to moving in, Felice made sure to have the place fumigated. She wasn't taking any chances and there were definitely signs of lead poison. The main attraction of the apartment was the location, size, and price. Eighteen hundred square feet in Prospect Heights for two hundred grand was a steal, even if she did have to invest thirty thousand to make it both livable and appealing.

Calvin walked into Felice's world on a Thursday evening. Felice arrived in her lobby at approximately 6:45 and the appointment with Calvin was scheduled for seven. However, before entering the elevator, the doorman informed Felice a gentleman awaited her. Felice scanned the immense marbled entrance hall and spotted a man in a suit relaxing on one of the available sofas. She had to ask the doorman where the man was and he pointed to the person sitting on the couch. He couldn't possibly be the plumber, Felice thought. She was expecting someone in dingy overalls, a Carthart jacket, and construction boots. The man seated on the other end of the atrium appeared dapper. Maybe there was another appointment she had overlooked. Felice walked over to meet the stranger.

"Hi, I'm Felice Jackson, and you are?" She extended her hand.

"Hi, I'm Calvin Hamilton." Calvin's six-foot-four frame towered over Felice as he greeted and shook her hand.

Both were in awe of each other as they allowed a moment to pass. Felice wore business attire, which usually consisted of a skirt suit barely covering her lean and sexy thighs. The blouse always managed to accentuate her ample breasts, and the jacket was rarely ever buttoned. Calvin wore a navy double-breasted suit with pinstripes, a flattering tie, polished wingtips, and a diamond stud in his ear. His skin was blemish-free, making his roasted coffee-bean complexion glow. His nose was large and flattering; he had sweet tantalizing lips and the whites of his eyes danced. Felice didn't know when plumbers began dressing and looking this way, but she wanted one in-house right away.

"Please excuse me," Felice said. "I didn't expect you to be in a business suit."

"No problem. A lot of people don't expect a well-dressed plumber. Nevertheless, I believe in first impressions."

"You've certainly impressed me," Felice said, beaming.

"Thanks."

"We can go to my apartment so you can see the area for yourself. Then we can discuss what it is you can do for me. Shall we," Felice said leading the way.

"Sure," Calvin smiled.

The air was suffocating during the ride in the elevator. Calvin was too beautiful for words. Felice felt a thin layer of perspiration beneath her underarms. The first thing Felice noticed was his left ring finger, which was absent of a shadow and a ring. When they appeared in front of her door, Felice nervously entered the key into the lock. It didn't work the first, second, or third time. Finally, Calvin tried for her and it failed. She later realized in her haste they were using her office keys to open the apartment door. Felice had a hard time hiding her embarrassment. Calvin merely brushed it off as an honest mistake.

Inside the apartment, Felice directed Calvin to the living room and excused herself. She ran to the bathroom for quick relief and then hurried to change into more comfortable clothes. Felice returned wearing a cute pink terry-cloth short outfit made for the beach and flip-flops. A quick pit stop was made in the kitchen to grab some drinks before she returned to the living room. Calvin had removed his jacket and loosened his tie. He was looking over his portfolio when Felice came back.

"Here you go," Felice said, handing him a glass of water.

"Thank you," Calvin said, taking the tumbler.

"So what are these?" Felice asked. She sat close enough to feel Calvin's body heat.

"Oh, these are some of the bathrooms I've done in the past."

Felice watched as he flipped through the assortment of photographs. Twenty or more bathrooms and kitchens were available for show.

"These are really nice." Felice gasped. "You defy all stereotypes of what a plumber is supposed to be. You're more like a carpenter or designer." Felice laughed and Calvin joined in.

"How is that?"

"First off, you have a portfolio. I've never heard of a plumber carrying around a portfolio."

"I'm a plumber who also specializes in providing the finishing touches of all plumbing needs."

"I'll leave that one alone." Felice said, chuckling. "Anyway, you don't dress like a plumber. I mean, I was expecting overalls and boots and you arrive in a suit, and walk around with a portfolio instead of a plunger and a ratchet or whatever it is that plumbers use." Felice paused because Calvin looked as if he were oblivious to everything she said. "Don't try to be slick, because you know exactly what I'm talking about."

"Yes, I know, but like I said, first impressions. Besides, I take my business seriously. I work for myself, and I learned a long time ago that people can be a bit wayward when dealing with plumbers or people in the blue-collar field. Now, if I come to you like this, then immediately I gain your respect. Am I correct?"

"I never gave it much thought, but I guess you're right. Okay, let's go look at my bathroom and kitchen, and I'll share my ideas and you can tell me what you recommend."

"Sounds like a plan."

A few hours later and Felice lay sprawled out on her bed with Calvin, who definitely knew how to plunge. He inserted his tool in Felice more times than she could remember. Calvin owned a tongue with such precision it made Felice dizzy. The relationship continued for two great months, which was the entire time it took for her new bathroom and kitchen to be installed. When he was through she began making excuses to stop seeing him. Somehow Felice was bothered by his occupation and a few other things she couldn't pinpoint. Shortly thereafter, Felice met Aaron with the bright basketball career and flushed the plumber down the drain. Calvin was a good prospect and didn't have any liabilities, had nice assets, was debt free, owned his home and drove a decent car. Felice's dentist vouched for him on every level. Still it wasn't enough.

♀♂

This was the first time Felice would see him in more than three years. He would probably be upset about her stopping by unannounced. There was also the possibility of him being married. Some lucky lady probably had snapped Calvin up. Felice hesitated as she let every scenario run through her head. She decided that if a woman answered, she would simply introduce herself as an old friend.

The ringing doorbell roused dogs that began barking. The sound was startling. Moments later, a face peered from behind the curtained windows. A stern voice commanded the dogs to stop barking.

"Give me a minute," the familiar voice beckoned. Felice began wondering why she decided to pay Calvin a visit after all this time. He had probably dislodged Felice from his mind long ago.

The locks on the door began opening one after the other. Lastly he removed the deadbolt. *New Yorkers go through so much trouble to safeguard their homes*, Felice thought while waiting. She reminisced

on how opposite it was in Cuba. The chances of a home getting bur-
glarized there had to be one out of twenty-five thousand. In New York,
it was probably one out of every twenty-five homes.

Calvin stood in his doorway, shirtless, a thin line of hair traced the
center of his broad muscular chest. He was unshaved, hair unkempt,
and sported blue dungarees. Calvin appeared sexier than Felice remembered, and she had to practice self-control. Age definitely proved
to be working in his favor.

"Felice! What a surprise," Calvin said, reaching for a hug.

This was better than she expected. After three years of no contact,
Felice was sure he'd be less hospitable, but Calvin was too nice to
behave any other way.

"How are you doing?"

"I'm good and you?" Calvin asked, scanning Felice.

"I couldn't be better."

"Come in, come in. The place is in a bit of a mess, so you have to
excuse me. Let me go put the dogs out in the backyard."

"Okay." Felice followed Calvin inside. Quickly she examined the
room. During their brief fling, Felice had only visited Calvin twice. Most
of their adventures took place in her apartment or in public places.

The room was sparsely decorated. There were bookshelves, an area
rug, love seat, sofa, a center table, two dead plants in a corner, and a
lamp. Several African masks garnished the drab ecru-colored wall, which
looked freshly painted. The mixture of dog, cigarettes, and deodorizer
permeated the air. Perhaps these were the reasons Felice never bothered to visit Calvin.

Calvin returned wearing a clean white undershirt.

"You didn't have to put on a shirt on my behalf."

"It's okay. Before you came, I was exercising."

Oh, well, you look good," Felice said. *Good enough to eat,* she
thought.

"Thanks. So what brings you by this neck of the woods?"

"Actually, I went to Akwaaba's for brunch with my girlfriends."

"Oh, they have great food. I go there every once in a while, but it's
no fun sitting at a table alone."

Great! He was still single. Calvin answered Felice's question without even being asked.

"Calvin, stop it. I'm sure you can find company if you want. Don't play coy with me."

"No, I'm not playing anything. Do you know how hard it is to find a good woman?"

"There are plenty of us out there, Calvin," Felice defended. "It's much easier to find a good woman than it is to find a good man."

"If you say so, but these women today are gold diggers coming to the table empty-handed, loaded with baggage, unable to make clear decisions and making demands before the ride even pulls off."

"Not all women. Anyway, are you going beyond skin deep?"

"Felice, I'm not shallow. If we have a few things in common, get along, have a sense of humor, communicate, and find each other attractive, there's a good chance at a fruitful relationship. If the woman happens to be as beautiful as you, then I've definitely lucked up!"

"I guess that's fair," Felice said.

"Besides, I'm a good man, so what happened with us? We had something good between us, didn't we?" Calvin asked.

Felice went three years without answering this question. She didn't want to insult him, so her answer had to be politically correct.

"What we had was great, but you know I was going through a divorce. I had baggage of my own and it wasn't fair to pull you in the middle of my mess."

"Oh yeah, I remember now. Did you ever remarry?"

"No, I came—close, at least I thought I was close." Felice's thoughts drifted back to Aaron. "It didn't work out." Felice was beginning to feel antsy. This visit was supposed to be pleasurable and light. Instead it felt dreadful and grave. Felice regretted dropping by. At least he hadn't offered anything to drink, so she wasn't completely settled.

"Where are my manners? What can I get you to drink?" Calvin asked.

Damn, damn, damn!

"Oh, nothing, I'm still trying to digest the food I ate at Akwaaba. I was quite predatory with my meal."

"You always were able to put away the food and maintain an adorable figure."

"Thank you," Felice said, smiling. "I should probably get going. I have a couple of errands to run."

"Anything pressing? I mean I'm enjoying your company," Calvin said, moving from the edge of the sofa to sit beside Felice.

Felice felt the body heat generating between them and began to unwind. "I guess I can hang around a little longer." Felice figured if her friends were going to call her a freak, she might as well live up to the title.

Calvin intertwined fingers with Felice's and leaned in for a little oral titillation. Finally, progress was being made.

Felice removed Calvin's undershirt and planted kisses from the nape of his neck to his navel. She remembered how much he enjoyed having his chest massaged and nipples pinched. Calvin made no effort to hide his interest. Instead, he unbuttoned his pants to accommodate the recent rise. Within minutes both were naked across the couch.

Felice heard the dogs scratching at the back door, so they moved the party into the upstairs bedroom. A few hours remained before the afternoon stretched into the evening. However, the maroon drapes dimmed Calvin's room. In the dark, they groped and enjoyed each other's textures, curves, and body parts. Felice feasted on Calvin's penis, and he firmly grabbed her head, bobbing it back and forth as a show of his pleasure and gratitude.

Calvin stopped Felice and made her stand. His hands began fondling her breasts and he massaged and rubbed her already ripe nipples while dropping to his knees. He trailed kisses down Felice's stomach, widening his lips until he got closer and closer to her pussy. He nuzzled his tongue between the opening until he found her clitoris. Felice's eyes were shut as she played with his thick tousled hair enjoying the pleasure of Calvin's tongue as it ran up and down and occasionally flicked her clitoris.

Shortly after, Calvin palmed Felice by the ass and flipped her into position. A minute later he was banging her from behind, providing Felice with the loving she remembered even after all these years. Calvin still knew how to unclog her drain.

♀♂

The drapes were still pulled shut and when Felice awoke she couldn't decipher the time. Calvin remained asleep, so Felice tried to sneak out of the bed. She managed to get downstairs and put on her clothes, but not before Calvin woke up. He came downstairs offering a big smile. Felice reciprocated, and he embraced her.

"Where you going?" Calvin asked, still groggy from sleep.

"I told you earlier I had a few errands to run, and it's late now."

"You sure you have to go? I can whip us up a nice dinner. Give me an hour."

Felice placed a foot into her shoe. "No, really, I have to get going, but thank you for a lovely afternoon." Suddenly Calvin's house felt claustrophobic. She knew there were no errands and absolutely nothing to rush home to, but she needed freedom from Calvin. Even if it meant going home and hearing another one of those much unwanted messages on the machine. Why didn't this huntsman get the message already? Nearly two months had passed and Felice had refused to return any of the nagging calls.

"No, thank you, and it was my pleasure. I love your company. I only wish you'd come around more often and make me an honest man."

"You are such a kidder. You're twisting the phrase around, aren't you?" Felice laughed.

"See, you never take me seriously. When will I see you again?"

"Calvin, stop it. I do take you seriously. I promise you'll see me around."

"If I don't, I'll call you."

"You can. You have my number," Felice said, knowing the number had changed since they last connected.

"You need a lift?"

"No, I'm good. I'll grab a cab."

"Are you sure?"

"Definitely." Felice headed for the exit. "I'll be in touch."

Calvin walked Felice to the door and grasped her by the hand before she could leave. He pulled her to his chest and kissed her long and sensuously. When the kiss ended, he held Felice's chin in the crook of his hand.

"Felice, I really would like to see you again. It would be nice to give us another chance."

"I'll think about it," Felice answered and left.

♀♂

It was after seven and the sun was hidden behind the sky. The cool air sent chills down Felice's spine as she tried to flag down a taxi. She walked to Fulton Street, which was a better location to hail a cab since very few drove through the residential areas. During the ride home, Felice retrieved the red phone book from her purse and located Calvin's name. He already had two descriptions, which read: MR. FIX-IT and LETHAL TONGUE. Now she had more entries to include beside his name: CLINGY/NEEDY/TOO EMOTIONALLY INVOLVED.

15

The Devil Was Once An Angel

Hours wrinkled into days, days creased into weeks, weeks seamed into months, and months bent into folds. Felice was slowly losing her mind. She knew what had to be done, yet she was still trying her best to avoid the inevitable.

Stacks of mail beckoned to be opened. Felice's cousin, Smith, was kind enough to visit her post office box to retrieve and deliver it to her house twice a week. This was a task that she had asked him to fulfill during her exodus, and he was nice enough to continue even though she was no longer away. Several pieces were junk mail—credit card offers for which she'd never in a thousand years apply—bills, letters, bank statements, fashion catalogs, coupons, free CD and DVD promotions, magazines, monthly book club selections, and four pieces of mail from Jackson & Jackson Financial Consultants, Inc. Three of the packages from her company were financial statements and legal documents that she'd review with the help of Sylvah, if necessary.

One piece stood out that had nothing to do with their finances or legal corporate nuances. The handwriting was peculiarly familiar. This particular envelope was unmistakably addressed by her ex-husband's secretary, Shirley. Though she was curious to find out what trick Bedford had up his sleeve, she conquered the urge to open it and allowed it remain among the abyss of unopened mail. Apparently, after weeks of numerous calls, all of which were unreturned, Bedford had decided to employ another tactic—mail. Felice was not moved. She would ignore the letter the way she did his messages: "Felice, please call me. It's really urgent." Bedford even had the gumption to try and pay her a surprise visit two weeks earlier. It was a smart thing she instructed the doormen not to let visitors in without her strict consent. She also had them red flag Bedford's name. Felice selected the bills to be paid, letters from new friends abroad, and her financial documents—bank statements, including the three Jackson and Jackson quarterly reports.

Felice plunked down on her plush velvet mustard-colored sofa and began sifting through the pieces she'd selected. She reviewed each piece carefully before making several neat piles so that she could file them away once she was done. While studying her bank finances and business reports she learned that Jackson and Jackson was doing pretty well, even during these hard times. However, she also saw new amendments and provisions had been made during her absence and without her consultation. But how could she have been consulted when she didn't allow her business partner to know of her whereabouts? From what she gathered, the changes made weren't earth shattering. Nonetheless, decisions were being made and she wasn't a part of the process. Felice had to pay Jackson and Jackson a visit.

$$♀♂$$

The tall, swaggering building stood majestically before Felice. A large hotel that looked out of place shimmied alongside it. The gargantuan multi-story structure that housed Jackson and Jackson was erected firmly in its post. The outside read, in silver bold Arial-style lettering, ELEVEN PENN PLAZA. This was the place that fulfilled her dreams almost ten years ago. It was Felice and Bedford's vision that landed them in this prestigious building. Felice watched as the revolving doors swallowed people in and spewed them out with a hearty belch. She stood across the street on the steps of Madison Square Garden, avoiding familiar faces steering in and out of the building. Her heart raced with anxiety as she tried to gather her thoughts of what she'd say once she actually entered the building. Did they still have the same doorman?

Were the same people who worked there during her six-year tenure, still there? Felice knew that none of this mattered or applied to the business she needed to take care of. Felice made slow, careful movements down the steps. The sound of her heart amplified in her ears.

Upon entering the building she was asked to show proof of I.D., her destination, and told to sign the visitors-log-in-book. No one there had the faintest idea who she was. None of the guards recognized her though she saw one or two familiar faces. She decided not to call attention to herself. It wasn't of importance anyway.

Felice made her way to the elevator banks. She was headed to the seventh floor. Her mind raced back to the first day they had moved their offices. Jackson and Jackson started out in a small dank space in lower Manhattan. Early on, they weren't even in the numbered streets. The space was claustrophobic. It had three cubicles, which the landlord had mistaken for offices, and a reception area in which the assistants worked. The reception area was affectionately called the children's playpen because of its size. They were embarrassed to have clients visit their 450-square-foot hole-in-the-wall. It was a sweatbox, but was better than working out of their home. They had to get a start somewhere and after two years of toiling twelve hours, five and six days a week, Felice and Bedford were able to move Jackson and Jackson to a better location. They even had to hire additional staff to accommodate all of the accounts which had been acquired.

Felice had a smile on her face when the elevator reached its destination. As she departed the space, two friendly faces greeted her and took her place in the tin box. Thinking back to that time gave Felice renewed energy. As she walked down the hall toward the office she stood tall and added confidence to her stride. She was only two doors away from Jackson and Jackson. She stopped in front of an office with which she was all too familiar: Professional African American Men's Association of New York Corporate Headquarters. This was the place where Ms. Cinnamon S. Wells had worked and was probably still gainfully employed. She was the woman with whom Sandy Jackson, Bedford's second wife, caught Bedford in the most uncompromising position. When would men learn? And why did they continue to be so stupid? That was Bedford's second time getting caught with his pants down. At least when women got involved in something silly they knew the result, even if they chose to ignore it. Men chose to wander anywhere their dick aimed. Earlier in the day, before Bedford had gotten caught by Sandy, he and Felice shared lunch to discuss a decision she had made. Felice held the wall and shook her head thinking about the occurrences of that afternoon. Felice was glad that it was Cinnamon who got caught and not her, because goodness knows it could have been. She and Bedford had shared many moments across his woodgrain lacquered desk fucking like they didn't get enough at home.

Less than five steps and she'd be directly before Jackson and Jackson. Goose bumps appeared on her arms and thighs. One step, two steps, three steps. She had arrived unscathed, however, the sign no longer read Jackson and Jackson Financial Consultants, Inc. It read, LIGHTNING AND QUICK HEADHUNTING AGENCY. What the hell was this? What happened to her company? Where were Jackson and Jackson? Felice's mind had already run the sixty-yard dash and was off to the next race. Instead of panicking she decided to enter this new establishment and ask some questions.

Before Felice could reach the door, it sprang open and a young twenty-something woman, accompanied by a slightly older balding man stepped out. Felice entered before the door could close.

"Hello," Felice walked up to the reception desk.

"Just one moment," the woman said, too busy to be distracted. She punched her fingers angrily into the computer keyboard. The woman was smartly dressed in a conservative two-piece pantsuit. Her fiery red hair resembled coils from a box spring mattress, her eyebrows were plucked to a thin line, and her lips curved like the Joker's. The woman behind the desk wasn't as clean cut as her attire indicated, since she had an earring in her eyebrow and a piercing in her tongue.

The phone rang and she answered, "Lightning and Quick Head Hunting Agency, if we don't find you a job you qualify for in two weeks, we'll give you a day's pay. How may I help you?"

The fiery redhead listened intently to the patron on the line before she responded with what must have been the same instructions she repeated to every caller. "Bring two copies of your résumé, three references, and photo ID. We're located at One Penn Plaza, on the seventh floor, the last office at the far end of the hall." More information was swapped before the call ended. The small scarlet haired woman with tiny-pursed lips spoke quickly, barely taking a moment to breathe.

Felice stood by patiently awaiting her turn. She looked around the office and the walls were still painted a pale tan, but the Berber carpet had changed from green to burgundy. The pictures and cultural masks, which once hung in their front office were replaced with cheap framed oil paintings. Other than that not much had changed about the space Jackson and Jackson once held.

It was apparent that between the hours of noon and 2:00 P.M. Lightning and Quick Headhunting Agency received a lot of business. The waiting area was filled with anxious applicants whose names were randomly called by faceless voices from offices beyond their sight. Upon hearing their names, applicants would spring into action like they had just won the lotto and head in the direction of the voice to claim their prize. The receptionist began to alphabetize the resumes accompanied by applications and got up to put them in mail slots assigned to various recruiters. The redhead attended to Felice when she returned.

"Hi. Do you have an appointment?" she asked.

"No, I'm here because…"

"Oh, I'm so sorry. We don't have room for walk-ins today. We're really busy," she said, cutting Felice off and dashing back to her position behind the desk. "But since you're here, you can complete an application—" she handed Felice a clipboard—, "and leave your résumé."

Felice declined the clipboard and pressed her body against the desk.

"I'm not interested in a job," Felice fired back, frustrated. "I simply want to ask if you knew what happened to Jackson and Jackson Financial Consultants, Inc."

"No, I don't," she snapped back, head twisting and curls recoiling.

"How long has Lightning and Quick been leasing this space?" Felice asked, controlling her temper.

"We've been here for three months."

Felice thought back to the parcel she had failed to open from Shirley.

Maybe it contained information about Jackson and Jackson's new whereabouts. She was mad at herself for not opening the package, all because she thought Bedford had some ulterior motive, which he probably did. Felice needed to focus and locate her company. She took out her cell phone to call the office, but she couldn't get a signal.

"Do you mind if I use your phone?" Felice asked pointing to a freestanding handset in the waiting area. The cell phone reception in the building was awful. It was almost like the walls were made of lead.

"That phone is not for outside calls."

Felice wasn't in the mood to argue. Why else would they have a phone in the front office? Was it simply there for show? Felice's attention darted to the nameplate sitting on the receptionist's desk.

"Thanks for all of your help, Ms. Stinking Perky," Felice said as she headed to the exit.

"It's Stephanie Perkins," the woman shot back.

"Who gives a damn?" Felice said and slammed the door.

Felice returned to the lobby and was about to leave when something tugged at her to turn around. She could ask the guards if they knew the whereabouts of Jackson and Jackson.

♀♂

The twenty-eighth floor was certainly different from the seventh. The walls leading to the office were painted pastel yellow. The wall motifs were nicer and the light fixtures were classier. Felice was caught off guard as she approached Jackson and Jackson. This time around there was no mistaking where she was headed. A large sign greeted her when she vacated the elevator delivering her to their new quarters. Instead of the single wooden entry that read the name of her company on the seventh floor, she now stood in front of two beautiful French doors, which illuminated both light and life as shadows marched behind the enclosure. The glass was frosted, so that one couldn't see who was behind the door, but you could see figures and silhouettes.

Felice took a deep breath as she opened the door. She didn't know what to expect after stepping inside. An immediate air of warmth engulfed her, knowing her business was thriving so well at a time when the economy was in a slump. At the same time, she felt like a stranger in her own house. A mix of emotions surged forward all at once. The familiar feeling of electricity jolted Felice, seeing bodies fly by with purpose, staff members stopping to chat for an idle moment, but nothing was really the same. She didn't recognize anyone who had walked by. Was this really Jackson and Jackson? The name on the door said so, and the large glass partition that resembled an ice sculpture beside her said it was. Nevertheless, the people and the surroundings were different. Had she really been gone that long? Felice missed the work environment, especially the one standing before her she had worked so hard to build. She didn't know how she could have possibly let this go.

A few more moments passed before Felice found her way to the reception desk. The young woman looked more like a model waiting to be discovered greeted Felice.

"Good afternoon. May I help you?"

"Yes, I'm here to see Mr. Bedford Jackson," Felice said, impressed with this young lady's demeanor and attitude. She didn't see any odd body piercings or obvious tattoos. Felice didn't see anything wrong with those things, but felt that it didn't fit every business environment.

"May I ask who is calling?"

Felice didn't want to give herself away. She knew once she said Felice Jackson the woman would probably call everyone from the back to come out and meet the 'missing in action partner' or 'silent partner', whichever description Bedford had conjured up for her.

"Ms. Pryce," Felice answered.

"Please have a seat while I call him."

The young woman directed Felice to a set of matching chairs facing a small round table displaying several different financial and business magazines including *Black Enterprise* and *The Network Journal.*

Felice selected a magazine and browsed the content. She had read an entire two-page article that spilled onto the back pages of classified and junk advertising before glancing at her watch.

Shirley, Bedford's right and sometimes left hand appeared, looking as elegant and regal as Felice remembered. Her hair sprouted more salt than pepper and the crows had paid her a little visit, pinching the corners of her eyes a bit, but she was aging beautifully. For a second Felice thought that she was looking at the jazz singer Nancy Wilson.

"I thought it was you!" Shirley said in her southern drawl. She came over to pull Felice into a tight hug. "Who in the world you trying to fool, talking 'bout Ms. Pryce? You ain't been Ms. Pryce since before I met you," Shirley teased, turning to the receptionist. "Sepia, this here is the other half of Jackson and Jackson. This is Mrs. Felice Jackson," Shirley said, nudging Felice over to meet their receptionist. Sepia stood and extended her hand to shake Felice's. She appeared thrilled to be in Felice's presence.

"Oh my goodness," Sepia gasped. "It's so nice to finally meet you. We've heard so much about you. I thought that you were a myth." A few more people lingering in the vicinity were called over by big mother Shirley, and soon Felice was being assailed by the entire office. The staff seemed to have almost tripled.

Felice's account team was still intact and her head director had been promoted to vice president during her absence. Everyone was smiling, grinning, shaking hands, laughing, and asking questions, and the feelings of uncertainty that crept through Felice earlier had vanished. It felt good to be back.

Shirley gave Felice a grand tour of the office, which had swelled to a space of thirty-two hundred square feet and now included both a conference and breakroom. The suite was a jump from their down-stairs space of nine hundred square feet. Felice even had a corner office on reserve. All of her things were transferred to the new space but something was missing. It lacked the vitality she saw in the offices down the hall. Sitting in her office she marveled at the progress. Felice was tempted to pay each team member a visit to see what she had been missing, but she'd save that for another day. Her mind was made up. Felice was ready to return to work.

♀♂

The stroll down the hall gave Felice peace of mind. She still hadn't seen Bedford since arriving in the office, but she was ready to face the devil, even if all she had was a spoon instead of a pitchfork. There were so many things to be said. She had headed to Cuba a tangled mess and hoped she would never have to look back, but even then Felice knew that was a lie. She couldn't just desert her family and friends, among other things. If she were the demon she wanted to be it would have been easy to cash in her money market, stocks, IRAs, annuities, and other investments, and say to hell with this life. But she wasn't. Felice had a conscience and a soul that served as constant reminder of the things she left behind. She couldn't sleep at night due to the way she left things. At the time leaving felt right, but now she knew it was selfish and wrong. Her dreams had proven this night after sleepless night.

Sylvah and Bedford were the only two people who held her secret and now her mother did too. Sylvah never judged or said a harsh word on the subject and Felice loved her for being so understanding. However, she knew it was more out of love that Sylvah kept her mouth shut from judgment. Love kept her from telling Felice how stupid and immature she was behaving. Love kept her from walking away from their friendship of more than twenty years. It was also love that made Sylvah come to Cuba and urge Felice to return home and stop being a coward. Now it was Felice's turn to love even harder and remove the burden from her friend's shoulder. It had been unfair of Felice to ask her friend to carry the burden of her secrets for so long.

♀♂

A gold placard announced, CEO, MR. BEDFORD JACKSON. Felice's door didn't have the same display. The thought distracted her.

Shirley sat in a sizeable space and her back was turned to Bedford's entrance. Bedford's office was behind Shirley's encasement. It wasn't like their previous space, where there was just an open area and Shirley just sat out front. Here, you couldn't just invite yourself in without having to pass through her space and Felice was sure this was done intentionally to ward off unwanted guests. It appeared Bedford was finally learning and taking precautions. When Shirley finally looked up, she smiled at Felice.

"How you doin', honey? You settlin' in?" Shirley asked.

"I'm doing well. I was just sitting back and taking everything in. I still can't believe how much things have changed in my absence."

"For the better of course." Shirley nodded her approval and Felice agreed. "Even that boss of mine has done a one-hundred-and-eighty-degree spin. I think after his last fiasco he decided to calm down some. He's still a man, but a different one. They say a tiger don't lose its stripes, and a leopard don't change its spots, but I reckon even a snake sheds its old skin."

Felice couldn't imagine Bedford changing his ways. He loved pussy too much. Bedford was a gambler. Granted he was no good at playing craps, but he had to throw the dice anyway.

"Shirley, I want to believe you, but I've known Bedford almost as long as I've been living now and—"

"And even a sinner can seek redemption," Shirley completed.

"Even the devil was once an angel, and he can trick us to believe anything he wants."

"Only if you allow him to fool you, and tricks and games of such are for the circus. Now I know you think that I don't know much about the goings on in this office, but I know more than you ever care to learn. There are stories that would drop you on your ass—excuse my French. I keep my ears open and my mouth shut. I'm not some old cluck who doesn't know a stem from a branch. I intervene when necessary. I treat Bedford as if he was my son, and I try not to meddle, but when he does something sour I offer him my grace and hope that he will heed my message."

Felice wondered if Shirley knew about the sexual encounters she and Bedford had after the disintegration of their marriage. She was curious, but didn't have the nerve to ask Shirley such a lewd question.

"Do you really think he listens or just pretends to in order to make you happy?" Felice questioned. She folded her arms and her eyebrows rose quizzically.

"Make me happy? Mr. Jackson will have to pay for his sins, not me. He never listened before and behaved like a rebellious child. Today, he calls me for advice and this is how I know there's progress."

"I have to see it to believe it," Felice said as she headed toward the closed door behind Shirley.

"He ain't in there," Shirley said, allowing Felice to step past her into Bedford's adjoining office.

"What time will he be back?" Felice asked, looking at her watch. It was close to four o'clock.

"He's not in today. Bedford took the day off."

"Mr. Jackson? Took the day off? Is he on vacation?" Felice asked.

Felice found it strange because Bedford wasn't the type to not show up for work. Bedford loved what he did too much. The only thing he loved besides himself was his business. He had to be forced to take vacation time.

"No, he called in sick," Shirley confirmed.

The sick routine again, Felice thought to herself and smirked. She wondered whom Bedford was doing now that was taking him away from his precious job. Felice was almost convinced with Shirley's little speech about snakes shedding their skin, but they were still slimy, slippery, and venomous. Felice wouldn't want to be locked in a cage with snakes. The risk was trying to determine which were harmful and harmless. By the time you figured it out, more than likely you'd already been bitten and poisoned.

"Don't give me that look," Shirley said, acknowledging Felice's sinister smile. "It's legitimate."

'I'm sure it is. Shirley, you are a good person and you mean well. You probably hate to see the bad in anybody. You're always searching for good, and maybe that makes you see things differently or turn a blind eye to the obvious. I've fallen for the sick routine once and when I went home to cater to him, you know what I was greeted with?"

"Yes, I do," Shirley said sternly. "I know you went home and got your heart broken. You discovered your husband's shit was just as stink as any other human beings. Felice, I'm sorry that you had to experience such pain. Even sorrier it was someone you trusted. I prayed on y'all's entire situation. I didn't know what to do, because I had a feeling things weren't right. My heart didn't take to your assistant the way it normally does with folk. She was always smiling and trying too hard, but that's how a lot of young folk act, and it ain't right to just label people just because you think they too friendly."

"So you knew about Bedford and Davonna?" Felice asked, shocked. She was hoping that Shirley would answer in the negative, but she just said she had a feeling things weren't right. If she felt that way, why didn't she warn Felice?

"I had a feeling, but I wasn't sure, and I can't go interfering in grown folks business, much less wreck a marriage, about something I wasn't even certain about." Shirley paused to grab hold of Felice's hand. "Trust me, if I had proof I would have spoken to him and you. I thought you two made a wonderful couple. Confirmation of the affair even startled me. Bedford never told me, and you never piped a word, but it was obvious when that girl didn't return. You came to work with your panties in a bunch and Bedford was just tight. Thereafter, you filed for divorce and no questions needed to be asked."

Felice felt ill listening to Shirley of all people rehash her memories of yesterday. Five years of pain rummaged through her brain, but they didn't defeat her. Felice had come a long way and was stronger and almost fully healed.

"Okay, so what makes you so convinced that he's really sick?"

"Nothing has me convinced and he's not the one who's sick," Shirley said.

Felice looked at her confused, hands flailing in surrender.

"His daughter, Nina, is sick," Shirley completed.

16

Bedford and Felice Sitting in a Tree

Felice was speechless. Nina. Bedford had named his daughter Nina. That was the name of his favorite artist, Nina Simone. Her middle name was probably Simone as well. Felice wanted to ask. A rush of questions rapidly ran through Felice's mind. Could this have been the reason Bedford had been so persistent in calling her? Nina. What could possibly be wrong with her? She hadn't thought about her since that fateful day in November.

Felice's heart raced, and she felt a little lightheaded. She needed to take a seat. What she really needed was to get out of there. She didn't want to make Shirley aware of her sudden jolt of angst. Shirley couldn't possibly know about this. Or did she? Shirley had just told Felice that she knew more than Felice would ever care to learn. That statement said a lot. She wasn't going to ask, because if Shirley didn't know, Felice wasn't going to let on.

"Shirley, I've got to go. I have another appointment I have to get to," Felice said as she stumbled backwards out of the office.

"Are you okay?" Shirley asked. Felice didn't now if Shirley was being facetious or sincere.

"Yes, I'm fine." Anxiety pangs swiped her like wipers on a windshield. That fateful day at the clinic came swarming back the way a bee returned to its hive, only the memory wasn't very sweet.

The day that Sandy walked in on Bedford and his playmate was the same day Felice and Bedford decided an abortion would be best. She was already three months pregnant creeping into four. She didn't want to have a baby for a married man, even if that married man was her ex-husband. How would that appear? The thought alone was detestable. Insolence, disregard, rearing a bastard child, and malevolence were not part of her upbringing. Her mother would detest such behavior. It simply wasn't to be.

Later that evening Bedford returned home only to find his belongings in the gate of what would become his former residence. Sandy had kicked him out and changed the locks. She refused to hear anything he had to say and threatened to call the police if he continued to harass her. And who could blame her? Sandy wasn't as naïve as Felice originally thought. A few hours later Bedford showed up at Felice's. She could have easily turned him away, but maybe there was a glimmer of hope. Aaron had proved to be a loser and at least she already knew this swindler, Bedford.

Felice had scheduled an appointment for the abortion the following week. Bedford accompanied her. It was mid-morning on a Friday. The day was stunning. When they exited her building, in-line skaters and bikers zoomed by on their way to Prospect Park. People were walking their dogs, pedestrians strolled by not appearing to be in a rush, and shiny, freshly washed cars drove passed. It was too bright a day for gloom and death. Yet, that's exactly what Felice and Bedford were on the way to do. In less than a week, Felice would be four months pregnant. She was considering murder. Her conscience was ripping her apart and it felt like her heart was being pulped by a juicer. The previous night had offered little rest. No sleep at all. Felice lay there staring at the ceiling. Visions of crying babies, babies in Dumpsters, scalded babies, drowned babies, babies being thrown out of windows and abused babies, every sorrowful story she had ever read in the newspaper clogged her mind. She couldn't think exactly why she was doing this now. It just didn't make sense. There were women who would die to be in her position, hundreds of thousands of women who couldn't conceive. At one time she thought she was one of those women. How would she feel afterward? Was this something she could live with? Would she ever be able to forget this day? There were alternatives.

The room was cheerful. Rich shades of blue plastered the walls. Expensive paintings draped them. A magazine display covered a small section of the wall. Selections from *Self* magazine, *Nutrition Today, Women's Health, Fit Pregnancy, Planned Parenthood, Parenting* magazine, *Us, Essence, Shades* and *Oprah* claimed the racks. The reception desk had a beautiful arrangement of lilies, the scent of which permeated the air. A soothing jazz ensemble played in the background. Doctors made brief appearances to collect charts along with their patients. Newcomers entered to fill vacant seats.

The office atmosphere was warm, cheery and inviting. It felt like she was there for a routine check-up or physical. However, this visit was anything but normal.

Patiently Felice and Bedford sat awaiting their turn in the sitting area. Felice didn't want to look at Bedford. The choice had been made, and everything was settled. She wouldn't go back on her word and trap him. They had a business to run. There was no time to raise a child now, anyway, and she didn't want to be added to the fastest-growing category: single mothers. Bedford was on the rebound from another failed marriage. It just wasn't fair to him or her.

Felice was called into the room by her gynecologist, Dr. Grand. He was not doing the actual procedure; however, he had arranged to be the attending physician, which wasn't really necessary. He was simply there for support. Dr. Grand and the attending physician provided Felice and Bedford with helpful information regarding the warnings and outcome. They were advised that because the abortion was being done before the second trimester, it would be a safe and simple procedure and done vaginally. The physician would use local anesthesia and something called a suction curette instrument that would be inserted into Felice's uterine cavity after her cervix was dilated, which would reduce the possibility of perforating her uterus. Felice wasn't really concerned with what was and wasn't being used. She simply wanted the procedure to be over with.

"Felice, you're in excellent shape," Dr. Grand announced. "We don't foresee any complications."

After explaining the entire course of action, Dr. Grand and the attending physician left the room to allow Felice time to change into the hospital gown. Bedford wanted to remain until they returned. Silently, Felice began removing her garments.

Bedford attempted to break the ice. "That sure sounds like a lot of stuff that they're going to be doing."

Under the circumstances, Felice wasn't in a talkative mood. Bedford waited a few more seconds hoping to gain a response. There was none.

"I know what we discussed before, but…"

"But what? Nothing has changed," Felice countered as she unbuttoned her dress.

"Felice, a lot has changed."

"Like what?" Felice was angry. She was scared and upset with herself for being so careless. She was too old to be sloppy and Felice knew there were consequences for every action.

"You're no longer with Aaron. Sandy and I, well, you know where that's headed. Why can't we do this?"

Felice listened. Bedford had a point. It was one that she had already thought about, but didn't voice aloud. Still, the child would be a bastard. She would never remarry Bedford. There would have to be an ice rink with igloos in hell before she plunged down that drain.

"Because…" Felice limited her words to avoid crying.

"Because what? You can't give me one good reason why we are sitting in this place." Bedford stood staunchly in front of Felice. She was staring at the ground. He used his index finger to lift her chin. Her eyes were wet with suspended tears.

"This child was not made out of love," Felice challenged.

"It doesn't matter," Bedford said thoughtfully. "I love you and I believe you still love me. How could you not?" Bedford tried to remove the melancholy that cloaked them. "Do you still love me, Felice?"

Felice inhaled deeply. She knew the answer. He knew the answer. It didn't change the situation. Why was he doing this to her now? She was almost in the clear, but the clear to what? Moments ago she was having regrets. She was questioning herself as to why she was there. It was only hours ago she was being tormented and couldn't sleep. If she actually went through with this, would the rest of her nights be spent the same way? She didn't want to live the rest of her life feeling like a murderer. No one else would know, but she would always have the memory. Something she would have to live with forever. This wouldn't be as easily placed to the back corner of the bottom shelf.

A knock came from the other side of the door. "Are you ready, Ms. Jackson?" a voice asked.

"No, not quite," Bedford answered. "Can you give us a little more time?"

"Sure, I'll be down the hall in my office. You can just give my door a tap when you're ready."

"Thanks."

Bedford's eyes returned to Felice. Her cheeks were shining with tears.

"We can do this, Felice. Forget everything I said before. None of it matters now. Last week is now part of the past. Together we can make this work and build a future. Please reconsider," Bedford pleaded.

Maybe this was all supposed to occur. Everything happened for a reason. There were no coincidences. It wasn't a fluke that Aaron turned out to be a fake and Sandy was divorcing Bedford. It seemed more like fate at work. Perhaps this was her destiny.

"Felice, do you love me?"

Felice was hesitant. "I think I do."

"Let's do this. We have nothing to hold us back. You know me and my habits, and I promise I'll curb my ways. We're both financially secure. I want a family and promise to be the best father in the world. I will never let either of you down. You know my adoration for children, especially my relationship with my nephew, Shiloh, before he was killed. Felice, I never stopped loving you. This baby is a part of us." Bedford paused to rub Felice's belly. "No one knows me like you do, and I know you better than anyone else on the face of this earth. Don't deny yourself this."

Shiloh. Felice remembered Bedford's nephew. She really wished Bedford hadn't gone that route. Felice had been very fond of Shiloh and knew that Bedford, along with his sister, Isis had practically raised him. Felice considered her options. There were two choices—a right one, and a wrong one. Realistically, the decision wasn't that difficult to make.

Bedford pulled Felice into his massive chest. "Please, please do this for us," he whispered.

Felice was choked up. "Okay," she answered.

Bedford withdrew and held Felice's face in his hands the way a parent would a child.

"Okay, as in, yes, you will have our baby?" Bedford asked. His voice lilted with surprise. "I mean, you will be the mother of my child? Our child? You'll give us another chance?"

"Yes, I will have the baby." Felice took a moment to sigh before continuing, "As for the relationship, we'll take it day by day."

Felice and Bedford had taken so long that the doctor returned on his own. He knocked and they responded for him to enter.

Bedford informed the physician about their sudden change of plans.

"Dr. Grand and I figured something like that was going on. We have many patients who have second thoughts once they actually get here. The majority of them go through with it anyway, because abortion is more often than not used as a method of birth control. Then we have a selected few, like you, who decide to give birth."

"We hope that this doesn't put you out or anything. I mean, I hope this isn't an inconvenience for you or Dr. Grand," Felice apologized.

"No, not at all. You've actually given me some free time, Ms. Jackson. You were my only morning patient. What is important to me is that you feel that you've made the right decision." The doctor quickly looked from Bedford to Felice.

"Yes, we're sure," both answered in unison.

"Great. I'll go inform Dr. Grand. I'm sure he'll want to see you before you leave."

Felice's life would change forever.

♀♂

Bedford moved in with Felice for a few weeks, however, Felice encouraged Bedford to get his own place. She wasn't quite ready for the full commitment that Bedford was offering. She had grown accustomed to being alone. Felice was overwhelmingly independent. Life after Bedford had taught her to be self-sufficient. Not to rely on others. Work with what you have and last in the end, the only person with your best interest at heart is you. These barriers made it tough for anyone to enter—even Bedford, and he tried.

Bedford quickly found another town home. His new place of residence was in the heart of Harlem. The structure was recently renovated and cost almost twice what he had paid for the brownstone in Stuyvesant Heights, Brooklyn. The area was beautiful and up and coming. It was even larger than his first home. Bedford told Felice he hoped they would fill it with children. Felice didn't comment. Instead, she helped him decorate, and every room, with the exception of his private office, was reminiscent of Felice and her flair for style. The rooms were boldly tinted with odd colors and incongruous pieces of art and furniture that all corresponded like pieces of a puzzle. After its completion, the house resembled a masterpiece which deserved to be showcased in *Architectural Digest* or *Southern Comfort* magazine.

When Bedford finally moved in, he tried to convince Felice to sell her apartment and cohabitate with him. It made practical sense. That is, if they had had the same objective. Bedford wanted to raise their child as a couple under one roof. Felice wasn't sure what she wanted. Bedford didn't put up much of a fight for fear of adding stress. He figured the pregnancy made Felice confused, and after the delivery she would once again become rational.

Bedford was hopeful about restoring the relationship he and Felice once had. Visions of Bedford and Felice sitting in a tree danced in his head. He was almost certain he could change his ways and did everything possible to prove this to Felice. He waited on her hand and foot. If Felice sneezed, Bedford was there to clean her nose with a Kleenex. As long as Bedford was around, Felice had no wants or cares in the world. He was ready to fulfill them all. Bedford was happy and prepared to become a proud father. Felice tried to piggyback on his joy and experience some of his excitement, but she couldn't. The only thing that brought her pleasure was work, so she tried to fill every waking minute and hour doing things related to the job. Felice also enjoyed decorating Bedford's new home, but she wasn't about to become an interior decorator. She should have been happy. Instead she felt nothing—almost empty. There was no bond between her and the child growing inside her.

Felice didn't want anyone at the office to know about her pregnancy. She wanted to avoid all assumptions and questions—"So when are you due?" "Who is the father?" "Aaron must be so happy!" "When is the wedding set for, again?" Felice could do without the curious stares, questions, and insinuations.

Felice had gained a little weight, but she wasn't showing and was still able to wear her suits. Nothing physically had changed. Felice even planned to alienate family and friends, except Sylvah, until everything was over. She didn't know how she would explain a baby afterward, but she was sure there had to be a way. There were a couple of months to hatch out a plan. She wasn't due until November, so it could be done.

An idea was born. It was a balmy summer day in late June. Saturdays were always best to visit her mother because Felice could avoid bumping into her mother's significant other, Gene. Although the relationship between Felice and her mother was fickle, she still paid Samantha a visit from time to time. Felice had always been curious as to why her mother and father divorced. That day the answer was more obvious, but it was a matter she and Samantha never discussed. Felice wanted both sides of the story.

Felice arrived at her mother's house fairly early in the afternoon. She knew that by one, Samantha would be returning from yoga lessons followed by bike riding through Prospect Park. She'd return to take a shower, freshen up. By two, she would be off to get her manicure, pedicure, and massage. This had been Samantha's routine for as long as Felice could remember. If there was one thing Felice admired about her mother, it was her ability to take care of herself. Samantha was a health and fitness nut. The result was that Felice's sixty year old mother didn't look a day over forty. They were often mistaken for sisters.

Felice always found the comments to be flattering, since she always had idolized her mother's features.

Felice knocked on the downstairs and upstairs doors and rang the bell twice. There was no answer. Felice took a seat on the top step of her mother's stoop. She removed her latest read from her satchel bag and began perusing the pages of *Getting Hers* by Donna Hill. She was already halfway through it and couldn't get enough of the book. Lately, reading had caught her attention. Sylvah kept feeding her books to help occupy her time, and Felice read them during the train rides to and from work. Felice was up to two books per week and she didn't know if there were enough black authors around to keep her busy. She briefly thought about the book she had completed earlier in the week, *Nothing Special, Just Friends* by Toni Staton Harris. What an incredible story, Felice thought.

The double doors on the parlor level opened and Samantha appeared, startling Felice. She closed her book and looked her mother over.

"What are you doing out here?" Samantha questioned. She wore brown sandals with two-inch heels, which showed off dainty feet that were not in need of a pedicure. Her short hair was now in braids and she donned a white linen dress that Felice was more than sure she had seen in Banana Republic. Samantha was always very casual and stylish in her dress.

"I thought I'd come by and pay you a visit," Felice answered.

"Well, you know I have my appointments today, and I'm on my way out."

"Yes, I know. I thought I'd tag along. Is that okay with you?" Felice inquired.

"Sure, but you may not be able to get a massage. They're probably booked."

"Okay. I'll get the manicure and pedicure and read my book while I'm waiting for you to finish."

"That's fine," Samantha said. She was busy bolting the three locks lining the door. She shook it to reassure that it was indeed locked, as if a crook wouldn't find other means of entry if he wanted.

♀♂

By two-fifteen, they were in front of the salon. Samantha's masseuse greeted her at the door and swept her away. There was a cancellation and Felice could have gotten a massage, too, but she declined. Instead she read and waited for the reemergence of Samantha. They sat side by side as they were pampered in plush chairs that vibrated and soaked their feet in the basins attached to the seats. Operators worked on their hands and feet simultaneously. An hour and a half later they were walking the streets of Boerum Hill, searching for a quaint restaurant to dine.

♀♂

"I can't eat another bite," Felice announced an hour later. She had eaten a bowl of soup, a lobster salad, and shrimp fettuccini. She was sipping on a latte and scraping the remains of her crème brûlée.

"I should hope not," Samantha said. "Since when have you started eating like that? You act like you're eating for two," Samantha said dismissively.

Oh Shit, Felice thought. For the first time she realized her appetite had increased. Prior to the pregnancy she picked at her food like a bird, unless it was her favorite dish. Other than that, she abstained from overeating.

"I was just hungry," Felice said a little too quickly, steering clear of her mothers last statement. "I've been so consumed with work lately I haven't had time to watch my diet."

"Well, you better start. You're beginning to gain a little weight. You may want to come bike riding with me next week, jog around the block a few times, or join an aerobics class before it gets out of hand."

"Mother, you've always been so direct."

"And you appreciate it, don't you?" Samantha gave a phony smile. "So what's new? Anything you care to share with me?"

Felice began to panic. Did it show? Maybe she just was waiting for Felice to tell her. They say that mothers always know when their daughters become pregnant. Maybe it was written all over Felice's face.

"What are you talking about?"

"Nothing. It's just we haven't seen each other in a while, and I thought you had some good gossip or news."

Felice was relieved. "Oh no, everything is the same. Actually, Aaron and I broke up and Bedford and his wife Sandy also broke up."

"Oh my! What a shame," Samantha said as she shook her head. "Same thing as before?"

"Yep, same thing," Felice answered.

"Oh well, at least you got out of the trap, safe and secure."

"Yeah," Felice said dismissively. *If only you knew,* Felice thought. She had no intentions of telling her mother about the pregnancy. Samantha would definitely think her daughter was a fool.

"Do you still keep in touch with my father?" Felice asked.

"No. You do realize he's in Cuba, don't you?"

"Yes, but still I figured that you wrote each other every once in a while."

"We stopped all correspondence long ago. After you turned eighteen, we rarely wrote. Then I moved, and never bothered to give him my new address, so who knows?"

"Do you still have his information?" Felice asked.

"It's somewhere in one of my old phone books. Why, you plan to contact him?"

"It would be nice. I mean, I barely remember the man, but all of a sudden I want to know more about him."

"Very understandable. I can tell you things I remember."

Samantha spent the remainder of the hour reminiscing about her past with Felice's father. Felice had seen pictures of him before, but they were old and faded. She vaguely remembered him. She was about seven when her parents divorced. By the end of her mother's narrative Felice's desire to reunite with her father had increased.

"He doesn't sound like a bad person," Felice commented.

"Carlos is a very good and sincere man."

"Then why the breakup? It doesn't make sense."

"There was a lot going on you just wouldn't understand. Plus, there was a huge disparity between our cultures. We tried and tried, but could never see eye to eye. It was simply easier to remain friends."

At the end of the conversation, Felice had convinced Samantha to provide her with Senór Carlos Fernando Pryce's information and shortly thereafter, Felice began making arrangements to visit him. She eventually moved in with Bedford and sublet her condominium for two years. There was no objection from Bedford. He was happy she had finally succumbed to his request. By the end of the sixth month she looked pregnant and took an indefinite leave of absence, giving Bedford full reign of Jackson and Jackson. She told Sylvah of her plans for an exodus. Sylvah pleaded with Felice, but Felice was on a mission and had already applied for a visa. Felice would not be stopped.

The evening of November 9, Felice's water broke. She was admitted to NYU Medical Center in lower Manhattan. Since she had cut off communication with almost everyone, only Bedford, his sister Isis, and Sylvah were by her side. On November 10 she gave birth to a seven-pound, eight-ounce, beautiful and healthy baby girl. The delivery was almost painless. The morning of November 11 Felice disappeared from the hospital, leaving the baby behind. Bedford was due to arrive at any moment and she wanted to make a quick escape. She was to be released the following day anyway since she had a natural childbirth and hadn't received any sutures. Felice went to the house she shared with Bedford and left a four-page letter explaining why she couldn't be a part of their lives and ended the note with an apology. Felice also wrote a letter to her mother explaining her spontaneous departure but omitted the birth of her baby. By evening Felice was at the airport with her luggage and an open ticket to Miami. From there she made arrangements to fly to Cuba. November 12 found Felice in a terminal in Havana, Cuba.

Hear No Evil, See No Evil, Scream Your Evil

Felice hit speed dial on the cell phone and the line rang instantly.

"Sylvah Lawrence, how may I help you?"

"Sylvah, it's me. I need to talk." Felice answered, sounding panicked.

"Felice, you sound frazzled! Is everything okay?"

"Not really. Nina is sick."

"Nina? Nina who?"

"My daughter, Nina."

"Oh, my goodness! Felice where are you now?"

"I'm standing in front of my office on Seventh Avenue."

"Okay, I'm in the middle of something, but I'll try to meet you in the next hour. In the meantime, hang out in the restaurant across the street from your office where we used to meet all the time."

"You mean Nick & Stef's Steakhouse?"

"Yeah, and keep your cell phone on, so if I'm running late I can call you."

"Okay," Felice said, releasing some of her anxiety.

"Everything will be fine," Sylvah said reassuringly.

"I hope so. Sylvah—"

"Yeah?"

"Thanks for always standing by my side. It means the world to me."

"Always unwavering, because that's what real friends are for. See you in a bit," Sylvah replied before hanging up.

♀♂

Felice entered the restaurant and was immediately seated. She was very familiar with the setting and the list of food options, so when the waitress came to take her drink selection and leave the menu, Felice placed her order without opening the leather bound booklet.

The ambiance was as dark as Felice's mood. She sank into the booth and began to ponder the situation. Nina, her daughter was sick. Was it a cold? Did Nina have an ear infection, a fever, chicken pox, measles or the mumps? Was God trying to tell her something?

Felice was on her second glass of Merlot and Sylvah still had not arrived. Felice wasn't much for drinking, but she was nervous and needed to dull the sensation in the pit of her stomach. The last time Felice consumed this much alcohol was during her sophomore year in college. Aleshia, her good friend, was celebrating her twenty-first birthday. Everyone had drinks in their hand except Felice. Trays of apple martinis, Tom Collins and tequila shots were being passed around along with the house special, which was called A Little Sumpt'in Sumpt'in. Felice was having a hard time finding a good old-fashioned soft drink, so she munched on the chips and salsa and drank water.

Aleshia approached Felice and asked what she was drinking.

"Water," Felice answered.

"All this liquor in the house and you're drinking water? It's my twenty-first birthday, girl, get yourself a grown folk's drink."

Felice laughed. "I don't indulge in alcoholic beverages. Do you know how much harm it can do to your body and how badly it impairs your judgment? Besides, alcohol tastes nasty. It either burns your throat or leaves a nasty after taste in your mouth."

"Hmm, lets skip the alcohol 101 lesson tonight, because I believe I left my mother at home. But even Barbara gets her drink on every now and again and not all alcohol tastes bad. No one said you had to have something strong. Here try the Tom Collins," Aleshia grabbed a cup off of the tray her boyfriend was carrying around.

Felice refused the cup Aleshia had thrust at her.

"Trust me, Tom Collins tastes like lemonade and you love sour drinks. Just take a sip and if you don't like it, I won't bother you anymore." Aleshia attempted to give Felice the cup one last time. Felice hesitated before finally accepting.

She took a sip and swooshed it around like mouthwash. Aleshia burst into laughter.

"Felice, this is liquor, not wine or mouthwash."

"Whatever," Felice said taking another sip. "You're right, this isn't half bad at all."

"See, I wouldn't steer you wrong. Now drink up, and get out there and dance with your boy KK, and stop frontin' like you don't want him as bad as he wants you."

The next time Aleshia saw Felice she was on the dance floor with KK, drink number four in hand and her extensions flying in every direction. Aleshia jokingly handed Felice a few braids that had fallen out during Felice's wild dancing tirade. She was so drunk KK had to take her back to the campus. The next morning Felice's head was pounding and after trying to find the bathroom, Felice realized she wasn't in her dorm room, but KK's. To her relief, nothing had transpired between them, but that was Felice's last encounter with alcohol.

The waitress returned with Felice's calamari and shrimp cocktail. "Would you like a refill on your drink?"

"Let me try something different. Give me a Ketel One and Tonic. Actually, make it two," Felice said. Ketel One and Tonic was Sylvah's favorite drink, so she decided to give it a try.

Just as Felice was about to dig into her food, a familiar voice beckoned her. Felice looked up and it was Kenneth King, better known as KK and he wasn't alone. Next to him was a tall, bronze, stunning woman with jet black long hair and almond-shaped eyes. If she lost twenty pounds, she could easily pass for a model.

Kenneth hovered over Felice as if he were in awe. He pulled Felice from the seat and gave her a big bear hug. The embrace lasted longer than necessary and Felice had to break away. After all, he was with another woman and his long embrace didn't look proper. Was he really that happy to see Felice? True, they dated for a couple of months in college, but it was never sexual—except for the time Felice allowed KK to devour her pussy with his tongue like it was the last supper. KK was Mr. Playa Playa and was nicknamed KK not only because those were his initials, but also derived from his constant chase of the kitty-kat.

"Kenneth." Felice slightly slurred. "It's funny seeing you after all these years. How are you?"

"I'm great and you look wonderful," Kenneth drank Felice in with one gulp and finished by licking his lips.

His behavior is completely inappropriate, considering he has someone with him, but maybe she was just a friend or family member, Felice thought.

"You're not looking too shabby yourself." Felice was actually being modest, because Kenneth looked good. He aged better with time and fine wine could never compare to what stood before Felice. Kenneth was about six-feet tall; medium build; very defined luscious lips; dimples deeper than the Grand Canyon; dark eyes and long lashes. He was edible, to say the least. However, her judgment could once again be somewhat impaired since she just polished off two drinks. Felice was trying her best not to appear interested in Kenneth, but she didn't know if she was successful or not.

"Last I heard, you got married to the guy you were dating, Bedford."

"Yeah, we were married for a while, but we're divorced now."

"Oh, I'm so sorry to hear," Kenneth said sympathetically.

"You know what they say, all's well that ends well." Felice giggled.

"I hear that," Kenneth countered.

The woman accompanying Kenneth didn't seem too pleased with the exchange between Felice and Kenneth, or that she had been excluded from the entire conversation. Finally, she coughed to gain attention.

"Excuse my manners. Felice, this is my wife Monica."

Felice extended her hand to Monica, and although Monica accepted the handshake, it was weak and insincere.

"It's nice to meet you. Kenneth is a great guy. We've known each other since college," Felice offered.

"That's nice," Monica said turning her attention back to Kenneth. "Can we go see if Joy and Pepsi arrived yet? I'm famished and I need a drink."

Joy and Pepsi, wasn't that a campaign for Pepsi? Felice questioned to herself. She started to ask, but figured it was best to let it be. She was almost sure it was the Joy of Pepsi or something. She was getting thirsty just thinking about soda.

"Sure thing. Well, Felice, it was nice seeing you after all these years. We should exchange business cards before you leave."

Felice saw the look of disapproval on Monica's face and decided to decline the offer to stay in touch. "Sounds great, but I don't have any business cards on me. I'm sure we'll see each other again."

"Okay, take care of yourself." Monica was already several feet ahead of Kenneth, as she was satisfied with Felice's decision to not keep in touch with her husband.

Sylvah arrived just as the waitress was replenishing the drinks. "Ooh chile, thanks for ordering my drink, but I don't need two. My day wasn't that bad," Sylvah quipped.

"No, girl. One of them is for me."

"Stop! Felice, your spirits must really be low, talk to me."

"After I release my bladder. Help yourself to some calamari and shrimp cocktail."

"I sure will."

Felice rushed into the unisex bathroom. Fortunately for her, one of the three bathrooms was available. Kenneth was waiting for one of the toilets to become free when Felice walked out.

"Hey, funny seeing you again," Kenneth said, all smiles.

"It sure is. So how long have you been married?" Felice asked curiously.

"Five long years."

"Oh, the same amount of time I've been divorced. You know what they say: for every death there is a birth."

"Is that a good thing or bad thing?" Kenneth asked.

"Who knows? I just felt like sharing."

"Felice, you really, really look good." Kenneth's eyes quickly zoomed the entire region of Felice's body.

"So do you."

"I wish I would have been smart enough to get with you in college."

"You did," Felice reminded him.

"No, really get with you."

"You tried, but I wouldn't let you, Kenneth. How quickly we forget."

"Damn, what was wrong with me?"

"You were a playa and I just wasn't ready to give it up since, I was still a virgin."

"Well, now that you're not a virgin, are you ready?" Kenneth asked.

"Let's find out," Felice backed Kenneth into the restroom she'd just left. Once inside, they closed the door and the games began.

Kenneth kissed Felice roughly on the neck and guided his juicy lips to her cleavage. Felice unbuttoned her blouse, providing Kenneth full reign. He unhooked the front of the bra, releasing her full mounds and very erect nipples.

"Damn, were your breasts always this beautiful?"

"Yes, now suck." Felice commanded.

Kenneth fondled and sucked her breasts, causing Felice's pussy to throb with pleasure and juices to overflow. Kenneth's penis was straining through his pants. It looked like his dick was begging for release. Quickly Felice unbuckled his belt, unbuttoned and unzipped his pants. Soon her hands were massaging his nicely-sized penis.

Kenneth hiked Felice's skirt up, lowered her panties and made her turn around. She handed him a condom from her purse. She was prepared to accept it doggy-style when instead, she felt a tongue darting in-and-out of her. His tongue was so thick it felt like a miniature penis.

"Damn, I need this right now, Felice. I've wanted you for years."

"Mmh-hmm," Felice answered.

Slowly he entered Felice from behind. "I need this right now, too." The alcohol was giving her a slight buzz. They grooved together, occasionally changing positions. The space didn't afford them too much leeway, but it didn't stop or keep them from being creative.

"Why couldn't my wife be more like you? More adventurous. She would never do it in the bathroom, not even at home."

Is that what this is, adventurous? We're fucking in a bathroom, a lavatory, a toilet, a restroom, a shit box for goodness sakes, Felice thought.

"She's so busy being Miss Prissy, she forgot how to please a man. She's obsessed with losing weight so she can start modeling again."

"Are you going to fuck me or talk?" Felice was becoming impatient with the banter.

"This is good. Oh, damn!" Kenneth shrieked.

Once again they were into their groove. For the grand finale, Kenneth lifted Felice while pressing her back against the wall.

Someone began knocking on the door, but both of them were so entranced they either didn't hear or simply chose to ignore the banging.

"Suppose your wife sees us coming out of the bathroom together?" Felice asked. "You've been gone for a while."

"Don't worry about her. She's too consumed with her friends to even notice my absence. See no evil, hear no evil."

Felice was losing it. "Oh, Kenneth, I'm cumming."

"Damn, wait for me! Baby, wait for me," Kenneth crooned.

Their bodies were interlocked. Moisture trickled down Felice's back and Kenneth's brow dripped with sweat.

"I can't wait…I'm about to cum."

"Wait or I'll pull it out," Kenneth teasingly threatened.

"You wouldn't dare."

"I would."

"You're evil," Felice screamed as she came. "Kenneth, you're fucking evil."

"But I'm good," Kenneth said as he came.

♀♂

"What in the world took you so long?" Sylvah asked. "I was about to send out the search team for your ass."

"Girl, I got a little busy," Felice said, grinning from ear to ear.

"I was about to eat all of the shrimp, but I figured I better leave you something."

"I appreciate it, especially since you ate all of the calamari."

"I did you a favor. Calamari doesn't taste good cold. Anyway, tell me the haps."

Felice's senses started coming back and it suddenly dawned on her that the problem she tried to drink and fuck away still existed.

"Apparently, Nina is sick. I found out today from Bedford's secretary, Shirley."

"Shirley? Why didn't Bedford tell you himself?"

"He wasn't at the office to tell me."

"I think that's really foul. I mean you finding out from his secretary. What kind of man is he?"

Felice was afraid to admit it was her fault, because she had been avoiding Bedford.

"Well, he's tried to contact me, but we've been missing each other."

"Oh, really," Sylvah speculated. "So how many times have you tried to return his calls?"

Felice watched as Monica and company walked past her table. Monica cut her eyes so deep into Felice, she could have drawn blood.

"What the hell is her problem?" Sylvah asked, not missing a beat.

Felice shrugged innocently. Shortly thereafter, Kenneth stopped by their table.

"Hello," Kenneth said to Sylvah and she nodded. "Felice, thanks for everything. I know you said you don't have business cards, but here's mine just in case you change your mind about keeping in touch. I'd love to see you again."

Both women watched as he exited the restaurant.

"Is he what took you so long to return from the bathroom? And is he the reason why that woman tried to impale you with her eyes?" Sylvah didn't wait for a reply. "Well, I must admit, brother is fine. Anyway, back to business. You need to get in touch with Bedford. If he's trying to get in touch with you, it must be important."

"I know and that's why I'm concerned. But I'm also afraid. It's been so long and—"

"And nothing, Felice. Get in touch with Bedford ASAP! You two have a past together and a future involving Nina, so stop wasting time. I know if you could take back the last couple of years, you would. Unfortunately, you can't, so let's work with the present."

Tears began to well in Felice's eyes. She knew everything Sylvah said was true, but when did everything begin spinning out of control? Felice wasn't prepared for the bomb dropped on her earlier today. She didn't have a game plan or a strategy in mind. For once, she was going to have to wing it and hope Bedford would be forgiving, but most importantly that her daughter, Nina, was well.

"Felice, everything is going to work out, but you need to be wherever your daughter is. Go find Bedford."

"Okay, let me finish my drink first." Felice took a sip of the drink and the Ketel One and tonic blew her away. "This shit is awful."

"Hon, it's not awful. It's just out of your league."

"I'll take your word for it. I'm ready to go. I need to do this and you're right, I have nothing to worry about, because everything is going to be fine."

They paid the bill, headed toward the exit and walked to the train station together.

Sylvah hugged Felice before separating. "Call me first thing in the morning to let me know how things went. I'll be out tonight."

"Hot date," Felice joked trying to remove some of the edge.

"Something like that."

"Which one?"

"Hunter," Sylvah said, smiling.

"Have fun."

"I always do," Sylvah replied. "Good luck, pray on it and everything will work out. I love you, chick."

"Same here, and thanks for being there for me."

18

Ignore It

Hunter smiled at Sylvah as he stood patiently in the lobby of her building, waiting for the elevator. Sylvah matched his gaze. It was now common for Hunter and Sylvah to end their date, park his car, talk, and then he'd walk her to the elevator. They had a late dinner and went dancing afterward. It was now three in the morning. Sylvah's life was definitely taking a turn for the best. All of a sudden, she was feeling like Cinderella at the ball. Sylvah had been going out with Hunter for two months and no sex was involved, because Jason was still in the picture. Sex was definitely involved there. Now she was getting more than she thought she could ever handle. Who would have thought that at the age of forty, she'd be living the life of a twenty-five-year-old? She was turning the heads of young, old, white, black, Asian or whatever men. If it was a man, she got his attention. Even men in her office flirted with her. Perhaps she always had this certain appeal, but was blinded to it because of her marriage.

"So are you going to invite me up this time for a nightcap?" Hunter asked.

"Hunter, I don't think that's such a good idea."

"Sylvah, why not? I just want to spend a little more time with you. You enjoy my company, don't you?" Hunter asked.

"Yes, I do. It's just that I don't want to rush things. I like the way our relationship is now. We are getting to know each other on many different levels, and that's a good thing. I don't want to bring you up for something that I don't feel I'm quite ready for. I hope that you understand," Sylvah replied. She was extremely attracted to Hunter. The rush of current passing through her body when they kissed was definitely shocking. There was also a mild case of curiosity. Sylvah's interest rested in learning if the myths about white men were true. Were they really attentive and sensitive lovers and were the penises big or small? The other setback was having two lovers at the same time. Twice this week alone Sylvah got sweaty and nasty with Jason. She didn't want to get in the habit of doing two men at the same time. It didn't feel ethical, especially since she couldn't get Jason out of her head.

Hunter stood quietly as if in thought. Sylvah hoped that he didn't press the issue. It was bad enough she was already sexually involved with one man who was thirteen years her junior—Jason was only seven years older than Zaire. Sylvah had only been out with Jason one time and that was late in the evening to the movie theater and back. She didn't want to be seen with him in the daytime for fear of someone thinking she was an older relative. Sylvah had seen enough movies where the young attractive man dated the older woman and people mistook the woman for his aunt, older sister, or even his mother. She wanted to be spared the humiliation, but he was definitely good enough to keep indoors. Sylvah really enjoyed Jason's company. They actually had a lot in common, and if he were older, Sylvah would've probably sought something a little more serious with him. Jason expressed his interest in taking the relationship to the next level. Sylvah didn't know what he considered the next level. As far as she was concerned, six floors up to her condominium were plenty of levels.

Truthfully, Sylvah found Hunter to be attractive. Very attractive, but she never considered a sexual relationship with him prior to their first night. It was a thought she had avoided having with herself. After each date they kissed, and even that was innocent. Purposely, she'd turn her head so Hunter's lips landed on her cheek, nose, or forehead. On one occasion, Hunter asked Sylvah if his breath smelled. Sylvah was trying her best to steer clear of another encounter like their first date. That kiss nearly sent her to the moon without an oxygen tank. She hated to admit it, but she was afraid to get serious with a white man. Then again she was also afraid to become involved with a younger man who was gainfully employed. Sylvah was in a no-win situation. What would people say if she got involved with either? How would she go about explaining the age difference to her children? How would her friends and colleagues react to her dating a white man, or a younger man? Hunter was also younger, but four years was nothing in comparison to thirteen. Sylvah felt it best to leave everything the way it was. This way, no one got his feelings hurt and there were no strings attached. A philosophy she picked up from Felice.

Sylvah returned her attention to Hunter, who looked almost pitiful. Why was he pressing her now? Didn't he see how good their relationship was without sex? Sex only served to complicate matters. There was already enough confusion going on in her life with her children, work, and Jason. She was having a hell of a time balancing her problems now and didn't need anything else on the tray to topple her over.

The elevator finally arrived. Hunter unexpectedly leaned in close to Sylvah, leaving her absolutely no breathing room. He tipped her head back and snatched the kiss that she worked so hard to evade. She was once again caught in his rapture. His tongue eagerly searched her orifice. Delicately he allowed his tongue to swab every angle of her mouth and ended the kiss by gliding his tongue smoothly across her pearly whites. The tip of his tongue lingered on her upper lip. Sylvah was stunned and didn't know exactly when they ended up in the elevator. Their bodies were so intertwined that Sylvah could smell the faint remnants of Dove soap mixed with aftershave lotion. Hunter's soft hands stroked her bare arms, sending chills down her spine. His body hardened against her, and for the first time she felt his manhood rise. The heat between her legs went from tepid to scorching, causing her nipples to become erect.

The doors to the elevator opened, delivering them to their destination, but Sylvah didn't remember pressing the button to her floor. Hunter pulled away from Sylvah, took her hand, and led them out. Hunter wasn't familiar with his surroundings and looked to Sylvah for direction. Breathless, she pointed toward the left. They walked until she stopped in front of her apartment. In the dimly lit hall, Sylvah rummaged through her purse for the house keys. Under normal circumstances, she would have had them out before exiting the elevator. Sylvah always made a habit to take them out before arriving at her doorstep, a self-defense mechanism that she'd learned long ago. She found the keys, but hesitated before opening the door. Sylvah had a decision to make. She could end the date now before things escalated, because she knew that once inside there would be no stopping. Or she could go with what she was feeling, continue, and throw all ethics out with the trash. Sylvah placed the key in the cylinder. Hunter grabbed her hand before she could turn the lock.

"Sylvah, I don't want you to think that I'm pushing you into anything," Hunter said, understanding filling his light green eyes.

"You're not pushing anything that wouldn't have eventually happened," Sylvah acknowledged to both him and herself.

"Are you sure?"

"If you allow me time to continue thinking about it, I might change my mind," Sylvah teased.

"Well, I wouldn't want you to do that," Hunter said as he helped Sylvah turn the lock.

Sylvah turned on the light as they entered the apartment. Hunter stepped in after her, removing his blazer. Sylvah took the jacket from him and hung it in the closet.

"What kind of music would you like to hear?" Sylvah asked, wanting to set the mood.

"Do you happen to have any Luther Vandross?" Hunter asked.

"What black household doesn't?" Sylvah laughed and Hunter nodded in agreement.

Sylvah browsed her selection and found Luther Vandross's greatest hits compilation. She placed it in the CD changer along with Sade and her all-time favorite artist, Barry White.

"Make yourself comfortable," Sylvah encouraged. "I'm going to change into something a little more relaxed." She smiled and headed into her bedroom. Sylvah had just acquired some new lingerie and wanted to break one of them in. They were all so nice, she was having a hard time choosing, and she didn't want Hunter to wait longer than necessary. She didn't want to wait longer than necessary, either. She finally selected a short pink lace nightgown and matching robe.

When Sylvah reentered the living room, Hunter was anxiously awaiting her return. He jumped from his seat and bolted over to where Sylvah stood. She had planned to walk over to him as if on a runway, but he didn't give her the chance.

"You look so good," Hunter whispered in her ear. He pinned her against the wall, combining their body heat. He nibbled on her earlobe and traced his tongue on the outside of her ear. Sylvah's breathing became labored. She buried her head between his chin and shoulder while kissing his neckline. Her hands dipped south and found his belt buckle. Sylvah unfastened it. Slowly she unbuttoned and unzipped his pants. Hunter helped her remove them as he quickly kicked off his shoes. His button-front shirt followed, leaving him in just his undershirt and cotton boxers. The chemistry between Sylvah and Hunter was intense.

Sylvah grabbed Hunter's shirt and pulled him into her room. She didn't bother to turn the light back on. They found their way to the king-sized bed and Sylvah pushed Hunter down, collapsing on top of him. She landed on his very hard penis. Slowly she grinded against him and he reciprocated. He wrapped his arms around her for a very slow, passionate kiss.

Only one myth remained, because from the feel of it, Hunter definitely had sizeable equipment.

The phone rang.

Sylvah jumped.

"Ignore it," Hunter said, covering her mouth with his. "Let the machine answer."

The phone chimed three more times before the voice activation took over. "You've reached the home of Sylvah Lawrence. I'm not available right now, but please leave your name, number, and message, and I'll return your call at my earliest convenience."

"Hello, Ma. Where are you? Where are you? I've been trying your cell phone." Sylvah never turned on her mobile phone while out on dates—with friends or otherwise. "Please, please call me as soon as you get this message," Kenya cried, sounding panicked. "Zaire's been in a bad accident and—"

Fear gripped Sylvah as she flew across the bed, kicking Hunter in his ribs. The tears rushed to her eyes as she thought about what could have happened to her one and only son.

"Kenya, hello," Sylvah answered. "Baby, speak to me. What happened?"

19

The Package

Felice headed straight to Bedford's after her meeting with Sylvah. Her mind refused to remain at ease during the fifteen-minute train ride to his house. Thoughts of what she would say consumed her. Was it appropriate to begin by saying, "Hi Bedford, sorry I didn't return any of your calls. I've been real busy. By the way, how is our daughter?" Nothing seemed fitting and Sylvah's words from three years prior came floating back from out of nowhere, "How can you just give up your child without a second thought?" After what felt like hours of debating, Sylvah ended with "I hope this doesn't come back to haunt you, because regret is a hard thing to live with." Sylvah always was the wise and objective one of the group. It didn't matter how hard it would be to swallow, Sylvah always fed friends, family, and strangers the truth, along with the implications. Sylvah always said the remedy could sometimes be nastier than the illness itself, and in some cases went hand in hand. If only Felice had realized the importance of those words. However, this afternoon Sylvah had let her off easy. She didn't scold or say "I told you so." Instead, Sylvah consoled Felice and told her to deal with the here and now.

In the beginning, it was easy. During the pregnancy, she fought hard not to bond with the baby. It was terribly hard, but doable. Felice ate properly, exercised, and swallowed the horse pills the doctor prescribed for her. Those things were for her health. Bedford was the one who sang lullabies, rubbed her belly, and got excited when he saw what could be identified as a hand or footprint. Felice refused to become engaged. She had a plan and in order for it to be fulfilled she didn't let "he" or "she," as Felice so nicely addressed the baby, distract her. After all, she was already doing the right thing by having the baby. The easy way out would have been an abortion, which was something Felice felt would haunt her for the rest of her life. There was no way that abandoning the baby could be disturbing. When Felice conjured up a departure scheme, there was no doubt in her mind that Bedford would be an excellent parent. However, doubts about her ability to be a good mother were overshadowing. She was a good person, at least up until recently. Nevertheless, it was not enough to determine the type of parent she would become. Aware of the fact that she couldn't run from this forever, Felice never calculated this far ahead. Now the day had arrived.

The walk from 145th Street to 138th and Convent avenues never felt so far. Students attending City College and A. Philip Randolph high school cluttered the pavement. It was still early in the afternoon, not quite breaking five o'clock. Felice was forced to walk carefully in the street. Fortunately for her, not many cars were driving by. Felice walked so swiftly she didn't feel the small trickle of sweat diving down her back and across her brow. April had never felt so hot before.

Entering the ground level of Bedford's home, Felice closed the gate behind her. She gazed at the entire structure and was more than sure that Bedford's top two floors were still vacant. He always hated the idea of renting to strangers. Felice rang the bell. She waited a few seconds before punching the button a second time. While waiting, she tried to look inside the windows, which only had sheer curtains. The lights were out and the house appeared still. Any stranger could view the entire lower level from front to back—living room, dining room, kitchen, and a fenced-in backyard. Felice left the gated area and climbed the steps to the parlor. Again she rang the bell with no success. Felice was at a loss. If only she'd returned Bedford's calls.

Ten minutes later Felice was standing on the curb in front of Blimpie's on 145th Street. She located her cell phone and began dialing furiously.

The cell phone number she had for Bedford was no longer in service. If she hadn't been in such a hurry to leave the office she could've asked Shirley for his numbers. She never even bothered to write down the numbers he left on her answering machine over and over again. Nothing Felice did of late was right.

It finally dawned on her to call Isis, Bedford's sister. Felice was certain Isis hadn't changed her numbers. She was the type of person who practiced longevity with everything. She held the same job for twenty years and counting. She moved into her parents' house and took over their mortgage. Their parents purchased the house after moving from the projects, and then retired and moved to Arizona. Isis never switched banks, insurance companies, or anything else if it wasn't necessary. She lived the old adage "if it ain't broke, don't fix it."

The number wasn't saved in Felice's cell phone and she had to retrieve her phone book. She decided to grab a seat inside of Blimpie's instead of standing on the corner like a whore. Once inside, Felice ordered black coffee with milk and sugar and purchased a prepackaged Danish with cream cheese filling. After paying, she located a booth in the rear of the restaurant.

Felice dialed the number. When the phone rang her hands began to tremble. Several rings later the phone was forwarded to an answering service. Isis hadn't arrived home from work yet. Felice hurried to dial Isis' office. It wasn't quite five o'clock yet. The possibility of catching her at work was strong.

"Hello, you have reached Isis Jackson, personnel director of Saks Fifth Avenue. I will be out of the office on vacation until Monday. If your call requires immediate attention, please contact my assistant by pressing the pound button followed by extension 1224. Otherwise, please leave a message with your name, date, number, and nature of your call. Thank you and have a nice day."

Felice didn't know if it made sense to leave a message. It was Friday evening and she wanted to locate Bedford today, not next week. Monday was forty-eight hours away. Before she could make a decision the phone beeped, indicating she should begin speaking.

"Hello, Isis. It's been a long time since we've last had the chance to speak. I just wanted to say hi and see how you were doing. When you get the chance, feel free to call me. My home number is still the same. Bye," Felice was in the process of disconnecting the call. Then quickly she realized she never left an identity. Felice hadn't spoken to Isis in more than two years and Isis probably no longer recognized her voice. "Oh, I almost forgot, it's your long-lost friend, Felice."

Felice hated leaving such empty messages. They always managed to sound insincere, no matter how genuine you really were. It was probably a mistake calling Isis. Suppose she was upset at her for leaving without a trace? Felice imagined Isis retrieving her messages on Monday. At first Isis would be genuinely surprised, but it would quickly be replaced with contempt. Isis was a God-fearing woman. Still everyone had their limits and what Felice had done would surely be unforgivable. Now Felice regretted ever placing the call, and there was no way to retrieve the message.

Unwrapping her Danish, Felice tried to think of next steps. She could sit around and wait for Bedford to return home, but she had no idea how long he would take. It didn't make sense to visit Isis, because she was probably traveling somewhere on vacation and Felice wasn't quite ready to face her, anyway. The phone was one matter, but face-to-face may not be the best idea. Felice was running out of options. She thought about Shirley, but decided against getting her involved. As far as Felice was concerned, Shirley was already too involved and it made her uncomfortable. There was no one left. Felice finished her Danish and coffee and decided to head home. Maybe she could think rationally in her own personal sanctuary.

It was a good thing Felice got on the A train at 145th Street, because by the time it hit Fifty-ninth Street, the train was filled to capacity. The conductor had to tell passengers another train was two minutes behind him, because people were stuffing themselves in the entrances and the doors couldn't close. This was the first time in years that Felice rode a train during rush hour. She definitely hadn't missed it. The day was humid, and people had either failed to apply deodorant or it had worn off. Others wore too much perfume. All those scents combined in such a small space became lethal. The woman sitting beside Felice smelled like an ashtray and the man standing above her insisted on spreading his newspaper all the way open, refusing to hold the railing or the metal holder dangling above his head. Therefore, when the train made a sudden jolt or turn he would practically fall over into Felice's lap, barely mumbling "sorry" each time. By the third incident, Felice kneed him sharply to show her displeasure, after which he folded the paper in half and held the pole with his free available hand. Felice switched trains at Broadway Nassau and hopped on to the Number 2 train. She wasn't as lucky and had to stand the entire ride home, but it was less eventful than the first train.

When Felice entered her building she stopped to talk to the doorman and inquired about Bedford. She was informed that he came by on two separate occasions. He didn't leave a message either time. She raced up to her apartment. Perhaps the mystery envelope would shed some light on the situation.

The mountain of neglected mail remained in the same spot Felice had left it days earlier. She sorted through it, quickly locating the letter from Jackson and Jackson with Shirley's handwriting on it. Carefully, she tore it open.

JACKSON & JACKSON FINANCIAL CONSULTANTS, INC.
MEMO

```
To:        All Staff
From:      Bedford Jackson, CEO
Cc:        Felice Jackson, COO
Re:        Office relocation and Promotions
```

It gives me great pleasure to announce the completion of our move from the seventh floor suite, 7-12, to our new home 28-07, on the twenty-eighth floor. This move could not have happened without the support of our dedicated and hard-working staff members.

Over the course of two years, numerous changes have taken place. Several divisions have been added to assist our influx of increased business and new positions have been appointed accordingly. Jackson and Jackson Financial Consultants, Inc., now has two vice presidents. We are a living, breathing, growing organization and as such we must continue to grow with the business.

Tanisha Little, former director of the Entertainment and Fashion division, has been promoted to vice president. Ms. Little has been with Jackson and Jackson for four years. During this time she has proven herself to be indispensable on numerous occasions, putting out fires, taking charge of accounts as well as bringing in new clientele. Please congratulate Ms. Little when you get the chance.

Greg Lovelace has been promoted to Vice President of the Small Business and Finance division. Mr. Lovelace has been with Jackson and Jackson since its inception. He has worked under my tutelage and has moved from the ranks of account executive to account director and now, vice president.

In addition, we've recently employed three new staff members. Please welcome Tonia Jones, account manager, reporting to our new vice president Greg Lovelace. Anthony Whitley, marketing and research manager, reporting to both Ms. Little and Mr. Lovelace; and Tina Williams, office assistant.

A celebration is mandatory. Please mark your calendars for Thursday evening at Justin's restaurant. See Shirley for further details. Bring your appetites. Bon Appetít!

Best regards,
Bedford Jackson

Felice was livid. This was not the information she was looking for or needed. She hoped for something in regard to Nina or a more personal note. Not some memo with information she already knew. However, if she had read the memo before arriving at the office earlier she could have avoided mass confusion and the surprise reorganization. Just when she prayed for Bedford to have an ulterior motive, he didn't. Bedford had failed her.

Felice needed to talk to someone. She thought about calling Sylvah. Then she remembered Sylvah telling her about yet another hot date with Hunter. *Things are certainly heating up between them,* Felice thought, smiling for the first time since entering the apartment.

A nice long bath in the Jacuzzi would help her unwind. Felice did some of her best thinking while sitting in a hot, steamy, soothing tub. She popped the latest Alicia Keys CD into the built-in Bose wall unit. Almost every inch of her body ached. Visits with her personal trainer showed great results but were causing a lot of pain. Felice was tired of the "No pain, no gain," routine he kept feeding his clients. There were times while at the gym, Felice felt as if she was in the army being drilled by a sergeant instead of a personal trainer. She was willing to put in the work and step it up a bit, but he was going overboard. After all, she was far from obese. Felice was merely trying to tone up. The Jacuzzi jets were turned on high while she leaned back, allowing them to massage away the pain.

The notion came out of nowhere. Samantha. Felice's mother might have Bedford's new information. During their last phone call, her mother mentioned to Felice that she knew something. Felice was more than sure it was about Nina. The baby would be the only reason Bedford had to contact her mother. Bedford and Samantha weren't the closest of friends while he and Felice were married, but were always respectful of each other. Unfortunately, her intuition regarding Bedford was to be true. Felice had nothing to lose by calling her mother and getting the information. It had been two months since they last spoke, anyway. Felice was curious to know what her mother was up to; she couldn't possibly still be upset with Felice.

Felice removed a turban-styled towel from her head. Lotion was applied to moisten her skin and a white cotton gauze robe adorned her flesh. Felice sauntered to the kitchen to prepare a cup of vanilla and caramel specialty coffee purchased at Trader Joe's.

The phone rang, startling Felice. Placing the empty mug on the counter, she dashed across the room to answer the call. If luck were on her side, it would be Bedford, Isis, or even Samantha.

"Hello," Felice said with her fingers crossed.

"Hey, Felice. You sound out of breath. Did I catch you at a bad time?" Candace asked.

"No, I was just in the kitchen making some coffee. What's going on with you?" Felice asked, trying not to show her disappointment.

"Nothing much. Thought I'd give you a call."

"No plans tonight?"

"Just sitting here watching some television. Shane is out on the prowl. He's working on a big case that's making headlines in the news."

"Which one? There are so many."

"The kidnapping and homicide case," Candace answered.

"Whoa, yeah, I've been hearing about it a lot lately on the news. The person is kidnapping children, right?"

"Yeah, it's pretty frightening, especially if you have children. I know it's hard for you to imagine since you don't have any. You don't even have nieces and nephews," Candace stated.

Felice was at a loss for words. She did have a child. A daughter she knew nothing about. All Felice remembered was a very light, pinkish-colored baby with a mass of curls and bright red lips. At the time the baby had no distinguishable features that either parent could claim. Nonetheless, now Felice wanted to know more concerning the welfare of this child. For a moment Felice thought about her reply to Candace. The honest response would have been, "Yes, actually I do have a daughter and her name is Nina," followed by a long explanation. But Felice couldn't spring such news on Candace. There was no way Candace would ever understand. This was the same woman who freaked out and completely shut down over a little harmless one-night rendezvous in Jamaica. Instead, Felice gave the expected answer.

"Yeah, you're right. Even so, the mere thought is unsettling."

"I mean, there seems to be no particular pattern, rhyme, or reason. It appears to be random—at least that's what Shane and his cronies seem to believe. I think there must be some connection somewhere and they need to find the right clues," Candace said, playing detective.

"I guess so," Felice said, not wanting to hear any grueling details regarding the children that were found murdered. "So, where are the kids?" Felice asked.

"Jasmine is with my parents for the weekend and James is spending the night at a friend's. Shane and I were supposed to be having a quiet evening at home when his pager went off. They must have a break in the case, or they found another body. So it's just me and one hundred stations of nothing."

"Ain't that the truth! I explore all of the channels and still can't find anything suitable to watch. Half the time I end up watching cartoons or I pop in a DVD."

"Me too," Candace said, laughing. "Hey, Felice, have you spoken to Shane lately?"

"No. I wouldn't really have a reason to unless I bumped into him on the street. Why?"

"Oh, it's probably nothing."

"Candace, if you asked me, it's got to be something."

"Well, Shane said someone left a note on his car and it said something about 'you better watch your wife' and then there was a message on his voice mail saying the same thing."

"Oh my goodness! Candace, do you think it has anything to do with this case?"

"I really don't know. I mean, this is the first time something like this has ever happened. A unit is positioned in front of our home, and the kids are being watched just in case, but our kids don't fit the MO of the children they've found so far. Those children are younger and have all been white."

"Maybe it's someone Shane has had dealings with in the past. I'm sure he's put a lot of people away, making plenty of enemies along the way," Felice said. She was genuinely concerned about her friend, and for the moment forgot her own problems. "Was the voice a male or female?"

"Shane says it's an engineered voice and the letter wasn't handwritten and there were no prints."

"Damn, girl, call me if you need anything. I'm really sorry to hear this. Have you spoken to Sylvah or Alana?"

"Yeah, I spoke to Sylvah last night and I'm not calling Alana."

"Oh yeah, I don't even know why I asked," Felice said as she laughed. The sweet aroma of coffee caught her attention. The large silver clock above the refrigerator stared. The time now read eight-thirty. It was much later than Felice thought. It was obvious Candace needed to talk, and Felice wanted to help, but she had to speak with her mother.

"Girl, what are you plans for tomorrow?" Candace asked.

"Nothing in particular," Felice said, getting antsy.

"If you and Sylvah aren't too busy, maybe we can go shopping. There is a major sale at Macy's. It's a spring clearance and you know we always get really great bargains during seasonal sales."

"I'll let you know tomorrow. I've been shopping almost too much lately, and I don't have enough room as it is. When I get the chance, I need to clean out my closet and give away some stuff to the Salvation Army. Anything I haven't worn in three years needs to go."

"I hear you. Anywho, if you change your mind, let me know. I'm free."

"Call me in the afternoon and we'll see."

"Sounds cool! Anyway, I'm going to go sort out the clothes and do a few loads of laundry so I can have a free day tomorrow. I tell you the life of a parent never ends."

"I hear you," Felice replied, wishing only for a moment she could trade places with Candace; a loving husband, house, kids. *"Hasta mañana!"*

"Si, hasta mañana, chica!"

Ending the call with Candace wasn't painful at all. Now Felice had the great task of getting her mother on the phone.

♀♂

First she needed to drink her coffee to calm her nerves, although caffeine actually made her jittery. Felice took a sip and the liquid was lukewarm. She stuck it in the microwave for thirty seconds. When the buzzer sounded she retrieved the mug, walked into the living room and placed it on the coaster. A deep breath was necessary before dialing.

"Hello."

"Hello, Gene, this is Felice. Is my mother home?" Felice asked cordially. It took every ounce out of Felice to be nice. She didn't know what it was, but she never cared for Gene.

"No, Felice. I'm sorry she's not."

"Okay, what time do you expect her back?"

"I'm not certain. Probably early next week," Gene answered.

"What? Where is she?" Felice asked, surprised. Her mother rarely went away on trips, especially without Gene. This was truly an unusual occurrence.

"Sam's in California."

"California? Is she on a business trip or something?"

"No," Gene answered.

"If you don't mind me asking, what is she doing out in California?"

"She's at the Children's Hospital of Los Angeles."

"Doing what?"

Gene hesitated for a moment, as if it was taking great labor to answer the question. "She went with Bedford, Nina, and Isis. The baby is sick."

Get A Grip!

Sylvah lay sprawled across the bed as she listened to the details of Zaire's accident. Hunter attempted to soothe her by massaging her shoulders. Sylvah's body grew tense from shock and the alarm of hearing Kenya's panic-filled voice describe what happened to Zaire. Kenya was so shaken up that she was speaking in circles. Sylvah patiently waited as she allowed Kenya time to get her thoughts together enough to tell her the story.

Apparently Zaire and a few friends visited Kenya in Atlanta to attend a party. Zaire and his two friends left at about two in the morning and headed back to Alabama. It was drizzling rain before they left, but then the rain became torrential. The guys decided to continue even though the visibility was extremely poor. They must have figured the Jeep they drove could handle the weather. They were wrong and it hydroplaned. The vehicle flipped several times and broke through a guardrail. None of the boys had on their seat belts. All of them were found unconscious and were airlifted to the hospital. Kenya was on her way to the hospital when she called. She didn't know the specifics or the condition of any of the three.

Sylvah didn't say much to Hunter other than "Excuse me" and "sorry" as she packed her bags to fly to Atlanta. Bags crashed against the bed. Dresser drawers flew open as she grabbed items and threw them inside the suitcases. Closet doors opened and clothes were tossed across the room narrowly missing the luggage. Sylvah was upset with herself for not listening to her initial instinct, which was to come upstairs alone. Instead she allowed herself to be coaxed into inviting Hunter to her apartment, wasting valuable time. If she had come directly upstairs she would have heard the message and been on her way to the airport. Sylvah would have been that much closer to coming to her son's aid.

Sylvah glanced at the answering machine and saw that there were five messages waiting. She was more than sure that at least three of those were from Kenya and Bläise. Sylvah didn't know what she'd do if anything ever happened to her babies. Zaire never even had so much as a broken arm in his life, and never had seen the inside of a hospital before now. The most he ever had to endure was a sprained ankle from playing basketball and a few bruises from football. Colds and flu rarely paid him visits. Now she was told that her son was in serious condition. Sylvah knew she had to be strong and have faith that her son was going to be fine. Zaire was a survivor. She had to believe he would get through this incident unscathed.

Hunter went back into the living room to gather his clothes while Sylvah hurried about in her room. Sylvah knew he heard most of the details and she could see he was trying hard not to get in the way. Suddenly Sylvah became angry and this was a side of her that he had never witnessed before. Hunter kind of guessed that Sylvah was blaming herself for what happened and couldn't understand why. Hunter decided not to leave. He was going to offer his support to Sylvah any way he could. He took a seat in the living room and waited to hear Sylvah's next steps. The phone rang. He walked back to Sylvah's room and stood in the doorway to see if there was any additional news.

"Hello," Sylvah answered. "No, I was out." Sylvah paused briefly and went into a procession of explanations and answers.

"No, you know that I rarely keep my cell phone on." Sylvah paused again becoming impatient with the caller.

"What difference does it make where I was? Would that have prevented this from occurring? No I don't know his condition. I only know what Kenya told me. Do you know which hospital he's in?"

Hunter could hear the voice of the person on the other line. He was firing a line of questions at Sylvah that seemed unwarranted. Sylvah was visibly upset as tears once again filled her eyes and her body trembled.

"Bläise, none of that matters now. I'm not going to stay on the phone and continue arguing with you. We have to get down there to the hospital immediately." Sylvah nodded her head. "Mmh hmm."

"Okay." Pause. "Which airport?"

Pause.

"I'll meet you there."

Pause.

"No, I'll catch a cab. I don't need you coming over here to pick me up."

Pause.

"I packed two bags. I should be able to take both of them onboard with me."

Pause.

"Thanks for buying the tickets."

Pause.

"Okay, I'll see you in about forty minutes."

Sylvah hung up the phone, grabbed her purse and travel bags and turned the light off in her room. Hunter moved cautiously as she stampeded out of the bedroom.

"Sylvah, I can take you to the airport." Hunter offered. "You don't have to catch a cab." These were the first words that Hunter had spoken since Sylvah received the first phone call. He didn't know what to say after she had hung up with Kenya, and she hadn't appeared to be in the mood for conversation.

"No, that's okay. I'll be fine. The doorman can flag me down a taxi."

"Sylvah, don't be silly. I'm here and I want to come with you. Please let me do this for you."

Sylvah would've preferred to just take a cab. Then she could attempt to clear her head. Sylvah wanted some time alone. She was about to board a plane with her ex-husband for two hours and the entire time she would be thinking about the welfare of her son. Not to mention, the present state of her personal and business affairs. The flight would be tense, as she knew that Bläise would try to drill her about things that weren't even in her control. He had already started on the call. Bläise was upset because he and Kenya had been trying to reach Sylvah for about an hour. He made her feel as if she wasn't allowed to have a social life as he reprimanded her on the phone. Sylvah was already feeling bad enough and didn't need Bläise to throw dirt on her grave. If she ever wondered why they divorced, this summoned up all memories.

Before Sylvah could object, Hunter was taking her bags and throwing them over his shoulder. He walked to the front door and she followed. On their way out Luther sang, "If This World Were Mine." Sylvah thought, *if this world were mine, Zaire wouldn't be lying in a hospital suffering, Bläise wouldn't be such an asshole, and there would be world peace.* Unfortunately, none of these things would ever come to pass. Therefore, she would read the instructions and follow the rules of the game.

Sylvah remained quiet during the ride to the airport, but Hunter felt compelled to tell her how sorry he was about Zaire. He was apologetic throughout the ride. Sylvah was tempted to tell him to stop talking, but found it easier to shut him out. She appreciated his kind words, but he didn't know what she was going through. Hunter probably never experienced any kind of loss or pain in his life. His parents were still alive and well. His siblings were all comfortable and had their own families. Hunter didn't have any children. He bought and sold businesses whenever he got bored and traveled to fill the void. It was as if he avoided commitment to control the amount of failure and happiness that could possibly enter his life.

They arrived at the airport in record time. It was after four in the morning and few cars were on the road, so it only took them twenty minutes. Hunter parked in front of the Delta terminal. He rushed out of the car to open Sylvah's door and then unloaded her luggage.

Sylvah went to the skycap and presented him with her I.D. The flight was scheduled to leave at five-thirty. The skycap provided her with a boarding pass and she was about to walk away when Hunter drew her attention by holding her hands.

"Sylvah, I want you to know that I really care for you, and Zaire is going to be fine." He held her firmly as he looked deeply into her chest-nut-brown eyes. "I'll be praying for you and your family. If you need anything, I'm just a phone call away." He embraced Sylvah and briefly kissed her on the lips. Sylvah was too tired to respond and accepted his generosity with a simple nod before she walked inside the terminal.

♀♂

Sylvah was seated at the gate when Bläise occupied the chair beside her. Deep thought consumed her and she wasn't aware of his presence until the weight of an arm fell heavily around her shoulders. Sylvah looked at him and saw the same anxious, weary, and concerned expression that she wore. She didn't expect any different. Bläise loved his kids just as much as she did. Love produced their two beautiful children. Bläise was the only man who could truly relate to what she was feeling now. Sylvah fell into his open embrace and wept. They were tears that she held back during her ride with Hunter to the airport. Tears she withheld while walking through the terminal, tears from her last update from Kenya two minutes earlier. Bläise hugged her tightly and his tears melted into Sylvah's hair. Their bodies heaved in unison.

"I just spoke to Kenya," Sylvah announced, regaining her composure.

Bläise made no attempt to hide his tears as he wiped the residue away. He took a deep breath and prepared himself as if for the worse.

"And?"

"Zaire is at Grady Memorial Hospital. Kenya's there now, but she hasn't been allowed to see him."

"Do they have any idea what his condition is yet?"

"Kenya said that they rushed him into surgery and he's still being attended to." Sylvah held Bläise even tighter as the reality of her last statement hit her.

"My son...my God, please help him," Bläise cried.

Sylvah couldn't sleep on the plane. She was too distraught. There was no telling how long they would be in Atlanta. The one thing that she did know was she would remain there as long as necessary. Sylvah would have to make arrangements with her office to cancel all appointments until further notice. Postpone all court appearances and call Felice, Candace and Alana to inform them of Zaire's accident. Zaire's failure to come home during his most recent school break drifted into her thoughts. This was the first time he opted not to visit since his attendance at college. Zaire usually returned home every chance he got. There were many occasions that he visited just because he missed home. Sylvah and Bläise had one discussion concerning Zaire, and Bläise concluded that he was simply having a tough semester. Sylvah knew otherwise and tried to convince Bläise, still he refused to believe that Zaire's depression had anything to do with their divorce.

♀♂

Two hours, a monorail ride, a rental car and seventy-five miles per hour on I-85 later, Sylvah and Bläise arrived at the hospital. Bläise made sure to maneuver the vehicle cautiously. The roads were still a little slick from the earlier storm that caused Zaire's accident.

Zaire was in the ICU recovery area. No one would be allowed to see him for another two hours. When Zaire had been thrown from the car, he suffered a mild concussion, broken ribs, and internal bleeding, and his spleen had to be removed. The driver's lungs were crushed by the airbag and he suffered serious head trauma, while the passenger in the rear seat broke both legs and had a few abrasions. Of the group, he had fared the best. Fortunately none of them had blood alcohol levels that would indicate driving under the influence. The only thing they could be found guilty of was being foolish for not pulling over in the rain. Sylvah and Bläise were somewhat relieved. They were thankful that Zaire was alive. They were comforted to be able to be by his side as he recovered. Still, something lingered in the air that felt unresolved between Sylvah and Bläise.

Kenya, along with her best friend a Spanish girl named Mojita (pronounced Moheeta), and Lavender, Zaire's ex-girlfriend, were in the waiting room. Lavender insisted on coming when Kenya received the initial call about Zaire. Kenya was awake but looked like a zombie. Her best friend was half asleep and Lavender held a paper cup, which was probably once filled with steaming hot liquid. There were a few other people sitting in the room, probably relatives of the other victims. When Kenya saw her parents enter she got up and ran over to them for an embrace. The three of them formed a circle and held onto one another firmly. No words needed to be said.

Lavender, a petite girl with long, dark hair who favored a little Indian princess, came over to introduce herself to Sylvah and Bläise. Both were cordial, considering the circumstances of their meeting. They exchanged pleasantries and Lavender returned to her seat opting to stay until Zaire was permitted to receive visitors. The family of the driver—his mother, older sister and grandfather—also introduced themselves and offered their apologies and compassion. The driver had undergone surgery and was placed in the intensive care unit. All three of them would be hospitalized until there were signs of recovery.

Sylvah, Bläise, and Kenya sat opposite the driver's family. Kenya's best friend, Mojíta offered to make a coffee run to Starbucks. They didn't want to chance the hospital coffee, which was usually hit or miss. It was already a few minutes before nine o'clock in the morning. Bläise offered to pay since Mojíta volunteered to take the trip. He gave her a one hundred-dollar bill. Everybody gave her their order and she left, accompanied by Lavender and the driver's sister, Christina.

"So where's the other guy's family?" 'Sylvah asked curiously.

"They live in California," Kenya replied over a weary yawn.

"Are they on their way?"

"Apparently his mother is on a business trip in Seattle, so she can't make it."

"What about his father?" Bläise asked, concerned and confused.

"His father is dead," Kenya answered.

"Oh, my. I'm sorry to hear." Sylvah gasped.

"Yeah, his mother killed him," Kenya revealed nonchalantly.

"What?" Bläise and Sylvah said, stunned at their daughter's accusation.

"Yeah. Trent tells the story to everyone. Apparently his father use to beat his mother. She reported him to the police, got restraining orders and all that stuff, but still he continued. He'd visit her job to harass her—break into her house and beat her. One day she got tired of it and bludgeoned him to death with one of those cast-iron Dutch pots. Trent was eleven years old at the time. He told us he never really cared much for his father, because he treated Trent with the same heavy fist."

"Is anyone coming to see about Trent?" Bläise asked.

"His family was notified and I think his aunt and uncle are flying in. Trent wasn't as badly injured, so I don't think that they're going to rush."

"My goodness," Sylvah said with a shudder. "What has the world come to?"

"And you say his mother's on a business trip?" Bläise questioned.

"Yeah, they're pretty well off. She owns her own business. She's a feature film set designer."

"Have mercy!" Sylvah moaned. "Now, this woman didn't serve any jail time or anything?"

"I guess not. It was self-defense," Kenya stated and shrugged.

"Hmm, maybe if I had killed my husband, I'd own my own business too." Sylvah interjected as she looked at Bläise.

"Not if I had killed you first and collected handsomely on the life insurance," Bläise retorted.

"You two be nice," Kenya ordered.

"You know that we're kidding," Sylvah said as she elbowed Bläise in the ribs.

"I don't know about you, but..." Bläise began to joke.

"Anyway," Kenya said. She glanced at her watch. "We should be able to see Zaire in a little bit. They're probably moving him out of recovery now."

"That's right. I'm glad that I still have a son to see." Bläise took a long deep breath. "It's a shame that it took me this long to get down here and see him, even though we're still not in Tennessee. You know what I mean."

"Yes, we do, Dad."

"I hope those ladies hurry up and come with my caramel café latte and sesame bagel. I'm starving," Sylvah declared. She stood and stretched her arms and legs. Her joints were beginning to feel tight. "I'm going to make a run to the bathroom."

"Me too." Bläise got up to follow.

The walk down the corridor seemed to last a lifetime. The hospital was very modern. The halls were decorated with wallpaper and the door frame of each room was painted sky blue. The passageway was well lit and the nurses who walked by all wore plastered smiles. It was unlike any hospital they had ever visited in New York. It was much nicer. Nevertheless, while passing the rooms they heard the beeping of machines pumping fluids and monitoring patients, which brought them back to reality; this place was for the sick and dying.

Sylvah exited the ladies room and Bläise was standing at the entrance patiently waiting.

"Are you okay?" Sylvah asked as they headed back to the waiting room.

"I'm as good as can be expected. And you?"

"The same," Sylvah responded.

A long moment of silence lingered between them. Sylvah's arms were folded across her chest and Bläise had his hands buried in his pockets.

"So, you're dating white men now?" Bläise blurted.

Sylvah was stunned and stopped in her tracks. She was thrown by his question. Bläise walked a few paces ahead before stopping to turn around.

"What?" Sylvah asked.

"You heard me."

"I beg your pardon?"

"Sylvah, come on. I saw you at the airport. The man who dropped you off in the Lexus. He certainly wasn't a taxi driver or your chauffeur and if he were then you really got awfully friendly. I'm sure a tip would've sufficed."

"Who I date is none of your business," Sylvah said. "You don't see me asking you about your love life."

"If you're dating a white man, it is my business."

Sylvah couldn't believe her ears. Even after their separation Bläise was still trying to run her life. She was tempted to ask him if there was any truth to him living with a younger woman. The idea was quickly dismissed as soon as she realized she would be stooping to his level.

"Bläise, do you hear yourself? You are telling me that I can't date whomever I choose."

"I'm not saying that. I'm saying that you cannot date a white man."

"Give me a break. We are not married anymore, remember? And I can't see what difference it makes who I date as long as he treats me with love, honesty, and respect."

"We have two very impressionable children. How do you think it will look if you're dating a white man?"

"Two impressionable children? You've got to be kidding. They are grown. Zaire will be twenty next month and Kenya is eighteen. You act as if they're still playing in a sandbox or in elementary school. Get a grip!"

"All I'm saying, is that we have to set examples for them. If Kenya sees you dating this white man then she'll think this kind of behavior is okay. The same thing goes for Zaire. We don't want to play *Guess Who's Coming to Dinner*," Bläise said and shifted closer to Sylvah.

"What era are you living in?"

"Seriously, Sylvah!"

"No, I'm serious. My children—our children—can date whomever they choose. I will never, ever tell them differently. I don't give a damn about race, religion, color, class, or creed. If they feel good about the person of their choice and are being treated right then it's none of my business."

"You're sound like an Equal Opportunity Employer advertisement." Bläise grunted. "I disagree, and there was a time we would have been on the same page. You've changed." Bläise shook his head in mock disgust.

"I don't recall us ever being racist nor did we raise our children to be that way. Now this conversation is over, and I'm going back. We have more important things to be concerned about, like the condition of our son." Sylvah sprinted past, leaving Bläise behind.

♀♂

Sylvah and Bläise returned to the waiting room separately. She stopped at the nurses' station to see if there were any updates. Bläise lagged behind. When she returned they sat opposite each other. Kenya noticed the sudden change and moved to sit next to her mother.

"Ma, what happened?"

"What are you talking about?" Sylvah asked. She was attempting to pretend as if nothing was wrong between Bläise and her; however, she was failing miserably.

"Ma, stop acting silly. I know something happened with you and Daddy. He's over there in the corner all huffed up and you're sitting way over here in this corner alone. Why can't you both just get along?"

"Kenya, we're fine. We simply have a difference of opinion. That's all."

"Well, you both need to settle your differences and make nice. This is not the time or place for ill behavior."

"Since when did you become the parent and me the child?" Sylvah looked at her daughter and smiled.

"Since you two want to be silly. Now I'm going over there to tell Dad the same thing."

"No need. I promise to be good," Sylvah said.

They hugged briefly. The door to the waiting room opened capturing everyone's attention. It was Lavender, Mojíta and Christina, returning with bags of breakfast treats and trays of coffee.

"Did they say anything yet?" Lavender asked, taking a seat beside Kenya.

"No, I just came back from the nurses station and they said the doctor is with Zaire now. We'll know soon." Sylvah replied.

Before Sylvah finished her statement, the doctor taking care of Zaire entered. He walked over to Sylvah and sat in the vacant chair beside her. Bläise rushed over.

Sylvah, Bläise, Kenya, Mojíta, and Lavender all huddled to hear the prognosis. They couldn't discern the look on the doctor's face, so all were curious. All prayed for good results.

"Mr. and Mrs. Lawrence, I just left Zaire. He's conscious now, but he's in a lot of pain, as can be expected. He'll be in and out for a while. We just administered some morphine. It will cause some drowsiness and will alleviate most of the pain."

"Can we see him now?" Sylvah asked.

"Yes, you can. Not too many at a time, though."

"Ma, can I go first?" Kenya asked. "That way you and Dad can take as long as you want afterward."

Sylvah turned to Bläise and he nodded his consent. Lavender and Mojíta followed. The doctor remained to tell Sylvah and Bläise the entire prognosis and the care that would be necessary to nurture Zaire back to health. When the doctor left, Sylvah and Bläise returned to their coffee and bagels. Bläise sat in the vacant seat adjacent to Sylvah. Neither uttered a word.

Ten minutes later Kenya and crew returned.

"How is he?" Sylvah exclaimed.

"He's okay. A little groggy though. He has a bruise around his eye, a couple of scratches, an I.V. machine and some other monitor hooked up to him to check his vitals," Kenya said.

"I'm going in to see him," Bläise announced.

"Well, he's asking for both of you, so go together," Kenya slyly suggested. "Anyway, you better hurry before he falls asleep."

♀♂

Sylvah and Bläise entered the room together. They heard the doctor's description of Zaire and even Kenya's depiction, still they weren't prepared for what they saw. Zaire was hooked up to three machines and there was a respirator on standby, which frightened Sylvah. Zaire was pumped up with morphine to help the pain. He had bandages above his forehead, a black eye, his lips were swollen and the other eye was swollen shut. Tubes and cords were coming from several parts of his body. The sight of him made Sylvah want to cry. Bläise saw the look on her face, held her hand, and gave it a slight squeeze.

"Hey, son. How's my man doing?" Bläise asked.

"Hi, baby," Sylvah said, holding back the waterworks. She kissed him on the only available spot on his forehead.

"I'm okay," Zaire slurred.

"You had us so worried," Sylvah said.

"You did give us quite a scare," Bläise admitted. "Man, next time pull your butt over," he joked.

"I will," Zaire said. He attempted to smile. Instead pain creased his face.

"You remember everything that happened to you?" Sylvah questioned.

"Yeah. The car spun out of control. The next thing I knew, I was laying beside a tree and then I woke up in the hospital."

"You broke your ribs, they removed your spleen, and you have a few cuts and bruises. Other than that you'll live," Bläise added.

"Thank God for that," Sylvah said, placing her arm around Bläise's waist.

"So when did you arrive?" Zaire asked.

"We came at…what time was it, Bläise?"

"A few minutes after seven. Your mother and I flew out together."

Zaire forced a smile across his weary face. Sylvah and Bläise were oblivious to the true reason for the grin. They were just happy to see their son smiling.

"You can probably book a suite at the Ritz Carlton or Embassy Suites. I hear those are nice places," Zaire hinted. His voice started trailing off as sleep crept up on him.

"We'll look into it later," Bläise responded.

"I'm just glad to see you together again," Zaire said before drifting off.

21

The Lion's Den

After speaking with Gene, Felice made arrangements to be on the next available flight out of LaGuardia airport. She was unrelenting in her quest to obtain more information. However, Gene was tight-lipped and failed to provide her with anything further. The city, state, and name of the hospital happened to be more than enough to put Felice on the right track. She was finally getting somewhere.

The penalty for purchasing a ticket without seven-day advance notice was equivalent to extortion. However, Felice wasn't in a position to complain. She just needed to get to the other side of the country as quickly as possible. Felice was armed with one small pulley and her handbag. If there was a need to get anything else, it could be bought. California was a different state, not a different country. The same luxuries afforded a New Yorker were available to Californians, with the exception of the food and culture.

Felice gave Henry, her friend at the airport a call to see if he could pull any additional strings for her. Unfortunately, it was his night off and he didn't know anyone at the terminal from which Felice was departing. It looked like coach would be the way to go this time around. Felice prayed the seat beside her was empty. Tonight was not a good time to instigate a conversation. There were too many things to sort through.

Nina was two years old now. Felice fooled around with the notion for a while. In November she would turn three. Her child was about to be three. Felice wondered if she had a right to refer to Nina as her child. In a court of law, if Bedford wanted to pursue the issue, Felice would lose all rights to her daughter on the grounds of abandonment. No woman of sound mind would just up and leave their child. It had been almost three years with no contact and no attempt at reuniting. Bedford even tried to extend himself to her. Felice was sure he expected a much better reception from her. After all, they did have a child together and a business. Felice chose to ignore both.

Five hours provided plenty of time for reflection. Felice pieced all of the dreams together for analysis. The delusions were mocking her, the baby, Aunt Leslie, the molestation, and of late her mother. Bizarre dreams had been occurring to Felice since her childhood. Sometimes they made sense and other times they didn't. Of course this was natural. Not all dreams were meant to have definition, but the segment with the baby was very disturbing. The woman in the white lab coat appeared nice in the beginning and suddenly she forcefully tried to hand Felice the baby. When Felice declines the woman became almost violent and began yelling obscenities at her. Perhaps the lab coat was significant of the hospital and Nina. Maybe it was more of a vision than a nightmare. It was possible. Felice wanted answers and hoped for closure.

♀♂

Felice disembarked the plane and headed straight to the rental area to get a car. Los Angeles was not the type of place to take taxis and ride mass transit. Public transportation was not a good option. Felice had traveled to L.A. enough to be aware of this fact. Since she didn't have a reservation, most of the places were out of cars for the weekend. However, Felice lucked up on her very last try and was able to secure a compact car. It wasn't exactly her pick of the litter. Still, the important thing was that she would be mobile and needn't depend on others.

Felice felt like Daniel walking into the lion's den. Bedford, Isis, Samantha, and her conscience were all going to eat her alive. Fear of facing her past and future startled her.

Anxiety gripped Felice causing her to lose the way several times. She made more wrong turns than a New York taxi driver. If only she had invested the extra cash for the GPS tracking system the salesperson recommended. Instead she opted for a map and it had more red circles and arrows than a treasure hunt. It made the drive all the more confusing.

The Children's Hospital of Los Angeles was vast. It almost resembled a luxury resort with all the luxuries. The interior was colorful and the doctors and nurses weren't nearly as serious-looking as their counterparts in New York. Everything was laid-back, almost inviting. The environment removed some of the edge off Felice's visit.

Though the reception area clearly supported a team of five or six people, only one person manned it at this excruciating hour. The woman behind the reception desk appeared to be between twenty-five and thirty, with extra-long, sunset-blond hair and matching eyebrows. She seemed fairly tall due to the length of her upper body, and had capped teeth and lips that had definitely seen the likes of collagen injections. Felice didn't have the faintest idea where to locate Nina, what was the nature of her sickness or, how long she had been there.

Sunset blonde was ensconced with the computer. She laughed as she tapped the keys. Felice walked up and surprised her, but not before catching the woman in some sort of online chat session that obviously had nothing to do with work.

"Good morning," Felice announced.

"Good morning to you too," the woman replied.

"I'm here to see Nina Jackson."

"Nina Jackson. Please wait one moment while I look up the name."

Felice waited and looked down the long hallway, which had large bright colorful arrows pointing to several different units.

"Okay, Miss Nina Jackson is in the other building, the Children's Center for Cancer and Blood Diseases, but you can't see her now. Visiting hours are between 8:00 A.M and 8:00 P.M. If you come back in a couple of hours, we can issue you a visitor's pass."

Felice was in a stupor and didn't hear a word beyond Children's Center for Cancer and Blood Diseases.

22

Inconsiderate, Selfish and Crazy Bitch

God wasn't making this easy for Felice. Did the receptionist actually say Nina was in some kind of center for cancer and blood diseases? Felice thought she heard incorrectly, and requested the woman repeat herself. She did, confirming Felice's worse nightmare yet. Felice felt as if she was being penalized for her past transgressions. She had come this far only to receive even more startling news. None of her questions had been answered because the receptionist wasn't at liberty to release information. She was Nina's mother for goodness' sake! Yet she was in the dark about everything having to do with Nina. For thirty-four years of her life, Felice had been a good person. Felice always did for others, gave to others, appeased others, listened and forgave others. Thirty-four years! Certainly that had to count for something. Felice was all alone with no one to share her plight. There was no one to run to.

After leaving the hospital Felice drove around for a while. Emotions battled within, causing her to pull over to the side of the road. Felice bawled. She cried until every bone in her body ached. There were only two times Felice allowed grieving of such magnitude; the passing of her great-aunt Leslie, and when she made the ultimate decision to divorce Bedford. She wanted to feel pain and deserved everything happening to her, but her two-year-old daughter didn't. Nina was only a baby. Was this what the Bible meant by "The children shall pay for their parents' sins?" If so, then it wasn't fair. These rules should not apply to her family. Felice wanted to repent for every sin she had ever committed. This burden was hers to carry.

Felice had been on the side of the road crying for more than an hour when a highway patrolman gave a disturbing knock. Felice gazed out the window and saw his motorcycle pulled up beside her. A flashlight was aimed inside the car. The sirens on the moped glowed from red to white to blue. The lights were blinding as Felice tried to peek at the male officer. What could he possibly want? She didn't commit any crime and her rental car wasn't stolen. Felice took her time opening the window.

"Yes," Felice said wearily. Her face was red and her eyes were puffy.

"Is everything all right here?" The officer asked.

"I'm fine," Felice hoped her quick answers would send the officer away.

"Well, ma'am, if your vehicle isn't disabled you need to get moving."

"I was just resting," Felice responded.

"This is not a rest stop. It is extremely hazardous to pull over on the side of the road. There's a rest stop about a half a mile down the highway. I'm going to have to ask you to please proceed."

Heartless, white son of a bitch, Felice wanted to scream. Any fool could see she had been crying. Felice didn't know why she expected any sympathy.

"Thank you," Felice said, starting the engine of the car.

"No problem. California Highway Patrol at your service." He waited for Felice to pull off and then followed her. By the next exit he was gone.

Felice didn't bother stopping at the rest area. She saw a Starbucks from the highway and got off at the exit. Her stomach was at war with her. The last time she ate was the day before at Blimpie's and that wasn't quite the most nutritious meal. The smell of the coffee brought life back into Felice's eyes.

"Hi. Can I have a Grande Caramel Macchiato and a cinnamon bagel with lite cream cheese?"

"Sure," the cashier replied. "Grande Caramel Macchiato, cinnamon with lite cream cheese," she yelled to the person preparing the orders. Since it was six in the morning on a Saturday, only Felice and two other people patronized the store.

Felice provided the cashier with a five-dollar bill.

"I'm sorry, it's $6.60 with tax," she corrected Felice.

Felice looked at the menu to check the prices. She couldn't imagine what she had ordered that would total $6.60. Grande Caramel Macchiato was $3.50 and her bagel was $2.65, plus tax. *Highway robbery,* Felice thought as she searched her change purse to provide the cashier with the difference. She had planned on sitting in the store to drink the coffee and eat, but was so upset over the cost of the food she decided to eat in the car.

An hour passed before Felice returned to the road. The highway began filling with Saturday morning workers, errand runners, people going to the gym and other places. Relieved to see a hotel on the opposite side of the freeway, Felice immediately got off at the next exit and decided to check in. It was the first hotel she had seen since leaving the Children's Hospital. Felice had a gold Marriott rewards card, which entitled her to a rapid check-in.

The receptionist at the hospital said visiting hours were from eight to eight. It didn't make sense to appear wild and disheveled, which was exactly how she looked. Felice didn't have much to unpack. She took a quick shower, put on a change of clothes, raked her hair with a comb and viewed herself quickly in the mirror before leaving.

The Marriott hotel was only three exits away from the hospital. Directions were necessary, so Felice returned to the main building. The same familiar face greeted Felice at the reception desk. After hearing, "take the elevator to the second floor, turn left, then continue to the end of the hall, make a right, go through the double doors, continue until you get to the gold unit, etc, etc," Felice decided to ask for a map or written directions. The day had been trying enough already without adding getting lost to the list.

After a ten-minute walk Felice arrived in front of Room 406. Voices could be heard on the opposite side of the door. The fear that engulfed Felice during the first visit seized her once again. This was for real. Her daughter was behind this particular door. There was no doubt as to whom the voices belonged. Reservations of entering the room were overwhelming. Tears began to well in her eyes again. Hands cloaked her face as she worked on controlling her breathing. Felice thought she'd be ready when this moment finally came, but she wasn't. The idea of visiting the chapel for prayer before going in buzzed in her brain. She needed to be forgiven by God, although church felt very foreign to Felice. She hadn't been in years. There were tons of Catholic cathedrals in Cuba, but she wasn't Catholic. Besides that, the priests spoke rapid Spanish and the churches weren't well attended.

Weakness rattled Felice and rendered her motionless. All she managed to do was crouch against the wall alongside the room. *Breathe, breathe, breathe. Take deep breaths,* Felice ordered herself. *Our Father, which art in heaven, hallowed be Thy name.* Felice tried to recall the rest of the prayer but wasn't successful. She opted to say something from the heart.

"Lord, please hear my cry. I know I've done a few wrongs things in my life, but I need you right now. I'm asking for your forgiveness. Of all the wrong I've done, I managed to accomplish one right. There's a little girl behind this door, my daughter Nina and she needs your help. I know people make empty promises every second, minute, hour, day, week, month and year, but God please believe me. If you answer my prayer, I will change my ways. I will do my best to live my life…"

The door to 406 opened and a breeze caused Felice to glance upward. Thoughts of her prayer remained suspended. Weary eyes resembling Felice's stared back. They quickly filled with shock and curiosity. Within seconds the look changed to anger, disgust, and disappointment. Steel-cold eyes gazed upon Felice, piercing a hole in her heart. A place that could bear no more misery.

Felice remembered applying the same expression to her mother nearly two decades before. It was a very bitter stare and it took years to rebuild their relationship. A relationship that had been rock solid from Felice's childhood until the revelation of her mother's sins. The discovery of her mother's alternate life was upsetting to Felice. Reflecting, Felice didn't know if she was hurt from her mother's betrayal or from sheer disgust of the notion that her mom was a lesbian. When Felice arrived home to find her mother with another woman, it had been very uncomfortable. How could her mother do something like this? Prior to that, Samantha had been the perfect mother. Afterward, it felt like everything her mother ever preached was a lie. Felice began analyzing every conversation she could remember having with her mom concerning boys. The whole, "boys only want one thing," and "learn to be an independent woman," etc., etc. Of course her mother would feel that way. Samantha didn't like men.

The day Felice observed her mother with Geneen, aka Gene, was the day their relationship collapsed. Samantha and Geneen weren't having a sexual encounter, though that would have been even more disturbing. Geneen and Samantha had been friends for years. Felice never saw anything out of the ordinary about their relationship. As far as she knew, Geneen and her mom were simply close. Geneen was her mom's shopping, gossip, travel, and hang-out partner. There wasn't a reason to suspect or believe that more existed. The revelation occurred during Felice's freshman year in college, when a few friends rented a car and drove to New York. Felice thought it would be nice to surprise her mother and tagged along. After all, the only time she visited home was during the holidays and the next one wasn't scheduled for another month, during spring break.

Felice entered their large Victorian home at approximately midnight. She was exhausted and figured her mother had to be sound asleep. Felice was tempted to head into the living room and fall asleep on the sofa where she and her mother often shared laughs, watched movies, cried on each other's shoulder and openly discussed anything that best friends talked about, but then she heard giggling from the floor above. Samantha usually went to bed early, so Felice was happy to know her mother was still awake, but with whom was she laughing?

Quietly Felice crossed the expanse of the living room taking caution not to knock anything over in the dark. She headed up the L-shaped stairwell. The wooden steps began to creak. Felice decided to tiptoe. Then it dawned on Felice that Samantha could be on a date. However, when she arrived at the second level, which housed the kitchen and formal dining room the laughter was coming from two women. Felice continued trekking to the third level where the bedrooms were located. Light shone from two rooms, Samantha's and the bathroom. Felice placed her bags in her bedroom and proceeded down the hall to her mother's room. She had to pass the bathroom first and the door was partially cracked. The shrill of laughter was resonating from the bathroom.

Felice stood in the doorway and what could only have been a moment felt like an era. Indeed, this had to be a bad dream or else she was having optical illusions. It was late and Felice was very tired. Then Geneen did something that remained etched in Felice's memory for years. It wasn't until Felice began seeing a therapist that she was able to eradicate those very unsettling visions. Felice witnessed as Geneen slowly dried her mother's body with a towel. Her approach was extremely sensual and appeared out of place. Sure they were best friends, but her mother was more than capable of drying off without assistance. The way she dried off each toe individually offering a foot massage in between. Slowly she brought the towel up the length of her mother's leg. First one, then the other. Geneen ended the rubdown upon arriving at Samantha's vaginal area. This touch appeared to be rehearsed and very stimulating. It wasn't until Geneen started suckling her mother's nipple that everything began to register in Felice's head. This was the most repulsive thing Felice had ever seen. The shock stunned Felice to shriek with enough volume to make unsettled spirits rise.

Alarmed, Geneen and Samantha rushed out of the bathroom. Neither expected Felice or anyone else to be in the house. Felice ran to her room before either could get to her, and she didn't emerge until the following day. That entire night her mother sat on the hardwood floor in front of her room, begging Felice to open the door and talk. Tears rained down Felice's face, but her heart wept from sadness and a feeling of betrayal. How could her mother do this to her? How long had she been this way? When was she going to tell Felice about her sexuality? Was this the real reason her mother and father weren't together? Did Felice's father know? Felice was full of questions. It took an undeterminable amount of strength for Felice not to open the door while her mother sobbed on the opposite side.

The following day, Felice decided not to stay the weekend. She also decided not to return home during the summer break and packed as much clothing as possible. It wasn't until her mother left to run errands that Felice attempted to exit. However, on the way to the train station with several bags in tow, she crossed paths with her mother. The scowl blazed across Felice's face articulated the words she couldn't say aloud. It was a mixture of shock, disgust, disappointment, sadness, and anger. Everything was left as is and Felice never allowed her mother the opportunity to speak her mind. Bad feelings were harbored for years.

When she returned to school, Felice quickly applied for a part-time job, found roommates and got an apartment off-campus to prevent from having to return home for future breaks and holidays. Felice began to seriously question her own sexuality, especially since she was the only person in her circle of friends who was still a virgin. Felice was in the second semester of her sophomore year when she finally allowed Bedford to dip into her treasure. By their senior year they were living together and shortly after graduation they were married.

Felice lost all respect for the woman she once compared to Mary, the mother of Jesus, a woman who could do no wrong. Prior to Felice gaining knowledge of her mother's sexuality, in her eyes Samantha was the epitome of a smart, successful, beautiful black woman who was single by choice.

Felice was raised with an open mind, but she wasn't ready to accept the harsh reality that her mother was a lesbian. Based on the teachings and stereotypes of society, being gay was unacceptable. It was the reason AIDS was prevalent today. Gay people were spreading the disease. Gay people were not to be trusted and were dirty. Gay people were promiscuous. God didn't love gay people. Did this now mean her mother was all of these things and should be punished? Though Felice knew today these theories were for the ignorant, it was how she was conditioned to feel then. She still didn't agree with the lifestyle her mother chose, but learned to love her in spite of it.

♀♂

"What are you doing here?" her mother asked. It took great effort to make Samantha react this way, but her tongue had the ability to splice people in chunks if provoked. Felice's mother was usually very jovial. She had a great sense of humor, wonderful personality, a positive outlook and was someone everyone could count on. The years following the dreadful incident, Samantha's behavior toward Felice remained loving and she expressed her apologies over and over. Still, Felice didn't talk to her mother for several years.

Felice expected to be greeted by bitterness; still she wasn't prepared. The pain etched in her mother's face was wounding. Felice had no excuse to offer for her erratic behavior or disappearance. It wasn't as if she was a child when she decided to pack up and run away leaving her baby behind. Felice was a grown woman who happened to have a very successful career and had several options available to her. She knew the thoughts sweeping her mother's head: "how could you abandon your own child?"

Felice's sad response was, "I don't know."

Felice stood straight and wiped her eyes. The last thing she wanted was a confrontation with her mother. Felice needed to see her daughter and hoped Bedford, her mother, or Isis wouldn't stand in the way.

"I'm here to visit Nina," Felice said calmly.

Samantha was livid as she pulled Felice a few feet away from the entrance so they wouldn't have a shouting match in front of Nina's room.

"After all this time? Felice, I'm very disappointed. We are all very disappointed. You left Bedford alone and your beautiful daughter motherless. You kept secrets…"

"Mom, you of all people should know about keeping secrets." Felice took the defensive approach even though she was in the wrong. The word *motherless* penetrated her body like a bullet in the flesh. The pleading look in her mother's eyes made it worse.

"Felice, this is not about me, okay? This is about you and your responsibilities. Besides, I had my reasons."

"I had mine as well, but right now I really need to see my child," Felice said, attempting to brush pass her mother.

Sadly Samantha sighed and shook her head in amazement. It didn't seem like Felice understood the magnitude of the situation, but she was about to school her. Samantha grabbed Felice's arm firmly, preventing her from taking another step. Felice didn't put up a fight and remained positioned.

"Do you believe you can simply waltz in here making demands?"

"I didn't make any demands. All I said was I want to see my daughter," Felice said softly. She couldn't recall ever seeing her mother this upset. A fire blazed behind honey-brown eyes, her lips curled placing emphasis on every word, and she had a solid grip on Felice's arm.

"The thing bothering me most is that you had the nerve to walk away from that little girl in there." Samantha released Felice's arm as she pointed to the door. "In the process you robbed me the opportunity of becoming a grandmother."

"Mom, I'm sorry." Felice began weeping again. "I'm not a terrible person. I don't know why I did it. I wasn't thinking straight."

"Felice, is that the best you can do? I don't know what came over you when you decided to just up and walk out of the hospital without giving anyone notice, leaving your newborn baby behind. Bedford went home to find a fucking letter, which didn't explain a damn thing, and he kept everything under wraps trying to protect you. He said he was embarrassed and confused and hoped you'd return. One year turns into two. Two years of no contact." Samantha lodged her hands on her hips as she spoke. "Only someone inconsiderate, selfish, careless, and crazy would behave this way. If you didn't want the baby, then you should have told somebody. My God, Bedford arrived at the hospital and you were gone. The hospital personnel reported you missing. Can you imagine how something like that must have felt?"

"Mom, please hear me out."

"You know what, nothing you can say will ever—and I mean ever—justify your actions. I'm hurt, Felice. I'm hurt for more reasons than one and can't bear to hear any of your sorry excuses. It pains me to talk to you in this manner and to say these next couple of words, but I'm gonna say them. I know I taught you better and right now, I'm ashamed to call you my daughter," Samantha said as she walked away in the opposite direction. Felice watched in tears, unable to say anything as her mother vanished down the hall.

23

Arrest Her Ass For Abandonment

Everything Samantha said rang true. Felice couldn't expect sympathy from anyone. Even her best friend had warned her before the execution of the grand scheme. Sylvah told Felice exactly how thoughtless she was being. She reminded Felice of the repercussions and even refused to deal with her for a stretch of time. It wasn't until Sylvah flew to Cuba demanding Felice return and accept her responsibilities, that their friendship resumed to normal. If only Felice had listened. She could chalk her actions up to post-partum depression. A lot of women suffered from it. Unfortunately, Felice's actions were premeditated. Her wheels had been in motion months before the baby was due.

Procrastination is such an easy trap for the human species. Samantha was long gone. All Felice had to do was open the door and walk in. If she was insane enough to walk out of her daughter's life, then she could be just as crazy and walk back in.

The door opened with little ease. Isis's chair faced the door and Bedford sat on the opposite side. There was an empty chair next to Bedford's. Neither turned their attention to Felice when she entered the room, but they were aware of another presence. More than likely they thought it was Samantha returning. Felice stood for a second, marveling over the doll-like child lying in the bed asleep as Bedford caressed her little hands. Nina was beautiful. Her plaited hair was thick and shiny like Felice's. She had pursed little pink lips and her lashes were long and curly. Monitors and machines were lined up against the wall. There were too many to count. Another wave of tears filled her eyes as Felice watched her daughter's chest heave deeply as if it were a struggle for her to breathe. Isis finally looked in Felice's direction.

"Samantha, I was wondering…Felice?" Isis said, shocked.

Bedford quickly spun around. Felice shook her head, but couldn't say a word. She wanted to grab her daughter and hold her for dear life. Felice wanted to go back in time and erase her wrongdoings. It probably wouldn't relieve her daughter of the illness, but at least she would have been there every step of the way. Now she was an outsider seeking forgiveness. She couldn't blame either of them if they asked her to leave.

Bedford didn't respond immediately. Instead he stared at Felice as if she were a ghost. His dark, brooding eyes were bloodshot, and he looked fatigued. Without a word, Isis stood and was about to walk over to Felice. Bedford quickly got out of his chair and intercepted. He detained Isis and pleaded for her to step outside for a moment.

"You should make that sorry bitch step outside," Isis spat.

"Isis, please, not here, not now."

"Bedford, it's your call, but I'm saying this one thing. They should arrest her ass for abandonment, because she ain't shit!"

Isis reluctantly left the room. Bedford returned to his seat and pointed for Felice to sit in the chair beside him.

"I didn't mean to cause a commotion," Felice said, realizing she had to tread lightly.

Bedford returned to caressing Nina's hand and remained silent. He reached for a cloth on the night table and wiped the sweat from her forehead.

Felice sat quietly not knowing what to say to Bedford. His subdued demeanor frightened her. Maybe it was best they didn't talk immediately. Felice now knew how both her mother and Isis felt, but Bedford's silence was troubling. She sat quietly and watched her daughter's labored breathing. This was where she needed to be. A sudden calm drifted through Felice and she couldn't resist the urge to touch this peaceful-looking child.

"Don't you touch her!" Bedford scowled and blocked Felice's hand. Felice became startled. "I wasn't going to hurt her."

"You've already done that."

Words could not reveal the way Felice's heart felt and she could blame no one except herself. Bedford had reached out to Felice on numerous occasions and she failed to take action. Sorry sounded lame, and forgiveness had to be earned. Felice didn't know which way to turn, but she was willing to walk on a ledge if she had to prove her worth.

"Bedford, I didn't mean to cause so much hurt. You know that I'm not a heartless person. That's why I'm here now. I promise you, I won't walk away ever again."

"You can walk your way to hell, because your promises mean nothing to me right now. My only concern is this little girl right here."

"Bedford, you can't mean that! I want another chance. Please give me the chance to be her mother," Felice pleaded as a rivulet of tears streamed down her face.

"I tried, Felice. I tried." Bedford stood and took measured steps toward the window across the room. He sighed slow and deep. It was evident his heart was tortured.

Felice yearned to touch and hold the softness of her baby, reassuring Nina of her mommy's love. While Bedford peered out the window, Felice stroked Nina's hand and her eyes fluttered but remained closed.

"Bedford, I realize my words mean little right now, and I can't blame you for feeling the way you do toward me. I expect you to be bitter, hate me, and lash out, but I'm begging you not to throw me out of your lives. I was such a fool and I'm a disappointment to myself."

"Felice, I can't hate you. You are the mother of my daughter." Bedford paused and turned to look at Felice. "We will always share this special bond, but you've let us down in a big way. I need to know why. Why you would leave your child in a facility with no plans of returning?"

"My mother summed it up best: I was selfish, Bedford. I was going through a lot of things and my life, as it was then, began to overwhelm me. When I first learned I was pregnant, my world began spinning faster and faster. I was losing control. Then I realized it wasn't Aaron's, the man I was engaged to marry. I was afraid to tell you and when I did, you treated me like shit."

"No, we resolved those issues. We moved past all of that stuff."

"Bedford, you moved forward and I remained stagnant. I functioned as necessary. I remained torn because you really never wanted the baby. It was a mistake and you even told me so."

"That's not true."

"Today, I know it wasn't a mistake, but it was difficult getting through the entire ordeal. The only reason you recanted was because Sandy left you. Otherwise, this little darling wouldn't have made it into this world. Some people are wise enough not to let obstacles obstruct them and others aren't. I classify myself as others. I defeated myself. I didn't know how to deal with my stumbling block. I saw it coming and couldn't go around it, so instead I tripped and fell in a bad way. I decided to run away from all of my problems, including you."

"You knew I loved you."

Nina coughed and her eyes popped open. Felice smiled while continuing to gently stroke her hand.

"Daddy," she whined.

"I'm right here, sunshine. Daddy is right here." Bedford returned to his seated position and Felice removed her hand.

"Good morning, Nina. How is my little sunshine today?" Bedford got up and kissed Nina on the forehead.

"Okay. Who's that?" Nina's little voice asked. Her words were very clear for a two-year old, but her voice was faint. Felice's heart ached to see her little girl in a place like this. Today marked her first official meeting with Nina, and they were in a hospital. Ironically, the hospital was the place she had left Nina two years ago. Hopefully this time around they would all go home together.

"Her name is Felice," Bedford answered.

I'm your mommy, Felice cried to herself. She knew Bedford had his reasons for not introducing her as such. Nevertheless, his casual introduction cheapened her existence in the room.

Samantha and Isis returned with cups of coffee and a small orange juice in a plastic cup with the peel-off silver lid.

Bedford turned his attention to Samantha and Isis. "Nina just woke up and she's looking a lot better today than yesterday."

"Yes, she is," Samantha answered, walking in Felice's direction to claim her chair. Felice got up.

Isis didn't respond, but she went over to the bed and kissed Nina on the cheek.

They circled Nina, creating a barrier, ignoring Felice's presence. Felice felt left out.

Bedford moved toward Felice and held her hand as he led her to the door.

"I think it's best if you left now. I still have lots of mixed feelings, and this is not the time or place to go into a discussion. Aside from that, I really want to discuss your sudden appearance over with my sister and your mother."

"I understand," Felice said, resigned to her fate. She was grateful enough that Bedford allowed her to stay this long. Felice knew time would heal the differences between Bedford and she, and even her mother. Isis was another story. She would be the challenge. If Bedford weren't present earlier, Isis would have attacked Felice. Isis had been known for holding grudges for extended periods. When Felice was married to Bedford, she made sure to never get on Isis' bad side. At this point, Purgatory would have been a better option and if Bedford sought Isis's opinion, Felice might as well pack her bags and leave.

"I'm not sure if bringing you into Nina's life right now is the right thing with all that's going on, but be patient."

"Can I ask you a question?" Felice asked while Bedford held the door open for her.

"Sure."

"What exactly is wrong with our baby?"

"She has a form of cancer called acute lymphoblastic leukemia."

Felice knew all about leukemia. Several of her family members had died from it. It was a trait in the family genes. Now she really felt responsible. Of all the people in her family to escape this disease, why did her child have to get it? Nina was a baby. It wasn't fair for her to suffer. Felice took a final look at Nina. She didn't want to leave. How could she walk out of her life again? But she knew Bedford was right. If she stayed, there was bound to be some mean words exchanged, and her daughter's recuperation was more important than anything else. Felice sincerely loved her child.

"Will she live?" Felice asked as she stepped over the threshold.

"We hope so," Bedford solemnly replied.

24

The Cosby's

Sylvah and Bläise took Zaire's advice and checked in a two-bed-room suite near the hospital. They thought it easier to share the space and receive updates together, as opposed to hearing the news separately and relaying it back and forth. It was also much more economical.

Sylvah invited Kenya to stay in her room and she agreed. Kenya was ecstatic to have her parents in the same space again. This was the first time they had been together since she left for college.

Each day they visited Zaire and his progress was good. He was soon moved out of ICU. The doctors reported they no longer had a reason to keep him under close watch. Zaire's friend, who had only sustained broken legs, had been released already. Sylvah was happy to see Zaire coming along so well, though she was concerned with the fact that Zaire had to lose his spleen in the process. Sylvah became relaxed after the doctors informed her of the spleen's function in the body. While it was a vital organ, Zaire would be able maintain a normal and healthy life.

Monday morning found Sylvah and Bläise driving to Tennessee on Zaire's behalf. Zaire would probably be unable to complete the semester while he recovered and would miss final examinations. Thus far, his grades were reasonable, but if he missed finals he stood the chance of receiving incompletes or perhaps failing, which would result in Zaire losing his scholarship. It was imperative for him to maintain a B plus average throughout his college career. To date, he had been successful. Then, when this semester came around, it was as if he stopped trying. Several of his professors reported he had missing assignments and hadn't shown up for a few classes. This was out of character for Zaire. Professors who had taught him in previous years expressed concern because they saw a difference in his behavior. One professor complained about his newly formed habit of goofing off in her class, and another said, "Zaire appears as if he just doesn't give a damn." Two claims, which neither parent had ever received from any of Zaire's teachers dating back from elementary school to high school. He had always been very studious and involved in several extracurricular activities. Although some of the professors had complaints about Zaire's recent behavior, they were sad to hear about his unfortunate turn of events and extremely sympathetic. Arrangements were made for him to take make-up exams during the summer session. Everyone felt he'd persevere physically and would achieve high grades, allowing him to maintain his average.

Sylvah wasn't completely shocked over the news, especially after the conversation they had. Zaire made a cry for help and neither Sylvah nor Bläise did much to resolve the situation. They couldn't allow his behavior to persist. If they did, things would only continue to get worse. This would be a challenge to Sylvah and Bläise, especially since they couldn't provide Zaire with the solution of his choice—them getting back together.

Since Zaire's health was improving Sylvah felt a little more at ease. She left messages on Felice's answering machine the day after Zaire's accident. Sylvah hadn't heard back from her immediately, which was strange. Felice was always very prompt when returning Sylvah's calls. When they finally did touch base, Sylvah learned about Felice's predicament. Sylvah's heart went out to Felice, but with the exception of the baby's illness, Sylvah saw this coming. It was impractical of Felice to believe that this process was going to be easy. Felice's behavior was disgraceful. Best friend or not, Sylvah was highly disappointed in her. The adage, *you never really know a person,* rang so true it frightened

Sylvah. Prior to this incident, Sylvah would've put all of her assets on the line if someone had told her that Felice planned to one day abandon her child. Today, she wouldn't bet her worn-out tennis shoes. Still, as a friend, Sylvah empathized with Felice. She already lost two years of being a mother, coupled with her baby having cancer and possibly dying, which made the situation more heartrending. Felice was suffering the worse hell imaginable—her conscience.

Sylvah also spoke to Candace and Alana, who both offered to come for support. Sylvah declined. All the family she needed was already present.

Sylvah broached the subject about Zaire's recent change in behavior during dinner with Kenya and Bläise. Sylvah wanted to avoid all confrontation, which was why she chose to discuss it at dinner. Sylvah knew if she tossed the topic out there while they were in the hotel room, voices would raise, tempers would flare, and in the end, nothing would have been accomplished. However, a scene was easily avoided while in a nice restaurant filled with people and a host of other distractions. Bläise would never misbehave in a place like this. Sylvah was simply trying to gauge everyone's feelings regarding Zaire. The accident, his nonchalant attitude in school, the breakup with Lavender, etc.; Sylvah wanted to be sure that she wasn't blowing things out of proportion. She wanted to keep her wits about her, but this was her child.

They dined at Black Pearls, a new upscale soul food restaurant located in Buckhead. The appetizers were tasty but expensive. The main course was delicious and they decided to dig into dessert and coffee.

"So, what did you think about our parent-teacher meetings yesterday?" Sylvah asked. She didn't look directly at Bläise, instead she dipped her spoon into an inviting red velvet cake with cream cheese frosting.

"I think the boy can try harder," Bläise responded.

"That's it?"

"What more do you want me to say? The pressure of school has intensified, and he's simply reacting. Do you ever think about how hard it must be to excel in every subject along with being an athlete? I mean, come on, Sylvah! It was bound to happen sooner or later."

"Are you talking about our son? Because Zaire has never had a problem maintaining grades, extracurricular activities, a job, girlfriends, or anything else for that matter. There's something more going on."

Bläise removed the napkin from his lap and wiped imaginary crumbs from his mouth. "Then do tell, since you're Miss Know It All!"

"I'm not trying to be Miss Know It All, Bläise. I'm simply acknowledging the fact that our son is troubled."

"You are overreacting. This is just a phase. He'll be back to normal. You'll see. He's already starting to cheer up."

"And do you know why?"

Kenya watched the exchange between her parents. It was obvious a storm was brewing. Hopefully, it wouldn't be a tornado leaving more bad feelings in its wake.

"Bläise, wake up. Zaire is pleased to see us together. As long as he feels things are copasetic between us and there's a possibility we'll stay together, he will be happy. Bläise, that's false hope."

"I don't think that's the reason at all," Bläise said, writing off Sylvah's statement as preposterous.

Sylvah was livid. She didn't understand how Bläise could be so blind to the obvious. He was so full of himself, always headstrong and heartwrong. This was part of the reason they couldn't get along and were no longer able to make it as a couple.

"When we were at the hospital today, do you remember the comment Zaire made earlier?"

"He made plenty of comments. We were there for three hours. You want me to record everything the boy said?" Bläise asked incredulously.

"Bläise, let's skip the sarcasm. I'm simply trying to make headway here, and I feel like I'm leaping headfirst into a brick wall." Sylvah turned to Kenya who was sipping on coffee. "Zaire said he loved having his family together like this."

"That's normal," Bläise replied.

"Yes, it is normal under different circumstances, but we're not together like this," Sylvah waved her hands back and forth from her to Bläise. "We are getting a divorce, and our son is insinuating a togetherness that no longer exists. Do you understand? None of this stuff began happening with his grades slipping, and him becoming sensitive to break-ups and such, until we announced our separation was permanent."

Bläise still appeared unconvinced.

"Okay, didn't you see how his face glowed when we mentioned our sharing a suite at the hotel?" Sylvah added.

Bläise shook his head in the negative.

"Now that you mention it, I noticed," Kenya interjected.

"Now you're agreeing with your mother?" Bläise asked mockingly. "I should have known this day was coming."

"No, just making an observation, Daddy. Besides, I speak to Zaire more than either of you. It was *me* that he came to Atlanta to visit."

Bläise raised his eyebrows questioningly. "I thought it was to see that girl, Lavender."

"Maybe it was a little of both, but I'm the main reason he comes to hang out in Atlanta. Before I started going to school here, I'm sure he didn't visit nearly as much."

"True," Sylvah said. "Since, of late, you seem to know him better than either of us, what are your thoughts? Do you think there is any truth to what I'm saying?"

"Don't expect me to crack any codes or anything. Everything that I say is simply my opinion and cannot be held against me in a court of law," Kenya quipped in an attempt to boost the solemn mood at the table. It worked, as Sylvah beckoned a smile and Bläise sat back in a more relaxed position. "Mom, I already told you my feelings on the subject. Zaire and I are both very sad about y'all divorcing. You're our parents and have always been together and been there for us."

"We'll always be there for you," Bläise offered. He affectionately reached to stroke Kenya's back. "Your mother and I getting a divorce will never stop us from loving either of you."

"That's right," Sylvah added and smiled.

"I know this, and I'm sure Zaire does, too, but in all of the years, and all of the friends we've ever had, you two are the only parents who stayed married. You always managed to pull through thick and thin and then the going gets tough and you suddenly decide to throw in the towel.

Mom, Dad, you were our model couple and everyone else's in the neighborhood. We were like the Cosby family, except Dad isn't a doctor. Still, all the other kids were envious of Zaire and me. This abrupt change is hard to swallow. Even for me. I'm dealing with it in my own way, and well...Zaire seems to be taking it harder."

Sylvah was saddened by her daughter's statement and pleased at the same time. For the first time in the past ten minutes Sylvah saw a shift in Bläise's demeanor. When she shared her beliefs, Bläise thought her to be a fool. As soon as their eighteen-year-old daughter revealed her thoughts and emotions, it was a totally different story. Sylvah was just glad they were finally making headway. It really didn't matter what it took to convince Bläise. The important thing was they were now on the same page and could unite to work on a solution.

25

Until Further Notice

The following day found Felice at the hospital bright and early. Determined to prove her loyalty, Felice decided to camp out front if necessary. Strategy: wear them down.

The first day is always the hardest day, Felice thought. The worst is over. However, she prepared herself for more chastisement. Deep down, Felice felt Bedford's heart would eventually cave in her favor. When it came to Felice he was Captain Caveman. Bedford was a complete sucker for her. Felice was usually the hard ass.

Yesterday, after leaving the hospital and returning to the hotel, the first thing Felice did was call Sylvah. There was no one else to turn to. Samantha was upset with her and reasonably so. Candace and Alana were out of the question. They didn't even know she had a baby. It was unthinkable to pull this rabbit out of a non-existent hat. Felice didn't need the when, where and why's. It was all too draining. Jermaine was another option, but Felice didn't know if she was ready to reveal or share this part of her life with him yet, or at all. That was the problem with keeping secrets. Secrets have pores and if they reside in the human vessel, at some point were bound to seep out. Hiding secrets and keeping up with the lies you created to cover them up was a full-time job. Gainfully employed at Jackson and Jackson, Felice didn't need a second full-time job. She was ready to resume her normal life, and this one would include her daughter.

Sylvah was experiencing her own trials. Felice wished she could be there for her girl. It had to be hard seeing your son in ICU. It was equally difficult for Felice to bear witness to her ailing daughter and not knowing her fate. The cancer Nina suffered from was curable. Acute lymphoblastic leukemia actually had the best recovery rate in children, so Felice prayed day and night for the Lord to give Nina another chance. She asked the Lord to provide her with another opportunity at being a mother as well. It was never too late to repent and seek forgiveness when it came to God.

Felice had been practicing her entrance. She wasn't going to stand in the hall again, allowing her mother, Isis or Bedford to find her loitering. If her mother or Isis planned another attack she intended to take her punishment like a big girl. No need to provoke them even further. Felice knew she was wrong. At least now she could admit it. It's sad and unfortunate that it took as long as it did to snap out of her daze.

When Felice entered everyone was once again seated in the same position she had left them in the day before. If it weren't for the change of clothes, Felice would have thought they didn't leave the hospital at all. However, this time Nina was alert and a doctor was performing what appeared to be a routine check-up.

"Daddy, it's Felice," Nina said as she saw Felice enter the room.

All heads turned as Felice debuted and Nina made the introductions. Isis wore a mean scowl while clucking her tongue, her mother nodded politely, and Bedford simply seemed indifferent. Felice didn't know if this was for her benefit or because he actually had a change of heart. As much as Felice wanted to be concerned, her main interest was Nina.

"Good morning, everyone. Good morning, Nina. How are you doing today?" Felice chirped. She smiled wide and bright at Nina.

"I'm fine."

The doctor changed the intravenous bag, said a few reassuring words to Nina and wrapped up his physical. Before leaving he pulled Bedford aside to share the latest prognosis. They were close enough for Felice to eavesdrop freely. However, she chose to wait for Bedford to tell her. Everything in due time, because Felice wanted to do this right. Missteps were not afforded right now.

The doctor left and Bedford returned with a smile stretching across his face. Isis walked over to squeeze his hand and her mother emulated his beam.

"Everything's looking good," Bedford said. The smile remained smeared across his face.

"Thank the Lord," Samantha said with raised arms above her head in praise.

♀♂

The cafeteria smelled more like antiseptic than it did food. A bright mural of children playing in a park was displayed on the far back wall. The signature below read: Trust, Hope, Happiness, Joy & Faith. However, the wall painting failed to bring cheer to anyone seated in the vast space. A few people sat at tables alone. Mourners, well-wishers, out patients, hospital employees and others filled the white starched room. The tepid mood served only to dampen the atmosphere and its guests.

Bedford and Felice were seated at a corner table. Half of a tuna sandwich remained in front of Bedford along with bottled water, while Felice drank Slim-Fast and a small salad. Both were quiet for an extended amount of time. Thoughts of Nina suffering haunted Felice. There were so many things she wanted to do to make up for lost time. Felice felt lower than scum after learning how Bedford had to rush Nina to the hospital time and time again before learning she had leukemia. Nina had suffered from fevers and fatigue. Nina was only an infant and was unable to tell Bedford that she was in pain, but upon her fourth emergency visit to the hospital the pediatrician did a thorough examination. It was then they became aware of Nina's condition. Her blood tests revealed an increase in white blood cells and low platelet counts. Additional tests classified Nina to be at low risk. The first two times Bedford went to the hospital alone. By the third visit, Isis had stepped in to do the job Felice had neglected and had been there ever since.

"Bedford," Felice said attempting to break the code of silence.

"Yes," Bedford answered, appearing preoccupied with his thoughts.

"Did the doctor say something about Nina's condition?"

"Yeah." Bedford stopped short and made no effort to further elaborate. Felice was anxious to learn more and couldn't hide her curiosity.

"Anything you want to share with me?" Her delivery sounded edgy although she tried to remain calm.

"Why do you care all of a sudden?" Bedford asked.

Bedford provided Felice with his full attention. The stone expression frightened her and the deliberate charge in his voice didn't help. For the first time in years, Felice felt intimidated. Felice decided to go with another strategy.

"Bedford, I want you to know how sorry I am about everything."

"Should I feel compassion in my heart for you right now?" Bedford slightly raised his hands in exasperation. "If you're looking for sympathy, I can't help you. You are not the one suffering and your feelings are not my priority."

"Bedford, I'm not seeking pity, sympathy or anything else along those lines. My only wish is to become active in Nina's life. I want a second chance. A chance to become her mother."

"We don't always get what we want, do we?" Bedford tossed back. Anger corroded Bedford's palate. Circumstance made Bedford behave cruelly towards Felice and she was well aware of this fact. Armed with this knowledge, she knew she had to tread lightly.

"No," Felice replied, disappointed.

"Why should I give you another chance? I mean, really. Do you know how many times I tried to find you? To reach out to you? You even went as far as to pretend it wasn't you on the phone once, and hung up on me. Even after that I left you message after message, to no avail. Felice, all I wanted from you was a family, a second chance. Don't you think I know I fucked up our marriage? I'm not a complete fool, but when we decided to have Nina, I thought we put all of the other garbage behind us."

"You'll never understand what I was going through," Felice said as the tears trickled down her face and her tongue began feeling thick and heavy.

"Try me."

"I would have to go back to the very beginning and, well, I started to tell you yesterday, but we were interrupted."

"Right now, I have nothing but time and no one is here to interrupt today," Bedford said, urging her to continue.

Felice sighed. She wasn't fully prepared, but if the future rested on honesty and revealing her inner most secrets, then so be it.

"It wasn't as easy as you think for me to leave the way I did. There were personal issues tormenting me from the past, making it difficult for me to keep my sanity. You were aware of the situation between Aaron and me," Felice paused to make sure she was holding Bedford's attention. He nodded. "Well, that combined with the pregnancy became too much for me to handle. I was slowly losing my mind. All my life I dreamt of having a family. I yearned to become a mother and when it finally happened, the entire situation was all wrong. At the time you were still married to Sandy and didn't want anything to do with the baby."

Bedford interjected. "That's not exactly true. I told you I wanted a family, but with my present wife, and you and I weren't married."

"Okay, either way I wasn't your present wife, but I was pregnant with your baby. Then Aaron and I split up and it was another painful blow for me, stacked with the grief I suffered from our failed marriage. Hurt isn't something I enjoy and I'm not a glutton for punishment, either. When you finally came around it felt like you were doing it out of pity or that I happened to be your last resort. I wanted to have the baby because I've never really condoned abortions, especially when so many people are unable to have children. Still, I doubted my ability to be a good mother and to make terrible mistakes that would impact negatively on our child. Besides that, I needed to find my father, to find out why he left and cut off all communication with me. Then I had to come to terms with something that happened to me as a child, and I never really did learn how to deal with my mother being a lesbian. I needed to know if that was why he left."

These thoughts had plagued Felice since her return from Cuba. Upon their release her head stopped spinning and everything felt lighter like layers of hot sweaty blankets were being removed.

"Felice, the only thing you have to do with regard to your mother is to love her. The lifestyle she has chosen has no bearing on your relationship."

"Yes, this is true and this may sound silly, but I was having a hard time forgiving her. I even hated her for a long time. Remember when we started dating in college and we would come home during the breaks, how I never wanted to introduce you to my mother? I was embarrassed."

"Yeah, but back then I wasn't in a rush to meet anybody's mother. You know what I mean, so I never put two and two together. You mentioned something about coming to terms with something from your childhood."

A moment passed before Felice responded. She didn't realize she had blurted that out and had to gather words carefully.

"Lately I've been having bad dreams. They include my Aunt Leslie, who you never had the pleasure of meeting because she passed away; my mother; the baby; and the gruesome incident I've blocked out for years. At first the nightmares didn't make any sense, especially the part with the baby."

Bedford shoved his tray to the side and placed his hands on the table for a more relaxed position. His eyes remained focused on Felice and his face wasn't as tense as it appeared earlier.

"I don't remember everything, but I was on my way from school and I was walking home by myself. This guy from the neighborhood followed me. I remember feeling his shadow creep up beside me and fear made me quicken my steps. I ducked into this alleyway near P.S. 117 Junior High School, which was the wrong move. The only things over there were abandoned buildings and old factories. My feet moved as fast as my little legs would allow, but my book bag was heavy and slowed me down. When he finally caught me I thought I was dead. He threatened to take my book bag and I was such a book worm that I vowed to do anything he asked. The boy felt me up and I remember how it made my skin crawl and my heart race. It was the worst feeling and made me nauseated. We fought when he tried to remove my pants and I fell really hard and bumped my head on the concrete and I blacked out. I must have been unconscious for a while, because when I came to he was zipping up his pants. Bedford, I don't remember much afterwards. However, I do recall running home with a throbbing headache and a huge knot on the back of my head and on the way I must have peed in my pants because I rushed into the bathroom and hand washed my clothes before Aunt Leslie arrived to baby-sit me."

Bedford's demeanor softened even further and became consoling. "Did he rape you?"

"I'm not sure if there was penetration or not."

"How can you not remember that?" Bedford asked.

"I passed out after hitting my head and I think there was pain, because I cried the entire way home. But that could have been for a number of reasons. The boy had thrown my book bag on the fire escape and I had to retrieve it by jumping on a huge Dumpster and climbing up the ladder. I didn't want my mother or Aunt Leslie to know that I had pissed my pants. I wanted to arrive home undetected so I could change and wash my clothes. I was fearful of getting home late and not completing my homework and chores before my mother came home. Aunt Leslie babysat me until my mother arrived home in the evening and every day, like clockwork, she sent me to the store to get her cigarettes and stuff. This had to be done before my mother came home because she didn't allow smoking in the house, so I didn't want to be late going to the store and risking Aunt Leslie being upset at me. Not one time did I worry about them finding out about what the boy had done to me. It's so strange how, as kids, we don't think straight, but these are the things that concerned me at the time."

"Felice, why didn't you tell anyone?"

"I was afraid that maybe people would say I asked for it or I was fast. And I was scared that if I did and no one believed me, he would come after me again."

"He could have come after you again, simply because you didn't tell."

"I know, but he didn't. I saw him several times afterward, but I always made sure to walk home with plenty of friends. He would stare at me in a threatening way, but he never took advantage of me again."

"Are you done with those trays?" a cafeteria custodian asked. She seemed to appear almost magically.

"Yes," Bedford answered handing both trays to the woman.

The custodian's footsteps were slow and lethargic, which was startling considering they didn't hear her approach. They waited for her to walk a few feet away before resuming their conversation.

"I don't ever want my daughter to keep things like that from me," Bedford said, shaking his head mournfully.

"Neither do I," Felice countered.

Bedford reached across the table and held Felice's hand in his. He appeared to be contemplating things in his head. Felice didn't want to start rambling, because she knew at any given moment tears would hastily begin traveling down her already wet cheeks. All she wanted was another chance. A chance to start fresh is all she asked for. There would be no more missteps. Bedford had to understand just how sorry she was for making such a stupid and grave mistake. After all, he was far from perfect. Taking care of Nina was the first thing Bedford had done right between them and that responsibility had been forced on him. Though there was no denying Bedford's ability to be a good parent, especially since he voluntarily stepped in to become his nephew Shiloh's surrogate father when his real dad died.

"Felice, I'm at a crossroad. On one hand, I'm sympathetic to you for two reasons. One, because you blessed me with a daughter and this has made me a very happy man. You do not understand the joy Nina has brought to my life. She has restored so much that was missing in my very hollow existence. This sickness is simply a minor setback. I believe this is something she will overcome. The second reason is because I never stopped loving you. Even after all of this, I still love you. It strikes me as bizarre, given all you've done to destroy the framework of our relationship."

The room felt still although chatter resounded from every direction. Nothing else mattered except the words coming from Bedford's mouth. Everything he said came from his core and it was so powerful, it reverberated to Felice's soul. She was touched and felt better about becoming active in Nina's life again. Felice felt the need to interject.

"Bedford," Felice now began to massage Bedford's hands and raised her eyes to meet his. "I think the problem is that I never fully got over you. I never stopped loving you. My heart still pined for you even after your betrayal. Why do you think I began sleeping with you again? I needed to somehow remain connected to you in one way or another and I needed it to be more than a professional level. The one thing I did come away with from my trip to Cuba is that we're all human and as much as we strive for perfection, it's not easily attained. We have to accept each other flaws included."

"Well, your love is definitely reciprocated, but there are other factors still at bay. I'm not comfortable introducing you to Nina as her mother. You've been away too long and as much as my heart goes out to you, I still don't trust you. I've also had this conversation with Isis and Samantha and…"

Bedford paused for a prolonged period. Felice's patience began eating away at her, but she knew he was searching for the right words.

"Let's just say that it's not looking very favorable for you right now. You're well aware of how Isis feels. If it were up to her, you would be made to suffer for the rest of your life. Your mother has mixed feelings. On one hand she is your mother and would love to see you play a role in the rearing of Nina. Then she's disturbed at how easily you were able to shirk such a major responsibility, and the impact it's had on her. Not knowing about her granddaughter for two years is a hard blow. I mean, you have to consider the relationship you two had before you did all of this. You both came a long way and then this happens."

"Bedford, in my defense, she has kept secrets from me as well."

"Felice, it's a poor argument. Samantha's being a lesbian is completely different and has no bearing on how you continue to live *your* life. Besides that, if she had told you about her lifestyle, would you have felt any differently?"

"Maybe."

"Then it seems your mother didn't stand a chance whether she told you or not. You already had your mind made up about how you felt about homosexuals. I'm not saying it's a bad thing, because it's your personal opinion."

"My mother is beautiful. She's not supposed to be gay."

"She's your mother and it never stopped her from being a good parent and providing for you. You can't hold being a lesbian against her forever. You have to release those repressed feelings and accept her for the beautiful person she is inside and out."

"I know."

"But you've decided to spite your mother by depriving her and withholding vital information, and it's not justified. And, despite everything that has transpired, upon learning about Nina's existence she has been extremely involved and supportive. I don't know if I could have endured these past few months without Samantha and Isis."

"So, Bedford, honestly, where do I stand?"

"I think what's best for everyone at this point is that you remain on the outside."

Felice was stunned and clung tightly to Bedford's hands, but he removed one hand to proffer her a napkin to wipe her face.

"Is this the way it has to be?" Felice asked through bouts of hiccups.

"Yes, until further notice."

26

It's All About Me

Felice felt as if she were losing her mind as she looked around at the white walls, the tables, and the hospital staff. She listened to all the voices chattering simultaneously, saying absolutely nothing worthwhile. It was like being in an asylum and Bedford was a visitor there to taunt her. The stream of tears was leaving chalky remnants on her face as she continued to wipe them away with the now wet tissue.

No, no, no, Felice thought. *Until further notice,* what the fuck was that supposed to mean? Yes, she did mess up, but she was here now and quite frankly was getting sick and tired of the bullshit. She allowed Isis to throw a tantrum, cuss her out and mistreat her. In addition, the relationship between Felice and her mother was even more strained now than before and her best friend had doubts about her integrity.

Enough was enough. It was time she took a stand for herself, because apparently if it were up to everyone else they would cut her out of the picture and Felice would not be erased so easily.

"I'm not clear on your last statement. What do you mean by until further notice?"

"Well, you turning up like this doesn't make it easy on everyone. It's going to take time for people to accept your return."

There was a time when Felice was a gum-chewing, around-the-way girl who didn't take shit from nobody. Over the years, she had managed to suppress that side of her. She simply grew up and the smart attitude was something that was left behind. Nonetheless, Felice could feel that dormant part of her personality begin to rise. Make it easy on everyone?" Who the hell cares about them? It's not about them; it's about the welfare of her daughter, Nina. Everyone did not give birth to their daughter.

"Bedford, I understand your concern and your feelings toward me right now, but the truth of the matter is I only care about my daughter. Bedford, we've been through a lot and I'm not going to use you as an excuse, but you know enough about my history to give me a second chance."

Bedford looked thoughtful as he sat adjacently from Felice. His dark brooding eyes softened. The smirk disappeared as his dimples began to melt an impression in his cheeks.

"Felice, if it were up to me I would, but I'm not the sole decision maker here. Not only that, but I have to do what's best for my daughter. I know you care about Nina, but you didn't love her enough to stick around the first time and I can't afford to have you abandon us again."

"I can't believe what I'm hearing. Are you out of your mind? Let's get this straight, and this is the last time, I'm going to say this—Nina is our daughter. You did not make her alone. I just admitted to screwing up and I have no intention of walking out of ..."

Bedford interjected. "I didn't say that I did."

"You implied that in your earlier statement, when you said you have to do what's best for your daughter. Whether it was intentional or not, she is our child. All of this nonsense about you not being the sole decision maker is just that, nonsense."

"You're starting to sound like a parrot. It's not about you. It's about Nina and her well-being, and right now she is fragile. Why are you so insistent on adding pressure to our lives?"

"See Bedford, that's where you're sadly mistaken. It's all about me and my daughter. If it weren't, we wouldn't be having this conversation right now. I'm her mother, yet I'm being told I have no right to see her, because of a decision you and everyone else has made. I bet you, a court of law would feel differently."

"Felice, lower your voice. People are beginning to stare at us."

"People, people people! When did you become so damn concerned about all of these freakin' people? Everyone seems to be running Bedford's life except Bedford. To hell with the people!"

"Felice, I run my life. What you have to understand is that while you were out gallivanting around the world, those people were extremely supportive and I'm not just going to shut them out now."

"Where were they when we built our business together? Where were they when you were constantly fucking me over and breaking up a perfectly good marriage? Where were those people when I was pregnant? Where were they then, huh? Answer me, Bedford!"

"Felice, you need to calm down. All of this is not necessary."

"Maybe it's not to you, but it damn sure is to me and until we are able to see eye to eye it will continue to be necessary."

"Is everything all right over here?" A tall lanky security guard asked.

"Yes, it is," Felice answered.

"No, it's not, and I'm going to take this as my cue to leave," Bedford said as he gathered his belongings to depart.

Felice hurried to follow him, and accidentally toppled over a cup of water, which splashed on the table, her hands and pants and left blotches of wetness behind. Blood boiling and heart racing, she trembled as she tried to repress the desire to attack Bedford for being so cocky, but she didn't want to be taken away in restraints. Still, he would pay. Felice wouldn't allow him to walk away so easily.

"Well, if you two can't lower your voices down to a decent conversation level, I'm going to have to ask you both to leave."

Felice ignored the security guard's request. She tailgated Bedford a few feet away from where they were seated.

"Where do you think you're going? This is not over."

"As far as I'm concerned, it is."

"If you continue to keep my daughter away from me you may not ever see her again, because this time when I pack my bags to go, she'll be with me."

"Woman, I will throw a restraining order on your ass so quick, you wouldn't know what hit you and I have a witness right here who overheard your stupid ass remark, too." Bedford said, acknowledging the hospital security guard.

Felice was fuming. *This shit is not going to go down like this,* she thought. It took her thirty years to be reunited with her father and she was not going to get the runaround to be with her daughter. *I will not be chumped, and no one is going to keep my daughter away from me.* Felice looked over at the table beside her and saw a tray with a few remains sitting idly. Without a second thought she snatched it up and swung it straight at Bedford. The food and the paper cup flew in another direction. Bedford didn't have time to duck and Felice had a clear shot. The tray hit him square on his chin and shoulder blade.

It happened so quickly no one saw it coming, but anyone looking at them didn't miss the look of horror and disdain on Bedford's face. Nor did they miss the security guard hem Felice face down against the table.

A woman came to Bedford's aide and proffered him a napkin to wipe the food stains off. He had smatterings of what appeared to be beef gravy on his white shirt and remnants of pumpkin or sweet potato pie.

"Fuck you and your eyewitness." Felice yelled.

Bedford was still too stunned for words. He should have known that if he got Felice riled she would behave irrationally. It was only a few years back when she had attacked him and Felice's poor assistant, Davonna.

Felice didn't know when the security guard called for backup, but within moments two more rent-a-cops showed, up along with a real police officer. She was surrounded and felt like a fugitive.

"Is that a threat?"

"When have you ever known me to make threats? I only make promises."

27

All Down Hill From Here!

This had to be the worse predicament yet. Felice was behind bars at the Los Angeles County police station. She couldn't believe Bedford had pressed charges against her. It was plain ridiculous. They hauled Felice out of the hospital so quickly she believed her being behind bars was merely a dream. However, after being told she could make one phone call, her dream quickly became a sick reality. Sadly, she couldn't bail herself out because they seized her belongings and refused to release Felice on her own recognizance because she wasn't a resident of the state of California. Therefore, she was considered high risk.

Now there was more drama added to the blend of Felice's big bag of mixed feelings. Her head pounded and the police refused to give her anything to help alleviate the pain. She asked politely several times for Tylenol, aspirin or any type of pain reliever they had available. Each request was met with a snide remark.

"This is not a pharmacy."

"You must have us confused with the general hospital, where they give a fuck."

"As soon as you make bail, you can visit the Wal-Mart and have your pick."

Three different officers offered three various responses, but they all had the same meaning; No!

Bedford was lucky she didn't beat his ass the way she really envisioned it. Instead of bashing his head with the tray, she wanted to crush his skull and watch as the bones disintegrated into dust. What made him so fit to be a father, other than the fact that he busted a nut and impregnated her? He was merely a sperm donor and the only reason he took responsibility was because she forced it on him. When she first announced the pregnancy to Bedford he didn't even want her to have the baby. As a matter of fact, he questioned if the baby was even his in the first place. It was insulting to think that he doubted or even thought Felice would play such a cruel trick. She wasn't into games and tricks were for kids.

Felice was at a loss. She didn't know who to call. Her mother was in Los Angeles, but she didn't know at which hotel and Samantha didn't believe in cell phones. Sylvah was in Atlanta and was dealing with her own problems. There was no way Felice was going to call Alana, and poor Candace would stress herself out and take this situation to an entirely different level of worry. Felice loved her friends to death, but she didn't have a soul to turn to. Felice's only option was to call Geneen and hope she would relay the message on her behalf.

Felice was hesitant, but she had no desire to spend an evening or a complimentary night at Chateau L.A.P.D. One of the kind policemen from earlier was passing by and Felice stretched her arms through the bars to touch him, and he flinched back.

"Don't you ever try to attack me like that again," the officer said.

"I was just trying to get your attention. I'm sorry if I startled you."

"Yeah, whatever. Next time for both our safety, I suggest you use your mouth to gain my attention. So what is it that you want now?"

Felice was feeling more and more like a criminal. There were people out there committing crimes far worse than her minor assault on Bedford and they were making Felice out to be a monster.

"Yes, I was wondering if I could make that phone call now?"

"Okay, let me see if they've processed and completed your paperwork yet. What's your name and the offense?"

"Felice Jackson and I'm here on assault charges."

"Oh, you're the chick that…" He laughed, said something inaudible and walked away. The officer could be heard yelling down the corridor, "Yo Jimmy, the fox you booked earlier wants to make her call now."

Felice shuddered. She was convinced all men were assholes.

Five minutes later Jimmy, the booking officer appeared and without saying two words he pressed the button to open the electronic cell gate. Before she could extend both legs out of the cell he placed handcuffs on her until they reached their destination.

At least their not as tight as they were earlier when they brought me in, Felice thought.

Jimmy took a few steps back to allow Felice some breathing room.

Felice's hand trembled as she dialed the eleven digits. The phone rang several times and she was about to hang up.

"Hello."

For the first time, Felice was actually happy to hear the voice on the other line.

"Hello, Gene. It's me, Felice."

"Hi. I heard you made it out there safely. That's good."

"Yes, I made it fine thanks to your lead. Listen, I need to get in touch with my mother. I'm kinda in a jam, but I need you to reach out to her for me."

"If you have a pen, I can give you the hotel and room number."

"No, I don't have a pen, but if you'd pass on my message for me it would be greatly appreciated."

"Oh, okay, you must be on a cell phone in the car without a headset. Let me run and get a pen so I can be accurate."

"Gene, no I don't have a lot of time," Felice yelled, but Gene was already gone.

"Okay, I'm back," Gene announced. "Now what's your message? It sounds like it's urgent."

"Actually it is," Felice answered.

"Okay, well I'm ready, so shoot."

"Tell her that I need her help as soon as possible. I need her to come down to the Los Angeles Police Department on…"

"Oh, you got stranded. No problem."

"No not quite. I got arrested. I'm in jail."

28

Two Hours Later

Two hours later, Samantha entered the Los Angeles County police station. She looked haggard and bewildered. The last thing she needed to hear was that Felice was incarcerated. Gene provided her with all of the particulars and Samantha immediately called the police station to fine tune the details, in order to retrieve the exact amount of cash needed to set bail.

The Los Angeles Police Department was everything one would envision on television. The unit bustled with activity. Individuals with handcuffs were being booked by officers. Some were rambunctious while others calmly tried to plead their innocence. Phones rang non-stop. Frustration lingered on impatient faces while tears ran down others. Police officers walked around, cocky in their domain, thrusting their superiority on civilians. There was commotion at every turn.

Samantha stood still while her eyes took a 180-degree tour. After swallowing everything in she quickly pulled herself together and began to walk with a purpose. This poke was no place for her daughter. Samantha approached a female officer, who appeared to be friendly, behind the main desk. She was engaged in conversation with a fellow officer.

"Hello ma'am," Samantha said, trying to sound pleasant.

"Yes, may I help you?" The officer asked turning her attention to Samantha, but the smile and the jovial mood disappeared.

"My name is Samantha Pryce. My daughter, Felice Jackson, is being held here on assault charges. I would like to make arrangements for her release."

"One moment," the officer walked over to an empty desk and Samantha followed. She pointed to an empty chair and told Samantha to take a seat while she typed information into the computer.

"Okay, you said Elise Jackson. I don't show an Elise in our system."

"No, I said Felice. That's F-E-L-I-C-E."

"All right, here she is. Yes, she's being held on assault charges. Payment of a cash bond is required."

"Is it possible to see the arresting officer or someone in charge here?"

♀♂

Felice was becoming fatigued, famished and frustrated. Her headache still remained, but it wasn't as pronounced. The only thing she ate all day was the food from the hospital earlier, and it hurt her brain to reflect on that scenario. One of the policemen took pity on Felice and brought her a cup of hot tea. It helped soothe her nerves and subside the hunger pangs.

Over the past three hours Felice had time to think. Felice believed things could have been handled differently, but Bedford still deserved what he got. He had it coming!

Still, this was the man she would have to deal with, whether she liked it or not, for the next sixteen years of her daughters life and even longer. She realized that as long as they shared a child they would forever be connected. It was better to have an amicable relationship as opposed to a bitter and nasty rapport. This would be best for all involved.

Deep in thought, Felice heard someone call her name and she snapped out of her trance. The electronic gates unlocked and an officer came to accompany Felice out. She was taken to an area where they returned her belongings, which she had to sign for, and then she was led back to the reception area. Immediately she spotted Samantha sitting on the bench. Samantha's face was painted in worry, because she hadn't spotted Felice yet. However, for a woman of sixty years, she looked extremely youthful and could pass for Felice's sister. Samantha wore a powder pink tank top with matching button front and drawstring linen pants. She had a fresh, clean makeup look with lip gloss and a little eye shadow, and her wavy hair was captured in a banana clip with wisps of hair escaping on the sides and in the back.

Felice raced over to her mother. At that moment, she was so grateful for Samantha. No matter what their differences, Felice knew that Samantha wouldn't let her down and then—Felice spotted Bedford.

Son of a bitch, Felice thought.

Upon seeing Felice, Bedford and Samantha stood. Felice was sure they could see the smoke emerge from her head. Because of Bedford she had to endure several painful hours behind bars. A place that Felice vowed she'd never ever visit again. Yet, she had to curb her attitude. After all, they were still in the police station.

"Samantha," Felice said coldly.

"Felice it's not what you think. We're here because this situation has gone far enough."

"What situation?" Felice asked.

"Felice, please don't play coy. Your mother is talking about us."

"Us? what about us?"

"Felice, Bedford dropped the charges against you, so I suggest you drop the attitude. Now do you want to resolve the condition of your present relationship so you can begin seeing your daughter, or do you want to continue being an asshole? See, because quite frankly, I'm sick and tired of your funky shit! I've been dealing with your disregard and disrespect of my lifestyle and we're going to change that. Now, this is not the place to have such a discussion. So I suggest we go someplace a little more private to carry on this conversation. Agreed?"

"Agreed," both Bedford and Felice chimed.

At Felice's suggestion they decided to have dinner at the home of the garlic flower. During Felice's last trip to Los Angeles a few years back she attended several restaurants and the Stinkin' Rose was her favorite. It was a slow night at the restaurant, so they were able to request a larger booth toward the rear. The scent of garlic wafted through the air. Soft music serenaded their ears and the plush seating embraced bodies. The waiter returned with a tray of water, warm garlic rolls and garlic butter and took their drink order.

"Well, like I was saying at the station house…," Samantha began.

"No, let me say something first," Felice interrupted. It took every ounce for her to make amends, but it was something she felt necessary. "Bedford, I want to apologize for attacking you today. I allowed my emotions to take over and I can't deny how good it felt at that moment to hit you, but I realize it was wrong."

"Felice, you don't have to be such a smart aleck."

"No, Samantha. It's okay. In Felice's own way, I know she means well and I accept your apology."

"Thank you," Felice said. "Samantha, I also want to apologize to you for being so insensitive and crude to you and Gene. You're right. I never took your feelings into account. I've been totally selfish, and I'm not saying this because it's expected. I'm sincere and I know that sorry can't make up for years of insolence, but I love you a great deal. And I'm happy that you've found someone to love you just as much. Gene is a good person. I hope you will forgive me?" Tears began to well in Felice's eyes and Bedford handed her a napkin.

"Of course I can," Samantha replied. She got up and went to Felice's side of the table to give her a big warm hug. "I love you too! You're my daughter and as your mother, it's my job to forgive you."

"Thanks," Felice said holding her mother tightly.

"Good, now it should all be water under the bridge. Now let's get down to business."

"Yes, we should. It's also about time we begin to discuss the arrangements for our daughter."

Felice's face lit up. "Are you sure?" she asked.

"Positive."

"Oh my goodness," Felice squealed. The smile on her face was so bright it could have made a rainbow seem dull. "Wait…should we be having this conversation without Isis being present?"

"Remember what you said earlier? Nina is our daughter." Bedford then placed his arm around her shoulders and placed his hand atop Felice's.

29

A License To Whore

Another week managed to pass and Zaire was recovering nicely. He would be discharged tomorrow. The only indication he was ever in an accident were a few minor cuts and bruises. This was great news to be received on such a beautiful Atlanta day. Yet, Sylvah and Bläise clucked at each other like two angry chickens in a coop.

The soft wind grazed Sylvah's face while Bläise's words stung her heart. She was tired of pretending and putting up a good front for Zaire. As soon as they left the facility they bickered about everything. The only thing they did was agree to disagree. Bläise was stubborn and in denial and Sylvah was troubled and tired. Troubled about Zaire and tired of Bläise being an asshole.

During every visit, Zaire made it hard on his parents by making insinuating and leading comments under the guise of innocence.

"What did you two do last night?"

"Maybe we can take another family vacation together this summer."

"Did you and dad send out the invitations for the family reunion? Where are you guys going to have it since you sold the house?"

"What did you do to celebrate your twenty-second anniversary?"

"Did you get the honeymoon suite at the hotel?"

"Where did you guys move to?"

"Where am I going to stay when I come home during the break?"

To which Bläise either changed the subject or left the room, claiming he was hungry or had to use the restroom. Sylvah however, gave answers that were very direct, but tactful, so as not to hurt Zaire's feelings. Sylvah's main concern was his recovery, but at the same time she wasn't going to mislead him.

Sylvah didn't understand why Zaire refused to accept the fate of his parent's marriage. For the first time, Sylvah realized she didn't even like Bläise as a person. It took this critical accident for her to become conscious of this fact. He was stubborn, bossy and chauvinistic. The three qualities were not very complimentary of each other.

"You're making this out to be much worse than it is... I mean, so what if the Zaire thinks we're still together? It's no big deal. It's surely not the end of the world."

"It is a big deal, because it's a lie, Bläise. Since when did we break into the habit of lying to our children?"

"He'll be out of the hospital tomorrow and we can break the news to him then. Does that work for you, Sylvah?"

"It works for me. I'd feel much better."

The normal bustle of the hotel lobby was absent. The usual shrill was down to a soft murmur. The hotel staff greeted Sylvah and Bläise as they entered the hotel. They had become fixtures over the last week and a half. Sylvah enjoyed the luxury accommodations of the hotel and the hospitality, but she was relieved to be checking out tomorrow. Another two nights alone in a room with Bläise would send her to the insanity ward.

"Sylvah," a voice called as she and Bläise walked to the elevator.

She recognized the voice, but most of the hotel employees were beginning to sound familiar. Then again, the workers had been calling her by Mrs. Lawrence.

"Sylvah."

The pitch was definitely familiar. Sylvah turned around to confirm her notion. Bläise stopped and also turned in the direction of the voice.

Sylvah's eyes searched the perimeter of the vestibule and no one turned up. She shrugged her shoulders continued her stroll to the elevator bank. Just as they were about to enter the pulley, someone called her name again and this time when she turned around she saw him. Sylvah's eyes had to be deceiving her.

"Who is that?" Bläise asked sounding annoyed.

Sylvah ignored Bläise as he stood at the entrance impatiently waiting.

"Oh my goodness what are you doing here?" Sylvah asked.

"I couldn't stay away any longer," Jason answered. He grabbed Sylvah by the waist and hoisted her a few inches from the ground. Then, without speaking another word, he gave her a closed mouth kiss.

"I missed you too," Sylvah whispered.

"And who might this be?" Bläise asked interrupting the mood.

"Oh Bläise, this is Jason. Jason, this is Bläise," Sylvah introduced.

"So who are you dating? First I see you kissing white men at the airport, and now this kid, who looks like he should be hanging out with our son."

"Excuse me?" Sylvah asked as steam rose from the top of her head, nose and ears.

"The divorce papers are not a license to become a whore," Bläise snapped.

The words whipped Sylvah's ears while embarrassment flushed her face.

"So now I'm a whore? You know what Bläise? Go to fucking hell!"

"That's certainly where you're going if you continue this behavior."

"This is your ex-husband?" Jason asked astonished. "Now I can see why."

"Young man, please mind your business."

"And if I don't?" Jason countered. He began to roll up the cuffs of his sleeves. Jason took one step closer and Sylvah placed herself between the two men.

"Jason, please don't stoop to his level. Bläise, I knew you were an asshole, I just didn't realize how deep." Sylvah tried to remain calm.

"You are the mother of his children and this is how he acts toward you? Sheer disrespect," Jason said in disgust.

They were still standing at the bank and patrons were coming in and out of the elevator. People stared at the exchange as they passed them by. A few lingered longer than necessary. Sylvah didn't like confrontations, especially in the presence of others.

"Jason, where are you staying?" Sylvah asked.

"Actually I have a condominium in Buckhead. It overlooks the downtown area."

"Great. If you wait a couple of minutes while I pack my belongings, I'll accompany you."

"Sounds like a plan. I will wait in the reception area."

"Great," Sylvah said again as she brushed past Bläise and into the elevator. He followed before the doors closed. Bläise's face became red with anger, jealousy and disdain. Sylvah focused on her reflection in an attempt to ignore Bläise's presence, though his heavy breathing and pacing in front of her made it quite difficult.

"Sylvah, I can't believe you! Did you have all of this shit planned before the divorce?"

They were alone. Sylvah folded her arms while agitation swept her face. Foul thoughts littered the empty pockets of her mind. Disregarding Bläise became impossible.

"Bläise, you stupid muthafucka! Don't you ever, ever disrespect me like that again! Don't you ever call me out of my name and if you don't have anything good to say to or about me, SHUT THE HELL UP!"

"Stop acting so ghetto. It's not attractive on you," Bläise said as he exited onto their floor.

"You're not very attractive, Bläise. You're starting to look more and more like a horse's ass. It may be because you are one."

"It's better than sleeping with the enemy or getting locked up for jail bait."

Sylvah froze. When Bläise no longer heard the clicking of her heels he paused and retraced his steps until they stood side by side. Sylvah's left hand swung with such force that Bläise's face spun one-hundred and eighty degrees. The negative thoughts dislodged with the slap. Sylvah felt good.

Bläise was about to return the favor to Sylvah.

"Uh- uh. Don't be stupid," Sylvah warned, wagging an index finger.

"This divorce must really have you rattled, because you've lost your damn mind! What gives you the right to slap me and think you can walk away without any repercussions?"

"Because you had it coming and the only person who's lost their mind is you."

"Have you ever heard of assault?" Bläise asked.

"Actually yes, I have. If you recall, I represented you two years ago for attacking the Asian man who hit your car and you had two other situations from the past. Therefore, it's your word against mine, so good luck."

Bläise fumed as he pounded a fist into his open hand. "Fuck you."

"Bläise, it's a wonder I didn't leave your sorry ass first. I would prefer that we not speak beyond our children. After we meet at the hospital tomorrow and speak to Zaire, I believe I'll be on my way because the more I'm around you, the less I like you."

$$♀♂$$

Jason patiently waited in the lobby. Sylvah had a suitcase with wheels and a duffel bag, which he immediately relieved her of upon her exit from the elevator. The concierge returned the keys to Jason's car and they vanished.

Sylvah replayed the scenario and Jason remained quiet. Ten minutes later they were heading to his apartment.

Once Sylvah settled in she realized neither of them had exchanged words since leaving the hotel.

"Jason, are you okay?"

"I'm good," he answered. His voice sounded despondent.

"You don't sound fine."

"You know what? I'm not good at playing games, so I won't. Your ex-husband mentioned something earlier and it's bothering me."

Sylvah figured as much. She didn't like being called a whore either. It was degrading and disheartening, especially coming from her ex-husband.

Sylvah removed her cardigan sweater and sat beside Jason. Her hands gently massaged his back. Jason pulled away.

"Talk to me," Sylvah urged.

"Who were you kissing at the airport?"

"What?" Sylvah asked. Then it hit her. She had forgotten Bläise's slight about her kissing some white guy.

"The white guy?"

"Oh," Sylvah said.

"So it's true?" Jason asked. He stood up and began pacing the room.

"Listen, Jason. Hunter is a friend. Besides, you and I never said we were dating exclusively."

"So am I just a friend too?"

"You're different. You're more than a friend?"

"Are you sleeping with Hunter too?"

"Excuse me? That's none of your business, but to answer your question, no. Contrary to what you might think, I'm not a whore."

"Sylvah, I never said you were," Jason defended. "It's just that…I like you and I thought we had something special. Then Bläise…never mind. I'm sorry."

"We do have something special and I value your friendship. Now as much as I'd like to go into this with you, I have other issues to deal with, like a recovering son who is in denial and an idiot ex-husband. My best friend's daughter is suffering from cancer. I'm supposed to be in court on Monday morning and I still have to make sure my daughter doesn't feel neglected at the same time. I already have a lot on my plate without you running a guilt trip on me and accusing me of things that I'm not."

Jason looked lost.

"Friends?"

"Jason, a number of things are going on in my life and if we can't enjoy each others company then I need to be moving on, because I can't deal with anymore aggravation."

"You can discount me that quickly? Sylvah, I came down here to support you and this is how you behave?"

Sylvah put her cardigan back on and began gathering her belongings.

"I appreciate you coming and it means a lot to me, but I didn't ask you to come. You know, maybe I should book myself into another hotel."

30

Suicide Mission

Sylvah smiled as she thought about her client, Dr. Scott's, victory in court. After several grueling months his ex-wife, Glenda attempted to get $3.5 million in damages, alimony, and the house. Sylvah felt that Dr. Scott was being far too generous by offering Glenda anything other than the door she came through. He was still willing to provide her with a monthly allowance of five thousand dollars and a lump sum of one million dollars if she dropped the claim for the house. However, God never liked ugly and Glenda was only rewarded one hundred thousand dollars. No alimony, no house.

Glenda had sauntered in the courtroom dressed to the nines as usual, but this time she brought a guest. Mr. Mandingo's arm was possessively placed around Glenda's waist. He bore a strong resemblance to the British rock musician, Seal. However, Mr. Mandingo's skin tone was smooth and even. He stood tall and his gait was confident—a little too confident—almost pretentious. *This must be the alleged suspect Dr. Scott found his wife with in the compromising position,* Sylvah thought.

Apparently Glenda had more important things to tend to. She entered the courtroom almost fifteen minutes late and Sylvah was in the process of asking the judge to dismiss the case.

Sylvah called Glenda to the stand. As she approached the bench Sylvah noticed something different about Glenda. Sylvah began her line of questioning and on a whim changed her direction.

"Mrs. Scott, exactly how many months are you?"

"I beg your pardon?" Glenda asked astonished.

"Objection," Glenda's attorney bellowed, to which the judge overruled.

Glenda looked horrified and didn't answer right away. She began fingering the pendant around her neck.

She had taken great effort to conceal her blooming belly, which Sylvah noticed immediately. On previous occasions when they were in arbitration Glenda's dress was usually very interesting and revealing, but never sleazy.

"Five months."

"And Mrs. Scott, who is the father of your unborn?" Sylvah already knew the answer, but wanted Glenda to answer for the record. "Please remember, you are still under oath." Sylvah reminded.

Sylvah rested her case and it didn't take long for the judge to declare a ruling, which was in Dr. Scott's favor. Sylvah wanted to gloat in Glenda's face, but it would have been completely out of character and highly unprofessional. Still, Sylvah felt that conniving women like Glenda made good men like Dr. Scott become bitter and untrustworthy.

Sylvah stirred sugar into chamomile tea when the phone rang.

"Hello," Sylvah answered, as she balanced the phone in one hand and the tea mug in the other.

"Hey Ma," Kenya replied.

"You miss me already, huh?"

"Actually, two weeks of you and Dad is more than enough. I know you must be glad to be back in your own bed."

"You know your mother too well. It was nice being down there with you guys, but I missed work and to be quite honest, your father got on my last nerve."

"I could tell. I guess the divorce is not such a bad thing. I never realized how much you two bicker at each other."

"Well, on the flight back we agreed to remain amicable. Especially when considering Zaire. He's taking this so hard."

"Actually, that's why I called."

"Is everything alright? Is Zaire hurt? Did he do something? Should I call your father?" Sylvah asked frantically while placing the cup on the countertop. Pacing the kitchen she circled the island twice.

"Ma, please calm down. Zaire is okay. It's just that I found something out."

"Kenya, you scared me," Sylvah said, as she pulled her hand through her hair. She sat down to relax and began sipping the tea. "So, what did you find out?"

"Zaire caused the accident."

"What do you mean, Zaire caused the accident?" Sylvah asked incredulously. "It was raining. Did Zaire cause the road to become slick? Did he force the car off the road?"

"No, but according to Trent, they told Zaire to pull over, because the rain became torrential…"

Sylvah scratched her head in confusion. "Kenya wait. You're not making any sense. Zaire wasn't driving."

"Yes, he was."

"The other guy…, um what's his name?" Sylvah paused. "Prince, right–he was driving."

"No, it was Zaire and both Prince and Trent said he was driving. He was upset about you and dad, his recent breakup with Lavender, and well, he was talking crazy."

"Kenya, that's nonsense. Prince got his lungs crushed by the airbag…remember?"

"We assumed it was the airbag on the driver side, but it was the passenger airbag. Ma, we can go back and forth on this forever, but you should call Zaire. Talk to him."

Sylvah tried to digest this late-breaking news. She didn't understand why Zaire would put his life at risk and also endanger the lives of his friends.

Sylvah remained deep in thought.

"Ma, are you still there?" Kenya asked.

"I'm here. I gotta go," Sylvah replied absently and hung up. Her palms became sweaty and she started feeling light headed. Sylvah remained seated rubbing her temples until the feeling passed.

Moments later Sylvah found herself in the bedroom. Quickly she pulled out her palm pilot and located Zaire's number and dialed.

"Zaire, I have a question to ask you."

"Ma! Hey, how are you?"

"I'm not doing so well. I just received some disturbing news."

"What happened? Are you and dad okay?"

"Yes, Zaire. Your father and I are doing just fine. You do realize we are divorced now and no longer live under the same roof, right?"

"Y'all are just tripping. He'll be back."

"No, he won't and if he wanted to return, I wouldn't take him back. Zaire, what your father and I had was beautiful and we have you and your sister to prove it. But we're now divorced. I've moved on and so has Bläise. I need you to really understand what I'm saying. I will always love your father and we'll remain friends for life, but it's over. We've accepted this fact and now it's important to us that you understand as well."

Zaire became silent.

"Zaire, do you hear me?"

"Yeah, I hear you."

Sylvah detected attitude in his voice, and Zaire knew better than to answer "yeah". It was either yes or no, but chastising him about his grammar wasn't important. However, getting him out of denial and to take responsibility for his actions was.

"Zaire, earlier I mentioned asking you a question. I actually have two questions. Why did you allow us to believe Prince was the driver? And were you on a suicide mission?"

31

Act of Forgiveness

F elice, what's wrong, baby?" her great aunt Leslie asked. She and Felice sat on the porch. The day sizzled from the richness of the sun. Aunt Leslie used the paper funeral home fan to cool herself down as she sipped the last of her 7-Up.

Felice's face gleamed with tears. She didn't answer immediately, because her body trembled with fear. Perspiration caused her plaits to cling to the side of her face.

"Auntie Leslie, please don't send me back to the store. I don't wanna go."

"Chile, stop being silly—now take this money and go buy my pickle, cigarettes, and pork rinds, and when you get back I'll have something special for you."

"OK."

Reluctantly, Felice took the money from her aunt and descended the porch steps.

"Felice," Aunt Leslie called. "Don't forget my 7-Up and no dilly-dallying."

"OK." Felice made it to the store safely—retrieved the items and departed. However, she decided to take a different route home in hopes of avoiding her assailants. Suddenly the afternoon turned into evening. The street lights illuminated the roads. Felice walked in the opposite direction, but she still ended up on the same path. She started running until she saw the Dumpster. However, she didn't hide behind it this time. Instead Felice continued to run and the guy who molested her in previous dreams ran after her. He eventually caught up and tackled Felice from behind, dropping them both on the ground. They struggled. She fought him with every limb in her ten-year old body. Shock covered his face as Felice rampaged. Felice scratched, pummeled, kicked and bit her attacker until she was able to get free and on her feet again, leaving the captor behind. Felice finally got away.

A large warehouse stood before her. There was a door on the side of the building. Felice turned the knob and the door gave way–she entered. Darkness smothered the room and disinfectant filled the air. Felice didn't know where she was, but she needed light. She straddled the wall while feeling for a switch. She pressed a button and a burst of light filled the room.

Felice was in the hospital where Nina was born. Hospital personnel walked swiftly past as if she weren't present. Felice walked from door to door in search of an exit. She came across a room filled with familiar voices and peeked inside.

The woman in the white lab coat held Felice's baby and walked her over to Aunt Leslie, who took Nina. Samantha and Bedford stood beside Aunt Leslie while she sung a lullaby, but the words were unfamiliar.

> *Through strife the slumbering soul awakes*
> *We learn on error's troubled route*
> *The truths we could not prize without*
> *The sorrow of our sad mistakes*

All eyes were transfixed on Felice as she entered the room. She was no longer a little girl. Aunt Leslie looked directly at Felice and spoke. "The act of forgiveness is a two-way street. In order to be forgiven, you must also learn to forgive."

The nurse turned to leave. She paused before Felice. "Your daughter is now safe."

32

Regret

Candace sat home patiently waiting for the arrival of her husband, Shane. For the first time in their marriage she was actually afraid for him and their family. Shane was the lead detective on the kidnapping case, which was now becoming extremely intense and receiving a vast amount of publicity.

The first child was discovered in the Dumbo district of Brooklyn, and after weeks of searching, a homeless man found the second missing child, dead beneath the Brooklyn Bridge. The murderer either had a fondness for Brooklyn or the crimes were happening nearby. Forensics was trying to determine how far the bodies traveled and place of death. Cause of death was already evident. However, there were no fibers, fingerprints, or anything else linking them to a suspect.

Shane described the condition of the latest victim as gruesome. The coroner tried to make the little girl more presentable as not to frighten the family. The girl was identified as Choice Hoyt, the daughter of a well-known city official. The murderer tortured and molested Choice. The entire situation was daunting, because there were still several other children reported missing.

The police investigative team discovered several distinctive patterns of the abductor. The children's ages were between eight and ten years old—male and female. They were taken from school playgrounds; all attended private schools; all were from middle-class families; and the children were loners.

The abductions were too close for comfort, especially with everything circling the Farewell household. Shane received two more disturbing phone calls. Again the voice was automated and untraceable. One message advised Shane to watch his back and the other informed him that people aren't always what they seem. The kidnapper didn't leave notes for the parents of the abducted children, so there was no direct link. Still, the department took precautions, because it could be someone Shane dealt with in the past who was seeking revenge.

Second, communication suddenly became a major issue between Candace and Shane. Candace didn't know if it were her imagination working overtime, but things felt strained. They didn't talk nearly as much as they use to. It was almost as if Shane knew Candace betrayed him. When the girls made preparations to go on the trip, Shane begged her not to go. They had never spent so much time apart and he wasn't comfortable with her going overseas. Jamaica wasn't like a weekend in Martha's Vineyard or Atlantic City. To make matters worse, Shane's job consumed his time and their children were having trouble in school. James was suspended for fighting and Jasmine had detention for back talking her teacher.

The anxiety coursing through Candace's body stemmed from guilt. Candace felt there was a direct correlation between the negative aura enveloping her household and her infidelity to Shane. It was karma. Nevertheless, she still couldn't eliminate the thoughts of her one-night stand with Clayton. She regretted the day she ever set eyes on him. Candace beat herself up daily, for engaging with Clayton in the first place and for enjoying the act. Just thinking about Clayton and the way he devoured her still made her body tingle.

Candace needed someone to confide in. Unfortunately, Felice was MIA, Sylvah was dealing with her own family issues, and Alana simply was not an option. Candace had been playing with the business card Clayton gave her in Jamaica. She was so desperate she considered calling him, but there was no point contacting Clayton since he was the problem—the root of her guilt. Nothing good could possibly come from Candace reaching out to Clayton. Candace didn't trust herself around him. It was obvious she lacked self-control, and common sense walked out the door once Clayton entered.

Candace tried to drown her problems by reading a novel when Shane opened the door. She immediately closed the book and focused on her husband. He appeared tired and a bit distraught. Creases almost like drapes when pulled formed in his forehead and dark circles shadowed the crescent of his eyes.

Shane's thoughts must have been elsewhere, because he didn't notice Candace sitting on the couch.

"Honey," Candace said before he could leave the room. "How was your day?"

Surprised, Shane stopped in his tracks. "Hey. Sorry, I didn't even see you sitting there. It's been a long one." Shane walked back to the couch and sat beside Candace.

"I can imagine," she said, after their lips brushed coarsely.

"We found another little girl," Shane said, sounding disgusted and disappointed at the same time.

"Oh goodness gracious!" Candace sighed while shaking her head. "Are you guys any closer to finding this lunatic?" Candace asked.

"We've narrowed it down, but nothing concrete."

"I know you'll be happy when you finally catch the creep. He deserves the chair for harming defenseless children. This person has to have a lot of mental issues."

"Yeah, we'll be happy, but for now, I'll be happy to know who keeps leaving me these messages and notes."

Candace's heart fluttered.

"I received another one today." Shane handed the paper over to Candace. She took the folded article and opened it. The typewritten note was in bold and all capital letters. Candace couldn't believe her eyes.

The message read: *NOT ALL MISTAKES ARE MEANT TO BE FORGIVEN.*

Candace didn't know the exact meaning of the message as her mind dashed and mixed thoughts filled her head. What mistakes? Was this a threat to her husband? Was this a threat to their family? Were their children next? Why would someone want to do harm to her family?

They needed to capture this person right away, because Candace wouldn't feel safe until they did.

In the End

The July night stormed heavily. Rain pelted against concrete, brick buildings, windows, cars; rattled gates and broke tree limbs; disturbing everything in its wake. Claps of thunder resonated like cymbals. Children and adults were frightened by the intensity of the storm. Network television interrupted regularly scheduled programming, while others flashed warning advisories, requesting citizens to remain indoors. It felt like a tempest was brewing. However, it was only the residue of a hurricane that had originated in the south. It traveled north to New York but upon its arrival had died down to a mere rainstorm.

By morning, the strength of the sun soaked up the wetness and the sewers drank the remains. Felice, Sylvah, Candace and Alana were scheduled to meet for their monthly Sunday brunch at Akwaaba's. Felice even went so far as to send out invitations to the ladies as reminders, since their last gathering had been over four months earlier.

Work was becoming routine again for Felice. She had officially returned to Jackson and Jackson two months ago. The staff members treated Felice as if she had always been there, even though the majority of them hadn't been present during her original tenure.

Felice's alarm clock sounded and she got up without hesitation. Today wasn't a day for procrastination. It marked a new day for cleansing, fresh starts, forgiveness and sharing. Felice realized, after years of blame, she had to take responsibility for her actions.

Otherwise, she would never be able to escape her past.

She was anxious to start her day and her first order of business was to run one lap around Prospect Park. Felice figured if she exercised now she would be absolved if she over ate during brunch. She hauled on her Nike tank top, matching running pants and socks. As she laced up her sneakers the telephone rang.

"Hello," Felice answered.

"Hey, how are you this morning?"

"Feeling good. I'm about to go running in the park. You're up pretty early."

"So are you, but something told me you'd be up already. You always said the early bird gets the worm."

"This is true, but…well, you know, today is the day," Felice said, a smile blanketed her face.

"So, we're still on?"

"Yes, we are."

"What time should I expect you so we can be ready?"

"Ten o'clock is good."

"Then ten it is. We'll see you then. Wait… Felice… I love you."

Felice hesitated. Her response was lodged in her throat. She drew a deep breath. "I love you too."

♀♂

The candles still flickered from the night before. They were almost burned down to the wick. The smell of vanilla and berries permeated the air. The drapes were pulled shut, eliminating the daylight. Caramel-colored skin layered vanilla wafer flesh. Two melded bodies lay comfortably, sharing the warmth of one bed.

The night before had been wonderful for both. Sylvah and Hunter enjoyed a helicopter ride around town and viewed the spectacular sights of New York City. Afterwards, they attended a charity banquet, benefitting the Breast Cancer Foundation.

Sylvah never thought she and Hunter would have come this far. He was very instrumental in her life, but there were a number of things that still bothered her. Like the way people stared at them whenever they went out. Females looked at her as if she were a woman scorned and the men's expression read "I know he can't possibly satisfy you the way a *brotha* can."

Sylvah liked public displays of affection. She had grown to love the adulation because of Bläise. He had always held her hand, kissed her on the lips or wrapped his arm around her shoulders, flaunting Sylvah as his prize possession. However, when Hunter did these things she received more than a hateful glance, which made her very uncomfortable. She often found herself pulling away from him to avoid malicious behavior. People snickered, made rude comments and even treated them like outcasts. They received poor service at restaurants, valets, stores, the country club, and other social gatherings. When Sylvah brought these incidents to Hunter's attention, he created excuses or brushed it off as nothing. Sylvah began to realize that as nice as Hunter was, they would never be on the same page.

"Good morning, beautiful," Hunter said, smiling as Sylvah stirred in the bed.

"Hi," Sylvah replied, rubbing her eyes. "What time is it?"

"A few minutes before ten," Hunter replied. He began stroking her hair.

"How long have you been up?"

"About forty-five minutes."

"Mmh…doing what?"

"Just staring at your beautiful face. Did you know you have three beauty marks on your face and two on your neck? Not one eyebrow hair out of place, cute ears, and the most sensuous lips I've ever tasted."

"Which ones?" Sylvah asked playing coy.

"Actually, both and I wouldn't mind tasting them now."

"Mmh…sounds tempting, but I have to get ready to leave. Today is Sunday brunch with the girls, and I can't miss it."

"Not even for this?" Hunter asked, rubbing his growing shaft beneath the covers, while his other hand navigated between Sylvah's thighs.

Raging hormones started warming her body. Sylvah knew if she remained beside him she would melt like butter on toast. Sylvah pulled the sheets back and slid out of the bed. She sauntered across the room nude.

A look of disappointment spread across Hunter's face. "Didn't you enjoy last night?" He asked.

"Last night and this morning were both wonderful, but I still have to go."

"OK," Hunter said, defeat lacing his voice. "Sylvah, last night, before we ended up in your apartment." He paused, and a smile immediately replaced his frown. "You said you had something you needed to talk to me about. It seemed pressing."

A look of horror covered Sylvah's face, but Hunter was oblivious to her scowl. She had her back to him. All at once, her mouth felt dry, Goosebumps popped up all over her flesh, and she suddenly became aware of her nakedness.

Sylvah had been avoiding this conversation for the past couple of weeks, but she couldn't continue to postpone the inevitable.

"Yes, there is something I'd like seriously discuss with you, but it can wait until after we shower."

♀♂

Candace was the first to arrive at Akwaaba's. She couldn't be seated until the majority of the party arrived, so she walked two doors down to Brownstone Books. Just as she was about to enter she saw Alana at the register. Candace quickly changed directions and decided to get a cup of coffee at the shop next door instead.

Candace didn't know if she could continue to stomach Alana or the façade they called a friendship. She never understood why Alana despised her and it always rested on Candace's heart. It wasn't until Jamaica that Candace realized Alana was envious of her, and there was nothing she could do to appease Alana. Therefore, she finally decided to release the negative thoughts and energy sifting in her head generated by Alana. Candace had more important things to concern herself with, like the welfare of her family.

As soon as school ended, Candace and Shane had reluctantly sent the children down south to his parents for the summer. They both agreed it would be safer, and hoped to find the captor before the new school year. Otherwise, there was a strong chance James and Jasmine would have to enroll in school and remain southbound until they were out of danger.

Candace departed the shop with the coffee in her hand and almost bumped into Alana, as she stared at Sylvah stepping out of a luxury car. There was a white man she had never seen before holding the door open for Sylvah.

Alana looked Candace up and down without uttering a word and walked to the restaurant entrance and stood in the doorway. Candace ignored her as she sipped her coffee and followed.

Sylvah spotted her friends and waved. She was about to walk over to them, but the man who held the door open called her name. Sylvah turned to face him and he caressed her cheek, and without warning he grabbed her for a long and very passionate kiss. Candace and Alana looked on in awe. It was like watching a black Scarlett O'Hara and Clark Gable in *Gone With the Wind*.

After the kiss, Sylvah headed over to her girls and forced a smile.

"Sylvah, I do love you," Hunter said, stunning Sylvah. She stood frozen before Candace and Alana. "For once in my life, I know what I want and it's you. I don't care what people think. We can be together and if you change your mind, I'll be here for you."

Sylvah's heart sank. Breaking up wasn't supposed to be this hard. She wasn't supposed to fall so hard for this man, but she wasn't ready for the weight of this relationship. And though Sylvah hated to admit it, Bläise was right. It was one thing to introduce another man to her children, but a white man would not be easily accepted. It had nothing to do with her being prejudiced, and everything to do about a lifestyle adjustment. Life would be too difficult and it was a sacrifice Sylvah didn't feel like making.

Sylvah closed her eyes to push back the tears and took a deep breath before turning to face Hunter. As much as she wanted to run back into his embrace she couldn't. It was time to let go. She stared into his eyes and mouthed the words, "I love you, too." She watched as he returned to the driver side, buckled up and pulled off.

After Hunter departed Candace, Alana, and Sylvah assembled for a group hug. Sylvah released a few more tears and when they were through, she composed herself and they entered the restaurant.

The place buzzed with people and contemporary jazz played softly in the background. The hostess seated them at a table toward the rear of the restaurant near the emergency exit, which was open, and since the day was so beautiful people were seated at the tables outside.

Felice arrived with a visitor. Alana's and Candace's backs faced the door and the waiter who was taking their drink orders blocked Sylvah's view. Felice spotted her friends and strolled in their direction.

Sylvah nodded her approval to Felice and they exchanged a smile.

"Hey girl," Alana said as she stood to give Felice a hug. "Long time, no see."

"Oh my God, who is this little angel? She is so adorable with her pig tails and big brown eyes!" Candace said, taking the little girl's hand.

"Yeah, I was about to ask the same thing, but somebody wouldn't give me chance," Alana bickered.

"Sweetie, tell them your name," Felice said.

Nina looked at her mother briefly before responding. Her warm brown eyes sparkled. "My name is Nina." Her voice was soft and timid when she spoke.

"Is this your little cousin or niece?" Alana asked.

"I thought Felice didn't have any siblings." Candace interjected.

"Maybe she does on her father's side or something," Alana snapped.

Sylvah sat back quietly, waiting for Felice to make the next move.

"Actually, Candace you're right. I don't have any siblings and both my mother and father are only children." Felice took a seat beside Sylvah and sat Nina on her lap. Nina wrapped one arm around Felice's neck and placed her thumb in her mouth. "Nina is my daughter."

"What?" Candace and Alana gasped. Shocked by the revelation, they looked at Felice and Sylvah.

"Yes," Sylvah said to affirm.

"Let me start again. I want to introduce you to my daughter, Nina. Nina, I want you to meet your aunties." She pointed while talking. "This is Auntie Candace and Alana. You already know Auntie Sylvah."

Nina took her thumb out of her mouth to smile and wave at Sylvah.

"Back it up," Alana said. "When did you have a child? This is not even possible."

Sylvah sighed in exasperation.

Felice already knew to expect doubt and antagonism. But in all fairness, this was a huge bomb to drop. She'd have to fill them in on the entire story and she was happy to have the opportunity to share, but it would have to wait for another day.

"Listen, please know that I wasn't in my right mind for a while and that's why I left for Cuba. I had to learn a few things and make corrections along the way and my daughter was a part of that."

"OK, so say she is your daughter, who is the father?" Alana asked.

"Bedford."

"Oh my goodness," Candace blurted. They looked at Candace. "Forgive me, but this is all so shocking. But I believe you. It actually answers a lot of questions I had."

"Really?" Felice asked and Candace nodded.

"So are you two an item again?" Alana asked.

"No we're not, but we are very good friends and will remain this way. We have a lot of things in common and a daughter to bind us for life."

"Sylvah, you knew about this all along and never peeped a word," Alana said.

"It wasn't my place," Sylvah answered.

The waiter returned with their drink orders and offered to bring another chair for Nina, but Felice declined the offer. They all got up to fix plates for themselves. Moments later they were all seated and eating.

"By the way, Sylvah, who was that man you were with earlier?" Candace asked shyly.

"What man?" Felice asked.

"That was Hunter," Sylvah said, trying to ignore Felice.

"Girl, that was a good-looking man. Where you been hiding him?" Alana asked.

Sylvah reached for the salt, when Felice pulled her hand into the light.

"What in the heck is this?" Felice asked ogling at the diamond ring sparkling on Sylvah's left hand.

"It's a ring," Sylvah said smiling.

"It's not just a ring," Alana replied. "It's a big-ass ring." Alana took Sylvah's hand to examine the diamond. "This setting is the bomb too. I know this is platinum."

"Please watch your mouth around my daughter," Felice said. She stopped to listen to her request and it felt really good to say *daughter*.

Alana apologized. "How many carats is it?" she asked.

"Three carats and yes, its platinum." Sylvah answered modeling the ring and the diamond sparkled from every angle.

"Did Hunter propose?" Felice asked.

"No, I broke it off with Hunter this morning. That's why he gave that spiel earlier." Sylvah explained to Candace and Alana.

"You turned that poor man out." Alana joked. "He was out there professing his love to you and what not. I thought he was going to cry before driving off in that nice ride." Everyone laughed.

"Why did you do that?" Candace asked. "It looked like he made you happy."

"Yeah, but it was too complicated. Anyway, another friend gave me this ring."

"Damn, we don't waste anytime, huh?" Alana said, stuffing her face.

"Jason gave you this ring?" Felice asked, and Sylvah smiled. "He is not playing. Girl, you do you."

"You have to tell us all about Jason," Alana said.

"Girl, I'll do you one better. He's coming here to pick me up, so you can all meet him."

"Sounds like a plan."

"Not to change the subject, but how are things going with Zaire?" Candace asked.

"He's doing well. For the most part he's staying with me for the summer and we're still seeing the family therapist. Kenya hates it, but she understands it's for the benefit of her brother and the family. Bläise is very supportive and hanging in there too. "

"That's good," Candace replied.

"Speaking of children, how are James and Jasmine?" Sylvah asked.

"They're doing well. They haven't really adjusted to southern living yet, and of course they miss their friends, but this is only temporary. I miss my kids so much," Candace said playing with her food. She seemed to be in a distant place.

"Are the threats still coming?" Felice asked.

"Not since school ended, but that doesn't mean anything."

"It sure doesn't," Alana mumbled.

"Excuse me, what did you say?" Candace asked.

"Nothing," Alana answered.

"It sure didn't sound like nothing," Candace snapped.

"You know what, Candace? Sometimes bad things happen when you do fucked-up shit."

"Alana, I think you should leave," Felice said. Nina was falling asleep until Alana raised her voice and Felice tried to lull her back to sleep. "I can't believe those words would come out of your mouth. Candace is our dear friend and we're talking about her children. This is something you wouldn't wish on your worse enemy, much less a friend."

Alana abruptly got up. "Speak for yourself." She dumped twenty dollars on the table and left.

"Candace, don't cry," Sylvah said moving to Alana's chair. "Trust that everything is going to be fine."

Jason was outside waiting for Sylvah, and Shane came to get Candace. They all chatted outside for a few minutes before parting ways.

"Felice, do you need a ride home?" Sylvah asked.

"No thank you. You guys have fun. I have one more stop to make before Nina and I head home."

"OK," Sylvah said as she stepped into Jason's Range Rover. He closed the door for Sylvah and returned to the driver side. Felice watched as Jason kissed Sylvah before putting the car into gear and driving off.

Ten minutes later Felice and Nina were standing in front of a familiar brownstone. Felice rung the bell and took a deep breath. Felice and Nina waited patiently.

"Who is it?" the person asked.

"It's Felice."

"Just a minute."

She heard the clicking sound of bolts being unlocked and the heavy gate opened. Calvin Hamilton stood before them. Felice's own *Mr. Fix It*. He invited Felice inside.

"Two visits in one year. I must be the luckiest man alive," Calvin joked. "So tell me, and to what do I owe the pleasure of this visit?"

"I wanted to introduce you to my daughter, Nina," Felice said. She was afraid Calvin might react funny or treat her differently.

"I didn't know you had a daughter," Calvin said taking notice of Nina for the first time. "She's beautiful, like her mother."

"Thanks for the compliment. I'm lucky to have her," Felice said relieved at Calvin's response.

"I agree." Calvin said, lifting Nina. She giggled.

"Calvin, there's a lot of things you don't know, but I wanted to tell you why I was so hesitant to become involved in the past. You deserve an explanation."

"Question? Are we still going to play your little game of cat and mouse?"

Felice observed how well Calvin handled Nina and was pleased.

"No. No more games.

"Good, then the past really doesn't matter."

And with that, Felice's motto of *no strings attached* had changed.

The saga continues in *One Night Stand*

Candace and Shane Farewell seem to have it all. In addition to a wonderful marriage, two beautiful children and a nice home, Shane has found success as a decorated veteran detective and Candace is making things happen as a high-powered advertising executive. Things couldn't be more perfect—until Candace goes to Jamaica and has an affair with gorgeous model Clayton Breeze.

As they struggle to try and rebuild their marriage, someone begins leaving disturbing notes during Shane's shifts, which adds to his pressure to solve one of New York's largest child murder cases. Candace immediately suspects Clayton, and when she and Shane see him one day, the fallout results in Candace questioning all she holds dear and wondering if a one-night stand was worth the price.

Coming Spring 2006

He Was My Man First

by
#1 Essence Bestselling Author

Nancey Flowers
and
Courtney Parker

"Love never loses its way home"

1
My Man

*H*e lives with me. We've been together for nine years and have been engaged for three of those years. I'm the one rocking the two-carat, princess cut platinum engagement ring diamond on my finger. Rich and I go back for many, many years and he was my man first and will always be *my man*. My friends always tell me to cut Rich off, because he's a dog. But they'll never understand our relationship and our commitment to one another. Those other chicks that he used to kick it with on the side wasn't nuthin' serious. He was just having some fun. I understand that men cheat and for those women out there that think their men don't cheat, they're only fooling themselves. If the notion that your man ain't sticking his dick in some other pussy helps you sleep better at night, then good for you. I like to keep my shit real!

Richard Washington and I met when I was seventeen years old and he was eighteen. I was fucking with this drug dealer named Colombo, who had Lafayette Garden and Marcy projects on lock. I was Colombo's number one chick and shit was always right with us, but whenever shit went wrong with his game I got the short end of the stick or the thick end of the belt, literally. Colombo was known for his quick temper and being violent. Nevertheless, my options were limited. My father pulled a Houdini and disappeared when I was ten years old. Two years later, my mother was robbed and stabbed to death on her way home from work; leaving me with an aunt who just didn't have the time or just didn't give a fuck. I didn't stick around long enough to figure out which it was, because by fifteen I was living the life with Colombo.

Rich was one of Colombo's many runners. Colombo operated out of an apartment in LG projects, but we didn't live there. Colombo was a follower of Biggie Small's *Ten Crack Commandment's* rule number five: *never sell no crack where you rest at/I don't care if they want a ounce, tell 'em bounce.*

I had seen Rich at the headquarters, and we would make small talk, but Colombo didn't like me associating with the hired help. Therefore, I kept my communication with all of his people to a minimum. Rich was different, though, and finer than a grain of sand. He's the kind of brother that you can carry to the club one night and a black tie affair the next. At six feet, one inch, burnt caramel skin, sensuous lips, silky eyebrows and lustrous hair to match, Rich put male models to shame. So even though I didn't say much, my eyes must have said a million words. Whenever Rich came by my heart would flutter and it didn't help that he was always so nice. All of Colombo's workers were polite to me because I was his girl. Most of them even had the nerve to proposition me on the low, but I knew better than to ever fuck with any of them niggas. If Colombo ever knew they were disrespecting him like that he would have popped their dumb asses, but I kept my mouth shut. I could handle myself.

Chief was one of Colombo's front men. Chief met with this cat that was a regular, but the guy and his two friends were trying to leave the parking lot without paying for the crack. Chief panicked and ran into the building, returned with his Glock and fired shots at the truck that they were riding in, killing two of the men. The third guy managed to escape. Needless to say this fucked up Colombo's entire shit because not only was it on his turf, but it was right in front of the building that he operated out of. Shit was chaotic and I tried to calm Colombo down. He was running around in circles like a kid without direction. I knew this was bad, and to make matters worse there was still one guy on the loose and Chief was so fucked up he couldn't even give a simple description. Colombo got so pissed with Chief that he beat him to the point where I had to intervene. One of Chief's eyes was already shut and if Colombo did the same thing to the other eye Chief definitely wouldn't be able to identify the survivor. Colombo thought I was taking up for Chief and started pummeling me to death. By the time he was done, I knew he had broken my arm, a few ribs and it felt like I was breathing under water. I didn't even want to see a mirror. Shit was a madhouse and Colombo took Chief, his crew and the rest of his shit and left me in it.

Rich heard about the shooting and what happened to Colombo and his crew. When he arrived to the apartment the only thing left of Colombo and his crew was me. I was much too weak to do anything other than remain still and wait for the police to find me, but that never happened. Instead, Rich came and rescued me. Rich was my savior. He picked me up and took me to his apartment, which was only two buildings over from where Colombo operated. When things cooled down and the cops left the scene, Rich drove me to the hospital. In the ER I found out I had a punctured lung and they admitted me.

Rich visited every day and when I was discharged, Rich carried me to his house, and nursed me until I fully recovered. However, before we arrived at Rich's crib, the first thing that came to my mind was that Colombo was going to kill us if he found out whom I was staying with. I later learned that Colombo, Chief and three of his boys were killed the same night he left me for dead in the apartment.

After that shit, I knew it was time to get out of the drug game. I barely escaped with my life and understood I had been given a second chance. At the time, Rich lived with his mother and older sister. Almost immediately they became the family I longed for and Rich the man of my dreams.

One night while Rich and I were up talking, I learned that he had aspirations that didn't include being a drug dealer. Rich had dreams of becoming the next big fashion designer. He had a big black sketchbook buried beneath his bed of urban clothing designs that he had drawn. No one knew about his ambitions because he didn't want to seem gay, but I told him that he really needed to pursue his dream. I pointed out that most of the biggest designers were men: Ralph Lauren, Tommy Hilfiger, Calvin Klein and Giorgio Armani, and as far as I knew none of them were gay. Rich deserved better, and so did I.

At my encouragement, Rich enrolled in Katharine Gibbs School of Fashion Design. While attending school, he was able to secure a job in the mailroom at Jorge Jacobs, which was one of the hottest up-and-coming fashion lines. I also returned to school, but I had to get my G.E.D. first, which didn't take long. I'd always been smart; I just needed motivation. I also attended Katharine Gibbs and received my degree in office administration, and now I'm a highly paid office manager. A lot has changed since Rich and I first hooked up, for better and for worse.

The better was that we were partners and relied on each other to survive. We worked hard and together we managed to save our money and move out of the 'hood. Rich and I still live in Brooklyn, but we recently purchased a two-bedroom condo in Clinton Hills. The worse is Rich's affinity for women.

The first trick to enter the picture was Qwanisha. Rich and I were going through our first major crisis in the relationship; money. At the time, the jobs we had barely paid us any real dough. At least not the kind of money we were used to receiving. Colombo had always kept my pockets padded and Rich managed to stack his cash, but that was dwindling to nothing and neither of us were used to living off measly funds much less paycheck to paycheck. We argued about any and everything, and started drifting apart.

Qwanisha was best described as a hood rat that I had to squash, because rodents deserved to be terminated. I heard from a friend of a friend that Rich was messing around with some girl. I approached him about it, but he craftily changed the subject and began caressing my breasts and nibbling on my ear. Rich knew I couldn't resist his touch then or now. After a few more minutes of foreplay, we ended up fucking right on the kitchen countertop. Although I didn't broach the subject again that night, Qwanisha never left my mind.

After about two months of the bullshit and a few nights of Rich not coming home, I had to put that shit to an end. The look of surprise on Qwanisha's face when I knocked on her door and asked for my man could only be described as stupefied. It was a Kodak moment. It wasn't until I punched that bitch square in her face that she snapped back to reality and Rich came to the door, looked at Qwanisha and took me home. We never discussed that night and things went back to normal for an entire year. Then there was LaToya, Elisa, Portia, Chantel and Monique. None of them hung around for long and I made sure of that. The one thing I wasn't going to tolerate was my man catching feelings for these bitches. That wasn't going to happen.

Now there's some new bitch named Vanessa. Rich never admitted when he was fucking around in the past and he wasn't going to start now, but I knew something was going on between them. Vanessa wasn't on the same level as the hoochies from Rich's past. She's a bourgeois chick who works at Jorge Jacobs with Rich, so they dealt with each other regularly. I can't get a whole lot of information from anyone because she wasn't in my network of friends. So for once I feel handicapped and at a huge disadvantage because I can't just go to his office and beat this ho down the way I want to. For once, I actually feel threatened by this bitch, Vanessa!

It's three o'clock in the morning and I'm wide awake. For the past few nights I've been unable to sleep soundly. I've been mulling over my present predicament in our relationship and as I look at Rich, now sleeping peacefully, I know that sacrifices must be made. Our relationship means everything to me and I will stop at no ends to allow no man or woman to put asunder all that we've built.

"I shall marry you"

2
But He's My Man Now!

Although her mouth was occupied at the moment, Vanessa's mind raced with exciting thoughts of Richard. How proud she was of him this morning in the board meeting! Of course he deserved a little mid-day mouth-to-head reward for a job well done. And she was more than happy to give him that reward. Vanessa had been looking for an in up the corporate ladder for years now. Vanessa's stagnated Director of Business Affairs position had long worn out its welcome, and she wanted nothing more than an opportunity at the Vice President position that would soon be up for grabs. Although corporately she knew she would never actually get the job, for her male-dominating office would never allow a woman of color such a high position, she didn't mind accepting the position via her new protégé, Richard.

"Oh baby, you give the best head...shit!" Richard moaned as Vanessa continued to stroke his penis with her tongue.

"You like that, daddy?" she teased in between slurps. "There's more of this to come." Vanessa curled her tongue and moved her lips faster against his erect skin, causing him to ejaculate in her mouth.

"Damn, you suck a mean dick! Shit, I don't know what the fuck I'm gonna do with you."

"The question is, what am I going to do with you?" Vanessa asked as she walked over to her desk. She wiped her mouth with Richard's handkerchief. "This is truly just the beginning. With my help, you're well on your way to making V.P. and all presidents have a first lady, so I'm going to do whatever I have to and for you, to ensure my spot." Vanessa reached for the bottle of Scope, took a swig, swooshed and spit it out in her trashcan. "Speaking of doing whatever we can for each other, have you left that woman yet?"

Vanessa could see the irritation on Richard's face. She couldn't understand why a man with such a prestigious future insisted on dwelling in an obviously hideous past, especially with a woman that clearly was stuck in that state. The nerve of Richard to even entertain his long time girlfriend, Chauncey, annoyed her. The little loyalty story about how she was there for him before he was who he'd become was becoming redundant and, even more, unimportant to Vanessa. This girl from his past clearly had nothing on her, the woman of his future. She was more determined than ever to prove that. Even if Chauncey had been there first, Vanessa knew she was here now, and to her now was all that matter.

"What is it, baby?" Vanessa reached for his tie. "Am I not everything you want?"

"I didn't say that, but..."

"But, nothing. Sooner or later you're going to have to let her go. Now I've been patient with you, have I not?" Vanessa stroked her tongue seductively against his lips. "And I've listened to your story of loyalty long enough, but I'm your future, baby, and the plans I have for us don't include company." Vanessa unbuttoned the top few buttons of her purple silk blouse after locking the door to her office. "Now I expect you to handle this. I'll give you a little more time, before assuming you need my help."

Her blouse fell to the floor. Her skirt and hose followed. All that remained was a chocolate-coated Vanessa in a black lace La Perla bra and thong. "Come here, daddy," she whispered while leaning back against her desk. "Let me show you why you need me and not her."

Vanessa could tell Richard couldn't resist her as he slid his legs out of his pants, which were already bagged around his ankles. He secured the condom and as his steel-plated penis entered her, she knew she had him exactly where she wanted him. Vanessa made sure that she fulfilled Richard in every way, exhausting him both mentally and physically to where even when he went home to Chauncey, his thoughts and energies remained with her. Vanessa sucked at his neck and clawed at his back and chest, ensuring the remains and evidence of their lovemaking. It was a gift she so graciously chose to send Richard home to Chauncey with. If nothing else, Vanessa needed Chauncey to know that they had been together and despite she and Richard's lengthy past, Vanessa didn't plan on going anywhere. She would fight for what she wanted, expecting nothing less than a victory.

If Chauncey wanted Richard half as bad as she did, then may the best woman win! And as it stood right now, with his penis knee deep in her vagina, victory was already hers.

Vanessa exited the ladies room, refreshed and headed back to her office. Nothing beat a little mid-day loving, especially with someone as fine and sexually talented as Richard. Although they hadn't been sleeping together for more than a month now, Vanessa knew she would have Richard eating out the palm of her hand the minute he came to the executive floor over a year ago. It took her that long to feel him out and deem him worthy of her good love and generosity. Vanessa never did anything that didn't benefit her, so Richard was no exception. The minute she established him as her corporate guinea pig, it was on.

Much to her surprise, Richard moved her. His rough-around-the edges persona intrigued and excited Vanessa. Granted, he was no Dexter, her corporate counterpart with whom she'd had a momentary fling. Yet Richard was just smart enough to welcome the grooming from the major partners, and naïve enough to fall prey to her charms, in order for her to get where she wanted to go.

After pulling Richard's file, Vanessa knew that any candidate from the Katharine Gibbs School of Fashion Design clearly was Jorge Jacobs's excuse for keeping well within the affirmative action guidelines for hiring. Richard did have potential and despite his lack of any true education, his good looks, charm and sexy personality were uncanny. The way he made her body feel more than compensated for his lack of proper upbringing. Besides, Vanessa loved the fact that Richard wasn't the protégé of one her parents' friends. With Vanessa's father, Justice William Montgomery Knight, being the only Black judicial Supreme Court Judge for the State of New York and her mother, Cornelia Elaine Mitchell-Knight, heiress to the Soul Shine Corporation, Vanessa was always being paired with the traditional *Who's Who*. Richard served as a healthy change, with the added bonus of pissing off her perfectionist mother.

"A Bachelors with honors from NYU and a Master's in Global Fashion Management from Fashion Institute of Technology, not to mention a year of studying in Paris, and you're dating some reject flunky from a design school no one's ever heard of," her mother taunted. "Nessa, you're breaking my heart."

This was something Vanessa knew to be untrue. The only thing valid about her mother's comment was that it broke her heart to not be able to control Vanessa's life. And if screwing Richard day in and day out helped Vanessa to define her independence, then she would just call Richard her Plymouth Rock.

"Ms. Knight, there is an urgent message from your mother. She'd like you to call ASAP. I've put a fresh cup of coffee on your desk, as well as left your other messages."

"Speak of the devil," Vanessa said aloud.

"Excuse me, Ms. Knight?"

Vanessa shook her head and smiled at her assistant, Cynthia. Nearly twice her age, Vanessa wondered why Cynthia never aspired to do more than be someone's secretary. To have to take orders from a twenty-nine year old senior executive had to be strange...or not.

Though Vanessa was accustomed to barking orders to the hired help, she always managed to keep her temperament with Cynthia to a minimum. Cynthia was great at what she did, and for nothing more than that deserved Vanessa's respect.

"Thank you Cynthia. Please hold all other calls until you see that I've finished with my mother. If I know her, this call will be a lengthy one." Vanessa smiled, then turned back to Cynthia, "Better yet, interrupt me in exactly fifteen minutes."

Vanessa entered her office and closed the door behind her. She had, by far, the most beautiful office in the entire building, all compliments of her parents. When the time came to decorate her quaint corner office, Vanessa insisted that she incur the cost of the décor. If she was going to work there indefinitely, she would have to design her office to her liking and not based on what her employers could afford.

Vanessa curled her back into her coffee-colored leather chair and smiled. Just hours before she and Richard's second romp in the office, he had her legs straddled on each arm of that very chair. She craved him…and was determined to have her appetite completely fulfilled.

The only deterrent to her otherwise happily-ever-after was Richard's hoodrat home girl Chauncey. But as with any proper fairy tale, there was always a little bad before the good in the end. If Vanessa, a princess, had to endure a few toads along the way to happiness, she would. For she knew beyond a shadow of a doubt that Richard definitely had the makings of a good Mr. Knight.

Flowers in Bloom titles are available on-line and at your local bookstores. If they do not carry your selection of choice, please request that the store order it.

Thanks in advance for your patronage!
Coming Soon to a store near you...

Down In The Dirty by J.M. Benjamin, 2005
He Was My Man First by Courtney Parker and Nancey Flowers
One Night Stand by Nancey Flowers, 2006
Silent Scream by Carol Chapman, 2006

Visit us on-line at www.flowersinbloompublishing.com
We'd love to hear your thoughts.
Enjoy!

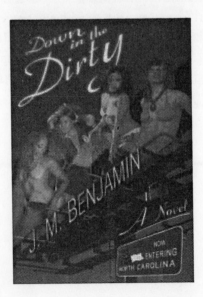

More Titles by Flowers In Bloom:

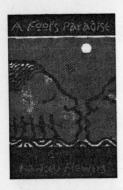